THEY HAVE HIDDEN AMONG US FOR CENTURIES.

BOOK ONE

THE DARK FACE OF EVIL

HANK MARTIN, HIS WIFE, LINDSEY, AND THEIR TEENAGE SON, TIM, battle an evil that permeates the government of Liberia to the very doors of the president's office.

This is a battle that, if Hank does not win, will cost him far more than his career; it will cost him the sacrifice of his son to the *endosym*, a creature that has hidden in the jungles of Liberia for centuries.

THE DOORWAY TO THE OTHER WORLD WILL OPEN
BOOK TWO

THE PLANTATION

WHEN DOCTOR GEORGE NAH SARDAY, THE LEADER OF THE NEW Age cult Dacari Mucomba, purchased the old Johnson Plantation in Johnsonville, Virginia, as the site for the School for West African Spiritual Studies, Chief of Police Brian Bishop had little reason to be concerned.

Little did he realize that it was far more than just another fake religion bilking money from its followers; the school was hiding the creature whose existence would threaten not only the city of Johnsonville but also the very existence of the human race. With time running out and marked for death, Chief Bishop finds an unlikely ally in Tim Martin, a senior at the University of Virginia who knows too well what they must face when they meet the *endosym*.

THE CONQUEST OF EARTH BEGINS
BOOK THREE

THE ACADEMY

HIDDEN IN THE FORGOTTEN TUNNELS BENEATH THE UNITED STATES Military Academy is a creature that should be dead. It was hanged in 1779. But it's not easy to destroy an *endosym*.

In order for the conquest of Earth to begin, the *endosym*—Duncan McDougal—knows that the unborn child of Samantha and Tim Martin must die. From the United States Military Academy, to New York City, to the jungles of West Africa, the battle between the *endosyms* and the Martins escalates.

ENDOSYM

BOOK FOUR:

RESURRECTION

By J Henry Thomson

The events and adventures in this novel are fiction. The names, characters, places, and incidents are either a product of the author's imagination or are used fictitiously, and any similarity to persons, living or dead, business establishments, events, or locales is entirely coincidental.

ENDOSYM: RESURRECTION
Copyright © October 23, 2015 J. Henry Thomson
All rights reserved.

ISBN: 0985742631
ISBN: 13: 9780985742638

ACKNOWLEDGMENTS

When writing a novel, there are always those individuals and places whose contributions make the novel come to life.

First I want to thank you, the readers. Whether you are a first reader or a follower of the Endosym series, thank you for your support.

The adventure for Amy Brown begins in Spokane, Washington. Many of the places and locations in this story are real. However I have used them only to add realism for the reader. All actual locations begot positive experiences, and in most cases, descriptions may not be totally accurate and are only used to set the stage.

Freeman High School and Gonzaga University (my alma mater) are both real institutions, and my character Amy Brown was proud to be a student at these two schools.

To Kim Holmes and Sarah Coleman-Campbell, thank you for your insight in educating me in the creation of a sixteen-year-old teenage girl character.

For this novel, I offer a thank-you to Dick Raymond and Larry Hicks, who read the draft and told it like it is.

As always, my editor, Irene Hicks, continues to provide the energy, unflagging support, and encouragement that get me through the difficult periods.

Finally, to my wife, Linda, thank you for listening to my ramblings as I developed the story.

Then I saw a heap of ragged clothes strewn across the floor. I noticed another pile by the entrance. Looking closer, I realized that these weren't heaps of discarded clothes—they were bodies. I dared approach one corpse. I felt bile rising in my throat. It was the remains of a disemboweled man; his intestines were lying on the floor; his arms and hands embraced the unruly guts as if he were trying to put them back in place. He had no face that I could see.

I turned away and ran.

Four Months Ago

SHE SAT AT THE KITCHEN COUNTER STARING AT THE HEADLINE ON THE DAY'S front-page story on her iPhone: "Dixon Withdraws." Below, in smaller print she read more:

> WASHINGTON: In a statement today to the media and supporters, Senator Allen Dixon, the front-runner for the Republican Party nomination, announced his withdrawal from the presidential election. According to sources at campaign headquarters, his wife has fewer than two months to live. Dixon, who was believed to have the best chance to become the second black president of the United States, will remain at his wife's side. The withdrawal has turned the campaign upside down.

She wiped a tear from her eye before looking back at her iPhone.

"No!" she whispered. "I must not do this."

She put the iPhone down, buried her head in her hands, and began to sob. It was so unfair. The world was unfair. She had sacrificed so much. Now this. Again she looked at the phone. Just sixty seconds. That's all. She picked up the phone again.

Taking a deep breath, she punched in a familiar number and held the phone firmly against her ear. It rang once, twice, and then on the third ring, a woman answered.

"Dixon residence."

"Hello?" she said. "My name is Angelia Swenson, and I'm a sorority sister of Mrs. Dixon. We were very close in college, and I was one of her bridesmaids. Is she well enough to talk to me?"

"She may be asleep. One moment, please," said the woman.

If she were asleep, she would hang up, and there would never be any attempt to call again.

After what seemed like minutes, but most likely was only a few seconds, a different woman's voice came on the line. It was barely a whisper.

"Angelia, I'm glad you called."

"I'm not Angelia," she said. There was a pause.

"You—it can't be. You died sixteen years ago."

"It's me, Mom," she said.

"Oh, God, that can't be possible. Where are you? What happened?"

"Mom, tell no one that we have spoken. I love you, Mom."

Before there was an answer, she hung up.

She stood up, wiped the tears from her eyes, and deleted the news story. She could do no more.

1

THEY SAY THAT TO LIVE YOU MUST ALMOST DIE. IF THAT'S TRUE, THEN during the last six years I have truly lived. It seems hard to believe that not only my life but also the fate of the entire human race changed on that fateful day. Let me take you back to that morning six years ago.

My name is Amy Brown. I'm seventeen. Well, actually, I will be seventeen in four months, so I guess I'm really sixteen. Even though I'm sixteen, I'm a senior at Freeman High School in Spokane, Washington, and I've been accepted to Gonzaga University in the fall.

I guess you could call me the typical teenager. If you asked me what I look like, I'd say I have green eyes and ash-blond hair, and I'm tall. To be exact, I'm six feet one. Which means that although some of my girl-friends claim I'm attractive, I feel gawky. My breasts are too small and my hips too narrow. One of my boyfriends said I have a cute butt. But to me, personally, it's smaller than it should be. Honestly, I wish I weighed twenty more pounds. I'm the runt of my family. Both Mom and Dad are taller than I am. Imagine being the runt, and you're still taller than 60 percent of the boys.

I guess I'm popular. I play volleyball, and I'm on the varsity cheer-leading team. Even though I'm taller than two of the boy cheerleaders, I do a pretty good job.

Oh, I almost forgot. I also have a black belt in karate. No, I am not a female Bruce Lee. It was my dad's idea. He enrolled me in the martial arts when I was six. In grade school and junior high, I loved it. But in high school, I was more interested in other things. Besides, a boy doesn't want to date a girl who can kick his butt. No, I have never used my martial arts training to protect myself. As a matter of fact, most of my friends don't know I have a black belt.

When you're as tall as I am, you feel weird in a dress. At least I do, and I am much happier in jeans than in a dress. Of course, I only like designer jeans, not some pair of Walmart specials. My taste in clothes comes from Mom.

We live near Hangman Hills. It's a development south of Spokane next to Hangman Valley Golf Course. My dad and I play golf sometimes, but it bores me. I love to talk, and some people don't like talkers on the course. I think they take golf too seriously.

We have lived in our house since I was four months old. It's big for just the three of us, but most of the homes out here are. We have ten acres and could have horses, but the only pet we own is Mr. P. He is a big gray tomcat. He's my cat. I found him when I was in fifth grade.

Dad sells stocks and bonds and works for ER Rogers Investments. I guess he does pretty well. He bought me a new Mustang when I started my senior year.

2

ON FRIDAY, MY LIFE CHANGED. IT STARTED OUT LIKE ANY OTHER school day. In the morning, I grabbed a Pop-Tart for breakfast and headed for the garage. Mom has always lectured me on my eating habits and that morning was no different. I of course mumbled one of the normal remarks that we teenagers are so good at.

I pushed the garage opener and climbed into my Mustang. It's only three months old and still has that cool, new car smell. It is bright red and has white racing stripes. It has a turbocharged engine and is fast. Dad and I both like fast cars. No, I don't drive recklessly. Hey, I'm a girl—no testosterone. I backed out of the garage, turned around, and headed down the long driveway to the main road.

Freeman High School is eleven miles from the house. I programmed in my favorite tunes and sang along as I drove. When I got to school, I parked in the student lot.

It was starting to rain. When my hair gets wet, it curls. I wear it long, and I hate it when that happens. But that's what your hair does when you are part black. Oh, I forgot to mention that. The truth is, I can pass for white, which is all right considering that there are only four African Americans in our school.

Mom's darker—well, sort of brown. One of her parents must have been black. She was a foster home child and knows nothing about her parents. I don't hide the fact that I am part black, and none of my friends seem to care. All my boyfriends have been white. Mom's real active in the PTA and church, and everyone seems to like her even if she is part black.

3

I RAN FOR THE FRONT DOOR AS THE RAINDROPS BEGAN TO FALL. As the door closed behind me, I entered to the noise of 316 students all talking at once as they waited for the first bell to ring. Talk about the Tower of Babel. This was it.

"Amy!" Riana Morrison shouted over the din. "Are we doing pizza after the game?"

"Sure," I answered.

We had a basketball game at five o'clock. After the game we would all gather at the Pizza Hut on Sprague Avenue. Mom and Dad knew that I wouldn't be home until around ten.

I know—most teenagers do what they want and stay out late, but not me. My folks trust me to do the right thing, and I want that trust. Besides, I had a major term paper due on Monday, and this weekend I was committed to that term paper.

Craig Henderson ran up.

"Hi, Craig," I said.

"Hi, Amy. What are you doing after the game?"

Craig had a big-time crush on me, but he just wasn't my type. Right now, I wasn't interested in any major commitment. Now, don't get me wrong, I like boys, but I am not gaga over them, and I'm one of those 20 percent who really is a virgin. Enough said about that subject.

"We're all going to Pizza Hut."

He smiled and said, "Maybe I'll see you there."

"Sure," I said, returning his smile.

I headed for my first class. English Literature. I actually like going to school and do very well. I especially like to write. I finished all of my required courses for graduation last year, and this year I'm taking college prep courses.

Freeman's senior class is only seventy-three students. Because we are a small high school, I take college prep courses on Tuesdays and Thursdays at West Valley High School. To me, the classes are interesting.

At lunch, we all gathered at our regular table in the cafeteria. My three closest friends are Riana, Justine Adams, and Marylyn Yurich. We all live in the Hangman Valley and attended grade school and junior high together. Riana's parents go to the same Methodist church we do.

"This food sucks," grumbled Justine.

"It looks like the school's on another health-food kick," I replied.

"Well, you're lucky, Amy. You could eat pizza all the time and not gain a pound. Unfortunately I need the health food," said Justine, who has always been overweight.

As was the case with our friendship, we always enjoyed our lunches together even though we traveled in different social groups. Personally, I think this social stuff is a bunch of bull. I like people in all groups. Maybe being from a different ethnic background than 90 percent of my classmates makes you look at life a little differently.

After school, I spent some time in the library, and then at four o'clock, I went down to the girls' locker room and got dressed in my cheerleader's uniform. A half hour later, we were in the gym warming up before the basketball game. Students began filing into the gym, and soon it was packed. It was the first game of the season. We were playing Ritzville, and both teams were considered first-place contenders in our division. It was going to be a good game.

No matter how the game ends, the cheerleaders must continue to keep the students supporting the team. With a close game, that can be tense. This was a close game. We didn't get a breather until halftime, and it was so hot, I was sweating like a pig. Funny, we say that. In biology we learned that pigs don't sweat. Anyway, I think my deodorant was failing.

We stood around waiting for the second half. I looked up in the stands. Craig Henderson waved at me. I waved back. Craig plays football and had on his letterman's sweater. Several other football players were with Craig. These guys usually spend the basketball season walking around the stands, scoping out girls. Right now, they were all staring at me. I glanced down at my sweater. Oh great, I had sweated enough that the sweater was sticking to my chest and my nipples could be seen through my sport's bra. Now, three horny ballplayers were busy undressing me with their eyes. Jeez, boys are stupid. Do they think we don't know what they're doing? I felt like walking into the stands and kicking all three in the nuts. Instead, I smiled and turned my back to them

The buzzer blared for the second half. For the next thirty minutes, the lead alternated back and forth. By the last two minutes, we were no longer cheering. We were all watching the game, each person holding our breath. With the score tied at sixty-nine each, there were only three seconds left on the clock. Ritzville got the ball. The player took a shot at half court. It sailed through the air toward the net. I willed the ball to miss the net, believing I had the power to move objects. With a whoosh, the basketball slid through the net, and the final buzzer went off. Ritzville had just won the game, seventy-two to sixty-nine.

A cheer rose from the other side of the gym. Defeated, we filed out of the gym. We were so close, but they always say that close only counts in horseshoes, whatever that means. In the locker room, we were all quiet. I showered, dressed, and headed out to my car. It was time for us to get over the game. It was time to gather at the Pizza Hut on Sprague.

$$\overline{\underline{4}}$$

I WALKED OUT TO THE STUDENT PARKING LOT. MOST OF THE CARS had already left. My Mustang was sitting by itself. I pulled out my key and pushed the unlock button. The horn beeped, and the lights went on.

As I approached the car, I heard a cat mew. Great, just what I needed was a stray cat looking for a home. Well, I already had a cat, and it would just have to find someone else. The cat jumped on the hood of my car. I was about to shoo it off when I looked again. It was Mr. P.

"Mr. P, what are you doing here?"

Maybe it just looked like my cat. The cat jumped off of the hood and ran over to me. Mr. P had a limp. When I first found him, the vet said that some time before we got him his back leg had been broken and had healed wrong, giving him a slight limp. But the injury didn't slow him down. It was definitely Mr. P.

He ran up to me, looking up with his big yellow eyes. Then he went back to the car and stood by the door. I opened the door, and he jumped in. As I slid into the driver's side, he butted his head against my arm. God, I loved this cat.

I was only eleven when he came into my life.

It was summer, and I had wandered down by the golf course. I was looking for golf balls in the woods. Mom had told me not to go into the woods, but you know how preteens are. We do our own thing. I was searching for balls when I saw the skeleton of a cat lying in the grass. It was lying on its side, like it was asleep. There was no meat or hair on the bones; it must have been there for years. I wondered what had killed the poor thing. Then, typical for an eleven-year-old, I pretended that I was a good witch with the power to bring the poor cat back to life. I picked up a stick, pretending it was my magic wand, touched the skeleton with the stick, and whispered, "Hocus pocus, I order you to live." Of course, nothing happened, and after a few moments, I wandered off searching for more balls.

"Hello, little girl. What are you doing here?"

I turned around. Standing in the shadow of a pine tree was a man. I couldn't explain it, but something told me that this was a bad man.

"Just looking for golf balls," I answered.

"Would you like to go for a ride with me?" asked the man.

"No!" I said, remembering my mother's warning never to talk to strangers. I turned and ran as fast as I could. I was tall for my age, and I could run fast. I could hear the man behind me, but I was pulling away.

Then I tripped on a root and fell flat on my stomach.

"I got you now, you little brat," he growled.

I felt his hand grab my shoulder. Then the man screamed.

"No, get away from me!" He screamed again. I rolled over and saw him running through the trees.

I sat up shaking and then started running for home. I didn't want to look for golf balls any more, and I would never go back there again. As I ran out of the woods, I saw something gray running beside me. It was a large gray cat. He looked up and kept pace with me. When I turned into our driveway, he followed.

When Mom saw the cat, she freaked at first. She had gone in and called my dad who came home early. When Dad saw the cat, he said, "Hello, Mr. P."

The cat answered as if he knew him. Dad explained that when he was a boy he had had a gray cat named Mr. P.

So we kept him, and that's how he got the name Mr. P. From that day on, he has slept on my bed every night.

$$\overline{\underline{5}}$$

"HOW DID YOU GET HERE?" I ASKED THE CAT.

I knew the cat could have come eleven miles, and I have read stories of cats traveling hundreds of miles to make it back home, but this wasn't home, and how did he find my car?

Suddenly, I had a bad feeling. I pushed the start button, and the engine fired up. I dropped the selector into drive and raced out of the parking lot. When I reached the road, I turned left, heading back home. I would not be going to the Pizza Hut until I satisfied myself that everything was OK at home.

When Dad bought me the car, he had said, "You can drive it as fast as you want, but if you get a speeding ticket, it goes in the garage until you are twenty-one."

Needless to say, I usually drove five miles under the speed limit. I love this car, and there was no way that I would risk losing it.

For the first time, I disregarded Dad's warning. I put the pedal to the metal, as they say, and four hundred fifty horses roared into action. The speedometer hit a hundred miles per hour going up the Palouse Highway. The car almost slid off the road as I made the sharp left onto Baltimore Road. I raced down the road, hit the brakes as our driveway approached, and pulled up to the front of the house.

I pushed the button, shutting off the engine. Everything looked OK. The outside lights were on. The living room lights were on. I felt stupid. What was I thinking? Well, now that I was home, I might as well poke my head in the door. I would also make the stupid cat stay home. He could have been eaten by a coyote or hit by a car. No way should he be following me to school.

Right after I had turned sixteen, I had gone to a movie. There was some kind of power outage at the theater, so I came home early. I parked the car in the garage and went upstairs. We have carpet on the stairs, so I made no sound. As I reached the top of the stairs, the double doors of Mom and Dad's bedroom were open, and the nightstand light was on. I decided I would let them know I was home. I walked up to the door, which was close enough to tell that they were naked on top of the bed, doing it. My God, Dad's over forty! Would you believe that someone that old would be doing it? I was so embarrassed that I sneaked back downstairs and hid in the den for three hours, and then went back upstairs pretending that I had just come home.

After that I always made sure that they knew I was home.

6

I WAS WALKING UP THE STEPS TO THE FRONT DOOR, KEYS IN HAND, WHEN I saw that the front door was standing open about an inch. No way! Dad is absolutely paranoid about security. We lock the doors even when we are sitting on the back porch. He makes us set the alarm every night once we go to bed. Even the windows are always locked. There is no way the front door should be unlocked and open. I pushed it open wider and stepped into the entryway. Mr. P was standing next to me. His tail was all blown up three time its normal size.

The last time I saw the cat's tail that size was when Mr. P first met Jesse, the neighbor's Australian shepherd. The dog had spotted Mr. P on the back porch and came racing through the yard toward the cat. Mr. P arched his back and let out a growl, his tail blown up like tonight. Jesse slammed on her brakes, came to a stop, and stared at the cat. After that, Jesse never went near Mr. P.

"Mom, Dad, I'm home," I shouted. No answer. I walked into the den and shouted again. "Mom, Dad, anybody home? Where are you?"

The TV was on, but muted. If they had gone next door to the neighbors, the TV would be off. Dad's also a stickler about wasting electricity.

He almost makes you pee in the dark to save a few kilowatts. Where were they? I stood listening. The only sound was the ticking of the grandfather clock in the hallway.

I headed for the kitchen. For the rest of my life, I would wish I had just turned and ran out of the house. I could feel cold air blowing from the kitchen as I approached. I figured that the back door must be open. Even with my coat on, I was shivering. As I walked into the kitchen, all I could say was, "Oh, my God," over and over again.

Blood was splattered everywhere. Both of my parents were covered in it. It was so bad that I was trying to convince myself that it was someone else but they were mom and dad and they were dead. Listen, I've seen enough of those bloody horror movies. I knew that they were dead. But this was not a movie. I didn't scream like they do in the horror movies. I didn't faint. I just stood there looking at my parents' corpses, paralyzed. I couldn't move.

7

I DON'T REMEMBER LEAVING THE KITCHEN, AND I DON'T REMEMBER dialing 911.

The first thing I did remember was a woman's voice saying, "911, what is your problem? Hello, this is 911—what is your problem?"

I found myself whispering into the phone, "My mom and dad have been killed."

"What is your name, miss?"

"Amy."

"You are calling from 14166 Baltimore Road. Is that where your parents are dead?"

"Yes," I said.

"Do you know what happened?" the operator asked.

"No," I said. "I just got home. They are on the kitchen floor."

"Are you sure they are dead?"

"Yes," I said.

"You said your name is Amy?"

"Yes," I said.

"Amy, the police are on the way. Do you want me to stay on the phone until they get there?"

"Yes," I said. "But I don't want to talk." I sat on the floor holding the phone.

When I saw the flashing red and blue lights, I said, "They are here."

The operator asked, "Where are you?"

"In the living room sitting on the floor."

"Do you have a gun or anything?" she asked.

"No," I said.

"Amy, you just sit there. The police will be coming in the front door. Do not make any fast moves or try to run."

I grabbed Mr. P and held him in my arms. Two officers came through the front door. Their guns were drawn. One of the officers looked at me.

"Are you OK?" he asked.

"I guess so," I answered.

I heard voices in the kitchen. At first I thought it was Mom and Dad. Then I heard what one officer was saying.

"I've got two dead in here from multiple gunshots."

"Search the property," said the officer who had first spoken to me. "Call Major Crimes Division."

8

UNLESS YOU HAVE LOST A LOVED ONE IN A TRAGIC DEATH WITH NO warning, you may not understand my emotions at that moment. I was sitting in the sitting room off of the living room. This had been Mom's favorite room. She would spend hours there with the two French doors closed while Dad and I watched a sports game on the TV in the living room. Mom had decorated the room with expensive wing chairs, a gold velvet camelback sofa, gold silk drapes, and a thick Indian carpet. With the doors closed, it had been a quiet and restful place to sit. The police officer asked me to take my cat and wait in the sitting room. He told me that someone would be in shortly to talk to me. They kept the doors open and a policeman was always watching me. It seemed like they expected me to suddenly bolt out of the room.

At this point, I couldn't even stand up. I had a splitting headache, and I felt sick to my stomach. Although I was on the verge of tears, I couldn't cry. I watched the Crime Scene Investigation people come and go. When I closed my eyes, I pictured Mom and Dad lying motionless on the floor. Then I imagined them laughing together at the kitchen table. I wanted to wake up from this nightmare, yet in my heart, I knew that would not happen. I prayed to God for strength to see me through this. I prayed for the hurt to go away.

Even in that moment, there was humor. In the six years we have owned Mr. P, the cat had never been allowed to place one paw in mom's sitting room. I was sitting on mom's gold velvet sofa, with Mr. P stretched out next to me. I started to shoo him off, then choked back a sob. Mom didn't care anymore whether the cat was in her sitting room. It was then the tears started to flow. I could feel them running down my face. I rubbed my arm across my face. I imagined my mascara smeared all over my face. I must look like hell, which was fine with me since I felt like hell.

9

I HEARD A SOFT RAPPING ON THE DOOR TO THE SITTING ROOM AND looked up.

A man and a woman were standing there. The man was wearing a tan sports coat, white shirt, and blue pants. He was wearing one of those skinny ties, the kind Mom and I had gotten rid of for Dad years ago.

This man looked about Dad's age. He had brown hair, graying at the sides. The woman was much younger, maybe in her late twenties or early thirties. She was wearing a pants suit. I remember thinking, "I would look good in that suit."

Her hair, jet black, was cut in a short bob, and her lipstick was light pink. She was wearing very little makeup, but her smooth complexion allowed her to get away with it. She had a pretty smile, revealing straight white teeth. I suspected we were sisters in the braces club. Mine had come off two years ago.

"Amy, I'm Detective Harriet Sims, and this is Detective Mark Baker. We would like to talk to you. May we come in?"

My nose was running. I sniffed and said, "Sure."

Detective Sims handed me a Kleenex, and I blew my nose. Sims sat next to me on the sofa. Detective Baker started to pick up Mr. P and move him. To my surprise, the cat let out a deep growl and bared his teeth. Detective Baker sat in a wing chair instead.

Baker pulled out a notebook and a pen.

"Is it OK if I call you Amy?" he asked.

"Sure, that's my name," I answered.

"Could you tell me what happened?" he asked. I went over everything that had happened. I left out Mr. P showing up at school. I just said that I had come back home following the basketball game and found my folks dead. One of the uniformed policemen stuck his head in the door.

"May I see you for a minute, Harriet?" he asked. Sims got up and spoke with the policeman. When she returned, she whispered to Detective Baker. He nodded and then looked at me.

"Amy, do you know how to shoot a pistol?" he asked.

"Yes, Dad taught me when I was seven."

"Do you have a lot of guns in the house?"

"Some," I said.

"What kind of guns?" he asked.

"I think there are a couple of Glocks and a snubbed-nose thirty-eight."

"What else?"

"A shotgun. Oh yeah, I think Dad keeps a gun in his car. He has a permit to carry a concealed weapon."

Detective Baker yelled out the door.

"Check Brown's car. There may be another one." He looked back at me. "Have you fired any guns today?"

"No," I answered.

"What about in the last week?"

"No, not for years. Dad and I used to go to the indoor range when I was in junior high, but since I've been in high school, we haven't gone shooting."

"How come your dad has so many guns?" asked Detective Baker while jotting something in his notebook.

"Dad's always been kind of paranoid. I guess he felt safer with the guns," I answered.

"What does your dad do?"

"He sells stocks for ER Rogers."

"How about your mom?"

"She's a stay-at-home mom. She's pretty smart. I think she went to college, but I don't remember her ever working. Oh, she keeps the books for the Methodist women's group and was president of the PTA last year. She also likes to read." I choked. "Liked to read."

Detective Sims sighed and spoke softly to me.

"Amy, we are going to take you down to the Public Safety Building. You're a minor. We will need to have a relative come with you. Can you give us the name of someone nearby that we can contact?"

"We don't have any relatives," I explained.

"You mean in Spokane?" asked Sims.

"No, I don't think I know of any relatives. Mom was in foster homes as a child and didn't know her parents. Dad's parents died when I was very young, and they never talked about any relatives."

"Are you telling me that your folks don't send Christmas greetings to relatives or talk to family members on Facebook?" asked Sims.

"No, Mom and Dad are not into Facebook, and I don't think I have ever heard them mention anyone outside of Spokane."

"Were your folks born and raised in Spokane?"

"No, they lived back East and came here just before I was born."

"Where back East?" asked Sims.

"I think Chicago. Listen, I don't know; we never discussed relatives, never in my life." I was becoming frustrated with all the questions. Baker looked perplexed. He stood up.

"Harriet, see if Amy needs to go to the bathroom." I did, and Detective Sims went with me to the one in the hallway. As we walked, Mr. P stayed plastered to my leg. I realized that he was going in with me too. To my surprise Sims came in also.

"Sorry," she said, "we can't leave you alone."

Do you realize how small a hall bathroom is? It would be crowded in there with the cat. I always have trouble peeing at the doctor's office. I did not feel comfortable with this woman standing there. What if she was gay or something? I pulled down my pants, closed my eyes, and concentrated on going. At first, I thought I wouldn't be able to go. But I really needed to go. When I finished, I washed my hands, seeing myself in the mirror above the sink. God, I looked horrible. I ran the water till it was hot, soaked and wrung out a washcloth, and wiped the makeup off. Then we all went back to the sitting room.

10

After about an hour, Baker returned with a white-haired woman. Her name was Mrs. Carlson. She was from Washington State Child Protective Services. Detective Baker explained that since I had no next of kin, a representative from Child Protective Services had to accompany me to the Public Safety Building.

"I would like to talk to Amy in private, please," said Mrs. Carlson. The detectives didn't look very happy about her request but nodded their assent. We went into the sitting room. Mr. P was right there beside me.

"Is that your cat?" she asked.

"Yes," I said. I didn't say it out loud, but I thought, "Of course it's my cat. Why do you think he's sitting here?"

"Is there someone you can leave the cat with?" she asked me.

"No," I said, "and he is all I have left." I started to tear up.

Mrs. Carlson frowned and asked, "Do you have a cat carrier, a litter box, and some cat sand?"

"Yes." I was sobbing now. "In the garage."

"OK, we'll put him in the cat cage, and you can take him with you. Now, dear, I need to ask you some serious questions. I have been told you have no known relatives. Is that correct?"

"Yes," I said.

"What is your date of birth?" I told her. "So, you will not be eighteen for fifteen months. OK. In the state of Washington, until you are eighteen years old, you are not legally able to make your own decisions. You will have to go into the foster care program. Do you understand what I am saying?"

"I can take care of myself or stay with one of our friends," I answered.

"I'm afraid it doesn't work that way. The law is very specific. As a minor you can't make that decision without the approval of a legal guardian. What about godparents?" she continued. "That would work."

"I don't have godparents. All I have are just friends of my family."

"Then it must be a foster home," she said. "Next, I have to ask you if the police have read you your Miranda rights. You know what that is?" she asked.

"I'm a senior in high school. Yes, I know what they are, and, no, they didn't read me my rights."

"Did you admit to them anything about hurting your parents?"

"No," I whispered. "Why would I do that? I never tried to hurt my parents." I suddenly realized why Baker had asked me so many questions about Dad's guns. The police suspected that I had killed my parents— which meant I could find myself in jail.

"The police want to take you down to the Public Safety Building and do a test for gun residue on your hands. If you haven't fired a gun, you will be released to me, and I will take you to a foster home while this investigation continues. This will only be a temporary home until we can find a more permanent residence closer to your high school. Do you understand all of this?" asked Mrs. Carlson. I nodded and asked Mrs. Carlson if I could have a drink of water. I was dying of thirst.

"They haven't offered you a drink?" she asked.

"No," I said. "They let me go to the bathroom; I guess I could have sipped water from the faucet, but I didn't."

"How long have you been in this room?"

I looked at my watch. It was three o'clock.

"All night," I said.

"When was the last time you had anything to eat?" she asked.

"At lunchtime."

"Cops," grumbled Mrs. Carlson. "Those insensitive bastards." She stormed over to the door. "Get this girl something to eat and drink," she yelled.

"Mrs. Carlson, could I also have an aspirin?"

"Of course, dear." She reached into her purse, withdrew a small case, took out two aspirin, and handed them to me. In less than twenty minutes, Detective Baker came in with a sandwich and a Coke.

"I'm sorry. I should have thought of this," he said as he handed them to me. I just nodded as I accepted the food and drink.

I never thought I would be able to eat, but I was starved and wolfed down the sandwich. A Coke had never tasted so good. When I finished, Mrs. Carlson directed a policeman to get the cat carrier and Mr. P's cat box.

"Do you have any suitcases?" asked Mrs. Carlson.

"There are a couple in the hall closet upstairs," I answered.

"Amy, let's go pack a few things. I want you to bring enough clothes to last a few weeks. Also bring your cosmetics and any personal items you will need."

Mrs. Carlson helped me pack my things, and then we put Mr. P in his carrier. Usually it's a battle to get him in his carrier. This time he walked right in and curled up.

We went out the front door, avoiding the kitchen. I glanced toward the kitchen door as we passed by, but I only caught a glimpse of several people in white coveralls.

Mr. P and I crawled into the back of a patrol car. There were no door handles, and a plastic shield separated the front and backseats. Except for no handcuffs, I felt like I was being arrested.

At the Public Safety Building, Mrs. Carlson would not let the police ask me any more questions. They sprayed some stuff on my hands and clothes and shined a light on the sprayed areas. I guess they found nothing, because they allowed the two of us to leave.

We went out to the parking lot and got into a gray Tahoe SUV with state exempt plates. We turned left onto Monroe Street and drove north past Rowan. We were entering an area with older homes. Two blocks later, we turned left onto a side street. I looked at my watch. It was seven o'clock on Saturday morning. I had been awake for twenty-four hours, and the world, as I knew it, had just ended.

11

Dad had always said that Child Protective Services (CPS) was a poorly run organization. That had been his standard comment after some lawsuit was settled, and there was a TV news story about CPS's failure.

Maybe his opinion was based on the fact that Mom had said she'd been in the system as a child. Or maybe it was just Dad. He had an opinion on just about everything. As for me, I thought Mrs. Carlson was an OK person. She definitely knew what she was doing. What I didn't know was that I was about to experience the other end of the CPS spectrum.

The neighborhood had old ranch-style homes. Old cars lined the streets. Although some of the homes appeared to be well kept, others were in a poor state of disrepair. We stopped at a house that clearly was on the poorly kept end. The dead grass in the front yard appeared to have never been mowed. Of course, in October everyone's grass was dead. The flowerbeds were full of tall weeds. Some reached the bottom of the windows. Two large straggly shrubs stood on each side. Each was taller than the house. A twenty-year-old Ford Taurus sedan was parked in the driveway. Even Spalding's Wrecking Yard would have rejected it. It had dents in the doors and trunk. It was so dirty that I didn't know exactly what color it was. A broken bike stood in the front yard. The house was a faded light green color with chipped brown trim. Most of the paint had peeled off, exposing the gray asbestos shingles. *Can you die from living in an asbestos-covered house?*

Mrs. Carlson helped me get my things, and Mr. P huddled in his cat carrier. On the way, we had stopped by a Safeway, and I bought a bag of Kitty Nibbles and a food and water dish for Mr. P.

As we walked up the broken concrete sidewalk, Mrs. Carlson smiled and reached out for a quick hug.

"Don't worry, Amy. I'll get you out of here as quick as I can."

Out? I didn't want in.

12

As we climbed the four steps to the porch, I leaned against the iron railing. It rattled back and forth, offering no support at all. The screen door was ripped in several places.

Mrs. Carlson rang the doorbell. I could hear a TV blaring. The door opened. Standing there was a fat lady in a bathrobe. She had reddish gray hair, which looked like it had never been combed or washed.

"Amy, this is Regina Hanson. You will be staying here for a few days."

Hey, I knew that. I assumed Mrs. Carlson was sending a message directly to this woman. Regina had one of those gravelly voices that are a result of smoking. She also had the cough that smokers get as they try to kill themselves with cigarettes.

We stepped cautiously into the house. When she closed the door, odors nearly overpowered me. Stale cigarette smoke, body odor, and just plan "uck." I almost barfed right there. The living room was a disaster. The floor was covered with a worn dark green shag carpet that was probably fifty years old. There was a mishmash of furniture that would never sell in a rummage sale. Papers and magazines were piled on the tables.

Doesn't CPS require foster parents to keep their houses clean? If things were not bad enough, Regina dropped the next bomb.

"The cat stays in the garage while you're here."

"What?" I asked.

"Toby will kill it if he finds it in the house," she answered.

Who the hell was Toby? Her husband? Would I have to talk to Toby and explain that Mr. P could do nothing to this pigpen, even if he took a dump on the floor? The smell might even improve the place. I kept my mouth closed. Gritting my teeth, I asked where the garage was.

"Through the kitchen," she said, pointing to the left. I picked up Mr. P's carrier, and Mrs. Carlson helped me carry the rest of his stuff to the garage.

Pushing open the garage door, I discovered why the Ford was parked outside. I had never seen so much junk. We had to push boxes of used clothes, dishes, toys, and tools out of the way to make room for his carrier and cat box.

Mrs. Carlson touched my shoulder.

"Honey, this is bad. I am going to notify my supervisor that this home needs an immediate inspection. I will get you out of here Monday, even if you have to stay in my apartment. Just hang on for two nights."

"All right," I said. "I guess this is better than putting him in an animal shelter."

I went back in the kitchen to get Mr. P some water. The counter and sink were full of dirty dishes. I had to stack some of the dishes just to reach the faucet. I took Mr. P's water dish back into the garage and filled the other dish with Kitty Nibbles before opening the door to his carrier.

"You stay here, Mr. P. I'll come back later and play with you."

He looked at me and then looked around the garage. Immediately, he jumped up on one of large boxes and began to sniff and do a visual search. He seemed happy in the garage. It must have been full of mice. Those were Mr. P's specialty. He was a committed mouser. He used to go out into the fields next to our house and hunt for mice whenever he could escape the confines of the house. Then he would devour their lifeless bodies on our back porch. It used to freak Mom out when she found mouse parts on the back porch.

13

WE WENT BACK INTO THE LIVING ROOM. REGINA WAS WATCHING THE big flat-screen TV. Two kids were standing next to her. One was a girl; the other, a boy. They looked like they might be eleven or twelve. They clearly were brother and sister. Maybe even twins.

"Hi, I'm Randy. This is my sister, Sherry. What's your name?"

"Amy," I said.

"Are you going to be staying with us?" asked Randy.

"For a few days," I replied. *The fewer, the better.*

"Cool," said Randy.

Mrs. Carlson turned to me.

"Amy, I will see you Monday." She then spoke to Regina. "Amy needs sleep. She has just experienced a tragedy and has been up for more than twenty-four hours."

"Randy, show her where she will be sleeping," said Regina.

Randy and I walked down the dark hallway.

"This is my bedroom," Randy said, pointing to the door on the right. "Mrs. Hanson wouldn't let me and Sherry sleep in the same room. That's yours and Sherry's room. Don't worry, she don't talk."

"Why?" I asked.

"Mom's boyfriend did something bad to her, and she hasn't talked since. That's why we have to stay with Mrs. Hanson. The last door is Mrs. Hanson and Toby's bedroom. Don't go near that room or Toby will bite you."

"Bite me? What kind of a guy is Toby?"

"He ain't a guy. He's a dog." Randy shouted. "Toby, come here and meet Amy."

"Holy smokes!" I exclaimed.

Walking out of Regina's bedroom was the largest pit bull I had ever seen. He must have weighed eighty pounds. His head was huge. He walked up and began sniffing my leg.

"He's OK," said Randy. "Once he knows you, you can pet him."

"I'll pass," I said.

"Just remember, never try to go into Regina's bedroom. He'll bite you," Randy warned again.

I decided that I would not talk to Toby about Mr. P coming into the house. I was now more worried that the kids might let Toby into the garage. Maybe I wouldn't tell them that I had a cat out there.

We pushed open the door to the bedroom where I would be staying. The floor had the same ancient green shag rug. There was no way I would walk barefoot on that filthy thing.

There were two twin beds in the room. Surprising enough, the room was very neat and as clean as you could get it. There was a suitcase at the end of one bed. I figured the other bed was mine, and I tossed my suitcase onto it.

"Where's the bathroom?" I asked.

"Right across the hall," said Randy. "The lock doesn't work. Don't worry. I won't open it." I saw a gleam in his eyes that told me just the opposite. Randy was a typical eleven-year-old boy, and I suspected that without a lock, he would definitely try to peek. My best friend had a younger brother who was always trying to sneak a peek when she was getting dressed. I decided that we would settle the issue right then and there. I reached over and grabbed Randy's shoulder. I have very long fingers and sharp nails. Randy was maybe just a little over four feet tall. I was almost two feet taller. I squeezed my hand tighter.

"Randy, if the bathroom door opens while I am in there or if the door to Sherry's and my bedroom opens while I am in there, I will kick your butt. Understand?" Randy's eyes became as big as saucers.

"I'd never do that," he said.

"Good. I'm sure you wouldn't. Now, I need to use the bathroom. You stay right here."

I stepped across the hall and into the bathroom. At least the floor wasn't covered with shag carpet. Unfortunately, the linoleum floor was filthy. The back of the toilet and the seat were splattered with dried pee. My girlfriend used to tell me that her brother had a problem aiming. This made me glad I was an only child. I soaked some toilet paper with water from the sink and cleaned off the seat before I sat down. I needed some bathroom cleaner. I wasn't about to live like this, not even for two days. I washed my hands in the sink, which looked like it hadn't been cleaned in years.

14

WHEN I GOT BACK FROM THE BEDROOM, SHERRY WAS STANDING NEXT to Randy.

"Hi," I said. "My name is Amy."

The girl just stood there. Toby stood next to the children. He just stared at me. When a pit bull the size of Toby stares at you, you're not sure whether to run or freeze. He walked over, sat down, and looked at me. I carefully reached down and patted his wide head. He seemed OK, but I knew enough about the breed that he might be friendly around us, yet kill a cat in an instant. No way would Mr. P get in this house.

"Sherry, we're going to be roommates. Is that OK with you?" I asked. She nodded but again said nothing.

"I told you she wouldn't talk," said Randy. "We're twins; that's why they kept us together. We're lucky to be here."

"What's Mrs. Hanson like?" I asked.

"She's OK, I guess. She pretty much leaves us alone. Most of the time she sits in front of the TV watching game shows and smoking cigarettes. Sometimes she takes us shopping with her. She's not mean. Some of the foster parents are," said Randy.

I had no idea what it was like to be a foster child. How lucky I had been.

"I heard the other lady say that you had something bad happen to you," said Randy.

"Yes," I said. "My parents were killed."

"That's a bummer," said Randy. "Our mom's in jail. The police are mad at her because of what her boyfriend did to Sherry."

I didn't want to talk about this anymore, so I changed the subject.

"Could Sherry talk before?" I asked.

"Sure. She was even a better student than I was. She goes to the doctor every week. I guess they are trying to get her to talk."

I stifled a yawn. I looked at my watch. It was almost noon.

"Do you guys eat lunch here?" I asked.

"Sure. On Saturdays we usually fix our own. Do you want a peanut butter and jelly sandwich?" asked Randy.

"Sure, let's go," I said.

We walked back into the living room. Regina Hanson was sitting in her chair, eating off a tray. She looked over at me.

"Did you find everything OK?" she asked.

"Yes," I said as Randy and I walked into the kitchen. "Who washes the dishes?" I asked.

"Me and Sherry," said Randy. "We need to do it this afternoon."

I opened the refrigerator, expecting to see stale bread and moldy cheese. To my surprise, it was well stocked with food. At least that was a plus. There were even fruit and vegetables. While the kids made peanut butter and jelly sandwiches, I made us a salad. We sat at the kitchen table to eat.

Suddenly Randy looked at the door to the garage.

"What's that noise?"

Oh, great, he heard the cat.

"I have a cat," I said. "He has to stay in the garage. Toby would kill him."

"Can we see him?" asked Randy.

"All right," I said. "But we must make sure that Toby is nowhere around. We can never let the cat indoors."

I went to the door. I stuck my foot out, ready to keep Mr. P from getting in the kitchen, but he made no attempt. Maybe he knew that the dog was in the house.

We stepped into the garage. Sherry immediately bent down and picked up Mr. P.

"Careful, he might scratch you," I warned. But the cat made no attempt to struggle. Sherry held the cat close to her face. Tears were running down her cheeks. I had to wipe tears from my eyes.

"What's his name?" asked Sherry.

It was as if lightning had struck the house. Randy and I stood there in disbelief.

"She just spoke," he said. "She hasn't said a word in six months."

I cleared my throat.

"His name is Mr. P," I said.

"That's a nice name," she said. "He told me everything will be all right," said Sherry.

"That's nice," I said.

Hey, I talk to my cat, but he doesn't talk to me.

Whatever the case, a minor miracle had just happened. Sherry's ability to speak began to soothe the hurt I was feeling about my parents' deaths. The three of us—plus Mr. P—stayed in the garage about an hour. When we came out, Randy went into the living room to tell Regina that Sherry had finally talked. At first, Regina didn't believe it. That is until Sherry walked up to Toby and said, "Hi, Toby."

As we were standing there, I started to feel dizzy. "I think I need to lie down," I said. I excused myself and walked back to the bedroom. I was going to unpack my bag, but first I needed to just close my eyes for a minute.

15

I OPENED BY EYES. THE ROOM WAS DARK.

That was strange; I had just closed my eyes for a few minutes.

I looked at my iPhone. It was one in the morning. The streetlight outside the window let in enough light that I could see Sherry asleep in her bed. I got up and went into the bathroom. I sat on the toilet, trying to figure out what might happen to me. This was the first chance I had had to reflect on the problems ahead me. Some of the greatest revelations occur while you are sitting on the toilet. I was now an orphan. I had no family, no job, and would not even graduate from high school until May. I wanted to find out who killed Mom and Dad. But I had nothing. I was only a ward of the state of Washington.

Then I had that revelation. I had everything. I was the heir to Mom and Dad's estate. I knew they paid cash for everything. The house had no mortgage. Dad paid the credit cards off every month, grumbling about how much I had spent on clothes. Dad had stocks and bonds. Mom and Dad had wills, and they had shown them to me. In the event they both died, all their assets went to me.

Would I have to wait until I was twenty-one? I needed to talk to Dad's attorney, and I should do it soon. To do this, I needed wheels. I needed my Mustang. Dad had the title in my name, and I wanted it. Maybe Regina would help me get my car. Then I realized that was unlikely. She wouldn't even get off her butt to fix lunch. Besides, the police weren't letting me near my own house.

Well, it's mine. I'll go home and move back in. Possession is nine-tenths of the law. Then I'll talk to the attorney. I may only be sixteen, but I have my rights.

I stood up and pulled up my pants, but I didn't flush the toilet. I wanted to be as quiet as possible. I went in the bedroom, grabbed my purse, and headed down the hall to the living room. My coat was hanging in the hall closet. I started out the front door and then stopped. I walked into the kitchen, opened the door to the garage. Mr. P stuck his head out of his carrier. Good, he was already in the carrier. There was no way I was leaving Mr. P in that house while I was out.

I walked west down the street to Maple, turned left, and continued down to Rowan. There was a convenience store on the corner of Maple and Rowan that was open twenty-four hours a day. I was glad it was only a few blocks away. Mr. P weighs twenty pounds. He's not fat; he's just a big cat. Try carrying a twenty-pound cat in a carrier for more than a couple of blocks. I had to switch the carrier between my sore arms as I walked.

At the convenience store, I bought a Diet Coke and a power bar. I pulled out my iPhone and punched in the Diamond Taxi Service in Spokane. When the dispatcher answered, I turned to the clerk, an Indian guy with one of those turban things on his head.

"What's the address here?"

He gave it to me and I gave it to the dispatcher. Twenty minutes later a taxi pulled up. I scrambled into the backseat, pushing the cat carrier in first.

The driver was a young guy who was in his senior year at Gonzaga U. He drove the taxi to help pay expenses. I was about to tell him I had been accepted to GU next year. Instead I told him I graduated from GU with an MBA last year. If you're six feet tall, you got an advantage. No one knows how old you are. He might freak out if he thought he had a sixteen-year-old in the backseat. I'm pretty sure he was hitting on me, but I ignored the direction that was going.

He pulled up into our driveway. I held my breath. I expected the place to be covered with crime tape. Fortunately, it wasn't. However, my car was not sitting in the driveway where I had left it. Then I remembered the police asking for the key fob. They were probably looking for the murder weapon.

Oh yeah, Amy Brown, mass murderer.

Had they impounded it? I hoped not. If that was the case, I could always take Dad's BMW. I prayed that the Mustang was in the garage. The title was in my name, and I figured that legally I would be on firmer ground.

The taxi's meter read $23.30. I pulled out one of the fifty-dollar bills I kept in my purse for emergencies. This was another of Dad's precautions. He made sure we always carried six fifty-dollar bills. I handed the driver a fifty and said, "Keep the change." After all, if I was an MBA graduate, I could afford to tip well. He beamed. He was kind of cute. Maybe under other circumstances, I would have taken a closer look.

16

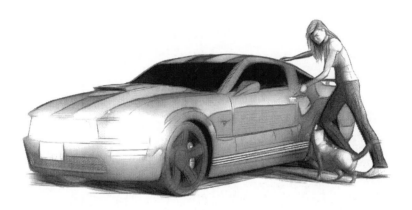

As he pulled away, I got my key out for the front door, which was covered in police sticky tape. A sign on the door read ENTRY PROHIBITED. ACTIVE CRIME SCENE. The tape had to be pulled off to enter. The bottom of the sign read, "Entry without specific permission of Spokane Police Department may result in a fine of $10,000 and/or imprisonment for up to five years." There was a phone number to call for more information.

Two days ago, I would have turned and walked away. After all, I'm the girl who drives five miles under the speed limit. But tonight, I slipped a fingernail under the tape, hoping I wouldn't break a nail, and carefully pulled the tape away from the door. I stuck the tape to the door's surface. After I got my car, I could reapply the tape.

I inserted the key, turned the lock, and pushed the door open. I expected to hear the alarm go off. But it was silent. Of course, the police didn't know the alarm code. I guess they assumed police tape and a warning would keep the bad guys out. *Or a determined daughter.* I turned on the hall light. It seemed as if—for just a moment—it had all been a dream. Then the weight of twenty pounds of cat in his carrier in my left hand brought back reality.

I put the carrier down, stooped over, and opened the carrier door. Mr. P stepped out, stretched, and padded toward the kitchen. That was the one place I did not want to go, but I had no choice. The extra keys to the cars hung on the wall next to the door to the garage. I walked over to the kitchen, turned on the light, and stepped in.

I don't know what I expected to find. The furniture had been pushed over to one side. The back door was boarded up with plywood. No, there was no blood. The floor was cleaned, and I could smell some kind of cleaning solution. There were a number of circled Xs on the wall and even on the refrigerator. I looked closer. Each X marked a bullet hole in the walls. There must have been at least twenty holes.

All I remembered seeing Friday night was Mom and Dad on the floor. I looked down and gasped. The silhouettes of where my parents' bodies had fallen were marked with masking tape. In a flash the emotions became overwhelming. I fell to my knees, sobbing. I cried like a baby. I would stop, and then I would start crying all over again. I yelled out Mom's and Dad's names. I don't know how long I sat there next to where their bodies had fallen. Then there just were no more tears.

I walked to the sink, turned on the cold water, and dampened my face before bending down and taking a drink. Then I grabbed a towel and blotted my face. Looking up, I saw there were two Mustang keys on the rack. Good news! I was right. My Mustang must be in the garage.

I heard a scratching sound. I turned around, and there was Mr. P standing on his back legs scratching on the front of the drawer where we kept his cat treats.

"You want a treat?" I asked. He looked at me. "OK, I'll take a few with me." I pulled open the drawer. Besides his treats, I saw his leash and harness. Yes, a cat can be leash trained, and he was. I would take it with me. I tried to pull the leash out, but it was stuck. The end of the leash was hung up on the back of the drawer. I pulled on the drawer, but it wouldn't budge. I was in no mood for this. I jerked the drawer as hard as I could. The whole drawer came out, and I fell flat on my rear, drawer in my lap. Mr. P's treats were scattered across the kitchen floor.

I stood up, pushing the drawer off my lap. It was then that I saw that something was taped to the underside of the drawer.

Probably another of Dad's emergency plans.

I pulled the tape off. It was holding two keys hooked on a ring. Attached to the ring was a nametag: Allied Storage. It had an address on East Trent. I pushed the keys into my front jeans pocket and grabbed the leash, the harness, and a handful of cat treats. I went back to the living room, picked up the cat carrier, and returned to the kitchen.

Inside the garage we had parked my Mustang, Mom's Lexus, Dad's BMW, and our ski boat. I almost broke down again. It was like our family sitting there, all together again. I stifled a sob and forced myself to keep on going. The cat carrier went into the trunk. Mr. P rushed for the passenger seat and sat patiently waiting for me. Once the garage door was fully open, I fired up the engine and backed out of the garage. I made sure to close the garage door.

At the front of the house, I left the engine running and went back inside through the front door. I scooped up the cat treats from the floor and repositioned the drawer back under the counter. I made sure all the lights were out, both inside and outside. Once on the front porch, I locked the front door and carefully reapplied the police tape. It didn't look perfect, but it would do. I got back in my Mustang, closed the door, patted the dash as if it were a real horse, and headed back to Regina's.

17

HAVE I MENTIONED HOW MUCH I LOVE MY CAR? YEAH, I GUESS I DID. Mr. P and I were cruising north on the Palouse Highway. My music was on as loud as I could stand it. The instrument panel looked like an airplane cockpit. An hour ago, I had thought my world had ended. Right now, I felt exhilarated. I was alive again.

I came to the stop light on Fifty-Seventh. I figured it would take me about thirty minutes to get back to Regina's. Then I felt something in my pocket poking into my right leg. I reached down and realized that I had the keys to the storage container. The keys—what was so important that it had to be kept in a storage container?

What was that address again? I tried to wiggle the keys out of my pocket. Holding the steering wheel with one hand, I struggled to get them out, but they were too tightly tucked into the pocket. I swerved across the centerline. This wouldn't work. I gave up and drove down Regal to Twenty-Ninth. I crossed the street into the parking lot of the McDonald's, pulled in, got out of the Mustang, and worked the keys out of my pocket. I wear tight jeans. I mean really tight. A lot of us girls do. It's kind of funny. Boys think it's cool to wear their jeans hanging down so far that their butt cracks show. Girls think it's cool to wear jeans so tight that they look as if they were painted on. My jeans are so tight that there is no way I could carry a wallet. I could barely get my fingers in my front pocket to retrieve the keys. Dad used to always bitch about how tight my jeans were. His comment was that I might as well be naked. Of course, Mom wore hers tight, too. He didn't complain about that. He used to pat her on the butt, assuming I didn't notice. Yeah, sure, I'm blind.

Finally, I got the keys out. I got back in my car, turned on the reading light, and looked at the address. The storage facility was on Trent out in the city of Spokane Valley. I punched in the address on the car's navigation screen. It was farther out than I realized, but I decided to check it out anyway.

When I finally reached the storage facility, the place was totally dark. A little voice in the back of my head seemed to tell me that this wasn't a smart idea. But my curiosity was stronger than the little voice. I pulled up to the front gate of the facility. There were two keys on the chain. One was for the front gate and the other for the storage container. I got out and walked up to the gate, looking for the lock. There wasn't one. I pushed on the gate, and it swung open. I drove in, got out, and went back and closed the gate behind me.

There were hundreds of storage sheds side by side. Some smaller facilities had doors only four feet wide. Others had garage doors that swung up. I looked at the number on the key: 211. I figured that must be the second row of containers. As I drove through the area, I put on my high beams. With no lights anywhere in the facility, I used my car's lights to guide me. The site had a road up the middle with rows of containers on each side. The containers were lined up like houses on a street. I turned left into the second row. The numbers on both sides were in the forties and increased as I slowly drove along looking for container 211. The sidelight from the headlights provided enough illumination to see the numbers.

I need to get a flashlight and keep it in the glove compartment.

I was going the wrong direction. I backed up, did a K-turn at the center road, and began driving slowly down the other side. Driver's education had paid off. Last year I wouldn't have had a clue what a K-turn was. The distance between the containers was wide enough that a vehicle could pull up directly in front of a unit. There it was—211. It was a large garage door–type container.

I pulled up, the Mustang facing the door. With my headlights on high, I left the Mustang running and looked over to Mr. P.

"You stay in the car." I did not need to be trying to find my cat in a dark storage facility.

18

I GOT OUT AND APPROACHED THE CONTAINER DOOR. I INSERTED THE key into the lock, turned it to the right, grabbed the handle, and rotated it. The door loosened. At the bottom of the door was another handle. I bent down and pulled up on the handle. The door came up, rotating into the ceiling of the container. It was just like the garage doors at home, except that those are electric. You don't have to lift them by hand.

With the door all the way up, I stood transfixed, looking at all the junk piled along the sides and back of the unit. And it was junk. There was old furniture, a refrigerator, kids' toys—none of which I remembered owning. The center of the container, the size of a single-car garage, was open enough that I could walk inside. Why in the world would Mom and Dad have all this junk? Mom would buy a new couch if ours got a stain on it. There was no way they could have owned all this. And why did they save it? I decided to open one of the cardboard boxes in the stack on the right. It was full of old school books. Another contained old clothes.

There must be some mistake. I must have opened the wrong door.

At the back of the container, more cartons were piled up to the ceiling. I spotted a corner of a small strongbox in my car's high beams. Dad had a portable strongbox that opened with a combination lock. He kept valuable papers there. Light gray, it was about twelve inches wide, eighteen inches long, and a foot deep with handles on top. I would never have spotted the box if I had not left on my car's high beams. I started pulling some of the cardboard boxes out of the way. The strongbox was on a top shelf. I reached up and pulled it down. Too heavy for me, it slipped out of my hands and dropped to the floor. I bent over to pick it up.

The next thing I knew, I was flying forward. I crashed into boxes, the side of my skull striking one of the shelves. Pain shot through my head as I fell backward. I finally landed on my back. Everything was going black, but I could hear voices. The noises scared the hell out of me. It sounded like more than one person. Rough hands grabbed my arms. The pain in my head was unbearable.

"Get her pants off! I get dibs first."

"Fuck you, Billy. If I'm pullin' off her pants, she's mine."

"You can have sloppy seconds."

"Hey, guys, look at this—a new Mustang! That and pussy all in one night!"

I could hear their voices. I knew what was coming, but I was totally helpless.

"Oh, God, please help me," I moaned. "Please help me!"

Then everything went black.

19

I COULD FEEL THE COLD CONCRETE AGAINST MY LEGS AND BOTTOM. I was naked from the waist down. I tried moving my legs, but they wouldn't budge. *My feet must be bound together.* I tried moving my arms— they weren't tied. My head hurt. I reached a hand up to check it out. There was a knot the size of an egg on the back of my head. My eyes were shut, but I could see light.

Something rough touched my face. I screamed, pushing my hand out. It connected with warm fur. I opened my eyes. At first everything was blurry. Then I found myself staring at the overhead door of the storage container. I heard a mewing; Mr. P was sitting there staring at me.

The realization hit me like an electrical shock. I had been raped and left lying in the storage container. I felt numb, then disbelief.

OK, Amy, think. What do I need to do now?

I had to get up and find help. I had to get to a doctor. I struggled to sit up. The bright lights blinded me. I could hear the Mustang's motor idling.

Were they sitting in the car, watching me, and waiting to rape me again?

I looked down. I saw that my jeans and panties were pulled down to my knees. It's funny what went through my mind. I might be have been a virgin, but I knew the mechanics of sex. It couldn't be possible with my pants around my knees. Then I saw the dark spots on my legs and stomach. I touched one. It was sticky. I brought my hand up to where I could see it. There was blood on it. I had been injured, maybe seriously.

I might be bleeding to death.

I felt a new sense of urgency. I reached down, pulled up my underpants, and then worked my jeans up. I got to my knees. I felt dizzy and thought I might vomit. It passed, and I shakily got to my feet and pulled my jeans the rest of the way up. I began to examine my injury. It was the middle of the night. No one was coming by to help me. The only sound I could hear was the purr of the Mustang's engine.

For the first time, I noticed the smell. Someone had pooped here. Actually, someone had pooped, peed, and done something else. The high intensity lights of the Mustang gave off a bluish white light. Black stuff was running down the sides of the boxes.

Then I saw a heap of ragged clothes strewn across the floor. I noticed another pile by the entrance. Looking closer, I realized that they weren't heaps of discarded clothes—they were bodies. I dared approach one corpse and felt bile rising in my throat. It was the remains of a disemboweled man; his intestines were lying on the floor; his arms and hands embraced the unruly guts as if he were trying to put them back in place. He had no face that I could see.

I turned and ran.

My feet started slipping. I looked down to see that I was walking in puddles of black, slippery fluid. I knew it was blood. I had to get out of there and fast.

I need to call the police. There must be a crazed killer hiding somewhere.

Then I remembered the strongbox. I saw it lying on the floor splattered with blood. OMG, I had blood on my sneakers. It was everywhere; maybe some of it was my blood. One of the cardboard boxes had tipped over. It was full of used clothes. I grabbed a cotton shirt and wiped the blood from the box. Picking up some more old clothes, I walked toward the door.

Where was the cat? I looked down. Mr. P was strolling along right beside me, totally unconcerned, like this was an everyday occurrence. How had he gotten out of the car? As I got closer to the door, I happened to glance to the right—and screamed. There was a man lying on the old stove, his eyes staring at me. He didn't move. He couldn't move. His entire throat had been ripped out, leaving a gaping hole. He was as dead as the other two.

I stepped out of the storage unit. I was shaking so badly that my teeth chattered. I reached inside the Mustang and popped the trunk. Using both hands, I struggled to lift the box into the trunk and put it next to Mr. P's carrier. It was really heavy. What had Dad put in it? It sure wasn't papers.

The passenger door was standing open, so I went around to close it. Mr. P started to jump in.

"Hold it, cat," I said. I picked him up and wiped his feet off with an old shirt. Then I stood on one of the shirts and wiped my sneakers, trying to remove the blood and whatever else was on them. I tossed the old clothes in the shed, reached up, pulled the door down, and turned the handle to lock it.

I kept expecting someone to come out of the dark and grab me. I honestly cannot tell you how I was able to function so rationally. I should have been running down the street screaming.

I got in my car and headed toward the front gate of the storage facility.

20

WHEN I REACHED THE GATE, I ALMOST DROVE STRAIGHT THROUGH.
My love for my Mustang made me stop. I got out, pushed the gate open,
and jumped back in. I dropped the gearshift into drive and pushed the
gas pedal to the floor. This time, I didn't close the gate. I raced down
Trent at nearly one hundred miles per hour. When I saw a traffic light
change ahead, I slowed down but didn't stop. I didn't see any cars on the
road, and I drove through the red light. As I got closer to town, I began
to settle down. I could feel no pain other than the bruised lump on my
head. I wiggled around trying to feel if there was any pain in my vagina.
I figured, if you've been raped, you must hurt down there. I couldn't feel
any discomfort.

Maybe I'm so scared I can't feel the pain.

In what seemed like minutes, I was pulling into the driveway at
Regina's house. I parked alongside her old Ford. Outside it was still dark.
I would sneak in and put Mr. P back in the garage. Then I needed a
shower and a closer examination of my body. If I had been raped, then I
would go to the emergency room.

I got out of the Mustang and went to the trunk to get Mr. P's cat
container. But he was following me like a dog. I figured that I would just
put him in the garage and then get the cat carrier.

Dumb move on my part, but now as I think about it, not the first
dumb move of the night. A storage container where all the lights were
out. Lights on poles throughout the site, but not working. Then no lock
on the gate. I should have never gone in there.

I entered a house where an eighty-pound pit bull lived with my cat under one arm. I made it to the kitchen. Then all hell broke loose. As I reached for the light, something big jumped against me, knocking the cat out of my arms. I heard a deep growl. Actually, I heard two deep growls and a hiss like a snake. I turned the light on and gasped. There were Toby and Mr. P facing each other like a pair of boxers. Mr. P's tail was blown up like a bottlebrush, and I swear he looked twice as big as he really is. Toby's hackles were raised, and he was showing a set of teeth that could break an ax handle in half. I lunged for the chair, picked it up, and was prepared to smash it over Toby's head when a strange thing happened. Just like with Jesse, our neighbor's dog, Toby suddenly stopped growling and walked over next to the wall and sat down. Mr. P came up to me and calmly sat down.

"I'll be darned," I said. "I guess you two can settle things by yourselves. Toby, go to bed." Without hesitating, the dog looked at me and headed out the kitchen door into the living room.

I paused to listen to see if anyone had been awakened by the noise. Nothing. I decided to get my shower.

"Come with me," I said to my cat. I quietly walked down the hallway, entered my bedroom and picked up my suitcase, took it into the bathroom, and set it on the floor. Mr. P came in with me.

I stripped off my clothes and checked myself out in the mirror. There were red smears of blood on my legs and stomach. Further examination made me fairly sure that I had not been raped and that the blood was not mine. I ran my fingers through my hair and checked out the lump on my head. It was still there, but the skin hadn't been broken. I would have a bruise on my rear where I fell on the concrete and one of my wrists was a little sore.

I stepped into the shower, turned the water on as hot as I could stand it, and scrubbed my body with soap. Normally I wash my hair separately and rinse with my special conditioner. Right now all I wanted was to get rid of the blood. Body wash worked just fine. I got out of the shower, applied powder, and put on clean jeans and my blue sweatshirt.

I took my worn and dirty clothes as well as my shoes back to the kitchen. I could hear Regina sound asleep and snoring in her bedroom. Mr. P followed me. I walked into the laundry room and threw my clothes, socks, and sneakers into the washing machine. Regina had some Clorox Stain Fighter. I poured in two cups. Hopefully the stuff would remove bloodstains. When I first started having my periods, I had a few accidents and got blood on my nightgown and sheets. Mom always used hydrogen peroxide to get the blood out. I didn't have hydrogen peroxide, so the stain fighter would have to work.

I walked back out into the kitchen. I looked at the clock on the wall. It was 6:45 a.m. To my surprise, the kids had washed the dishes. I looked under the sink and found a container of Ajax cleaner. There was also an old rag. I began to work on the sink. I then did the stove and countertops. Maybe later, I would buy some real floor cleaner.

I heard the click of doggie toenails on the floor; Toby came in and looked at Mr. P, who sat on a throw rug next to me. He stood long enough to get a drink out of his bowl and then plopped down on the floor. He let out a low growl.

I was frying bacon and eggs when Regina walked in. She looked around, obviously surprised that I was cooking breakfast. Then she saw the cat and frowned.

"I told you to keep that cat in the garage. If Toby sees him, he'll kill him, and I won't be responsible, young lady."

"They get along fine," I said.

"I doubt that. I got him because he killed cats, and I promised the people that I would never allow him near a cat," she said firmly.

Just then Toby, who had been lying next to the wall, got up to greet Regina, his tail wagging. He sat down next to Regina. Mr. P walked over to them and plopped down in front of the dog. His tail twitched as he watched me. Regina almost lost the cigarette that was hanging between her lips.

"I don't believe it," she said.

"Breakfast will be ready in twenty minutes," I said with a smile. "Why don't you wake up Randy and Sherry?"

21

I FOUND FOUR MATCHING PLATES TO USE FOR BREAKFAST. I HAD FRIED bacon, putting it in the oven to keep warm. I scrambled the eggs with milk and paprika and topped it all with a little cheddar cheese. I made toast and prepared fruit bowls.

I actually liked to cook. Even as a small girl, I loved to cook alongside Mom. She had never cooked before I was born. When she decided to stay at home with me, she was determined to learn how to cook.

She said she worked at a TV station before I was born. She never said what she did, but I couldn't imagine her as a TV anchorperson or anything like that. Don't get me wrong—she was a beautiful woman. But, her hairstyle hadn't changed in years, and she wore an ugly pair of glasses. I was always trying to get her to buy cooler glasses or contacts. Dad was the same way. He wore "old man" glasses.

With the table set and breakfast ready, I began wondering where Regina and the kids had gone. I heard a giggle and looked up. The three of them stood in the doorway. Regina was wearing a dress, her hair had been combed, and she had on lipstick. Judging from Sherry and Randy's wet hair, they had both taken showers. I couldn't help but grin.

"Breakfast is ready," I said.

I busied myself getting the food out of the oven and then handed everyone a paper napkin.

"Randy, it's Sunday, and it's your turn to say grace," Regina said.

Grace? She has the kids say grace before breakfast? Is this the Regina I met yesterday? We bowed our heads.

"God is good. God is great. Let us thank him for this food. Amen," said Randy.

"Amen," we all said together.

It was short and sweet, but the only time we ever said grace at home was at Thanksgiving and maybe Easter. After breakfast, everything seemed to be going great when Randy dropped a bomb.

"Mrs. Hanson, there's a new car in the driveway."

"What?" asked Regina, obviously astonished.

"A red Mustang," answered Randy. *Whoops, now what?*

"It's mine," I said.

"Yours?" asked Regina. "Did you steal a car?" She looked at me and frowned.

"No, it's really mine," I answered emphatically.

"Where did it come from?" Regina asked.

Come from? That's a good question. Think, Amy. How did it get here?

"My girlfriend borrowed it. She called me and asked if I wanted the car. She dropped it off this morning," I answered confidently.

"Young lady, you cannot have a car like that," said Regina, not believing me.

"It's mine," I said. I handed Regina the registration. "See, it's mine. My name is on the registration."

"Well, it is yours," said a surprised Regina after looking at the paper. "You mean to tell me that your parents gave you a new car?"

"Yes, for my birthday."

"Well, you can't have a car," Regina said with her arms folded across her chest.

"Why not?" I argued. "Is there some law that says that a foster kid can't own a car?"

"I don't know," said Regina. "All my foster care kids have been young. I guess since it is really yours, at least until I talk to Mrs. Carlson, you can keep it."

Round one goes to Amy. But I wasn't sure if convincing Mrs. Carlson would be as easy. *Oh, well, I'll worry about that hurdle when I get to it.*

With the car ownership issue settled, Randy wanted to go for a ride in the car.

"After you guys wash the dishes, we'll see about going for a ride," I said.

"Cool," said Randy. "Come on, Sherry; let's clean up the kitchen."

22

WHILE THE KIDS CLEANED THE KITCHEN, I CHECKED TWITTER ON MY iPhone. My generation was born tweeting. I was able to use an iPhone by the time I was five and could send a text message faster than I could speak it.

I hadn't looked at my account since Friday night. It was now eight o'clock Sunday morning. That long without tweeting is considered terminal. There were a few routine tweets from Friday night. By Saturday morning, the news of the deaths of my parents must have gotten out. From there on, I had messages from friends and classmates sending their condolences. I didn't want to respond, so I sent a message to all. "Thx for the msgs. Talk soon." That should hold off any more messages. Then my iPhone chirped. *Didn't you guys get my message?* It was from my best friend Riana.

"Rv J wants 2 c u."

Reverend John Nelson was our minister. In the Methodist church, the ministers change every five years. This one was better than the last one, and he related to teenagers. He was old, maybe fifty. He had one of those Amish beards where the men shave above the upper lip and just have a beard along the side of the face on the chin. He was tall and soft-spoken.

I needed to talk to someone, and he would be fine. I texted back to Riana.

"When?"

"2day," she answered.

"OK," I wrote.

"4 OK?"

"Yes."

"W r u?" she asked. I typed in the address and went to find Regina.

"Regina, my minister is coming over at four o'clock today," I said as I walked into the living room.

"Oh, dear." She looked around. "This place is such a mess."

"Maybe we can clean it up?" I suggested.

"We could, but the vacuum is broken. I don't have the money to buy a new one."

"I'll get one," I said.

"You can't do that, dear. I'm supposed to be taking care of you."

"Not a problem. I'll get a cheap one," I answered.

Just then Randy walked in.

"You said you would take me for a ride."

"I did, didn't I?"

"Can Sherry come too?" he asked.

"Sure, I guess so," I said. "Is it all right if I take them for a short ride? I'll stop by Sears and pick up a vacuum. When we get back, we can clean up the place for Reverend John."

"Let me give you some money toward the vacuum," said Regina. I tried to turn her down, but Regina insisted. She gave me thirty-five dollars.

"We'll be back in an hour or so," I told her and I gave her my cell phone number. I also programmed her phone number into my phone.

23

WE HEADED OUT TO THE MUSTANG.

"Wow," exclaimed Randy. "That's a GT. It's absolutely cool. I want to ride up front."

"Sorry, guys, you have to ride in the backseat until you're twelve. It's the law."

"Bummer," said Randy.

I made sure the kids buckled up and then walked around to the driver's side. As I headed around the front of the car, I saw spots on the grill and hood. It was blood. I couldn't leave it like that in the mall parking lot. Someone might realize that the stuff was human blood. I turned to Randy.

"Is there a car wash anywhere?"

"There's one on Ash and Garland," he answered.

I headed down to the car wash. It was one of those operations where guys scrub off the main dirt with buckets of soap and water before you go through a high-pressure wash and rinse. No one was ahead of me this early on a Sunday morning, but I knew that, after the church services, the car wash would get busy.

I paid for the special that included a towel dry after the wash and left a three-dollar tip for the two guys. They were so enthralled with the Mustang and me that they might have paid me to wash my car. Neither noticed that the dirty spots were blood. It helped that the Mustang was red.

After the car had been washed, we headed to the mall. I parked next to Sears, and we trooped in.

"I want you kids to stay close," I said. As an only child, I wasn't used to dealing with younger children.

We headed to the appliance section. The clerk almost pounced on me.

"May I help you, miss?" he said, smiling.

"Yes, I would like to purchase a vacuum," I said. Mom owned a Dyson vacuum cleaner and loved it. "Do you have Dysons?"

"Yes, they are our best models," he said, realizing he was about to make a big sale. "I want the one with the rotating base," I said.

"That will be six hundred and ninety dollars, plus tax."

I pulled out my MasterCard and driver's license. The man went over and ran the card. For a moment I feared that the card might be rejected, but it went through with no problem. Of course, why would the police freeze my cards? My parents were murdered; it wasn't like they were bank robbers. The clerk handed me my receipt, saying we could pick up the vacuum at the loading dock.

As we headed for the exit, we walked by the clothing section. I glanced over at Sherry and Randy. They were wearing the same clothes they had had on the day before. I remembered the small suitcase next to Sherry's bed. They didn't have many clothes.

I spotted the preteens section.

"When will you guys be twelve?" I asked.

"In three months," Randy answered. I walked over to the dresses.

"Do you like this one?" I asked Sherry.

"Oh, yes," she said. I picked out two other outfits and then underwear and shoes.

I made Randy stay put while we went into the dressing room. Sherry pulled off her jeans and T-shirt. I saw her small breasts budding out. Sherry was close to puberty.

"We need a couple of training bras," I said.

"Bras? What for?" asked Sherry.

"I'll show you when we get home," I answered. *God, I bet nobody's even told her about periods*, I realized.

Next it was Randy's turn. That was a little more difficult. We finally ended up with a new pair of sneakers, two pair of jeans, and two shirts.

He couldn't understand why he needed underwear—he already had two pairs. But I insisted. Before I bought the pants, I wanted him to try them on. He refused. I reached over, grabbed his shoulder, and squeezed like I had the day before.

"Ouch! I'm going." He stormed off to the dressing room. It was a good thing I checked; the pants were too small. I got the next larger size.

With the clothes shopping done, I picked up some cosmetics for Regina. I looked at my watch. We had been gone more than two hours. I called Regina. She answered, sounding like a worried mother.

"It took us a little longer. We're on our way back. I want to stop by Safeway and get some cleaning supplies," I said.

"I'll have lunch ready when you get home," said Regina.

Lugging the shopping bags out the door, we got in the Mustang and drove to the delivery entrance. The Dyson was in a big box. I popped the trunk. There was the cat carrier and the strongbox. I had forgotten about the strongbox. I slid it over to one side. *God, this is heavy. What's in it? Lead sinkers?*

I'd wait until night to find out. I didn't want anyone else to know about the box. With the Dyson in the trunk, I placed the cat carrier in the front seat. I stopped at Safeway for cleaning supplies and a dozen doughnuts before we headed back to Regina's house.

So I had dropped about eighteen hundred dollars on my MasterCard. *Dad's gonna freak-out when he sees the charges.* Then it hit me like a slap in the face. Dad was dead. I stifled a sob and wiped a tear from the corner of my eye.

When I pulled into the drive, I quickly pulled the Dyson vacuum out of the trunk and closed it so no one would see the strongbox. The twins were so excited, they couldn't stop talking. Regina was livid. I shouldn't have spent my money. It was against the law for her to take anything from foster children in her care, she complained. I told her that I wasn't a poor foster child. I had tons of money, and she could just consider it an anonymous donation.

"Well, I'll pay you back," she grumbled.

"I'll tell anybody who asks that you gave me the money. After all, you did, remember?" I told her.

"Not enough for all this," she said, pointing at the shopping bags.

"I found some great bargains," I said. Then I handed her the lip gloss, perfume, and foundation. It sounded like she snorted as she walked down the hall to her bedroom, where I thought I heard her sobbing.

Shortly she returned. "Thank you. Lunch is ready in the kitchen."

<h1 style="text-align:center">24</h1>

WE STARTED ON THE HOUSE AFTER LUNCH. WE ONLY HAD FOUR hours before Reverend John arrived. I suggested that perhaps Regina could smoke outdoors. She said nothing but did go out on the porch.

Three hours later, the place looked a lot better, but it would take days to get it really clean. The Dyson worked great. No one would believe how many loads of dirt we dumped in the garbage. When we had an hour to go, we all got cleaned up. Regina put on the dress she always wore when she met with CPS. She was wearing the Chantilly. I was struck with another moment of sadness. Mom wore Chantilly.

When the doorbell rang, Regina answered it. The twins and I were sitting in the living room. Randy and Sherry looked great in their new clothes. Reverend John and Regina walked into the room. He was wearing a black suit with one of those white minister collars. I had said I would never cry again. What did I do? I started crying. He placed his arms around me.

"It's OK, Amy. God will help you through this. In time, the pain will lessen," he whispered to me.

"I know," I sobbed, "but I miss them so much."

Reverend John sat down and began talking. He was a cool man—when he started talking, everyone else did too.

Randy and Sherry told him they used to go to Sunday school. They didn't know who their dad was. Their mom had lots of boyfriends, and the last one had done a bad thing to Sherry. Now their mother was in jail. Reverend John just said that sometimes adults do bad things, but that God will always see us through the hardest times.

Regina told him that she and her husband, Frank, worked as custodians for the Spokane School District. They had no children and loved to go camping and fishing. They were proud of being school custodians. Ten years ago she had fallen off a ladder at work and injured her back. She retired with a modest disability pension. Frank had continued to work. They were doing all right until the day Frank started coughing up blood. She begged him to go to the doctor, but he was stubborn. By the time he finally did, he was diagnosed with Stage IV lung cancer. He lived one more year. The expenses were astronomical.

After Frank's death, Regina lost their home and she only had enough money to rent this house.

Again, Reverend John listened and sympathized. At that moment, I felt closer to Regina, Sherry, and Randy than to anyone else on this earth. I had just lost my parents, and I shared in their misery.

Then Reverend John turned to me.

"Would you all hold hands?" he asked. He held my hand and Regina's, and we reached out for the twins' hands. We bowed our heads, and he began to pray.

"Lord, we rejoice in the fact that you have given us your son, Jesus, to carry us through this time of trial and tribulation. We do not understand your master plan for our lives. We do not understand why men do evil things to the innocent. We reach out to your son, Jesus, with our aching hearts. We know that his love will be there for us in the darkest hours.

"Lord, I just ask that you be with each of your children seated here. For Regina, show her that you still love her and have a plan for her life. For Randy, show him that he is a child of your creation and that he can be someone special. For Sherry, show her that there are good people willing to be here for her. Take away the hurt and fear. And, Lord, for Amy, dear Amy, I know in my heart that you have a special plan for her. During these days of sorrow, be there with her. Walk with her as she finds her destiny. We ask this in Jesus's name. Amen."

I will always remember those words. After the prayer, it seemed easier to talk about what must be done. Until that moment, I had not thought much about the future. We had to plan a memorial service. We decided to schedule a celebration of my parents' lives at the church the Saturday after next.

The next topic was more difficult. Since I had no next of kin, someone would have to deal with the estate. I would need a legal guardian until I was eighteen years old. Reverend John asked about wills. There were wills. I remembered when we went to the lawyer. His name was Paul Dino, and his office was in downtown Spokane. I had been with my parents when Mr. Dino had prepared wills, powers of attorney, and living wills. He was a nice man and would know where the wills were kept.

"Do you think Mr. Dino would be willing to represent you?" asked Reverend John.

"I believe so," I said, although I really hadn't thought about it.

"Then someone will have to act as your legal guardian until you are of age," he said.

"Mrs. Hanson," I said.

"Who?"

"Regina Hanson. She's licensed as a state foster home caregiver. The state sets the stupid rules, and I want her. I'll talk to Dad's attorney and see if he can help me do that."

Reverend John and Regina were both looking at me like I had just lost my mind. Less than thirty-six hours ago, I had thought she was the Wicked Witch of the West. But since then I had learned a great deal about Regina. I also wanted the twins to be part of this deal. That was, of course, if their mother stayed in jail. I didn't know how I was going to accomplish all that, but I was going to try.

The final issue was the most difficult.

"Do you know when your parents' bodies will be released by the police?" asked Reverend John. *Released?* I hadn't thought of that either.

"They have to go to a funeral home. Then there is internment in a cemetery," he continued. That was another subject I had not even thought about. We had never talked about cemeteries or internment.

"The police haven't told me anything," I said.

"I'll make some inquiries as your minister. Unless you have an objection, I'll have the bodies sent to the Smith and Jones Funeral Home. Then you can decide what to do."

I was sobbing again. I managed to get out, "That's OK. Thank you."

Reverend John stood and got ready to leave. I gave him my phone number. He hugged each one of us and said, "God will be with each of you."

As she closed the front door, Regina looked at me. "Dear, I am not sure that Mrs. Carlson will allow you to stay with me. She was pretty emphatic that you would only be here a few days."

"I'll talk to Mrs. Carlson tomorrow," I said. "Let's get dinner."

25

AFTER DINNER, AS A REWARD FOR GETTING THEIR HOMEWORK DONE, Regina allowed the twins to watch *America's Funniest Videos* before bed. The school bus would pick them up at seven o'clock in the morning. She had prepared a note for the middle school special education counselor explaining that Sherry was now talking. Several times she asked Sherry a question to see if the speaking was just a fluke, but Sherry answered the questions with ease.

After the twins went to bed, I learned more about what had happened to Sherry. Sherry and Randy's mom, Vicky Johnston, was one of those women who always seemed to find the wrong guy. I saw that in high school. Some of my friends dated real losers. For some reason, they seemed unable to leave even when the guy two-timed them. It was like they were afraid that if they broke up with the jerks, no one would ask them to prom. I was never that hung up on boys. Anyway, their mother had slept with so many guys that she didn't even know which guy was Sherry and Randy's father. *How can a woman be so nieve?*

Vicky tried to raise the kids as best she could. They even attended church and went to Sunday school. Then she met Mike Douglas. Mike was a petty thief and had a number of minor brushes with the law. He also abused women, as evidenced by a no-contact order with his last girlfriend.

Douglas swept the twins' mother off her feet. He moved in and things got bad. He had no job and spent most of the time hanging around the house while Vicky worked as a waitress. For over six months, Douglas molested Sherry, who was just eleven years old. He told Sherry if she told anyone, he would kill her. Vicky was aware of what was going on and did nothing to stop it. As Sherry withdrew into a shell of silence, the school district called in CPS. An examination of Sherry showed that she was being molested. The police arrested both Vicky and Mike.

Regina had had the kids for the last three months.

"What will happen to the twins?" I asked.

"If the court proves that their mother knew that that dirtbag Douglas was molesting Sherry, they both would be doing jail time, and the kids would end up in foster care until they were eighteen. I've discussed keeping them with me. Thank God Sherry is talking again. The state was getting ready to separate her and Randy and send Sherry to a special care facility," explained Regina.

"What about me?" I asked. Regina smiled. "You are a special person, Amy. It seems unbelievable that you would be placed in the foster care program. You come from a well-to-do family. In my experience, someone like you ends up with relatives. You're more like an adult than a child. Yet it could take months for the state to figure out what to do. I would love to have you stay here," said Regina. Then she laughed. "You've got me smoking outside of my house. If you hang around long enough, you'll be making me quit."

We were sitting on the sofa in front of the LCD TV that was mounted on the wall. Mr. P was curled up on the sofa against my leg, purring. Toby, who was lying by the front door, stood up and scratched the front door.

"You want out, Toby?" asked Regina. Toby barked.

"Won't he run off if you let him out the front door?" I asked.

"The previous owner had one of those invisible fences. Unless I have him on a leash, he will not set foot on the sidewalk," said Regina as she got up and walked to the door. Mr. P got down and followed her.

"I think my cat wants out too."

"Honey, your cat's only been here two days. He might run off, or Toby might go after him outside," said Regina with a look of concern.

"We can go out with them. I know that Mr. P doesn't like to use his cat box if he doesn't have to," I said as I walked over to Regina, who was getting ready to open the door.

When she opened the door, Toby zipped out. Mr. P followed right behind him. Regina turned on the porch light, and we watched the two animals. Toby sniffed the shrubs in the flowerbed before lifting his leg and peeing on one. Then he kicked up his back feet, sending dirt against the bush. Mr. P walked over, sniffed where Toby had peed, and turned around to send a stream of pee at the exact same spot. People say that animals do not have expressions, but I wish you could have seen the look on Toby's face. He was shocked.

"A little turf battle between two males," said Regina, smiling.

Both animals walked back up the steps, and we let them in. Mr. P led the way with Toby following. Mr. P walked back over to the sofa, jumped up, and stretched out. Toby plopped down and let out what sounded like a groan. Regina and I stood there, laughing so hard that we had tears in our eyes.

We had been watching the Fox TV network. The ten o'clock news was just starting.

"I'll shut that off, honey. I'm sure that you don't want to see it," said Regina.

"No," I said. "Wait a minute. It's OK. Maybe they have a lead on who killed my parents."

I recognized the two anchors. Many times Mom, Dad, and I would watch them before heading off to bed.

The anchorwoman began speaking:

For the second time in fewer than two days, murder is our top story. As the community struggles to understand the brutal execution-style murders of a couple in Hangman Hills, Spokane Valley police are investigating a triple homicide, apparently gang related.

The bodies of three members of the Skulls Gang were found dead in a storage container. The three young men's bodies had been mutilated, according to a source in the coroner's office. Identification was made from fingerprints. The bodies were discovered following a call from the owner of Allied Storage. When Walter Kincaid arrived this morning, he discovered the front gates standing open. A pickup truck was found in the rear area filled with items stolen from storage containers. Police were called. As they were investigating the scene, they discovered what appeared to be blood running out from under the door of a container.

A search warrant was acquired, and the container was opened. The three bodies were discovered inside. Police believe that this may be retaliation by a rival gang. The investigation continues.

As for the murder in Hangman Hills, the names of the victims have been released. They were James and Sally Brown. Mr. Brown worked for ER Rogers Investments, and they lived in Hangman Hills for more than sixteen years. Interviews with neighbors indicate they were a well-liked family. There have never been any problems involving the police. Needless to say the entire community is terrified that this may not be an isolated incident. Apparently nothing was stolen, and police believe that the Browns were specifically targeted.

The police have been unable to find any known relatives to the Browns. They have a sixteen-year-old daughter who is a senior at Freeman High School. We have been unable to locate the Browns' daughter.

And now, Lisa Yang with the weather.

26

"I'M SORRY, DEAR," SAID REGINA.

"It's OK," I said. "I have to know what is going on. But now I think I'll go to bed. Tomorrow I need to go see Dad's lawyer and find out what he can do to help me. Good night, Regina."

"Good night, dear."

I got up and walked down the hallway to the bathroom. I brushed my teeth and washed my face and was getting ready to put on my T-shirt—I sleep in a large T-shirt and boxers—when I remembered the strongbox in the trunk of my car. I needed to find out what was in it. I kept my clothes on and walked into the bedroom, climbed into bed fully clothed, pulled the covers over me, and stared at the ceiling. Mr. P jumped on the bed. He wasn't very happy. At home, I had a queen-sized bed, but this bed was much smaller.

"Hey, I need some room too," I said as the cat kicked my legs.

I lay there thinking about the next steps I had to take. I started counting off on my fingers what I needed to do. One: I needed to know what my legal status was. Two: I needed to know where my parents' wills were. Three: I needed to know when I could get into my home. Four: I needed to find out when the police would release my parents' bodies. Five: I needed to plan a memorial service. Six: I needed to figure out what to do about school. I didn't want to go back. I didn't think I could face all those kids, looking at me like I had the plague or something.

Perhaps the school issue was the easiest. I had already passed all of my required subjects. My senior year was supposed to be college prep and fun. I could take the GED and get my diploma. The GED was a written exam that had to be passed to receive a high school diploma if you dropped out of school. I could take the GED in November and graduate. I didn't need to return to school.

God, four days ago I was worried about what color nail polish to wear and whether I'd have a date for senior prom. Now all this. None of those things seemed important any longer.

I heard the door handle turn, so I closed my eyes, pretending I was asleep. The door opened. Then it closed. I heard Regina whisper, "Come on, Toby," and the door to her bedroom close. I lay there. The toilet flushed in Regina's bathroom. I waited thirty minutes and then quietly got up. Sherry mumbled something in her sleep. I walked to the door, Mr. P right beside me. I couldn't leave him in the bedroom. He might start meowing or scratching at the door.

"Come on," I whispered.

I quietly made my way outside to my Mustang. As Mr. P and I walked by the bush where he and Toby had peed, he dashed over to the bush, backed up, and sprayed the spot again. He then ran up to me.

"Don't overdo it, buster," I whispered. He looked up at me, his golden eyes reflecting the streetlight by the curb. It almost looked like he was smiling.

I held the fob for the Mustang and pushed the trunk button. The trunk popped up. I reached in and lifted out the strongbox. I had to use both hands. The thing was heavy. It must have weighed thirty or forty pounds.

I lugged the box up the steps, set it down, and pushed the front door open. I carried it in and placed it on the floor, closing and locking the door behind me. With Mr. P still right beside me, I lugged the strongbox through the kitchen and into the garage.

Mr. P went over to his box and began moving cat sand around. *Oh, great. He's going to take a dump.* If that happened, I would never be able to stand it. His poop really stinks. But all he did was push the sand up in a corner. He was apparently trying to cover up a small spot of past pee so Toby wouldn't know. He started wandering around all the stacks of boxes, probably checking for wayward mice.

I sat down next to the strongbox. It was locked with a four-dial combination lock. The numbers were from *0* to *9* for a total of ten. With four dials, that's ten thousand possible combinations. *I could spend two weeks trying to open this box! If I had tools, I might be able break into it, though.* These boxes were pretty well built. The hinges were internal, and it was made of heavy steel sheeting and had an inner fireproof liner. You could use a cutting tool to open the box, but that might damage whatever was in it.

I decided that, because this belonged to my father, I might be able to figure out the combination. I knew that Dad would have a combination that he wouldn't forget. I spun the combination, turned up all zeros. Normally when you buy one of these boxes, they initially open on zeros. Then you use a little key that comes with the box to reset the combination. Four zeros didn't work, and I wasn't surprised. I tried *1, 2, 3, 4*, then *4, 3, 2, 1*. Nothing. We had a combination lock on the boat trailer. It was the last four of Dad's social security number. I dialed in *3, 1, 7, 2*. No result. I tried our birthdays, other special dates, still with no success. Maybe this wasn't our strongbox. The storage shed contained junk that I had never seen. I might have ripped off someone else's strongbox.

Maybe I should get rid of the thing. I quickly rejected the idea. That wasn't going to happen. I had to find out what was inside. I closed my eyes. Was there any number sequence I had forgotten that Dad would not forget? There was one other. I dialed in *7, 2, 6, 4*. Those were the last four digits of my social security number. I looked at the box. Was that the right combination? I took a deep breath and lifted the handle. It opened.

I realized that I had closed my eyes. What was I expecting? An explosion, a blinding flash of light? I looked in. If a human skull was staring back at me, I wouldn't have been surprised. There was something wrapped in a small towel. I took it out and unwrapped the towel. There was a badge and a 40-caliber Glock 22 in it. I could smell the gun oil. A magazine was in the pistol. I released the magazine and pulled the slide back; a round popped out and landed on the concrete. There was still a round in the chamber. All you would have to do was pull the trigger. Lucky for me that Dad had instructed me in the use of these guns.

If someone like Randy had found this, he might have accidently shot himself.

I examined the badge more closely. It was numbered and read FBI. This was a weapon used by FBI agents. When I was in junior high, Dad and I used to shoot at an indoor gun range. A number of people used the range. We had 9mm Glocks. A gentleman was shooting next to us. As we pulled our targets back, he had looked at my target. I had hit five out of ten bulls. He had remarked about my shooting. He introduced himself. He was an FBI agent. He asked if I would like to see his service weapon. It had been a Glock 22 just like ours except the larger .40-caliber round. He told me that all FBI weapons used the larger caliber because of the stopping power.

I had a bad feeling about this. What was an FBI badge doing in the strongbox? Since the last four of my social security number opened that box, I could no longer believe it was someone else's. A noise drew my attention back to the box—there was my cat, pawing through the contents.

"Hey, what are you doing? Get out of there!" I ordered. He was persistent. His claws hooked on a gold necklace. He pulled it out. "Give that to me," I said.

It was a large tooth attached to a gold necklace. It felt warm in my hand even though it was cold in the garage. I looked closer. It was big, maybe from an alligator or crocodile. No, I remembered from biology, reptile teeth were straight. This was slightly curved. *A carnivore, like maybe a big cat, perhaps a lion*, I concluded.

I set it down on the floor next to the pistol. Mr. P sprawled in front of the tooth, just staring at it. The cat was really acting weird, but I wanted to check out what else was in the box. I saw two velvet bags and lifted them out. Each one was about the size of my fist. They had little drawstrings. I opened the first one and looked in. It was full of pieces of glass, like when you break a piece of tempered safety glass. I reached in and removed one. It was a diamond the size of my thumb. Bigger than one you could mount on a ring. How did I know it was a diamond? I'm a girl. It's in my DNA. I sat down, still holding the bag. My hands were shaking. I opened the other bag to find it filled with rubies and emeralds.

Were my folks international jewel thieves? I looked back in the box. I saw two green notebooks. Below them were a bunch of rolled coins. They looked like they might be old silver dollars.

I picked up the two little notebooks to find that they were actually passports. We had enhanced driver's licenses that allowed us entry into Canada, but we never had passports. The farthest I had ever been in my life was Canada. Most of our summer vacations were at Lake Coeur d'Alene. Several of our family friends owned places on the lake. We would take our ski boat and spend weekends with them.

I opened one of the passports. The picture was of Mom when she was younger. She wore her hair long and had no glasses. She was gorgeous. I opened the other. It was my dad. His hair was cut short. Dad had never worn his hair short. He, too, had no glasses. The greatest shock was the names on the passports. The name on Mom's passport was Samantha Lynn Dixon-Martin. Dad's passport had the name Timothy Henry Martin. *Holy smokes—they used false names on the passports.* Were they spies?

All that was left in the box were the rolls of coins. I lifted one out. It was heavy. I unwrapped the coins. They were shiny gold. I looked at one closer. It was a gold Krugerrand. It read ONE TROY OUNCE OF GOLD. In my hand was ten ounces of pure gold. I didn't follow gold prices, but I was pretty sure that an ounce of gold was about two thousand dollars. How many coins were there in the strongbox? I begin lifting out the rolls of coins. I set them on the floor. Counting the one in my hand, there were twenty rolls. That was two hundred one-ounce coins. *No wonder the box is heavy—that's over thirteen pounds of gold.* I quickly calculated. *At two thousand dollars an ounce, that's four hundred thousand dollars.* Then there were the jewels. They could be worth millions.

My heart was racing. This made no sense at all. I began to put everything back in the box. I kept out two of the gold coins and a red gemstone about the size of a walnut. I pushed them into my jeans pocket.

As I reached for the tooth, Mr. P growled at me. I looked at him sternly.

"No! You don't do that," I said sternly. "It's going in the box." I dropped it in the strongbox, closed it, and locked it. *OK, now what do I do with it?* I couldn't leave it in the Mustang. The answer was simple: Dad had hid it in junk in a storage container. I could hide it at least temporally in Regina's garage.

I started moving cardboard boxes. I opened one. It was full on men's clothes. They probably belonged to Regina's husband. I pulled the clothes out, put the strongbox in, and covered it with clothes. I then pushed other boxes around it and placed other cartons on top of the one with the strongbox in it.

I turned off the light in the garage, walked back into the kitchen, closed the door, and went back to bed. Apparently Mr. P was no longer mad at me because he jumped up on the bed and curled against my leg.

I wondered if I would have been better off not finding the strongbox. Who were my parents? All my life, I just assumed that we were the typical family. Everything we did was typical. I had thumbed through the passports. They had traveled around the world. The last stamp in the passports was Sudan in North Africa. Were they spies? Crooks? Murderers? It couldn't be possible. I knew them, and I loved them. We went to church; we prayed together; we laughed together. There had to be a mistake.

But whom do you know who has millions in jewels and tens of thousands in gold coins, fake passports, and an FBI badge, all ready to load in your car and run? Why did they call themselves the Martins? There was too much information; I couldn't rationally explain what was happening. At some point, I must have fallen asleep.

Had I known what was going on at the Public Safety Building earlier in the day, I would never had been able to sleep.

27

In the Major Crimes Division, all the desks but one was unoccupied. In a police department the size of the one in the city of Spokane, even on Sundays, the offices were open. But, other than patrolmen who worked shifts, detectives in the Major Crimes Division spent most of their hours working either in the field or on weekdays, when they could make contacts.

SPD was located in the new Public Safety Building on Mallon next to the Spokane County Courthouse. The building housed both the County Sheriff and Spokane Police departments. Although totally separate law enforcement agencies, they not only shared building space but worked closely together.

Mark Baker finished the last bite of a second Sausage McMuffin and took another sip of coffee. He spread the crime scene photos out on his desk. They were eight-by-ten-inch glossy prints. The murders had occurred in Spokane County and normally the Sheriff's Department would have handled this case. But they were short two detectives in their division, and the chief had offered up Mark and his partner to be the lead team on the case.

This had been no problem for Mark. He was happiest when he was working a case, and there was little in his life other than police work. It wasn't always like that. Things had changed five years ago when Tami divorced him. They had met when he was a rookie and she worked at Starbucks. When he got coffee, she was always there with her big smile. They got married and had one daughter, Carrie, who was now all grown-up and married with two children of her own.

Tami was diabetic, and, five years earlier, she had been hospitalized for six days. It was during a big police investigation, and Mark tried to visit the hospital as time allowed. He blamed Tami for part of the health problem. She often forgot to use her insulin or she ate forbidden food. It wasn't like she was dying. Quinn, her older sister, was with her every day. Mark never liked Quinn. During the hospitalization, Quinn convinced Tami to leave him. After she was discharged from the hospital, Tami moved in with Quinn. The next thing he knew, he had been served with divorce papers. Mark didn't fight it. To be honest, they had fallen out of love long before the hospital stay. As divorces go, it was fairly amicable. They split up their property, and Tami moved to Newcastle near Seattle where their daughter and son-in-law lived. She would be closer to the grandchildren. At Christmas when they all got together, he and Tami were cordial, but they no longer had any feelings for each other.

At forty-seven, Mark was young enough to start over, but since the divorce, he had had zero social life. He lived in a small rental. Other than a weekly poker night or attending a sporting event with the guys, most of his nights were spent alone in front of the TV. He preferred being in the office to doing anything else. He often wondered what would happen when he retired. He understood why many old cops committed suicide when they retire. There was nothing left.

Then there was his partner, Harriet Sims. When Hector Remarus retired, Sims was moved up from the street to become a detective. She was fifteen years younger than Mark. It didn't matter. The day that Harriet walked into the Major Crimes Division, he had fallen in love. What a joke! First of all, Harriet was almost young enough to be his daughter, and the gold band on her left ring finger should have been a deterrent. But even worse, her partner in life—a petite, blond second-grade teacher—was also a woman. Harriet was blatantly gay and happily partnered.

But Mark couldn't help himself. He loved Harriet. He often wondered if she even realized how he felt. He had not dated a woman in the last four years. Every day he looked forward to being with Harriet. He didn't even bother to apply when a lieutenant's position came open.

That would have meant that he and Harriet would no longer be working together. He realized that Harriet would move on in the department, and their days of working together would sooner or later come to an end, but for now, he cherished each day.

He stared at the two pictures of the victims. Brown was his own age; his wife, a year younger. The wife was African American with light skin. She had probably been a beautiful woman. Each victim had been shot multiple times. Recovered rounds were 9mm. None of the neighbors had heard any shots, indicating weapons with suppressors. After they had been killed, the bodies were rolled face-up. Two small entry wounds were visible on their foreheads. This was classic Russian Mafia. Two rounds fired into the victim's head at point-blank range from a .22 automatic pistol. Clearly this was not a random shooting. The Browns had been killed for a reason.

He placed the photos in a folder and turned on his computer.

"OK, Mr. and Mrs. Brown, let's find out who and what you are."

With the Browns' social security numbers and fingerprints and his access to the FBI, Homeland Security, and the IRS databases, Mark began to develop a picture of the Browns' life in Spokane, Washington. In the old days, cops spent hundreds of hours following up on leads. That still had to be done, but a lot of the work could be done with technology. Mark planned to spend the day developing information packages on each of the victims. Then on Monday when Harriet came to work, they could follow up on what he had learned.

28

MARK'S CELL PHONE BUZZED IN HIS POCKET. HE PULLED IT OUT AND looked at the caller ID—Spokane Valley Police Department.

"Detective Baker, Major Crimes Division," answered Mark.

"Detective Baker, I'm Lieutenant Borston. I understand that you are the lead on the Brown murders."

"Yeah," said Mark. "What can I do for you?"

"We have an ongoing investigation that may be linked to your case. We received a call from Allied Storage this morning about a break-in. When our man arrived, he found a pickup truck in the rear of the lot. It was filled with stolen items. In the storage unit, a number of containers had been opened. There was no one in the area. We began to do a more thorough search of the contents. We found a locked container with what looked like blood seeping under the door. Forensics confirmed that it was human blood. We're getting a search warrant to open the container. It turns out the container is being rented by one James Brown in Hangman Hills. Looks like he has rented the container for more than ten years."

"You've got my interest," said Mark. "May I be there when you open it?"

"Not a problem."

"Great. I'm on my way."

Mark started to leave the office. He stopped. Harriet would want to be in on this. He pulled out his phone and punched in her number.

"Hello," answered a female voice.

"June, this is Mark. May I speak to Harriet?"

"Hi, Mark. Just a minute."

About ten seconds later, Harried answered.

"What's happening, partner?"

Mark's heart jumped a few beats just hearing her voice.

"I hate to bother you on a Sunday morning, but Spokane Valley PD has an active crime scene, and it may be linked to our murder case."

"Pick me up in twenty minutes. I just got out of the shower. Give me time to get dressed."

"See you then," said Mark. He hung up. He would have loved to see her stepping out of that shower. He headed down to the garage to pick up their car.

Twenty minutes later he pulled up in front of Harriet and June's house on Twenty-Seventh Avenue. When they said good-bye, Harriet kissed June and headed down the sidewalk to the car.

As always she was stunning. She was wearing a maroon pants suit and black flats and carried her coat. The sun was already up and the temperatures would be in the fifties by afternoon. She could be a fashion model if it weren't for the shoulder holster with the .40-caliber Glock and the detective badge pinned to her pants pocket. She opened the car door and slid in. Mark detected the smell of fresh soap and perfume.

"So, what have we got?" asked Harriet.

"Not sure," he said. He told her what had happened. As they headed out on East Trent, he told her what he had found on the computer.

"So far, I can't find anything on the Browns going back more that seventeen years. It's as if they didn't exist before that."

"Could it be witness protection?" asked Harriet.

"That's possible. This sure looks like a mob hit. It also looks like they were wealthy."

"Yeah," said Harriet. "June and I couldn't live in that house with both of our salaries, and he gave his daughter a new Mustang GT."

"No, more wealth than that."

"What do you mean?"

"From the tax records, it looks like Brown was worth hundreds of millions of dollars. With that kind of wealth, where they were living was like a shack on the other side of the tracks."

"What were you doing? Working the case this weekend?"

"Yeah, I didn't have anything else to do."

"Mark, you need to get a life. You can't be working all the time."

"I'm OK. Besides, this murder bothers me. It was so ruthless, and I'm still not sure what to make of their daughter, Amy."

"You think she was involved in their murders?" asked Harriet.

"No, but something isn't right," answered Mark.

Mark saw the police cars up ahead next to Allied Storage. He pulled across Trent and parked behind a police cruiser. They got out and walked up to a patrolman standing at the entrance.

"Detectives Baker and Sims. We're here to see Lieutenant Borston."

The patrolman said, "Go on in. Take the second lane to the right. You'll see the CSI truck."

Harriet and Mark went into the storage facility. They spotted the large white van with several people standing around. Most were in uniforms. A short rotund guy in a blue suit walked toward Mark and Harriet.

"I'm Matt Borston."

"Mark Baker. This is Harriet Sims."

"We're getting ready to open the door," said Matt. "Let me get you some booties and latex gloves." They slipped the plastic booties over their street shoes and placed on the latex gloves. CSI would be the first to enter, checking the area for evidence and then telling the detectives where they were allowed to step.

Mark looked at the white rolltop door that came to the concrete floor in front of the unopened container. A dark congealed substance had seeped through the crack under the door. A line of yellow crime tape indicated the no-step zone.

"We've got a good bloody handprint on the door," said Borston.

"Can you provide us a copy of the print?" asked Mark. "We can check it against prints we pulled from our crime scene." He doubted there would be any match. At the Browns' house, it was clear the perps had worn latex gloves.

Mark looked around the area in front of the container. The roadway was asphalt, but the building was on slab concrete. At each entrance was a concrete pad, part of the building. Next to where the blood had gone under the door, Mark saw what looked like small animal prints.

"What are those?" asked Mark.

A middle-aged woman in a white suit with a FORENSICS tag stapled on her pocket answered.

"It looks like a cat walked in the blood before it dried. Probably a stray cat attracted by the blood."

Finally it was time to open the door. One of the technicians inserted the key.

"Would everyone step to the side, away from the door?" ordered the technician.

Since they had no idea what was behind the door, he wanted everyone back in case it was booby-trapped. He slowly lifted the door. It seemed like it was taking forever, but it was only a matter of a few seconds.

With the door open, sunlight streamed in. The technician took a tentative step into the building. He had maybe taken two steps when he shouted.

"Holy shit!"

Then he bolted out of the container, ran outside of the tape, and proceeded to vomit.

"That doesn't bode well," whispered Harriet to Mark. Working homicide, Harriet and Mark had learned to expect and prepare for the worst. Mark looked at Matt Borston, took a deep breath, and walked carefully toward the storage container, being careful not to step on any evidence. He pulled out his high-intensity LED flashlight. As he reached the door, he could smell the carnage. Last time he had smelled this was when a guy strapped with explosives blew himself to pieces.

He wasn't surprised to find the mutilated bodies on the floor. He approached one that lay near the door. It was the body of a man. His intestines had spilled out on the floor. He had no face. To his right was a third man. The eyes were open. The man's entire throat had been ripped out, leaving an empty space between the head and the shoulders. For the next two hours, the police team carefully examined the grisly scene. Everyone spoke in whispers. Even the seasoned veterans were affected by the carnage. Finally, Harriet and Mark left Lieutenant Borston and headed back to Spokane.

"I'm hungry," said Harriet.

"You're hungry?" asked Mark, surprised after what they had just witnessed.

"Yeah, we had just gotten up when you called. I didn't get any breakfast."

They pulled into Denny's. They settled into a booth. It always amazed Mark how Harriet drew stares. Here was this knockout woman, packing heat. He really enjoyed being with her. She ordered the Grand Slam breakfast, orange juice, and coffee. Mark ordered coffee wondering how Harriet kept her figure eating like that. He was still feeling a bit queasy.

"I guess we'll know more once the autopsies are complete," said Harriet. "What do you make of it, Mark?"

"It looks to me like they were ripped apart by some large animal," said Mark. "There were puncture wounds on the head of the guy on the stove. If it were an animal, it had huge fangs and claws."

"Come on, Mark, that isn't possible. I'll bet it was some kind of gang thing. You know, it's weird. Two of those guys were packing, yet they never pulled their guns," said Harriet. "Also, that handprint on the door is small like a woman's hand. Then there were those cat tracks."

"The Browns' daughter has that gray cat," added Mark.

"Right," said Harriet. "Her cat killed those guys."

"I'm not saying that, but I'll bet that Miss Amy Brown and her cat were out at that storage container."

Harriet laughed.

"We sound like Scully and Mulder."

"Who?" asked Mark.

"You know, those two FBI agents in the old TV series *The X-Files*. They investigated mysterious happenings."

"Maybe not that," Mark said softly. "But, I will tell you, the Browns' homicide is definitely not your neighborhood-variety murder."

29

I JUMPED AT THE BUZZING SOUND, OPENING MY EYES. WHAT IN THE world was that? I sat up in my bed. The sound was coming from the other side of the room. Sherry got up, walked to the dresser, and shut off the alarm clock. An alarm clock, would you believe that? It was three minutes past six. I stretched and yawned.

Sherry headed for the bathroom. A few minutes later she returned.

"School day, huh?" I asked.

"Yes," she answered.

"You going to be OK?" I asked.

"I think so," she answered. "Sometimes I still feel bad." Sherry looked at the floor.

Child molesting is such a terrible crime, I thought.

Sherry put on one of the dresses I had bought her at the mall.

"I want to look pretty today. Will you help me with my hair?" she asked.

"Sure," I said. "Let me get dressed first."

I heard Randy leave the bathroom, so I headed quickly for it. I washed my face and underarms, brushed my teeth, applied deodorant, and got dressed. *I need to get more of my clothes. How long will the police keep me out?* At home I had a whole closet plus dressers full of clothes. I didn't like having such a limited wardrobe.

Once dressed, I brought Sherry into the bathroom and had her sit on the toilet seat while I brushed her hair. She was an attractive little thing with reddish-brown hair, blue eyes, and a smattering of freckles. She would be a beautiful woman.

After I got Sherry ready, we headed for the kitchen.

"Good morning," said Regina. She held a cup of coffee. To my surprise, she had no cigarette. We sat at the table eating cereal, toast, and bananas. The last two mornings, I'd eaten more breakfast than I had eaten in the last four years.

With the twins off to school, I helped Regina with the dishes.

"What are you going to do today?" she asked me.

"I need to meet with Dad's attorney. He has an office downtown. I'll call and make an appointment as soon as their offices open at nine o'clock," I answered.

Paul Dino's secretary told me that he would be pleased to see me. I had an appointment for two o'clock at his law office in the Wells Fargo/ American West Bank Building on Riverside.

At ten, I left Regina, Toby, and Mr. P watching game shows on TV and headed for town. I planned to do some shopping, eat lunch, and get to the appointment with Mr. Dino just before two. My parents had been murdered just two days ago, and here I was going shopping. With no family, I just couldn't sit staring at the wall, though, feeling sorry for myself. I had to get my mind off my situation for a few hours. The loss and hurt didn't go away. I just pushed them to the back of my mind.

When I got to town, I parked in the mall's garage. Like most malls, it had large department stores connected to each other with covered walkways. There weren't many shoppers. After all, most kids were in school. Not me. I felt like I was playing hooky. Had I been in school, I would be in Advanced Calculus.

I looked in the store windows. As I walked along, I saw a small jewelry shop with a sign reading GOLD BOUGHT AND SOLD. I walked in. A buzzer sounded as I entered the shop. An older guy with white hair and thick glasses looked up from the table where he was working. His glasses had additional magnifying lenses attached to the right eye. The lenses could be rotated to provide magnification for close work. He was working on an old pocket watch.

"May I help you, miss?"

"Yes," I said, using my most adult voice. I had used a little extra pancake makeup and put on Regina's red lipstick. I usually wore very little makeup and preferred a light peach lipstick, but red lipstick and more makeup ages a woman. When I looked at the mirror behind the man, I wasn't sure that I liked what I saw. I not only looked older—I looked like a hooker. I guarantee you that the guy would have no idea that I was only sixteen.

"I have a gold coin I would like to sell, and I also have a question about a gemstone," I said.

He smiled.

"Let's see the coin first."

I reached into my purse and withdrew one of the gold Krugerrand coins. I handed it to him.

"Ah, a Krugerrand. Excellent choice," he said as he held the coin up to his glasses. "You said you want to sell it. Let me see what the market for gold was yesterday. We purchase gold based on current value. There is a five percent fee for cashing in the coin. Do you still want to sell it?"

"Yes," I said.

"The current rate is $2,484 per ounce. I will purchase it from you for $2,359.80."

He took the coin, walked over to a large safe, opened it, and withdrew some currency. Right in front of me, he counted out twenty-three hundred-dollar bills, one fifty-dollar bill, and nine dollars and eighty cents in change. I placed the wad of bills in my purse.

"Do I need to sign any papers or anything?" I asked.

"Only if the amount of gold sold exceeds ten thousand dollars. Then I must notify the IRS," he said, smiling. That was an interesting piece of information that I would tuck away.

I next pulled out the ruby. I handed it to him. He pulled down the little magnifying glasses attached to his glasses.

"Where did you get this?" he asked. My heart jumped. I was about ready to run out the door. I visualized him pressing a button on the floor and the police rushing in.

Instead I answered, "It belonged to my great-grandfather. He found it in Europe during World War II."

I usually don't lie, not even a little fib. Now, over the last few days, I'd lied like a trooper.

"Well, it's not originally from Europe. Might be from the Middle East. Very poorly cut, but a ruby," he said, more to himself than to me. He rubbed it against a plate. "Maximum hardness, minimum flaws," he continued.

"Is it worth anything?" I asked.

"Oh, yes," he said. "Unfortunately, I have no idea how much. You would have to take it to a gemologist who deals with antique stones. There's probably one in Seattle. I would recommend that you keep it in a safe deposit box," he said.

"It's worth that much?" I asked.

"Thousands of dollars," he said. "Maybe even more."

"Wow," I said. "I never dreamed it was worth anything at all."

"It's old, miss, very old. Maybe two or three thousand years old."

"Thank you," I said as I returned the gem to my purse.

As I walked out of the store, he said, "Miss, you need to get that in a safe place. You shouldn't be carrying it around in your purse."

"I will," I said.

I hurried down the escalator to the main floor. I kept looking behind me to make sure no one was following me. If that ruby was worth thousands, how much were all those gemstones in the strongbox worth? Maybe millions.

I was no longer interested in shopping. I walked down Main Street. It was a beautiful sunny October day. I walked into Auntie's Book Store. It's in the historic Liberty Building on the northwest corner of Main Avenue at Washington Street and has been an independent bookstore since 1978. I asked the clerk where I could find books on rare gems. He showed me the section. I pulled out a couple of books. Auntie's is a cool bookstore. They have all kinds of interesting things. There are benches and chairs throughout the store, and you can sit down and look at the books. In the third book, I found a stone similar to the one in my pocket. It was found in a tomb in Egypt. It had been auctioned at Sotheby's and sold for thirty million dollars. I looked around, reached in my purse, and pulled out the ruby. It looked almost identical. I felt how one of those winners of the Mega Millions jackpot must feel when he or she has the winning ticket worth millions. Was there a big flashing sign over my head saying, "She's got millions of dollars in her purse"?

I placed the books back on the shelves, walked over to the coffee shop, and ordered a mocha espresso. Mom and I were really hooked on mocha espressos. Any time we went shopping, we would always get one. She loved books, and we would spend an hour in Auntie's before we bought our espressos. I sipped my espresso and tried to figure out what was happening. What in the world were Mom and Dad involved in? A strongbox with millions in it? Were they killed because of their past lives? Had something or someone from their past found them? I would find out. I had to.

I looked at my iPhone. It was twenty minutes to two. Wells Fargo was four blocks from Auntie's on Riverside. When I got to the building, I entered the lobby. I looked at the directory. I found Barnes, Dino, Peterson, and Robertson, Attorneys at Law in suite 501. I took the elevator to the fifth floor and followed the signs to suite 501. I entered the office. It was a big spacious office, with a well-dressed lady sitting behind a large desk.

"May I help you, miss?"

"Yes," I said. "I'm Amy Brown. I have a two o'clock appointment with Mr. Dino."

She looked at a schedule on her desk.

"Yes, here it is," she said. "Would you please come with me?" She took me over to a waiting room filled with plush furniture. The carpet was so thick that I could feel my heels sink in about an inch. "May I get you a cup of coffee or a glass of water?"

"No, no thank you," I said.

"Please have a seat. Mr. Dino will join you shortly," she said as she walked out of the room and closed the door.

I walked to the window. I could see the river and Riverfront Park. When I was young, my parents would take me to the park to ride the carousel. As I stood there looking out the window, the door opened and Mr. Dino walked in. It had been six years ago that my parents and I had met with Mr. Dino when he updated my parents' wills. He was shorter than I remembered him. He had jet-black hair, combed back over what I suspected was a bald spot. He was on the heavy side—not fat, but not skinny either. He was wearing a dark blue suit, white shirt, and blue tie. He looked like an attorney. In his left hand, he had a folder. I think I caught him by surprise. I was wearing a blue pants suit, a white blouse, and two-inch heels. I was five inches taller than Mr. Dino. He probably expected a young girl with tears in her eyes.

"I am so sorry to hear about your parents. I didn't find out until last night. Had I known, I would have come right out to see you. I have their wills right here. They had us keep copies of them. Please sit down," he said.

I spent about an hour with Mr. Dino. The wills were very straight-forward. I was the sole heir. In the event that both my parents were dead, Mr. Dino was to be the executor for the will. He explained that it was unusual for an attorney to be designated executor. Normally, a next of kin or close friend was named as the executor. He explained that he was honored to assist me. We discussed my age and the fact that I would not be eighteen for sixteen months. We also talked about the issue of the release of my parents' bodies and access to the house. When I left Mr. Dino's office, I felt better. I believed that he would be able to help me.

30

I WALKED BACK DOWN RIVERSIDE OVER TO MAIN AND RETURNED TO the parking garage to get my Mustang. I paid the attendant seven dollars, pulled out, drove one block, and turned right onto Monroe. As I crossed the Monroe Street Bridge, my thoughts were somewhere else. The light changed to red at Mallon Avenue. I had to slam on my brakes to stop in time. I sat there waiting for the light to change to green. Then I took off. I had gone about two blocks when the sound of a siren made me jump. I looked in my rearview mirror. There was a black car with flashing red-and-blue lights in the grill and windshield. *Great. I stopped in time back there. What's the big deal?* I pulled over to the curb.

The police car was right behind me. A man wearing a sports coat stepped out. It was Detective Baker. Then Detective Sims got out of the other side. They came to the driver's window.

"What did I do?" I asked, somewhat agitated.

"I thought it was you, Miss Brown. Nice of you to get our attention right in front of the Public Safety Building," said Baker. "Detective Sims and I were just talking about you. Seems your folks had a storage container in Spokane Valley. We were just on our way for a second meeting with the Spokane Valley Police Department."

"Oh," I said somewhat sheepishly.

"Is this your Mustang?"

"Yes," I whispered.

"Miss Brown, if you lie to me, I will arrest you on the spot and book you in juvenile hall," said Detective Baker. "Now, how did you get this Mustang?"

"I took it," I whispered.

"She took it, Sims," he said to his partner. "What makes you think you can take it?" Baker asked me with a smug look.

"It's mine," I said.

"Your house is a crime scene," said Baker.

"The crime did not happen in my Mustang," I argued.

"Didn't you see the crime scene tape?" he asked.

"There wasn't any on the garage doors," I answered.

"So how did you get in?" he asked.

"With a door opener," I replied.

"We need to talk to you, Miss Brown," said Detective Baker.

"Mrs. Carlson told me not to talk to you without a lawyer," I answered.

"Let's go to the Starbucks over there. We'll buy you a cup of coffee," said Detective Sims.

"What if I refuse?"

"Then we will handcuff you and take you to juvenile hall and book you. You can then call a lawyer, and tomorrow or maybe the next day, you might get out," said Detective Baker.

I was in a major bind. I didn't dare tell them when I had taken the Mustang or what had happened in that storage shed.

"All right," I said.

They got back in the police car and pulled out around me. I followed them in my Mustang to the Starbucks parking lot. The three of us walked into the place. We picked a table next to the window. Detectives Sims and Baker faced me.

"You know, Miss Brown, you're an interesting teenager. You're qualified with a pistol and trained in martial arts," Detective Sims said.

"It's only because Dad wanted a boy, that's all. He enjoyed doing those things with me," I said.

Detective Baker pulled out that little notebook he had the night my parents were killed. He opened it, flipped the pages, looked at me, and started talking.

"The Brown family is quite an anomaly. You guys didn't exist until seventeen years ago. Where were you born, Miss Brown?"

"Here in Spokane," I answered.

"Do you know what hospital?"

"Sacred Heart Hospital. I saw the birth certificate when we got our enhanced driver's licenses," I said.

"Strange. There is no record of your birth in the county records at any of the area hospitals. I tried to run your parents' social security numbers. There's nothing back past seventeen years ago. IRS shows that your parents paid taxes every year, but they only keep records for ten years. Your dad worked for an investment firm. What did your mom do?"

"She was a stay-at home mom," I answered.

He continued reading his notebook.

"There is no mortgage on your house. I did a credit check. Your folks paid cash for everything."

"Is that against the law?" I asked. Baker ignored my question.

"But with your social security numbers, I was able to track stock dividends. Have your folks ever talked about finances with you?"

"No," I said.

"Did they ever talk about stocks and bonds?"

"No," I repeated. I was starting to get worried. *What is Detective Baker getting at?*

"What about funds in your name?" he asked.

"They had some funds to pay for my college," I answered.

"Where are you going to go to college?"

"Gonzaga."

"Pretty expensive?" he asked.

"I guess so."

"How much do you think?"

"Around thirty thousand a year," I guessed.

"So why would your folks have funds in your account adding up to thirty-five million dollars?"

"Thirty-five million!" I squeaked. "That's not possible."

"Not only possible, Miss Brown, but that's only a drop in the bucket. Your folks are worth at least six hundred million, and that's only the legitimate stuff attached to their social security numbers. I have no idea what else there is," said Detective Brown.

As this revelation sunk in, I thought of the strongbox in Regina's garage hidden in that cardboard box.

"I don't believe it," I said. "We lived all right, but we weren't millionaires."

"You're right there. You lived in an upper-middle-class neighborhood. Under the radar, so to speak. Miss Brown, your parents did not exist until they came to Spokane, and you were not born here. Do you know what that tells me?"

"No," I said.

"They were in some kind of witness protection program. I can tell you one more thing. It's very sophisticated, and someone with a great deal of power is behind this. I believe your parents' death had something to do with their past, and I am convinced that you know more than you're telling me," said Detective Baker.

"I swear that I had no idea that we had all that money," I answered honestly. Detective Baker looked at me.

"I'll be watching you, Miss Brown." He closed his notebook. "You're free to go."

The detectives got up and walked out of Starbucks. I sat there staring at the table. Where did my parents get millions of dollars? Obviously, the strongbox offered no clues. There was no receipt in the box telling me that they had won the Mega Millions jackpot.

Who were they? What was I going to do?

31

THE NEXT MORNING, REGINA RECEIVED A CALL FROM MRS. CARLSON, who informed her that she would be arriving to meet with Regina and me at ten o'clock.

We were waiting for her in the living room. I told Regina that I wanted to remain with her and the twins until I reached eighteen years old.

My fingers were crossed when we heard the doorbell ring. Regina got up and opened the door. She asked Mrs. Carlson to come in. I watched Mrs. Carlson as she entered the living room. She looked around, somewhat surprised by the appearance. The last time she had been here, the place looked like a pigpen. The furniture was still old and secondhand, but the room was now neat and clean. Perhaps the greatest surprise was Toby sitting by the hallway door. Mr. P was stretched out by the heat register.

Regina asked Mrs. Carlson to have a seat and offered her a cup of coffee. Mrs. Carlson declined, saying she could only stay a few minutes. *Uh oh*, I thought. *She's planning to whisk me out of the house immediately.*

She frowned, looking like she was trying to pick her words carefully. Then she looked at both of us.

"Amy," she said regretfully, "I told you that you would be staying here only temporarily. I know that I was supposed to get back to you yesterday, but I was not able to meet with the executive director for Spokane County until this morning. I'm afraid I do not have good news. Mrs. Haskins, the executive director, sees no reason why you should be relocated to another home. I am afraid that you will just have to stay with Mrs. Hanson until you are of legal age."

I sat there registering what she had just said. *I'll be darned,* I thought. *I got what I wanted.* I gave a weak smile.

"That's OK, Mrs. Carlson. I believe Mrs. Hanson and I will get by just fine. My cat gets along with her dog. Right now, I wouldn't feel like going somewhere else." I lowered my eyes to the floor, like this was a difficult decision, but I would be able to handle it.

"Dear, I am so pleased that you're taking this so well," said Mrs. Carlson. She turned to Regina. "Mrs. Hanson, is this any problem for you?"

"Oh no, Mrs. Carlson. Amy is fitting in just fine," said Regina.

"Excellent. I have some papers for each of you to sign. As she pulled the papers out of her briefcase, she said, "The state has issued you temporary custodial powers over Amy. You have the authority to authorize medical treatment, meet with Amy's school authorities, and make legal decisions for Amy's welfare."

Once the papers had been signed and copies were provided to Regina, Mrs. Carlson seemed to be satisfied.

"Well, it seems everything is under control. I must be going." Regina and I stood up and shook Mrs. Carlson's hand. When we closed the door, I let out a little squeal and threw my arms around Regina.

"Thank you for being here for me."

"It's all right," said Regina. "I just hope that I can be of some help."

"You know," I said, "I expected a fight. I guess I'm a little disappointed that the decision was already made before Mrs. Carlson got here."

"Honey, that is the way the bureaucracy of CPS works. Unfortunately, the young victims have very little to say in the matter. I am amazed more of the poor children don't become criminals. You said that you wanted to go to Freeman High School to meet with the counselor. We need to leave soon. I want to get back before the twins get home," said Regina.

"All right," I said, "but we're taking my Mustang. It knows the way to FHS."

It seemed like, at last, everything was going to be all right. I knew I had a long way to go, but at least we had made steps in the right direction.

32

WE ARRIVED AT FREEMAN RIGHT AFTER THE LAST LUNCH BREAK. Fortunately, I wouldn't have to talk to any of my friends. This was going to be difficult enough without talking about the death of my parents.

We entered the front door and then left into the office. Mrs. Ziegler, the secretary, looked up as we came in.

"Amy, I am so sorry about the loss of your parents," she said.

Understand that in a high school with only seventy-three seniors, the administration and staff knows most of us by name. I thanked her for her concern.

"I need to see Mrs. Phillips," I said.

"Of course, I understand. Let me call her office."

Mrs. Phillips was the guidance counselor. As we waited, Mr. Martin, the principal, walked by.

"Amy, we didn't expect to see you back this soon," said Mr. Martin.

"I won't be coming back yet, Mr. Martin. I need to talk to Mrs. Phillips about my courses and graduation. This is Mrs. Hanson; she's my temporary guardian and has the authority to make legal decisions for me."

Mr. Martin shook Regina's hand.

"Amy is one of our brightest and most popular students. I do hope the state will allow her to finish up her senior year with us," said Principal Martin.

"I'm sure that we will do what is in Amy's best interests," answered Regina.

"Oh, here is Mrs. Phillips. I will turn you over to her," Mr. Martin said and excused himself.

I introduced Regina to the guidance counselor. The three of us went into Mrs. Phillips's office, and Regina and I sat down in front of her desk. She pulled out my file and began paging through it.

"You're in the top five percent of the class; your SATs are in the top tenth percentile. You have already been accepted to Gonzaga University. This is one of the earliest acceptance letters for this year's class. You will be eligible for a number of scholarships in the spring," said Mrs. Phillips, looking more at Regina than at me.

Obviously, Mrs. Philips knew all this by heart, but she wanted Regina to know what a great student I was. I figured that it was time to make my point.

"Mrs. Philips, I would like to take the GED in November and graduate this semester," I said.

"Oh, Amy, that wouldn't be a good idea. I know you have suffered a horrible tragedy, but you would miss walking up the aisle with your class, the senior prom, and all the other senior activities.

This was the standard speech that Mrs. Phillips used on every kid planning to drop out of high school. I believed that my situation was different. Six months from now when I graduated, the fact that my parents were brutally murdered in their home would still be fresh in everyone's minds. As a matter of fact, at my ten-year reunion, people would probably say, "Oh, there's Amy Brown. Why, she hasn't changed one bit since the day her parents were murdered."

Six days ago, my life changed and all those senior things mean nothing to me anymore, I thought. But I didn't say it.

Instead I said, "Mrs. Phillips, I'm having difficulties coping with my parents' deaths. I don't think I'll be able to come back to school."

"I'm sure you will get past those problems. We can give you your assignments to do at home."

Obviously, this was going to be a major battle. Then Regina stepped in.

"Excuse me, Mrs. Phillips, of course you realize that at this moment I am considered by state law as Amy's legal guardian, and I'm empowered to make decisions in her best interest. Why don't we let Amy take the GED in November? She still could graduate with her class in June."

"Well, I guess that would work," said Mrs. Philips.

Then Regina continued. "What classes must she take for the rest of this semester to make sure she is on course for graduation?"

"Let me see," said Mrs. Philips. She looked at my records again. "Actually, Amy is taking only advanced placement courses. None of them are required for graduation. But she will be able to do so much better in college with these courses."

"Based on what you have told me, it sounds like she will do well without the courses," said Regina.

"Yes, but it is unusual to do this," answered Mrs. Phillips.

"Why don't we just drop the courses this semester, and then next semester we can sign her up for those courses you deem necessary," Regina suggested. She squeezed my arm, probably expecting me to argue, but I kept quiet.

Mrs. Philips sat there quietly for a few moments. "Very well, Mrs. Hanson. I'll schedule Amy for the November GED."

"Thank you for your assistance. Now I must get Amy back home. This has been a very tiring day. We've had her on medication since the loss of her parents." Regina took my arm and helped me get ready to leave. "Come along, dear. We'll go home now."

33

WE WALKED OUT OF THE SCHOOL. AS SOON AS I GOT IN THE MUSTANG, I turned to her.

"What's this drugged thing?" I asked.

She laughed. "Amy, during the years I have worked as a foster parent, I learned how to work the school system. I tell them what they want to hear. If they believe that you are traumatized, they will let you take that test next month, and then you decide what you want to do next. I'll be there for you."

"You know, Regina, each day I'm happier that our paths crossed. Would you like a cup of coffee at the coolest place?" I asked.

"As long as it's not too long. Remember, we need to get home," said Regina.

"It's just a couple of miles from here in Valleyford. We go right by it on the Palouse Highway," I said as I started up the car.

I drove back toward Spokane and turned left onto the Palouse Highway. After about a mile, just past Madison, I made a left turn into a gravel driveway.

We pulled through a small group of trees, and to the left was a large building. It was painted bright blue and had a red metal roof. The windows were trimmed in white. The doors were red. On the peaked roof was a sign that read ON SACRED GROUNDS COFFEE SHOP.

We pulled around back to a small parking lot that could accommodate maybe seven cars. On busy days people parked along the driveway and across Madison in another lot. I think it was a converted older house. We got out of our car and entered the building.

It was the coolest place. The walls were white pine and covered with all kinds of old pictures and other old stuff. Along one wall were bookshelves filled with old books. Over the counter were all kinds of old women's hats—the kind that women wore back in the early 1900s—hanging on pegs. Small wood tables with real tablecloths were set to accommodate four people in old wing-backed side chairs.

We could smell the fresh coffee brewing. An old glass front counter was filled with muffins, cookies, and pastries.

I explained to Regina that this was my favorite eating spot on the way home from school. Unfortunately, other than the Freeman store, this was the only place you could get snack foods. Otherwise, people had to drive twenty five minutes to the next nearest eating establishment.

There were only three other customers in the coffee house. We took a seat next to the bookcase. On wall shelves, old coffee grinders were incorporated into the decor. On each table was a crystal oil lamp. The place had the feeling of a country store.

"Why, this is such a nice place!" said Regina. "I wonder why I have never heard about it before."

The woman from behind the counter came over to take our order. She looked to be in her early sixties. She wore a red hat, a flowered blouse, and a long blue skirt.

"Welcome to On Sacred Grounds Coffee Shop. Our special today is egg-salad sandwich, muffin, and your choice of coffee, tea, or espresso," she said with a smile as she handed us menus.

We each decided to order the special. I ordered mine on whole wheat bread and added a blueberry muffin. Regina requested white bread. She also ordered two blueberry muffins to take back for the twins.

"I'm paying," she said. I didn't argue. Imagine what she would have done if I has said, "Oh, let me pay, I have twenty-two hundred dollars in my purse from selling one of my gold Krugerrrands" that might have been more information than Regina could handle. I guess a greater shock would be the fact that I might be worth more than six hundred million dollars.

"Thank you," I said with a smile.

After we finished our lunch, we continued sipping our drinks. Regina had the special blend coffee, and I had my mocha espresso. A couple of older ladies who had also been having a late lunch got up, paid, and left. One other customer remained. I glanced over to where she sat. She was staring at me. I looked down to see if anything was out of place. Nothing was. I looked back in her direction and smiled. Maybe I had met her before. Maybe she worked for the school district. To my surprise, she got up and came to our table.

I'm not real accurate at guessing people's ages, but I think she was in her forties. She was as wide as she was tall, and she was short, maybe five feet tall. She was wearing a single-piece dress that looked like it had been made from those old flower-seed bags. She had thick glasses with dumb frames like Mom used to wear. Her hair was red, streaked with gray, and it hung to her waist. She wore gold earrings and a gold nose ring.

"Hello," she said. "My name is Leona Erickson."

When she spoke, she had a voice like a little girl.

"Hello," Regina and I both said. I tried to search my brain as to whether I knew her. I didn't bother to give her my name.

"Are you members of a local coven or are you independents?" she asked. Now, that's not the expected question you get in a restaurant in Spokane.

"No," I answered, feeling more and more uncomfortable.

"Oh, I was sure you were one of us," she said, looking me straight in the eye.

"I'm afraid not," I said, beginning to feel like I was talking to a member of one of those religious groups who comes to your house and hands out flyers informing you that the end is near.

"I could see your aura all the way across the room. I have never seen such a powerful aura. If you aren't practicing, you might want to join us." She reached in a pocket and handed me a business card. I looked at the card. It read, "Leona Erickson, White Witch, Potions and Spells. Psychic Readings. Phone: 347-8967. Call night or day." She turned and headed for the cash register, paid her bill, and left.

"What was all that about?" asked Regina.

"I haven't a clue. I've never seen her before," I answered. I handed Regina the business card.

"A witch," she said. "That's not someone you encounter every day."

"No," I said. "We've had our share of religious nuts show up at our house, but never a witch."

"She said you have a great aura," said Regina, frowning.

"What's the big deal about aura?" I asked.

"There was a special on the History Channel about the aura," answered Regina. "According to the show, the aura is a field of luminous radiation surrounding a person. The depiction of an aura often connotes a person of particular power or holiness. Most religions discuss the aura. On the show, a person's aura had been photographed."

"She was a nut case," I remarked. "I'm surprised she didn't ask for money for the old witches' home. I guess we better leave so we get back before Randy and Sherry get home."

We paid, left the Sacred Grounds, and walked to the Mustang. As I was getting in, I glanced over at an older white van parked on the other side of the lot. Leona Erickson was looking out the window. That gave me a definite case of the creeps. As we headed toward the city, I pushed the Mustang to sixty-five, ten miles over the speed limit. I kept looking in the rearview mirror, making sure that the white van was not following me.

34

THE NEXT DAY WAS A SATURDAY, AND EVERYONE SLEPT IN. AFTER breakfast, the twins and I watched a teen high school flick on the Disney Channel. It was the typical crazy-antics show that goes beyond the reality of high school.

I normally didn't watch these shows, but I found myself laughing at some of the scenes, and I enjoyed watching the twins' reactions. Eleven-year-olds are a unique bunch of individuals. Puberty is just around the corner. Randy's voice had the squeak that occurs just before a male's voice deepens. Sherry was gaga over one of the teen male stars, saying how cool he was.

"Is high school really like that?" asked Randy.

"Sometimes," I said, "but you also have lots of studying to do."

"I wish it was all just fun," he said.

We had just finished breakfast, and Regina was cleaning up in the kitchen. I had started to help, but she ran me out.

"You kids go watch TV. I'll clean up, and then I want to get the pot roast in the CROCK-POT."

Being an only child, I had never experienced a Saturday morning with other kids. I was actually having fun. That hadn't happened in the last seven days.

Then I thought of the next Saturday. My parents' memorial service. I dreaded that more than anything else. At times, it seemed like Mom and Dad were just on vacation. Then the reality of what actually happened would overpower me once again.

"Do the older kids pick on you in high school like they do to the younger kids in middle school?" asked Randy.

Now, that question caught my attention. I told him that at Freeman the faculty does not tolerate bullying. Sure, it still happens, but if caught, that person is expelled.

"Does someone pick on you?" I asked Randy.

"Yeah, sometimes they pick on both Sherry and me. We wear second-hand clothes. Once they find out you're in a foster home, some kids make fun of you."

God, here was another part of society that I was clueless about. I never realized what it must be like to be foster kid.

"Just ignore them," I said.

"There are a couple of older guys that shove me when no one is looking," said Randy.

"Well, shove them back. You need to take karate lessons. My dad enrolled me in karate classes when I was seven," I said.

"Wow, you took karate?" asked Sherry.

"Until I was thirteen, which was about six years," I answered.

"What kind of belt do you have?" asked Randy.

"A black belt," I said.

"Whoa, I'd like a black belt," chortled Randy. "You can take on ten bad guys, break bricks with your bare hands, and I'll bet everyone in your school is afraid of you." Obviously Randy had the wrong impression of the martial arts.

"The purpose of learning karate is to allow you to defend yourself. You don't go around beating up people. Then you would be the bully," I explained. "Remember, I got my black belt in junior high. I competed against kids my age and weight class. Just because I have a black belt doesn't mean I can take down a two hundred and fifty–pound man. Of course, I might be able to slow him down enough to be able to run away."

"Well, you did break bricks, didn't you?" asked Sherry.

"No, we didn't break bricks, but we had to break boards to progress to the high-degree belts. We also had to demonstrate different techniques for the instructor, and then we had to participate in matches, but we used boxing-type gloves on our hands and feet to make sure we didn't hurt each other."

"In the movies, the martial arts guys strike walls with their hands, and it doesn't hurt them. When you broke a board, did it hurt your hand?" asked Randy.

"They taught us to direct the force of our blow, using our inner body strength. It's called ki. But I don't think my ki was that well focused. Although I didn't break my hand or anything, I sure felt it when I broke the boards and after a tough match with a good opponent. I often would have bruises everywhere. Don't get me wrong, Randy—karate gave me confidence. In volleyball when I serve, I focus on the ball, and I have a wicked serve."

"So after you took karate, kids didn't bully you or tease you?" asked Randy.

I had to laugh.

"Randy, when I was your age, I was the tallest kid in my class, so no one bullied me, but they did tease me. Behind my back, they called me string bean or stretch. It used to hurt my feelings, but I didn't dwell on it; I just ignored them. When I got into high school, the boys caught up with me. Then I guess I kind of filled out, and it was no longer a problem."

"Would you teach us some karate?" asked Sherry.

"I think it would be better if you enrolled in karate classes," I said.

"Ah, we could never afford that," moaned Randy.

"Oh, you might be surprised," I said. I vowed right then that if I had anything to do with it, these kids would have a better life in the future.

35

SUDDENLY WE HEARD GLASS BREAKING IN THE KITCHEN. I JUMPED TO
my feet as I heard Regina say, "Oh, my God."

"What happened?" I yelled.

She answered with a sense of urgency in her voice.

"Amy, take Randy and Sherry into my bedroom and lock the door."

"What?" I asked.

"Go now!" she screamed.

I didn't hesitate any longer.

"Come on, guys. Let's do what Regina wants!"

We hurried down the hall to her bedroom. I told them to go in. Toby
was in the bedroom.

"Toby, you stay here. I'm going to find out what is going on." I pushed
the button on the lock and closed the door.

As I headed back to the living room, I heard banging at the front
door. I also heard Regina yell, "You go away, Mike Douglas, or I'll call
the police."

I ran down the hall toward the living room. I could hear a muffled
voice through the door.

"Open the goddamn door, lady, or I'll kick it in."

There was a loud crash and one of the panes of glass in the front door
broke. I could feel my heart rate increase. Then I heard another crash
against the door. When I got to the living room, Regina had both hands
pressing against the front door. Then with a loud crash, the front door
burst open. I could see pieces of wood flying through the air.

Regina was thrown back, her head striking the wall as she fell. I stood frozen in place. A man stood on the threshold. He was big, at least six five. His shoulders were so wide that they filled the entire door opening. He wore a black leather jacket, like the bikers in the movies wear, faded blue jeans, and black wide-toed leather boots. His hair was buzz cut like those white supremacists from Idaho. Under different circumstances, I might have said that he was rather good-looking in a rugged way. He had that unshaven look that the Hollywood heartthrobs wore. But the wild look in his eyes scared the hell out of me.

He looked around almost like he didn't know where he was. I suspected that he was on meth or something. He looked at Regina sitting on the floor.

"Where's Sherry?" he demanded.

Sherry. And the name Regina used, Mike Douglas. *This is the bastard who molested Sherry.*

"Woman, I will beat the crap out of you if you don't tell me where Sherry is!" he shouted. "Sherry, where are you, girl? You're going for a ride with Uncle Mike."

He looked past me down the hallway to the bedrooms.

"I'll bet that little cunt is hiding under her bed," he muttered, apparently to himself.

For the first time, he seemed to notice me.

"Who are you?" he growled, frowning at me.

I was so scared that I started to answer him. It was as if he had some power over me. Then I thought about what he had done to Sherry.

"None of your business!" I shouted. I could feel the blood rushing to my face and guessed I was red as a beet.

"Get out of my way, you skinny bitch. I'm going to get that little girl, and we're out of here."

"No!" I said, surprising myself with the firmness of my voice.

"What?" he screamed. "I'll break you in two." As he came toward me, I rotated my body to the left and lashed out with my right leg with a kick to his face. His hand snaked out, grabbed my leg, lifted it up, and tipped me over backward. Then he walked right past me. I scrambled to my feet and leaped on his back, trying to scratch his face. He grabbed my sweatshirt and flung me off his back as if I were a rag doll. I hit the wall with sufficient force to knock the wind out of me. I crumpled to the ground and curled up in the fetal position. My ears rang.

His voice sounded like it was coming from a deep well.

"That did it," I heard him say. "You scratched my face. I'm going to kick the shit out of you!"

I saw only his legs and those leather boots as he came toward me. I saw him pull back his foot, and then I saw the toe of his boot coming toward my face.

"No!" I screamed as I brought my hand up to try to stop the boot from crushing my face. My fingers connected with the boot. The force of it should have mangled my hand and continued into my nose and teeth. Instead, my hand interrupted the momentum of his leg. Gripping the boot, I reached out with my arm. It felt like I was lifting a papier-mâché mannequin. Mike Douglas seemed to literally fly across the room, hitting the wall with so much force that the plasterboard shattered. He slid down the wall, landing hard on his lower back.

I jumped to my feet, ready to grab anything I could to keep him down. That's when things really got bad. He reached under his jacket and pulled out a large revolver. He pointed it directly at me.

"You're dead, you fucking bitch!"

I've never had anyone point a gun at me. At that moment, I knew that I was going to die. I stared at the gun, Mike's finger curled around the trigger. I could actually see his finger slowly and deliberately drawing back the trigger. He was doing it intentionally to make me suffer. He grinned as he prepared to kill me in cold blood.

Then there was a sudden gray blur before my eyes. I heard a scream followed by a deafening explosion. I expected excruciating pain but felt nothing. Deafened by the blast, I focused on Mike. He thrashed around the room with something on his face. I couldn't believe what I was seeing. It was my cat, Mr. P. The cat was clawing at Mike, and Mike was trying to pull it off with both hands. The revolver had landed at his feet.

Suddenly he was able to pull the cat from his head. He grabbed him and hurled him against the wall.

"No!" I screamed. *Oh my God, he killed my cat!* The man stood before me, bloody and covered with deep scratches. Instantly, I dashed forward, grabbed the gun, and stepped back. Tears ran down my cheeks. Then I heard a deep growl. I looked down. Standing by my right leg was Mr. P. I couldn't believe it. I've heard the stories of cats falling several stories and walking away, but the way that evil man had thrown Mr. P I couldn't believe that Mr. P hadn't been seriously injured.

Mike Douglas wiped the blood from his face. Deep claw scratches had torn his face, and the fabric on the shoulder and front of his leather jacket had been shredded. He looked at me as I stood facing him, the gun in my hand. I held the weapon steady, using both hands, just the way Dad had taught me.

"Sit on the floor!" I ordered.

"Fuck you!"

"If you don't sit down right now, I'll shoot you!" My voice quivered slightly.

"Listen, girly, it takes balls to shoot someone. Why don't you give me the gun so you don't hurt yourself?" he said, staring at me with those piercing eyes.

He took a step toward me. *This idiot is going to try to take the gun away.* I pulled back the trigger, locking the revolver's hammer to the rear. It was bigger and heavier than Dad's .38 revolver.

"If you take one more step, I'll kill you!" I said in the bravest voice I could muster. *Can I really kill a person?* I didn't know, but I had to do something.

Even though his face was streaked with bloody scratches, he stood solidly in front of me. His lips formed a cruel smile. I sighted down the barrel of the revolver, lining up the front and rear sights, and pulled the trigger. When the gun went off, I flew backward, unsteadied by the force of the blast. My ears felt like they'd been stuffed with cotton. My forearms shook with the intensity of the recoil.

"You almost shot me!" he shouted.

Yet I didn't falter. I aimed the gun at his chest.

"I missed," I said. "I was aiming at your balls, but they must be too small. Now sit down or the next shot will be in your chest."

He immediately sat down. Regina was still sitting on the floor. I had no idea how much time had passed, but I would guess it was only seconds.

"Are you OK, Regina?" I asked.

"I believe so. I hit my head on the wall, but I think I can get up," she said as she clutched the cabinet and struggled to her feet.

"Call 911, and then tell the twins to stay in the bedroom," I told her.

"I can't leave you alone with him," said Regina, concerned about me.

"That's OK. Mike and I have an understanding, don't we, Mike?" I said in all sincerity.

"Fuck you!" he replied.

Regina went into the kitchen. A few seconds later she came back.

"The police are on their way," she said before heading down the hall to the bedrooms.

36

"LISTEN," SAID MIKE. "I HAVE TO GET OUT OF HERE BEFORE THE police arrive. Come on, let me go."

Mr. P let out a deep growl. I looked down and saw that the cat was plastered against my leg.

"I don't think my cat wants you to leave," I said.

He started to say something more but then stopped abruptly. He stared at the cat. I could see fear in his eyes. Not a surprise, considering the deep scratches from cat claws that ran in parallel lines down both cheeks. One cut had barely missed his left eye. Blood oozed from the wounds. He would need stitches to sew up some of the deeper gashes.

I was surprised at how fast the police got there. In fewer than five minutes, two police officers stood at the door, their guns drawn. I had heard no siren. They must have arrived without using it.

One of the officers spoke with authority.

"Drop the gun!" he said. *Who has a gun?* Then I realized they both had their guns pointed directly at me. *Oops.* I didn't want to get shot. I let the revolver fall in front of me, gritting my teeth and praying the weapon wouldn't discharge when it struck the floor. Fortunately, it didn't go off.

"Place your hands on your head, lady!" one of the officers ordered.

At first, I didn't react. I was momentarily confused. *Wait a minute, guys—I'm not the bad person here.* I put my hands on my head and stood still. Two officers stepped into the room.

"Thank God you're here, officers," said Mike, trying to take the upper hand. "That crazy bitch tried to shoot me. Then she had that cat come after me. Look at my face! All I did was ask for directions," he continued, acting like a victim. "Next thing I knew I was being assaulted. I'm going to sue. Look at what that cat did to my face and jacket. You guys need to shoot that crazy animal right now before it attacks you."

"That's not true," I yelled. "His name is Mike Douglas, and he's supposed to be in jail. He molested an eleven-year-old girl. He came here to stop her from testifying."

The taller officer turned to Mike.

"Is that your name?" he asked.

"No, no, officer. My name is Bill Smith," replied Mike.

"Stand up, Mr. Smith," said the officer.

"What?" I asked. "You believe that animal?"

"Turn around, Mr. Smith, and place your hands against the wall. Spread your feet apart."

Now I wasn't so sure. Maybe the cop was smarter than I thought.

"I'm the victim," wailed Mike. "You can't do this to me."

"Against the wall now, Mr. Smith, or I will tase you," said the officer.

Mike got up slowly, faced the wall, and leaned against it with his hands and feet spread apart. It was obvious that this wasn't Mike's first time dealing with police. The officer holstered his gun and walked up behind Mike. The other officer kept his gun pointed in the general direction of both Mike and me. The officer patted him down and withdrew a black leather wallet from Mike's coat pocket. As the officer stepped back, he flipped open the wallet and looked inside.

"Well, well," said the officer. "You must have stolen Mike Douglas's wallet. That's probable cause for me to arrest you."

He pulled Mike's right arm around his back. Then he pulled the other arm around and handcuffed his two wrists together. He told Mike to sit back down on the floor and talked into the shoulder mic on his uniform.

"I'll be darned," he said to the other officer. "This dirtball is supposed to be in jail with a half million dollar bail. Would you believe there was a computer error? It showed a five thousand dollar bail. A friend of his sprung him."

Now it was my turn.

"All right, miss, you can lower your hands and have a seat on the davenport."

He pulled out a notebook and began asking questions.

"What's your name, miss?"

"Amy Brown," I said. He jotted down information in his notebook as I explained what had happened. By now, four other officers had arrived. One of the officers went down the hallway to speak with Regina and the twins.

Then the front door opened, and in walked detectives Baker and Sims.

"Miss Brown, it seems that violence follows you everywhere you go," said Baker. "What do we have here, Sergeant Lawrence?" he asked. The policeman who had been interviewing me briefed him on what had happened.

"The cat did what?" I heard Baker say.

Baker walked over and knelt down next to Mike.

"The cat did that to you?"

"Yes," yelled Mike. "I'm going to sue. That cat needs to be in a cage."

"I doubt that," said Baker. He stood up and came over to where I was sitting. Mr. P sat beside me. The cat stared at Baker.

"Are you OK, Amy?" he asked.

"Yes, I think so. I'll have a few bruises, but nothing is broken. Regina hit her head on the wall. I thought he had killed my cat, but he seems OK," I said.

"All right," Baker said. "We have medics on the way to check you guys out."

He stood and then turned back to me.

"You don't own a bigger cat do you?"

"A bigger cat?" I asked, somewhat confused.

"Yes, like a mountain lion or a panther?"

"No, just Mr. P here," I answered.

"OK," he said.

What in the world was that all about?

37

THE REST OF SUNDAY WAS PRETTY WELL SHOT. THE POLICE WERE there for four hours. They dug the bullets out of the walls. One went into the wall behind Mike when I had fired the gun. The other was buried in the wall higher up near the ceiling.

They had a hard time figuring out what had happened. They concluded that Mike must have tripped when he was preparing to kick me in the face. They didn't seem convinced that a cat would attack an adult man. Obviously, the wounds on Mike's face and his torn leather jacket attested to the fact that it had happened.

After Mike had been hauled off to jail, the kids were allowed back in the living room. Sherry sat on the couch with Mr. P in her lap. He was purring up a storm. When the medics came, I begged them to check out Mr. P. Even though they were not veterinarians, I knew that they could tell how badly he was hurt. One of the medics said that he couldn't do it. But the younger one agreed to do it while the other one was looking at Regina. He was young and cute and more than happy to check out the cat as long as I held Mr. P. He kept glancing over to me, and it was obvious he liked what he saw.

Other than Mike Douglas, we all came out pretty well. On the way to jail, Mike was taken to Holy Family Hospital's emergency room. I heard one of the policemen say that it took thirty stitches to sew up Mike's face. They also had to sew up Mike's right ear, which was almost torn off. While they were talking, they kept looking a Mr. P sitting in Sherry's lap.

"I've heard about attack dogs, and I've seen what a police dog can do," said the other cop, "but I've never heard of an attack cat."

The police called a carpenter who fixed the broken door and said he would come by next week to fix the holes in the walls. There was also Mike's blood on the carpet. I figured we could handle that with hydrogen peroxide and water.

Regina looked at her watch.

"My gosh, it's a quarter to seven. We've had no lunch, and the pot roast never got on. Let's go to Denny's for dinner," she suggested.

"Come on, everyone," I said heading for the door. "We'll take the Mustang!"

38

THE CORONER RELEASED MOM'S AND DAD'S BODIES ON THURSDAY. Regina and I had gone down to Smith and Jones Funeral Home and met with the director. I chose cremation because I didn't know where I wanted them buried. I wasn't sure Spokane would be their final resting place.

Regina's husband, Frank, had been cremated. As we were driving to the funeral home, she warned me that they would try to rip me off.

I had never been in a funeral home before. It was quiet. There were plush carpets on the floor. A man in a dark suit met us at the door and escorted us into a waiting area filled with leather chairs. A tall, older guy came in. He wore a black suit, crisp white shirt, and maroon tie. I noticed his gold cuff links.

"Miss Brown, I'm Martin Zinski. Please accept my condolences." I shook his hand.

"This is my aunt, Regina." Regina looked at me, her mouth open. I called her my aunt because they would not allow her to help me with the decisions if she wasn't an immediate relative. It's funny—it kind of felt good calling her my aunt.

"A pleasure to meet you, miss...?"

"Hanson," said Regina.

"Would you ladies care to sit down?"

We took our seats. Mr. Zinski folded his hands and said, "As you know, the remains were severely damaged. I would recommend a closed casket funeral. Of course, we could prepare them for viewing if you desire. We can work wonders, but there will be an additional expense."

Regina spoke up.

"We would like them cremated."

"Cremated?" asked Mr. Zinski. To him, it seemed like Regina had said a dirty word.

"Yes, cremated," I said, confirming Regina's request.

"Of course, of course. Now, about the choice of caskets," said Mr. Zinski with a thin grin. But he was interrupted immediately by Regina.

"No caskets," said Regina.

"Mrs. Hanson, you will have to have caskets for the viewing times."

"There will be no viewing times," said Regina. "We want immediate cremation. The memorial service will be this Saturday at Hills United Methodist Church."

"I see," said Mr. Zinski with a scowl. "Of course, we have special containers for the ashes."

Regina was about to say something more. I put my hand gently on her arm. I would like to see what was available. I was worried that Regina might say that we wanted the ashes in two brown paper bags.

Mr. Zinski had a catalog of cremation urns and boxes. They varied in price from several hundred dollars to jewel-encased containers costing more than ten thousand dollars. I settled for a box for each set of ashes for four hundred dollars, plus a brass plaque with Mom's and Dad's names and their birth and death dates for an additional seventy-five dollars.

That part of the business complete, Mr. Zinski next brought up preparation for cremation. Did we want to dress my parents?

"No," said Regina. "They came into this world naked, and they can go out naked."

"How about a flower arrangement?" asked Mr. Zinski.

"You mean you burn the bodies with flowers?" I asked, more than a little astonished.

"Of course, dear. It's a loving gesture to you parents," he answered with a note of sorrow.

"I don't want burned flowers with my parents," I said.

Mr. Zinski didn't give up easily.

"We have special hardwood boxes that can be used during the cremation. It is more dignified than just rolling the naked bodies into the crematorium."

I was getting mad this guy was trying to take advantage of my parents death.

"What do you think, dear?" asked Regina.

"I don't know," I said. "Dad never liked barbecued stuff. I don't want their ashes smelling like burned wood. We just want them cremated."

Mr. Zinski must have known that he wasn't getting anything else out of us. The total bill was $2,146, including state tax. Gads, how much natural gas for the furnace does it take to cremate a body?

"We will cremate your parents this afternoon. You will be able to pick up the remains tomorrow morning," concluded Mr. Zinski.

"I would like to see them first," I said.

"Oh no, my dear, I do not advise that," said Mr. Zinski.

He turned to Regina.

"Mrs. Hanson, you need to talk to your niece. The bodies were damaged severely. The sight of them could cause an irreversible injury to this young woman."

There was plenty I could say about my "irreversible injury." I saw them lying on the floor in their own blood; I saw three men brutally ripped apart by what, I have no idea; and I was almost shot by a pervert. *If I haven't suffered irreversible injury by now, it won't happen.*

Fortunately, Regina solved the problem.

"Mr. Zinski, if my niece wants to see her parents' bodies, then you cannot stop her. I will be right there by her side."

"This is most irregular," he continued before giving in. "Very well, will you follow me?"

We left the office and followed Mr. Zinski down the hallway to an elevator. He pushed B2. The elevator quietly descended. When the doors opened, we saw no carpet, just bare concrete walls, tile floors, and stark fluorescent lights. At a metal door, Mr. Zinski inserted a card into a lock, and I heard a click. Vaults lined the walls, just like the morgues in those CSI TV shows.

He opened one of the vaults. The first body was Mom. Strange, she looked like a balloon that the air had gone out of. There was no fullness to her body. She had been split open and then sewn back together. Her eyes were closed. Her head was misshapen. Two dark holes in the middle of her forehead were spaced about an inch apart. Other wounds in her body indicated that she had been shot a number of times.

"Show me my dad," I said, biting my lip so hard that it started to bleed.

He opened the vault next to Mom and pulled out Dad. That was harder. It's had to explain. I was just closer to dad than mom. The autopsy incisions were identical. Dad also had been shot a number of times. Two holes in his forehead were just like those on Mom. Even though they were probably already dead, someone had shot each of them twice in the head. That seemed crueler than the fact that they had been shot in the first place.

"I will find whoever did this and kill them," I whispered through gritted teeth. "Let's go home, Regina."

We turned and walked out.

39

HILLS UNITED METHODIST CHURCH WAS BUILT MORE THAN SIXTY years ago when small community churches were popping up in every American town. I guess the church should have been named Hangman Hills United Methodist Church, but the congregation felt it wasn't appropriate to name a church after an area where people were hanged. They name churches Calvary after the place where Christ was crucified, so I didn't get why Hangman Hills was so bad.

Megachurches seating thousands seem to be the norm these days, but I liked our little church. It sat about 150 people, who entered the narthex through double doors. To the right was the sanctuary; to the left were a fellowship hall and a small kitchen. Classrooms, offices, and the library filled up the rest of the space. The ceilings were made of dark tongue-and-groove wood planks bisected by large wooden beams. The pews were constructed of real oak. A stained glass wall stood at the front of the sanctuary. Until I was twelve, I had thought the glass was a real window. Of course, I never considered the fact that it was lit, even at night. Fluorescent lights behind the stained glass could turn night into day.

We arrived about ninety minutes before the ceremony. We had to ride in the Mustang. The police were still playing games with me and had not released my house and property yet. Paul was going to court Monday to force the police to release my home back to me. Thank God I had my Mustang. Otherwise, we would be riding in Regina's old Ford.

I bought new clothes for all four of us. Randy wore a sweater and a tie. Sherry had a blue-and-white dress with frilly sleeves. She wore a white bow in her hair. Regina had a brown pants suit. We had all gone to the hairdresser and had our hair done. Even Randy had a new haircut. I wore a cool pants suit that made me look like one of those female lawyers on TV and three-inch heels. I wore my diamond stud earrings and light peach lipstick. Regina helped me apply my eye makeup.

To my surprise, people were already at the church. Of course, I knew almost everyone. I was baptized in this church when I was just a year old. I attended Sunday school and youth group here. The church was a part of my life. Mom was involved with the Methodist women's group, and I could see the sympathy in their eyes. Other members of the church had died over the years, but they were all old. Mom and Dad were young, only in their forties. The fact that they had been brutally murdered added to the congregation's grief and shock over their loss. At that moment I would just as soon have been anywhere else than there. But Reverend John had explained that a service was part of closure and allowing everyone to go forward.

A table set up in the narthex had photos of my parents. None of the pictures showed them in their early years. All the photos seemed to have been taken since they move to Spokane. Neither of my parents had any pictures of themselves as babies, children, teenagers, or young adults. There were no photos of any other family members—grandparents, aunts, uncles, or cousins. No one ever explained to me why their lives seemed to start in Spokane just in the last seventeen years. Nor could anyone explain to me why their lives had ended so quickly and violently.

I had been allowed to go home with Regina while a police officer followed us around as we gathered pictures for the service. He wouldn't let us have anything other than the photos. I explained to Reverend John that the older pictures were stored in boxes and the police wouldn't let us go through those boxes. The truth was, I honestly do not remember ever seeing any pictures from before we arrived in Spokane.

That added to my fear that my parents were into something unlawful. I was still too paranoid to type in the names on the passports on Google. I imagined those names setting off some type of government alarm system.

Reverend John said it was time for me to go inside and be seated. I looked around. I could not believe the turnout. The doors and windows had been removed from the back of the sanctuary. Chairs had been added along the aisles and in the narthex. The fellowship hall was filled to capacity. There were also TV cameras from the local stations. When an upper-middle-class couple is murdered execution style, that's big news most anywhere. The media wanted to cover the funeral.

Regina said they would meet me after the service.

"No," I said. "I want you guys to sit with me."

"Honey, that's only for your immediate family," explained Regina.

"Regina, you, Randy, and Sherry are the only family I have," I insisted.

The four of us walked down the center aisle and took a seat in the front pew.

Sitting on a table next to the cross was a small double box holding my parents' ashes. Behind the box was an enlarged picture of my parents taken on their last anniversary.

I heard very few of Reverend John's words. I stared straight ahead at those small boxes that contained all that was left of my parents and all that was left of my life as I knew it.

All this in just seventeen days.

40

"PLEASE STAND AS WE SING THE FIRST TWO VERSES OF 'AMAZING Grace,'" said Reverend John.

Is it over? I didn't even remember what had been said or who had spoken. I started to stand but felt a little dizzy. Three hundred voices began singing together. I felt my tears start to flow. Then I felt an arm around me, pulling me closer. Regina held me as the song concluded. At that moment, she truly felt like my aunt or the grandmother I never knew. Her presence would see me through the rest of the ceremony.

So many people attended the reception; I don't remember who all I talked to. Many of my school friends came to the service. All expressed how sorry they were about my parents' deaths. Finally, after about an hour, Randy showed up with a tray of food, and Sherry, beside him, offered a glass of punch.

"Mrs. Hanson said you need to eat and drink something," said Sherry.

"Thanks, guys," I said as I munched on a finger sandwich and sipped the punch.

Then it was over. I thanked Reverend John. As we spoke, I glanced into the sanctuary. Randy and Sherry walked together. Randy carried the box of ashes down the aisle toward me. They had sober expressions and walked very slowly. I know that kids this age shouldn't be handling human ashes. But after what those two had gone through, I was thankful to entrust them with my parents' remains. They carefully carried their small burden out the door, and we placed the container in the Mustang's trunk.

"Let's go home and see if Mr. P and Toby are still speaking," I said as we piled into the Mustang.

We had left the cat and dog with the run of the house. I was convinced there would be no problem. Regina was still worried that Toby would suddenly become a cat killer. From what I had seen of their interactions, I knew that would never happen, at least not with Mr. P.

"My feet hurt," groaned Regina. "I'm not used to wearing shoes like these. It will be good to get home."

I started the Mustang and pulled away from the church.

41

MARK AND HARRIET ATTENDED THE MEMORIAL SERVICE FOR THE Browns. They had arrived early and watched the mourners file in. Mark looked like an FBI agent, dressed in a black suit and a blue tie. He wore shiny black shoes. He kept on his overcoat as the weather was crisp. Harriet wore a dark blue pants suit, and she, too, kept on her short overcoat. Their weapons and badges were concealed.

Because of the news coverage on the murders, a number of uniforms were assigned to the funeral service to control the media and onlookers. The chief said he really didn't feel there was any threat to the Brown girl. He was convinced that the parents were the targets, not the girl. Mark wasn't so sure. They were taken out on a Friday evening when the entire family would likely be home. If the girl had not gone to the basketball game, she would have been dead. Whoever committed the murders struck right at dinnertime, taking out both the husband and wife in the kitchen. Nothing was taken from the house. Doors, including closet doors, were open. That likely indicated that they were searching for something more.

Mark and Harriet took a position in the back of the overflow crowd in the fellowship hall. Mark scanned the people sitting in the chairs. He wasn't sure what he was even looking for. Maybe something out of place?

When the service ended, the minister asked that everyone remain seated until the family left the sanctuary. Amy, the two foster kids, and the woman caring for them walked down the aisle. Last time Mark had seen Regina, she had just dealt with the trauma of someone breaking into her house. Today she looked a lot better. She was a little overweight but definitely attractive. She had red hair and a pale white complexion. She was probably in her early forties. She was maybe five feet seven. The foster kids also looked more together than before.

Then there was the Brown girl. What was it about her? Every time he saw her, he felt an emotional attachment, not sexual, almost spiritual. She was stunning in her own unique way. She had long, straight auburn hair. Her green eyes almost seemed to glow. She looked like she spent hours in a tanning booth, but he suspected that was her natural skin color. After all, her mother was African American. Then there was her height. With the heels she was wearing, she had to be six feet five inches. She had one of those fashion model figures. Her complexion was spotless. He found it hard to believe she was only sixteen. In some ways, she appeared ageless, like an Egyptian goddess.

During the reception that followed, he and Harriet stayed near the door watching as people passed.

"I feel bad that we have to come down hard on her next week," whispered Harriet.

"I know," said Mark. "But she knows more about this than she told us. Now with a confirmed match that the bloody handprint on the storage container was hers, we know that Amy Brown was not only in the storage unit, but was there after the three hoods were killed. Maybe she was there when they were actually killed. We have no choice but to come down hard on the girl."

Finally, most of the crowd had left.

"Shall we go?" asked Harriet.

"Let's wait until the family leaves. We might as well sit in the car." They went outside to the unmarked car. Mark started it up and turned on the heater. After a few minutes, they were warm enough to take off their coats.

42

Only a few vehicles remained in the church parking lot. Mark leaned back and started to close his eyes when he noticed a blue Lincoln parked on the street about a block from the church. Two men, smoking cigarettes, leaned against the fender.

"Give me the binoculars," Mark said.

Harriet took out the compact ten-power glasses from the glove compartment. Mark adjusted the focus. Both men wore black leather jackets and looked to be in their late thirties with closely cropped hair. Maybe military. They were big and well built.

"Russians," said Mark.

"What?"

"I'll bet those guys could very well be the perps who killed the Browns."

"Are you sure?" asked Harriet.

"No, just a gut feeling." He studied them through the glasses once again. "Call in this license number," he told Harriet. She picked up the mic and asked dispatch to run a check on the plates. A few minutes later, they had an answer.

"It's a rental out of Spokane International Airport. Rented to Bill Jones from New York."

"When was it rented?" asked Mark.

"Three weeks ago," said Harriet. "That tracks with the time frame of the murders. You can bet Bill Jones is a fake name. But what do we do? We don't have any cause to stop them. They're parked blocks from the church on a public street."

"Let's see where they go," said Mark.

Just then Amy walked out of the church with Regina and the twins. They all climbed into Amy's Mustang and drove toward Spokane. As they passed the blue Lincoln, the two men got in the rental car, started it up, and followed the Mustang. Mark dropped the gearshift into drive and followed along about a block behind the Lincoln. Harriet pulled her Glock, pulled the slide back, and checked to be sure that a round was in the chamber. Mark grabbed the mic.

"Dispatch, this is Baker and Sims. Do you have any patrol cars between Sixty-second and Twenty-ninth on the Palouse Highway?"

"We've got one on Twenty-ninth and Thor."

"Could you send it toward our GPS location?" asked Mark. "We may have a situation."

"Roger, it's on the way."

"We might be overacting," said Harriet with a short laugh.

"Yeah, but I just have a bad feeling."

"Come on, Mark; they're not going to pull something in broad daylight on a Saturday afternoon."

The Mustang and the Lincoln continued down the road at exactly the thirty-five-mile-per-hour speed limit. Mark continued to follow at about a block back from them. At the intersection of Regal and Southeast Boulevard, the Mustang slowed and turned onto Southeast. The light changed as the Mustang made the turn. Instead of stopping, the Lincoln went through the red light. Fortunately, there were no cars coming south on Regal. Mark's heart beat faster. He shoved the gas pedal down and ran the red, accelerating to catch up with the Lincoln. As he rounded the corner, he saw the Lincoln race toward the Mustang, still traveling at thirty-five miles per hour, Amy was unaware of the threat behind her. The heavy Lincoln struck the lighter Mustang on the left rear bumper. The Mustang was forced to the right, traveled across the curb, and struck a power pole. It came to a sudden stop, steam boiling out of its radiator.

The Lincoln screeched to a stop behind the Mustang. Both doors flew open and the two men, holding automatic pistols with long black suppressors, exited. Mark did not even think. For the two officers, everything they did was automatic. Jumping from their car, Mark shouted orders to his partner.

"I've got the guy on the left; you've got the one on the right. Don't ask questions. Shoot to kill. This is a hit going down!"

43

Following the memorial service Regina and I decided it would be a good idea to head to a restaurant to settle down away from all of the mourners. We decided to treat the twins to dinner at Applebee's on Twenty-Ninth.

The service started at eleven o'clock, and it was now four in the afternoon. I had to admit that I was actually hungry. Moreover, since I didn't normally wear high heels, my feet hurt like hell. I decided it would feel good just to forget everything except food and family for an hour or so.

As we headed north to town, no one spoke. That gave me time to think about my future. January 17 would be my seventeenth birthday. That was only two months away. During the two weeks I had been working with Paul Dino, Dad's attorney, I discovered what a jewel the man was. He had already met with the state of Washington and discovered that once children reach the age of seventeen, they no longer fall under the foster care regulations as long as there is a designated guardian. At age eighteen, they become legal adults.

For this reason, I had Paul draw up the paperwork to make Regina Hanson my legal guardian until my eighteenth birthday. Paul was a cautious man and wanted to make sure that the guardian could not take my inheritance, so he proposed that for that one year, Regina would have half a million dollars for expenses. The rest of my millions would come directly to me on my eighteenth birthday. *Millions. Six hundred million.* I couldn't get my head around that figure.

I also wanted the twins to be part of the deal. Paul was monitoring the charges against their mother and her dirtball boyfriend. If only the police could find out who killed my parents. I knew that I would never get over the loss of my parents but that would at least give me some closure.

44

I WAS TRAVELING NORTH ON REGAL AND MOVED INTO THE LEFT TURN lane for Southeast Boulevard. The light was green, so I pulled onto Southeast Boulevard and headed toward Twenty-Ninth Avenue. Suddenly, there was a loud crash, and the steering wheel was almost ripped from my hands. Before I could figure out what was going on, there was another crash, and the window on my door shattered into a thousand pieces. We headed directly toward a utility pole. I slammed my brake pedal to the floor. It pulsated against my foot as the antilock brakes worked to bring the car to a halt in the shortest possible distance. But it was too late. The Mustang connected with the pole before the brakes could stop the car.

Two things happened on impact. First, the windshield cracked. Second, the side and front airbags deployed. Yes, they save lives, but the initial impact of the bags really compresses a person's body. They use some kind of powder to keep the airbags flexible, and the stuff irritates a person's eyes and throat.

I had powder in my hair, nose, and eyes as I slapped at the bags, trying to get them out of my way. *What just happened?* I could hear the hot catalytic converters ticking under my feet. Steam from the broken radiator poured out from under the hood. My three passengers were all coughing as they reacted to the powder. Sherry had burst into tears. My first thought was to be grateful that we were all alive. My next concern was to get out all of us out of the car. I was worried about fire.

I pushed the button for the door. It clicked open. Thank God there was still power to the latches. The front fenders had been shoved back from the impact, and the door didn't open easily. I had to physically lift my legs up with my arms to shift them to the open door. Part of the dash had dropped down on my legs. I felt a trickle of blood from a cut on my right knee.

Still seated in the car with the door pushed open, I looked up, and my heart caught in my throat. Standing directly in front of me was a man wearing a black leather jacket. I remembered seeing him and another man standing by a blue car as we left the church. I had paid little attention to them as we drove by; I had assumed they were with the press. But this man was not here to render aid. In his right hand, he held a gun with a long black silencer attached to the barrel, just like in those spy movies. When he looked at me, his eyes seemed to glow. He smiled and pointed the gun directly at my face. He was going to kill me, and there was nothing I could do to stop him.

45

"POLICE! DROP YOUR WEAPON!"

Someone was yelling at the man with the gun. He whirled to his right, and I heard several loud discharges and several quieter pops, which I assumed were from the silenced gun. The man was still standing, grinning, and looking toward the rear of the Mustang. I looked in that direction. There, on his knees, was Detective Baker. He held his right shoulder firmly with his left hand. It wasn't enough. I could see blood seeping freely through his fingers. Out of reach, his service weapon sat useless on the pavement in front of him.

The gunman laughed out loud and aimed his weapon at Detective Baker. He was going to shoot the detective in cold blood.

"No!" I screamed. I watched in slow motion as the man's finger squeezed the trigger. I closed my eyes—I couldn't watch what I knew was going to happen. I heard two soft spits from the silenced weapon, and then I heard three loud shots. I opened my eyes. The killer was lying flat on his back, blood pooling around his head.

I looked back to where I had seen Detective Baker kneeling on the ground. He was still on his knees, but he held his service Glock in his left hand. I struggled to my feet and scrambled to Detective Baker. He looked directly at me. I could see blood running out of the corner of his mouth.

"There are two of them," he whispered. "Sims went after the other one."

"Where is she?" I asked.

"On the other side of the car," he said, grimacing in pain. "Take my gun." He pushed it toward me.

I took the Glock; it was just like Dad's. Using a two-hand hold, I managed to carry it steadily to the back of the car. I could see that the entire left side and rear end of the Mustang were smashed in. About thirty feet behind the Mustang sat a blue Lincoln. Its right fender and grill were badly damaged. Behind the Lincoln I could see an unmarked police car with both doors standing wide open.

I cautiously moved to the back of my car. Then I saw the legs and short high heels and blue slacks. It was Detective Sims. As I went a little further, I could see that she was lying on her side, her face toward me. Her eyes were wide open, but she was seeing nothing. Just like when I saw Mom in the morgue at Smith and Jones, she looked like a balloon with the air let out. Detective Harriet Sims was clearly deceased.

The Glock now began to shake in my hands. Where was the other guy? For a split second, I didn't know whether I should run back to Detective Baker, stay where I was, or run like hell the other way. But I could not desert Regina and the twins, who still sat in the Mustang. The other guy would find a way to kill them.

I got down on my knees and crawled around the back of the Mustang. Keeping the gun pointed toward the back fender, I eased around the right rear. There, leaning against the fender, was the other man. He held a silenced Glock in his right hand. He had blood on one leg, and his sports coat was stained with a wide circle of blood. A large chunk of his head was gone. He should be dead, but he continued to stare at me.

He raised his arm and aimed the pistol unsteadily at me. I've never killed anything in my entire life, but I knew I had no choice. I regained control of Baker's pistol and pointed it directly at the man's head. But before I could do anything more, the light in his eyes vanished, and he slumped forward, his chin resting on his chest. I saw the right door start to open.

"Regina! Stay in the car, and don't let the twins out. They don't need to see this!"

I turned and hurried back around the car to Detective Baker. Now he was lying on his side. I knew that he could die, too. I rolled him to his back. He looked up at me and blinked. He was still alive. He coughed. He was foaming blood and spit.

"A bullet punctured my lung," he gasped. "You've got to stop the air. Place something over the wound."

Without hesitation, I pulled open his jacket and shirt, ripping the buttons from the shirt. He wasn't wearing an undershirt. I saw only a round hole about the size of my little finger above his right nipple. *Plug the wound? With what?* I started to panic. I had to do something. In desperation, I pressed my hand, palm down, against the bullet wound. I held it firmly in place.

"That's better," he said. "Is Harriet OK?"

I remembered Dad's account of witnessing a car wreck on the way to Leavenworth, Washington, a number of years ago. The young woman involved in the accident had asked about the other driver. Dad had lied to her, telling her that the other driver was only injured, when in reality, he had died. I found myself doing the same thing.

"She's been shot in the leg, but otherwise she is OK," I said.

"What about the other perp?" he asked.

"He's dead also," I said.

"Good," he said.

I could hear the sirens nearing as I held my hand against the chest wound.

"I don't feel too good," he mumbled.

"You are not going to die," I cried. "I won't let you."

I looked upward and prayed quietly. *Oh God, please don't let him die!*

Suddenly, I felt a hand on my shoulder.

"We can take him from here, miss." It was a paramedic. I don't know how long I had knelt there, holding my hand over Detective Baker's wound.

As the medics started working on Baker, I said to them, "He won't die; I know it."

Finally losing grip on my self-control, I began to sob.

46

THE SIX MONTHS AFTER THE CAR ACCIDENT BROUGHT LOTS OF changes—all for the better. I still remember that horrible day—the second worst day of my life—as if it happened yesterday. I can see Detective Sims lying on the ground, dead. I can see the wound in Detective Baker's chest.

We spent hours at the scene of the shooting as dozens of police surrounded the site. When we finally got home that night, every local channel led off its broadcast with the story of the shooting. When a police officer is killed and another wounded, it makes local and national news. To make matters worse, someone had taken pictures of me with my hand holding back the flow of blood from Detective Baker's chest wound. The news made me some kind of teenage hero. In the picture, my face was smeared with powder from the airbags. Dirt and ruined makeup was not only on the front page of the *Spokesman Review*; I also showed up on the front page of *TIME Magazine*. I received calls from national TV morning shows and syndicated talk shows wanting me to come in for interviews. I declined those appearances, but I couldn't escape the presentation of the Civilian Medal for Heroism by the chief of police. We also attended the memorial service for Detective Sims.

Detective Baker was still hospitalized when the memorial service took place. The good news was that he would recover from his wounds.

It turned out the two men who had tried to kill me had ties with the Russian Mafia. Ballistics showed that their weapons were the same ones used to kill my parents. The chief of police announced that they believed the deaths of my parents were a case of mistaken identities. The hit men had mistakenly targeted my parents. Apparently, for some reason, they believed I might be able to identify them as the assailants. For that reason, they attacked us. The case of my parents' deaths was officially closed.

Two weeks after the attack, I was allowed to move back into my home. Regina and I walked through the house. When she saw the kitchen, she said that I needed to completely remodel it. It had to look different. It shouldn't offer any memories of the place where my parents died. Once we got started, we decided to do an extensive remodel of the entire house. I kept my old bedroom, giving Regina my folks' bedroom. I told her to furnish it to her own taste. Two separate bedrooms were prepared for the twins. The den, living room, and Mom's sitting room, however, were left untouched.

Once the remodeling was complete, the four of us moved in before Christmas. Regina's Christmas present was our Chevrolet Silverado pickup. I offered Regina the choice of Dad's or Mom's car. We had an eight-year-old pickup that we used to tow the boat. Dad also used it on winter days when the roads had not been plowed. We kept it in the barn. When Regina saw it, she burst into tears. It was the same model and color as the truck that had been repossessed when her husband, Frank, was dying from cancer. She got the truck, and we kept the Lexus, selling Dad's BMW.

The insurance company wanted to total my Mustang following the shootout. I battled with them, demanding that it be fixed. It was the last gift I had received from my parents. In the end, I won. After a bit of work, my car looked as good as it did the day it left the showroom.

On Christmas Eve, we attended services at Hills United Methodist Church. We had not been there since the memorial service. Everyone greeted us warmly. The next Sunday we attended the ten o'clock service and didn't miss a Sunday after that. Regina joined the Methodist women's group, and Randy and Sherry the youth group. Sherry even started singing in the choir.

47

WHEN THE SECOND SEMESTER STARTED, I WAS BACK IN FREEMAN. I argued with Regina for over a month that I didn't want to go back. Finally, she put her foot down and said I would go back to school. There were no "buts" about it.

Gads, she is acting like my mother. I wasn't happy about going, but I did it just to get her off my case. Once back in Freeman, I realized that she had made the best decision. Within a few weeks, I was back to the old routine with all my old friends.

I started taking karate lessons again. I was trying to find that inner ki that I experienced when I confronted Mike Douglas, but nothing seemed to happen. Both Randy and Sherry started taking karate, though. I also joined cross-country. On a lark, Just for kicks I tried out for the track team and discovered I was a natural for girls' cross-country, taking third in state competition. The Gonzaga University track coach even asked me to run cross-country in college.

March 17 was a very special day for the twins. Regina officially adopted them. Paul Dino worked with their mother on the adoption. He offered to provide free legal services and got the twins' mother a reduced sentence for her testimony against Mike Douglas. He also offered her financial assistance when she was released if she agreed to allow Regina to adopt them. I got into the habit of calling Regina my aunt, so it was natural to start seeing the twins as my cousins. I guess you could say that I created the family I'd never had.

I even went to my senior prom. I went with Craig Henderson—that football player who had had a crush on me at the first of the year. We had a great time. Despite wanting more, all he got was a good-night kiss. Craig was not a guy I wanted to spend the rest of my life with. And—to be honest—he really didn't turn me on.

48

As the small Freeman High School orchestra played "Pomp and Circumstance," the seventy-three graduating seniors marched single file into the gymnasium. A gray tarpaulin had been placed on the floor to protect the hardwood from damage. Chairs for the audience were set up with the senior class sitting to the left and the faculty sitting to the right. The more than two hundred friends and relatives of the graduating class took up the remainder of the chairs.

"Amy, did you ever believe that that this day would come?" whispered Carrie Bruner.

"Not really," I said. The class filed into four rows of chairs and remained standing until the principal said, "Please be seated." Well, the time had come. Everyone in our row stood up. It was time to go up on the stage and accept the diplomas. We marched up to the stage in our blue caps and gowns. I had to remember to flip my tassel to the other side as soon as I received the diploma. I listened to the names being called. We stood on the floor at the bottom of the steps leading to the portable stage. When our names were called, we walked up on stage, accepted the diploma from the president of the school board, and shook her hand. Then we walked down the other set of stairs.

"Amy Lynn Brown, summa cum laude, will attend Gonzaga University."

I walked up, followed the procedure, and said, "Thank you." I made my way toward my seat. Regina, in the aisle with her camera, smiled like a proud parent. I felt my eyes begin to fill with tears. I was thankful for her love, but how I wished Mom and Dad could have been there. I knew I wouldn't be able to control my emotions, but I didn't care. I sat down and wiped my eyes with my sleeve. By the time everyone received diplomas, I had regained my composure.

49

After the last diploma was awarded, the benediction was given, and we all marched outside to meet our families.

"Boy, I can't wait until I graduate from high school!" exclaimed Randy. "Then I'm joining the marines."

"You're only in seventh grade, dummy," said Sherry. "You've got to graduate first."

I loved these kids. It was so much like having a younger brother and sister. Regina came to my side and hugged me.

"Congratulations, dear."

"Thank you," I said. Then I added, "You were right. I'm glad I finished high school."

She smiled at me with a look that said she knew she'd been right all along.

"Excuse me," I heard someone say. I turned around. It was Detective Baker. "I wanted to congratulate you," he said.

"Thank you, Detective Baker."

"Not Detective Baker anymore. I'm just Mark Baker. Call me Mark."

"I'm glad to see you doing so well," I said. To be honest, he didn't look that good. He had dark circles under his eyes, and I could tell in the way he held his right hand that there might be some paralysis from his wounds.

I realized that Regina was standing right next to me.

"You remember my guardian, Regina Hanson."

He looked over at Regina. Actually, he looked like a number of men did when they saw Regina. Mom had a StairMaster exercise machine in the dressing room off of the bedroom. Regina had not only kept the StairMaster, but she used it regularly—daily as a matter of fact. She quit smoking and lost sixty pounds. She had her hair done weekly, and there were at least three bachelors at church who were hot on her heels. It was obvious Mark Baker thought that she looked pretty good.

"Nice to see you again." He turned back to me. "Amy, would it be possible for me to meet with you in the next few days? There is some information about your parents' case that I would like to turn over to you."

"Of course," I said

"How about I buy you lunch at Applebee's on Twenty-ninth? Say Monday at noon?"

"I'll see you then," I said.

He turned and walked away. His right shoulder was slightly lower than his left. I realized how seriously he had been injured.

"He seems like a nice man," said Regina as she watched him walk away.

"Everyone is meeting at Pizza Hut now to celebrate. We need to hurry so we get good seats," I reminded her and the twins.

50

MONDAY SAW ME ARRIVE AT APPLEBEE'S FIFTEEN MINUTES EARLY FOR my lunch with Detective Baker—that is, Mark Baker. Why he wanted to meet was still a mystery to me. He had said he wanted to give me some information about my parents' case, but I really had no idea what he would have to say. As far as I was concerned, that part of my life was over. Detective Baker had seemed so different when he had come to my graduation. *Maybe he had been in pain still?* I wondered. I parked the Mustang facing the front entrance to the restaurant.

At exactly half past eleven, an older Toyota pulled into the parking lot. Mark Baker got out and approached the entrance. *God, he looks as if the world is coming to an end.* His shoulders were hunched, and he shuffled like an old man. *Why not?* I reasoned. *He is old, at least as old as Dad was, maybe in his midforties.* But as he approached the restaurant, he looked like a really old man, perhaps sixty or more.

I hopped out of the Mustang and jogged until I caught up with Mark at the door.

"Good morning," I said.

"Well, right on time," he said.

"So, Mark, what information do you have for me?"

"Why don't we have lunch first?" he asked. "Then we can talk."

We were seated at a table next to the window. I ordered a chef's salad. Mark ordered a cheeseburger and a beer. He laughed when the beer arrived.

"We could never drink alcohol when we were on duty, which in homicide seemed like twenty-four hours a day. Harriet used to say we were married to the job."

I thought I saw his eyes begin to tear up.

"You and your partner were very close?"

"Hell, I was in love with Harriet."

"In love? I thought that she was...well," I stammered.

"Gay?" he said. "Yeah, she never knew I was in love with her. When we became partners, we really clicked. The more we worked together, the closer we became. I've been divorced five years. I'm not real good at developing new relationships, so all I had was Harriet. You know, I used to fantasize about us together. But, I knew she loved her partner. God, I've never told anyone this before."

He looked so sad. I didn't know what to say.

"Maybe she knew," I said, hoping I wouldn't upset him even more.

We sat silently for a few minutes before the meals arrived. We ate because we had to, not because we wanted to. Finally, Mark laid down his half-eaten hamburger.

"Do you know anything about Catholics?" he asked.

"Not much," I said. "Why?"

"Well, for people to become saints, they must have performed three miracles. I always thought that was a bunch of baloney until I witnessed two on the same day."

"The same day?" I asked, confused.

"Yes. The day I died twice."

"I don't understand," I said, concerned about Mark's emotional state.

"Harriet and I attended your parents' funeral because we had some new evidence concerning the case. It involved the deaths of three gang members in your folks' storage unit. Remember when I asked you about the container?"

"Yes," I said, wondering where this was all going.

"Well, you told us that you knew nothing about the container. That was a lie."

"The case is closed," I said, my anger beginning to build. "I don't have to listen to this."

"Calm down, Amy; I'm not trying to follow the case into my retirement. I'm trying to save your life."

"Save my life? What do you mean?"

"Amy, I don't believe your parents were the target."

"I know that," I said. "It was a mistaken identity."

"Just hear me out," he said. "Your parents weren't the target. You were."

"Me? That's not possible. Why would I be the target?"

"Let me tell you the facts. You are not going to like what you hear, but please wait until I finish before you say anything. That's all I am asking. Then you can walk out of here, and I will never talk to you again. Do we have a deal?"

"All right," I said, but I didn't like the way this was going. *Did Detective Baker lose his mind? Should I get up and leave?* Instead, I sat patiently and forced myself to listen to what he had to say.

"We had new evidence that indicated that you had been in the storage container the night of the murders."

"Evidence?" I asked.

"Yes. You left a bloody handprint on the roll-up door. It wasn't your blood. It was blood from one of the victims. When they ran the prints, you were not in the database, so the police didn't know whose prints they were. The night your folks were murdered, we took your prints so we could eliminate them from the forensic evidence in the kitchen. We compared your prints to the prints on the roll-up door in the storage container, and they came up a match. You were there, weren't you?" he asked.

"Yes," I whispered.

"Look, I'm not a cop anymore, and I am not trying to do anything other than get closure for Harriet's death. Would you tell me what happened?"

I told Mark basically what happened that night. I left out the part about finding the strongbox.

"So you saw nothing and heard nothing?" he asked cautiously.

"No," I said.

"Your cat was there?"

"Yes."

"Let me show you the autopsies on the three guys found in the container." He handed me five sheets of paper. "Read the highlighted portion."

I read aloud what was written on page four: "The wounds on all three victims are consistent with the damage that would occur from a large cat. Puncture wounds in the skull of victim one indicated that the cat's fangs were at least two and one half inches in length. This would match a cat the size of a male Bengal tiger. Lacerations on the legs and torsos of the victims again indicated a cat of immense size. Based on two smeared paw prints found on the floor of the storage container, I would estimate the weight of the cat to be well over eight hundred pounds. The only place in Spokane County with large cats is the Cat Tales sanctuary, north of town on the Newport highway. It is also possible that someone in the area has a large illegal cat in captivity."

I handed Baker back the report.

"I didn't see any tiger that night."

"Well, there was your cat," he said.

"Mr. P only weighs twenty pounds, not eight hundred."

"I know," he said. "But there was one other incident."

"What incident?"

"With Mike Douglas. Remember when I showed up at Regina's house?"

"Yes."

"Remember when I asked you if you owned another cat?"

"Yeah," I said. "I don't own any other cats."

"Mike told me the weirdest story. Do you want to hear it?"

"I'm not sure." I frowned.

"Well, it might help with what I am trying to say here. Anyway, you need to know who Mike is."

"He's that bastard that molested Sherry."

"More than that. He's a member of the Avenger's Motorcycle Gang. They make Hell's Angels seem like choirboys. In addition, Mike was the enforcer for the gang. He was one mean son of a bitch. Mike told me that while lying on the floor, you grabbed his foot and threw him all the way across the room. Nonsense, right? I figured it was a bunch of bull. Then he tells me about your cat."

"You saw what Mr. P did to him?" I said.

"Not that part. He said when he pulled the cat off of his face, he broke the cat's neck. He said he felt the neck snap, and then he threw the cat against the wall as hard as he could. That cat was dead when it hit the wall. Then when he saw the cat standing beside you, he believed it was a ghost. He was scared to death."

"He was mistaken," I argued. "He didn't hurt my cat. He tripped and fell."

"Amy, please, just listen to my story."

I could feel tears beginning to well up in my eyes. The waitress laid the bill on the table.

"I'll be the cashier," she said. Mark looked at the bill, handed her a fifty, and told her to keep the change. She smiled and walked away. We had been having an animated conservation and I was sure that my face was flushed. I'm not sure why, but I hoped she assumed that we were father and daughter, not some old man hitting on a young chick. After she left the table, Mark continued.

"Amy, I was a cop for twenty-five years, and I would still be today, if they would allow a cop with a partially paralyzed right hand to serve. For twelve years I was a homicide cop, and I was a good one.

"Murder is the greatest of all the puzzles. You gather notes and information, and the pieces begin to form a picture. The picture tells a story. The end of the story is a conviction. Your parents' murders turned out to be a blurry scene with no end. The more I gathered, the more confusing it became. I couldn't let it go. For that reason, Harriet and I were hanging around following the memorial service.

"We were looking for something to clarify the picture. I spotted the two Russian guys leaning against a Lincoln a block from the church. When you, Mrs. Hanson, and the two kids left in your car, the two guys followed you. We were following a block behind them. When you turned off Regal to Southeast Boulevard, the Lincoln ran the red light. We raced after them. When we turned onto Southeast, it was already going down. My God, we never dreamed that they would try to take you out in broad daylight on a Saturday afternoon. We had to move and move fast. The real bummer was that homicide detectives don't wear vests except when they are about to make an arrest. Our vests were in the trunk of the car. It cost both Harriet and me our lives."

"But you survived," I said, confused.

"No, Amy. I died—twice."

"What are you talking about?" Obviously, Mark was having some kind of breakdown. "Look, Detective Baker—ah, Mark—you've been seriously wounded and are still recovering."

"No, Amy. Think back to what happened."

"I'd rather not," I said.

"Close your eyes. What did you see?"

"The man was going to kill me. Then you said, 'Police!' There were shots. I looked, and you were on your knees. Your gun was lying on the pavement. I screamed, 'No!' He was going to shoot you. I then closed my eyes and didn't see what happened."

"Did you ever wonder how I was able to retrieve my gun from the pavement, pick it up with my left hand while seriously wounded, and then shoot the son of a bitch, all while he was aiming his gun at me?"

"You're faster," I offered optimistically.

"No, Amy. He had me in his sights. I was a dead man. Then a miracle happened. As he pulled the trigger, his gun arm was physically pushed aside. He tried to bring the gun back into position, but he couldn't. It was like an invisible hand held his arm. It allowed me to retrieve my gun, aim, and shoot him."

"I think it just seemed that way," I said. I didn't like what he was saying.

"There's more."

"More? What more?"

"Remember when I asked you to hold your hand over the chest wound?"

"Yes."

"Well, what I didn't know was that the bullet had nicked my aorta. I was bleeding out and would be dead in less than five minutes."

"But you didn't die."

"No, I didn't. The doctors cannot explain what happened. The aorta sealed itself shut before I got to the emergency room. Two miracles occurred that day, and I don't know how or why, but, Amy, you caused them."

"That's impossible!" I said so loudly that several people in the restaurant looked at us.

"I know that it isn't possible. But I believe it happened. I also believe you were—and still are—the target, not your folks."

I'm not sure exactly when I stopped listening to Mark's ramblings. I didn't believe a word he was saying. Clearly he had suffered some kind of mental breakdown from being so severely wounded. I was a normal seventeen-year-old. I was born in Spokane and lived there my entire life. I didn't believe in ghosts or that stupid vampire stuff that teenage girls get all gaga about. My life was getting back to normal, and I didn't need some old guy looking at me like I was the next messiah. Even if Mark had saved my life, I didn't want to hear this ridiculous crap. I tried to reason logically with him. I told him that once those bastards who shot my parents were dead, no one else had tried to kill me. I was perfectly fine.

He countered with the fact that I had become a big news item following the shooting. Whoever ordered me killed had to back off for a while. He said, next time, it would appear to be an accident.

I stood up, knocking my chair over. I did not want to hear any more. I turned and stormed out of Applebee's. All eyes were on me as I headed for the exit, but I didn't care; I was angry at what he had said, angrier than I'd been about anything since my parents had died.

51

I RAN TO MY CAR, JUMPED IN, STARTED IT. I HIT THE GAS AND RACED out of the parking lot onto Southeast Boulevard, driving past the place where the shooting had occurred. I glanced over at the exact spot, expecting to see the ghosts of the killers standing there. There was nothing, of course, not even any marks or disturbed gravel on the shoulder. In six months every trace of evidence of the incident had vanished.

I drove straight home, my heads-up display showing my speed at seventy-five miles per hour. I didn't gave I damn. If the police wanted to give me a ticket, so be it. I pulled into our driveway in record time. I slammed on my brakes, shut off the engine, and got out of the Mustang, slamming the door as hard as I could.

Damn you, Mark—why the hell did you have to ruin my day? I inserted my electronic key into the lock and walked into the house. Toby and Mr. P greeted me with their normal enthusiasm. It was obvious Regina was out. Of course, the twins were still in school. The graduating seniors were out two weeks earlier than the rest of the students in the district.

I looked at the grandfather clock. It was only half past one. I probably would be alone in the house for several hours. I looked down at my cat.

"You're not some kind of devil cat are you?" I asked him. He just looked at me, probably hoping that I would feed him early. I stared at the wall. I wasn't sure whether I wanted to scream, cry, or just kick the wall. I went to the sitting room, opened one side of the double French doors, and walked in.

Both the dog and the cat sat down at the threshold. They both knew that this room was off-limits for furry animals. I sat down on the gold velvet sofa, rubbing my hand on the soft material. I looked at the bookshelves that lined one wall. The bottoms of the bookshelves were closed cabinets. Above them were shelves filled with Mom's favorite novels. She had an extensive collection of books, some first-edition classics. At one end there was a small drop leaf table that converted to a small desk. This is where we had put the oak boxes with my parents' ashes. Some people might think it strange to keep human remains in a home, but I found great comfort in the fact that the boxes were in Mom's favorite room. Sometimes I would come down and talk to them. No, they didn't answer, but I felt that they listened to me.

I closed my eyes, trying to clear my mind of the troubling things Mark Baker had said. The more I tried to forget, the more I replayed his words.

"Damn you," I shouted. Both animals scurried away from the door. "Sorry, guys; I wasn't talking to you." I got up and called them back to the door. I reached down and patted both their heads.

"Lay down," I said. Both the dog and cat obediently stretched out at the door. Since I was already up, I went to one of the cabinets and opened the door. A number of books were piled on top of each other. I pulled the books out and restacked them on the floor. Behind the books was the strongbox. I had not looked into it since that night six months ago.

I dialed in the last four of my social security number and opened the box. The minute I opened the lid, Mr. P was sitting beside me, seemingly curious about its contents.

"You're not supposed to be here, cat," I said sternly. He just stared at the box. I figured it must be that stupid lion tooth that fascinated him. On top were the two passports. I pulled them out. The next thing was the ruby that I had taken to the jeweler six months ago. I took it out too. Then I closed and locked the box.

As soon as the box was closed, the cat lost interest and went back to the doorway.

"Weird!" I said out loud.

I pushed the ruby into my front jeans pocket, set the two passports on the coffee table, put the strongbox back in the cabinet, and piled some books in front of it to conceal it. I sat down on the couch and opened the passports. Once again, I looked at the photos of my parents. I had not attempted to find out who they really were. I think I didn't want to admit that they had led different lives in the past. If they were mass murderers or spies, I don't think I could have lived with that knowledge. The fact that the men who killed them were Russian Mafia led me to believe Mom and Dad were involved in something bad. Maybe they were Russians spying on our country, living under the cover of being a typical American family that would include a child.

Maybe I wasn't even their child. They might have bought me to use as part of their cover. I was about ready to destroy the passports and just go along with the previous reality—my folks had always been the Browns—but my curiosity got the better of me. I wanted to know who they were.

With passports in hand, I headed up to my bedroom, sat at my desk, and turned on my computer. I typed in "Timothy Henry Martin" in the Google search box. There were hundreds of Martins. For thirty minutes I played with both Mom and Dad's real names—not the Browns, but the Martins. I started playing around with the dates and finally hit the jackpot. By going back to my birthday and moving forward, six months after my birth, I found the information I was looking for: articles. This one summarized what happened:

Prominent Washington attorney Allen Dixon's daughter and son-in-law were eulogized in a private ceremony this week in Alexandria. The couple disappeared when their plane crashed into dense jungle in a tragic accident in Liberia, West Africa, six months ago. Witnesses said the twin-engine plane was engulfed in flames as it vanished into triple-canopy jungle north of the remote village of Zigda, Liberia. Searchers were unable to locate the wreckage. After looking for them for two weeks, government and military efforts were called off, and the pilot and the Martins were declared dead. Samantha Dixon-Martin was an anchor for NYN TV. She was doing research for a news story on Africa. Her husband, Tim Martin, was an FBI agent and had taken a three-month leave of absence to accompany her to Africa.

Oh my God! Is this the Allen Dixon who was a candidate for president last year? Is he my grandfather? I shut down the computer. Everyone would be home soon. I would have to do more research, but later.

52

THE HEAT WAS STIFLING. I COULDN'T BREATHE, AND MY ARMS AND legs would not move. I opened my eyes. *What?* I was totally blinded by a bright light. I threw my hands over my eyes. Gradually, my eyes adjusted to my surroundings. I was lying in a fetal position on my side on a hot rough surface.

"Holy smokes!" I exclaimed. Mr. P let out a low growl as he stood looking into my face. "I'm dreaming, Mr. P."

I was lying on the red dirt in a primitive village in what I thought were the Amazon jungles. It had to be a dream, I decided, because I was in the same T-shirt and boxer shorts I had worn to bed. I struggled to my feet.

The village was nestled on a stretch of low-lying land. Around the village were rugged mountains and impenetrable dense undergrowth. Unlike so many other forested lands that clear-cutting had maimed, this forest was old growth—truly a virgin forest. Not far from the village to the east rose a massive tabletop mountain with jungle forest on its top. I could feel the hot tropical sun on my back. I could feel the humidity. I had never been to the tropics in my life, but I had watched those National Geographic specials, and this was clearly one of those villages.

The huts were covered with natural thatch. Here, no rusty tin roofs marred the landscape. I could see well-tended farms, herds of healthy goats, and orderly rows of crops. The scene was so sharp and real. I very seldom dreamed, and I remembered very little of my dreams if I did. This was more real than a dream should be. Smoke rose from the small fires behind huts, and there was a smell of burning charcoal mixed with the odor of cooking food.

Strange, I didn't see a single person in the village.

I walked toward one of the huts. My cat, Mr. P, followed. I looked in.

"Hello? Anyone here?" I called out. There was no answer. I checked several other huts with the same result. As I walked toward the other side of the village, my feet hurt from touching the ground scorched by the tropical sun.

"Ouch!" I exclaimed. I reached down and rubbed my foot. "I thought you couldn't feel pain in dreams," I said to my cat, as I stood on one foot and then alternated to the other.

I moved into the shade of one of the huts. Suddenly, Mr. P ran around the corner of the hut and disappeared.

I hurried after him. I stopped when I came to the back of the hut.

"No!" I screamed. Twenty-five feet in front of me stood a huge leopard. My cat was walking right up to the massive animal.

"Mr. P, stop! You come back here, cat. You might be able to intimidate a pit bull, but that leopard will kill and eat you."

I held my hands over my eyes to avoid the horrifying sight of the death of my cat. I waited for the cat's scream of agony and the victorious growl from the huge beast. When I heard no sound, I spread the fingers of one hand and peeked through before dropping both hands to my side.

I couldn't believe what I was seeing. The leopard sat on his haunches. Sitting next to him was Mr. P. Both cats were looking to their right. I followed their gaze. There on a wooden bench were a man and a woman.

Since both were dark-skinned, I decided that the village was in Africa, not South America. Both were barefoot and shirtless. They looked really old. The man's head had a bald spot fringed with snow-white hair. The woman's hair was thin. It, too, was snow white, and her skin was deeply wrinkled. They smiled and waved at me.

"Please, come closer," the man said, gesturing as he spoke.

The old woman laughed. "I see you have my cat."

"Your cat?" I said. "He's my cat. I've had him for more than six years."

"Girl, be mine long before he be yours," she chortled.

"Where am I?" I asked.

"You're home," said the old man.

"Home?" I asked, confused by his response.

"Dis be where your mother gave birth to you. Duh birth took place in duh hut behind me," he said.

"And who are you?" I asked.

"Why I'm Chea Geebe, duh greatest zo in all of Liberia!" He laughed. "Except for your mama's mama's mama's mama's mama."

"How did I get here?" I asked.

"Duh greatest of zos, dey travel from place to place outside of der body and can talk with duh spirits of duh dead," he answered.

I shivered as I thought about what Mark Baker had said to me yesterday. Perhaps that was what was causing me to dream.

"Why am I here?" I asked.

"Because of duh *endosyms*," he answered.

"The *endosyms*?" I asked.

"Dem have great power, and since your birth, many of der kind are coming into dis world each day. Soon it be too late for mankind and wimmens too. You will all become slaves to des creatures," explained the old man.

"What does this have to do with me?" I asked him.

"Why, dear, you be the chosen one, duh one with duh power to distroy dem *endosyms*."

"Listen, I'm a seventeen-year-old girl. My name is Amy Brown, and I was born in Spokane, Washington. That's in the United States, by the way. There is no such thing as *endosyms* that are going to take over the world."

"Anaya, I have seen dem *endosyms*. Dey have horns and tails. In Haiti where I be born, we calls dem *ezu*. Dey be bad, real bad. But you, Anaya, will be more powerful dan duh greatest of the voodoo priests, greater dan duh most powerful of dem witches. You, girl, will save duh world!" said the old woman.

"I knew it," I said. "You've got the wrong person!"

"Oh, no," said the old man. "You be Anaya Martin. Yous daddy was Tim Martin and when I departed dis body, I gave him duh power of duh great leopard spirit. Yous mama was Samantha Dixon. In her veins flowed duh blood of duh greatest of all zos. Deys union created you, and your power will come soon."

The old man stood up and came toward me. He had something in his hand, which he gave to me. It was a small square piece of leopard fur.

"Dis be duh key to duh chamber of duh Mountain of Darkness. It will open duh door. Dat leopard tooth I give to yous grandmother will show duh way. To learn duh truth, you must return to duh place of yous birth. When you enter dat Mountain of Darkness, den you will know yous destiny."

"Whoa!" I said. "This dream is getting out of control!"

"It no dream, Anaya. Now you will return to where you come from."

Everything began to fade. Then there was only darkness.

53

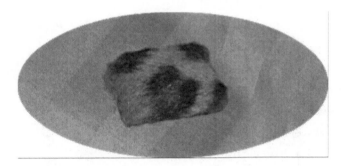

I OPENED MY EYES AND COULD SEE LIGHT OUTSIDE MY BEDROOM WINDOW. I looked at my iPhone. It was already six o'clock in the morning. Mr. P was curled up on my other pillow. He wasn't supposed to do that. I stretched and threw my covers back. I needed a shower. Then I'd help make breakfast. The twins had two more weeks of school.

"Come on, cat, get off the pillow!" Mr. P jumped off the bed.

I looked at the pillow and noticed that there was red dirt on the pillow where the cat had slept.

"What did you get into, cat?"

Then I looked at my bare feet before continuing to inspect the rest of me. I also had red dirt on my feet, on my boxer shorts, and on my T-shirt. I started getting a knot in the pit of my stomach. All that was bad enough, but then I noticed something more—a piece of leopard fur on the pillow. I nearly panicked. *Perhaps the fur would vanish, just like my dream, if I try to touch it,* I hoped. I touched it with the tips of my fingers. It was still there.

This is impossible. I'm not into stuff like this. Perhaps it was some sort of a prank. But who could be responsible? Who could have possibly produced a dream that remained so vividly in my mind?

I was scared. I mean I was really scared. Could I have a brain tumor? Was this all a hallucination? I pulled off the sheets and pillowslips and threw them in a pile near my door. I stripped off my T-shirt and shorts and headed for the shower. I scrubbed my body like I was getting rid of radioactive dust. Gosh, maybe it really was radioactive!

I put on fresh clothes and took the bedding to the laundry room. Then I remade my bed with clean sheets. I laid the piece of fur on my desk. I took out a small ruler and measured it. It was one inch by one and a quarter inches. The back had brown leather sewed to the hide. It was like a small pouch. I smelled it. I swear it smelled like the village in my dream. I rubbed my finger on the fur. It was soft like cat fur. Clearly the hide was real. I remembered the old mans words: "The leopard hide was the key to the chamber of the Mountain of Darkness." This was crazy.

I put the piece of leopard fur in my pocket. When I got to the kitchen, Regina was already up.

"Good morning, honey," she said.

"Good morning," I said. I pulled out the piece of fur. "Have you ever seen anything like this before?" I laid it on the table.

"It looks like a piece of leopard fur," she said. "Where did you get it?"

"I found it," I said.

"Do you think it's real fur?"

"Yes," I said. "You can see the hide on the back of it."

"Where did you find it?"

"Lying on the curb by Applebee's," I answered. Obviously, I wasn't about to say that an old black witch doctor gave it to me in a dream. If I admitted to that, I would soon be sitting in a padded psycho cell at Medical Lake Hospital.

"You know it's illegal to have leopard hide; you'll never find out who lost it," said Regina.

"I think I'll just keep it," I said as I pushed it back into my pocket.

Once breakfast was ready, we all sat down. The kids chatted away. I sat there fingering the piece of leopard fur. My first reaction was to blame Mark Baker. He said that I was different. Then when I found out who Mom and Dad really were, a dream could have occurred as a result of those two events happening on the same day.

But what I was holding was real. The red dirt from the village was real.

"Are you OK, dear?"

"What?" I asked.

"You seem preoccupied," said Regina.

"I just didn't sleep well," I replied. "I'm OK."

I tried to get into the conversation, but all I could think about was the strange dream. Was my name really Anaya Martin? Was I really the target of those evil men? Did they mean to kill me, not my parents? Was I some kind of witch or something? That wasn't even possible. This was the twenty-first century, not the Middle Ages.

Sure, I believe in God, but only crazy people believed in out of body visits to Africa and magic pieces of leopard hide —right?

54

I TURNED RIGHT OFF TWENTY-NINTH ONTO GRAND BOULEVARD. ON the left was Manito Park. I had called the number on the business card given to me at the coffee shop back in October.

Leona Erickson, White Witch
Potions and Spells, Psychic Readings
Phone: 347-8967
Call night or day.

On the back I had written the address the woman gave me. It was a house across from Manito Park.

I had spent an hour on the Internet the night before, researching Wiccans, witchcraft, and even devil worship. It clearly was something I had never even thought of doing in my whole life. Every time I went on one of the websites, I envisioned someone on the other end knowing my IP and jotting down my address. Gads, I would have felt more comfortable surfing porn sites. I was worried that reading all this crazy stuff would make me have even stranger dreams.

I had now gained a basic understanding of witchcraft. It appears in every country and culture and goes back thousands of years. Some witches are good; others are bad. They are capable of creating magic potions, spells, and charms. They can make totems and sometimes use physical items like scraps of leopard fur in their rituals. Besides witches, there are demon and devil worshipers. Ancient warriors from long-dead civilizations continue to reappear throughout history. What really surprised me was the fact that hundreds of witches live in the Spokane area. Their covens even meet in Manito Park. Perhaps that was why Leona Erickson had chosen to live across from the park.

I checked the address; there it was. I pulled into the driveway. It was one of those huge old homes built more than a hundred years ago. Some of the richest families in Spokane once lived in this neighborhood. Many of these homes had been converted into apartments. Now people bought them and tried to restore them to their original glory.

I didn't know what to expect. Maybe it was a house like in *The Munsters* on Nickelodeon. Immaculately maintained, the flowerbeds were filled with multicolored flowers, and the lawn was freshly mowed. Huge oak trees shaded the entire front yard. The exterior white paint and gray shutters were in such good condition that the place could have been built yesterday. A wide front porch was furnished with standing flowerpots, small side tables, and large wicker chairs. Wide steps led up to the front door. It was made of solid oak and featured leaded glass windows.

I opened the door to the Mustang, glancing in the mirror to make sure my lipstick wasn't smeared. I wore brown slacks, a white short-sleeved blouse, and low-heeled loafers. I remembered Leona Erickson as being very short and plump. I didn't want to appear too tall. I almost laughed. I had actually tried to figure out how to dress to visit a witch. Should I wear earrings or not? I guess I could have bought little pentagram earrings. As it was, I decided to go without any earrings.

"I'm so glad you decided to visit, dear," she said when she came to the door. "Please come in."

I stepped into the entryway. The interior was much larger than I had imagined. The hallway was at least twelve feet wide. A grand staircase led to the second floor. On the right I saw the formal dining room; on the left was the parlor. Highly polished hardwood flooring was dotted with thick oriental carpets. Finishing off the walls were dark oak wainscoting and crown molding. In between, wallpaper with tiny colored flowers tied together the entire downstairs area. Coming here was like walking into the past.

I could smell the odor of incense with a hint of apple and cinnamon.

"Please come into the parlor," she said with a knowing smile. *Said the spider to the fly*, I thought.

One person was already seated in the room. At first she was hard to see in the semidarkness. Some light came in through the slits in the drapery panels, but the only other lighting came from the low-watt bulbs in the table lamps. The person stood. I could hardly control my reaction. This woman was a giant, close to seven feet tall and as thin as a rail. As tall as I am, I was short compared to her.

"This is my life partner, Greta."

"How are you, Miss Brown?" said Greta in a voice as low as Leona's voice was high.

"Call me Amy," I said.

"Please sit down, Amy. May we get you something to eat or drink, dear?" asked Leona.

"No, thank you," I said. I remembered the story of Hansel and Gretel, the story of the two kids who went to the witch's house in the woods. I felt a little like those two kids, and I wasn't sure I wanted to drink or eat anything in this house.

"When I saw her at the teahouse, I knew she was one," said Leona to Greta.

"Yes, a true Wiccan," said Greta.

"I'm really not a Wiccan or witch or whatever," I said.

"Dear, I have never seen such aura, even in a high priestess. Since you said you do not belong to a coven, you must practice as a solitary Wiccan," said Leona, frowning.

"Afraid not. I'm just a Methodist," I mumbled.

"Many followers of the Christian faith are also Wiccans. Just like the Freemasons, our beliefs are ancient and are open to anyone willing to follow the way of enlightenment," explained Leona.

"How does that happen?" I asked.

"First, you must be asked to join a coven. We would be willing to introduce you to the priest and priestess of one of our covens that has a vacancy," said Greta.

"A vacancy?" I asked.

"Yes, a coven can be no more than thirteen members. Once the coven reaches thirteen, no additional members are admitted. A new coven must be formed. Our conclave has two hundred and thirty eight members in the Spokane area, so I'm sure you could find one, perhaps in your own neighborhood."

As they were talking to me, a large gray tabby cat jumped on the sofa and walked up to me. I started to pet him.

"Don't touch him. He bites," warned Leona.

"Yes, he bites," echoed Greta. I pulled my hand back. The cat climbed into my lap and curled up. He rubbed his wide head against my hand.

"You smell my cat don't you, buddy?" I said.

"Most strange," said Leona.

"Most strange," echoed Greta.

I looked at the two women.

"I've got a cat too. I guess he thinks I'm OK," I explained.

"You don't understand," said Leona. "Smokey is our familiar. A witch's familiar will never go to anyone else."

"Well, he sure seems to like me," I said.

"You said you also had a cat?" asked Leona.

"Yes."

"How long have you had your cat?" asked Greta.

"I found him when I was eleven," I answered.

"Eleven!" exclaimed Leona. "The magic age."

"Yes, the magic age!" agreed Greta.

"The magic age?" I asked.

"In the history of the witches of Ireland, it was believed that the familiar would come to a witch on her eleventh birthday," explained Leona.

"Well, I don't think it was on my birthday," I said.

"Was your cat still a kitten?" she asked.

"No, he was full grown," I said.

"Has he ever done anything special for you?"

"Special?" I asked. "Like what?"

"Protect you, for example," replied Greta. I thought about Mr. P attacking Mike Douglas. *Could Mark be right?* What had happened in the storage container may have just been an act of protection.

"No," I said. "He just acts like a normal cat."

"Too bad," said Leona.

"Too bad," echoed Greta. *What is it with these two women? They act like parrots.*

I picked up Smokey and set him down on the rug. He took one more glance at me before climbing into Greta's lap.

"Where were we?" asked Leona who had seemed to lose track of the conversation. "Oh, yes," she recalled. "I was talking about joining a coven. To become a member of a coven takes one full year plus one day. That is the timeframe that it takes to prepare the novice. She must study the craft before being initiated. We often initiate the new members on one of the sabbats."

"What's a sabbat?" I asked.

"Those are specials days for the Wiccans. There is Samhain on October thirty-first, Yuletide on December twenty-first, and Imbolc on February first, for example. All together each year there are eight sabbats. On those days the conclave of covens will gather in a sacred place to honor our gods and initiate new members," she explained.

"Well, right now, I don't think I want to join a coven. I was just interested in what you guys did."

"All Wiccans start out wondering if there is more to life. We learn how to use the elements of air, fire, water, and earth to tune our bodies into the spirit world. Ours is no different than any other religious quest that seeks the inner person. I can assure you that once you find your inner self through Wiccan ritual, you will never turn back to the everyday world. It's a wonderful experience." Greta sighed.

"Oh, there was one other thing," I said. I reached into my purse and withdrew the small piece of leopard fur. "Does this have anything to do with witchcraft?" I asked.

"Let me see it," said Leona. She stood and approached me.

I held out the piece of fur, and she reached out to take it from me. When her fingers were about an inch away from the fur, we all heard a loud snap. A blue-tinged spark arced from the fur to her finger. Leona jumped back faster than I thought a woman of her girth could do. She looked terrified.

"Where did you get that?" she asked.

"I found it," I said.

"You couldn't have found it!" Her voice was shrill; fear seemed to grip her entire being. Greta had rushed to her side. Leona rubbed her hand vigorously.

During Spokane's cold winters, it can get very dry. Just rubbing your shoes on a carpet can build up static electricity. If a person touches another person, a static discharge can spark between the two people. That's the only way I knew how to explain what had happened.

But Leona was acting really weird.

"What are you?" she asked, gasping more like she had stuck her finger in a light socket than just experienced a little charge of static electricity.

"Are you a *zoutari* or one of the *endosyms*?"

"I'm just me," I said, my curiosity now turning into outright fear.

"Go now!" she screamed. "Get out of our house!"

"Yes, get out of our house," echoed Greta. They both raised their right arms and pointed toward the front door.

I didn't need any encouragement. I stuffed the leopard fur back into my purse and bolted to the front door. Once outside, I dashed to the Mustang. I heard Leona yelling behind me.

"Never come back here again!" she shouted. "You are not welcome!"

I climbed into my Mustang and backed out of the driveway without looking. A horn blared as I pulled onto Grand Boulevard.

"All right! All right! Sorry about that," I yelled to the driver behind me. I dropped the gearshift into drive and headed toward downtown.

55

GOD, WHAT WAS ALL THAT ABOUT? TALK ABOUT TWO CRAZY DAYS. I started to laugh. In the last forty-eight hours, I had a weird dream that resulted in a piece of leopard fur turning up in my bedroom, and now two witches had kicked me out of their house. I was truly going nuts. If I told anyone about this, I would be committed to a mental intuition.

What should I do? I didn't have to think too long before I realized that there was only one person I could turn to—Mark Baker. He was the only one who believed that something weird was going on. I pulled into the parking lot of the dry cleaners on Grand Boulevard. I pulled out my iPhone and dialed Mark's number.

"Hello?" said a male voice.

"May I speak to Mark Baker?" I asked.

"This is Baker."

"This is Amy Brown."

"Yes," he said, somewhat hesitatingly. After what I had said the day before, his reaction was to be expected.

"I need to talk to you," I admitted. "I believe what you told me."

"All right, meet me at Shari's on Division, say in thirty minutes," he said.

"I'll be there."

I wondered why he didn't invite me to his house. Then it dawned on me. A forty-seven-year-old single man doesn't invite a seventeen-year-old girl to his house. That was a quick way to end up in jail. Mark Baker may not trust me. Shari's was a safe, public place. I put my phone back in my purse and headed for Division Street.

56

When I arrived at Shari's on Division, I saw Mark standing by the entrance. *God, he looks worse than he did two days ago.* He hadn't shaved, and it looked like he was wearing the same rumpled clothes.

I pulled into a parking spot, got out of my car, and approached him.

"Hi," I said.

"Hi," he said.

"I guess we had better stop meeting like this," I said, trying to add a little humor to the situation. It was good to get indoors with the air conditioning.

"Two," said Mark to the hostess at the counter. She took us to a booth by the window. I could see her looking at us, trying to figure out what was going on. Here was a nicely dressed young woman with an older guy who looked like a homeless man. "Menus?" she asked.

"I'll just have coffee," said Mark.

"I would like a piece of coconut cream pie and a diet Pepsi," I said. "You know, we used to go to Shari's at least once a month. Dad liked the food and the prices. It's funny that he was concerned about the prices. He could have bought the entire restaurant." We sat silently until the coffee, pie, and soft drink came.

Mark sipped his coffee before speaking.

"I never thought I would see you again."

"I know. I was pretty freaked out. I'm sorry," I said.

"I just didn't know how to approach the subject. After you left, I haven't felt like doing anything. You know, my life has been nothing but police work for years. If I had been younger they might have given me a desk job. But since I was retirement age, they gave me my pension and sent me on my way. Now that it's over, I have no idea what I will do. I understand why some retired cops eat their guns," said Mark.

"Eat their gun?" I asked.

"Suicide," he said.

"Jeez, don't talk like that," I said. "There is always something to do. There is always hope."

"Yeah, sure," he muttered.

I needed to get him away from this depression. He was my only hope, and I decided that I had to come totally clean with him.

"Mark, you remember when I told you I didn't believe that something strange or supernatural was happening."

"Actually, I said 'miraculous.'"

"OK, 'miraculous.' Well, since then something even stranger has happened. It's something so strange that everything you told me now seems true."

I reached into my purse and withdrew the piece of leopard fur. I held it between by thumb and forefinger.

"Touch it," I said.

"What?"

"Just touch it, and try not to yell."

"I don't understand," said Mark, puzzled by my request.

"Please, just try to touch it," I asked again.

"All right," he said.

He reached toward the fur. Just like when Leona tried to touch it, when Mark's fingers were about an inch from the fur, there was a sharp crack and a spark jumped to his finger. I have to give him credit. He didn't scream. But he jerked his hand back, rubbing his finger. The snap was loud enough that several people looked over at us. I thought I could smell ozone.

"What is that? Some kind of miniature Taser concealed in fake fur?" asked Mark.

"No. It's only a piece of leopard fur, but apparently I am the only one who can hold it," I said. "The weird thing is that an old black man in an

African village gave it to me in a dream." I paused to give Mark a chance to react, but he just looked at me. "The problem is that, right now, you and I believe that things are happening that cannot be explained in normal terms. You're a retired cop recovering from serious wounds, and I'm a seventeen-year-old whose parents were murdered. Then I was almost killed myself. We can't tell anyone else this story. For me, even more damning is I could lose my entire inheritance."

Mark sat there staring at me, rubbing the hand that had been struck by the spark. Because of the partial paralysis in his right hand, he was having some difficulty massaging it.

"Now it's time for me to tell you everything I know," I told him. "I will leave nothing out. The reason I'm going to do this is because you are the only person who might understand."

For the next hour, I told Mark everything that had happened, right down to the stuff I found in the strongbox. He sat there staring at me like I was some kind of nut. I expected him to reverse the role of two days ago and get up and walk out. Instead, he rubbed his eyes with his fists.

"Amy, you could not have made up a story like that. I don't understand what is happening, but I believe you."

57

I FELT TEARS BEGIN TO RUN DOWN MY CHEEKS. I WAS RELIEVED THAT I had been able tell someone, but, at the same time, I was afraid of what might happen to me.

"Maybe I'm possessed by a demon or something," I whispered.

"I don't believe that," said Mark. "In ten years in homicide, I've seen people that, even if not possessed by demons, are in some ways just as bad. I don't see that in you. Whatever you are dealing with, I will do my best to help you."

"Thank you," I said. "But after I tell you the next thing, you may want to refuse. You see, I have major problems and only you can help me."

"No, Amy, you have just given me a reason to live. What do you need?"

I held my breath, and then I said, "On January seventeenth, I will be eighteen years old. On that date, I will be of legal age and will inherit over six hundred million dollars.

"My birthday is seven and a half months away. Until that time, Regina is my legal guardian, and I am not about to tell her what is going on. Then there's my attorney, Paul Dino. I know there are things like client confidentiality, but as the executor of my parents' will, he could take court action to have me committed if I were to tell him any of this.

"For this reason, I need you to work for me for the next seven months without anyone else knowing, but I want you to know what you're getting yourself into. Imagine if they find out that a divorced older male is meeting secretly with a seventeen-year-old girl."

"I understand it's jail time," said Mark. "But I will still help you."

"OK," I said. "Here is what I need during the next seven and a half months. First of all, if my life is in danger, what can be done to keep me alive without getting Paul and Regina involved? Next, I told you my parents' real names. I want to find out what happened to them and what family I have. Finally, I want to find out more about the gems in the strongbox. Since Dad was an FBI agent and Mom was a reporter, I don't believe that the gems are stolen. But where did they come from? How valuable are they?"

I pulled out the ruby and handed it to Mark.

"A jeweler downtown told me that it was very old, and he thought very rare. He said there was a buyer of antique gems in Seattle who might know its value. I would like you to go to Seattle and sell it. I'll give you twenty percent of what you sell it for."

"That isn't necessary," said Mark. "I'll do it for nothing."

"No, Mark. If you agree, you will work as my chief of security. I will pay what a security chief guarding a multimillionaire gets paid. Until my eighteenth birthday, when I can draw up an official contract, I will use the gold Krugerrands to pay expenses."

"Amy, what kind of chief of security can I be? I'm a cripple. I can barely use my right hand," said Mark, holding it up for inspection.

"Then use your left hand," I said. "I saw you shoot with your left hand. Get better at it. Without you, apparently, I would have been dead."

"All right," he said. "Let me see what I can do."

I looked down. I hadn't touched my pie. Finally, I dug into it and drank my Pepsi. Mark sipped his coffee. We got up, and I took the bill.

"This one is on me," I said.

As I headed to the Mustang, Mark shouted back at me. "Give me two weeks, and I will come up with something."

"I'm counting on it," I said. *Hopefully, some bad guy won't kill me before then.* I waved good-bye and grasped the steering wheel. I felt a shiver run down my spine.

58

Two weeks after my meeting at Shari's, the doorbell rang. Regina answered. It was Mark.

"Amy, guess who's here," said Regina. They walked into the living room, but I hardly recognized the man. I couldn't believe my eyes. Mark was a changed person, and I mean really changed. He wore a tailored suit and shiny shoes. He was clean-shaven and had a fresh haircut. He looked like an entirely different person.

"Hi, Miss Brown, I just wanted to stop by and see how you all were doing."

"We're doing great, Mr. Baker. Please call me Amy," I said.

"All right, as long as you call me Mark," he said. *What's going on?* I wondered.

"I have a new job," said Mark. "Here's my business card." He handed one to Regina and one to me. I looked at the card. At the top was the law enforcement motto—"Protect and Serve"—and below that it read "Baker Security Incorporated, Investigations, Protection, and Security, Mark A. Baker, President." It included a phone number and e-mail address.

"I just started my own business," said Mark with a confident grin. "I rented offices downtown. I have six employees, and it's going to grow. Gary Ellis, the most recent Spokane County sheriff, is on my team. I also have Fred Richardson, who just retired as regional FBI chief; a couple of former detectives; and, on my desk, I have a dozen résumés from retired military and former law enforcement personnel. We already have two contracts, and this is just our first week. Would you believe that Northern Quest Casino has contacted us?"

"That's wonderful," said Regina. "Please, I would like to hear more. Would you care for a cup of coffee?"

"Great! Black is fine," said Mark.

"Amy, would you like a soft drink?" asked Regina.

"Sure," I said.

Regina headed for the kitchen. When she was out of earshot, Mark said, "Our agreement still stands."

"Thank you," I said. The next question caught me by surprise.

"Regina is a widow, isn't she?" asked Mark.

"Yes," I said.

"Is she dating anyone?"

"Not really," I said, somewhat confused.

"She sure is a fine-looking woman," said Mark, apparently to himself. He was looking toward the kitchen like a lovesick teenager.

When Regina came out of the kitchen, she had put on lipstick and was sort of blushing. *What's going on here?* I watched the two of them talking and felt sort of left out. *Hello, I'm here too!*

Yes, I knew that Regina had lost weight and had quit smoking, but I had never realized how good-looking she had become. She had a pretty face, but she was a little heavy in the hips. Her boobs were too big. But what did I know? My A-cup never garnished a second stare.

Mark gave us more info about his new company. He explained they had just purchased three used black Dodge Charger SRT8 HEMI-powered four-door pursuit cars. He had even driven one of them to my house.

Suddenly, he stopped talking and took a look at his watch.

"Oh, I must be going now. By the way, would you like to go out to dinner?"

I was a little confused. I was about to say I wasn't sure when I realized he hadn't been talking to me. He was looking at Regina. He was asking her out on a date. Regina nodded her head. They agreed on Friday evening.

59

ON FRIDAY, SHERRY, REGINA, AND I ALL HAD OUR HAIR AND NAILS done while Randy spent the afternoon with a couple of his buddies. When we got home, Sherry and I helped Regina get ready for her big date. We accepted and then rejected several outfits until we were all satisfied. We chose jewelry and even the best shade of lipstick. Regina was like a teenager on her first date.

I was concerned Mark might be doing this to set up security to keep someone from killing me.

"What if you and Mark don't hit it off?" I asked. I wondered if I was being too snoopy.

"Honey, at my age, a good dinner is a success. Anything else is gravy. I do have to admit that I am flattered that he asked me."

"He told me that he thought you were a fine-looking woman," I said.

"He did?" Regina blushed. "My goodness."

When Mark arrived, the twins and I stood at the door like parents checking out their daughter's first date. I jokingly said, "Now I want you home by ten o'clock." I bowed out of a party with a gang of friends to spend the evening with Sherry and Randy instead. At their age, they could have stayed home alone, but we planned to watch double-feature DVDs.

We had the two final episodes in the classic vampire series where the teenage girl falls in love with a vampire. We had popcorn and soft drinks and watched it on the big screen in the den. Both Randy and Sherry were enthralled with the movies. Personally, I found it a little hard to believe.

But after everything that happened to me, I didn't know what to believe anymore. By the time it was over, it was almost one o'clock.

At the end, Randy scooped up my cat, Mr. P.

"Mr. P and I will be vampires. Toby, since you're a dog, you can be a werewolf," chortled Randy. Mr. P was wearing the "I don't believe he is doing this" cat expression.

"All right, guys, bedtime for all of us," I suggested.

"We need to stay up until Regina gets home," Randy argued.

"Isn't going to happen," I said in my best big-sister voice. "Off to bed. I'm coming too," I added as consolation.

As we headed up the stairs, Sherry, still with her head in the movie, asked a question.

"Amy, do you believe that there are werewolves and vampires, and that they could have a child that is part human and part vampire that can do magic things?"

"No, Sherry, I think it's just a fun story, like those Disney stories."

"Gee, it seemed so real," she said.

"They can do neat things with computers to make it look real," I said. "Now get to bed."

She reached up by standing on her toes and kissed me on the cheek.

"Good night, Amy," she said. I couldn't help thinking how much I loved those kids.

Toby followed Randy to his room. Mr. P headed for my bedroom. As I closed the door and got ready for bed, I thought about what I had told Sherry about the movie being just make-believe. *I've had an out-of-body experience where an object came back to me and is hidden in a locked storage box. Maybe some of those movies are more real than we thought.*

Mark Baker believed that I could heal and move objects with my mind. I had to laugh—two old lesbian witches had even thrown me out of their house. Maybe I should be in a movie.

The good news was that I slept that night with no dreams or nightmares.

60

THE NEXT MORNING, I SLEPT IN UNTIL NINE O'CLOCK. I NEVER DID hear Regina come home. Since I could smell bacon cooking, I assumed that she made it back OK. I slipped on a pair of jeans, a sweatshirt, and flip-flops and headed for the kitchen.

As I walked in, I saw Regina standing at the stove. To my surprise, right next to her was Mark. He had his hand on her rear. I had to get out of there. I turned and ran back to my bedroom, slamming the door. I fell onto my bed sobbing.

I heard Regina at the door.

"Honey, can I come in?" she asked.

"Ok," I said between sobs. Regina walked into my bedroom.

"Oh, Amy, I am so sorry. Mark and I should never have come back here. It just happened. It's been so long, and I just didn't think. Can you ever forgive me?" cried Regina.

"Regina," I sobbed, "this has nothing to do with you and Mark."

"It doesn't?" she asked.

"No," I said. "When I saw Mark with his hand on your bottom, it was the way I would find Mom and Dad some mornings."

Regina finally regained her composure. She put her arm around me.

"Honey, it isn't going to be easy. Your parents have been gone for less than a year."

"Regina, just when I think I'm getting better, something happens to bring it all back. I miss them so much." I was still sobbing.

"I know, honey," said Regina. "Frank's been dead for six years, but some nights I feel him lying beside me in bed. I wake up and realize he is gone, and I cry myself back to sleep."

Then Regina looked at me and smiled. "Mark sure helps me realize that life goes on. Come on, dry those eyes, and let's get some breakfast."

We went downstairs together. Randy and Sherry were sitting at the kitchen table talking to Mark. When we came in, Mark glanced up. He had a guilty look on his face. Out of the corner of my eye, I saw Regina mouthing the words, "It's fine."

"Hey, Amy, Mark said he is going to take us fishing next Saturday. You've got to come too," said Randy, his excitement bubbling over.

I smiled and said, "Sorry, I've got something to do next Saturday." Fishing is not my thing. I did not want to sit in a boat for hours.

That Saturday Mark became more than just my chief of security. He became a member of our family. No, he didn't move in the next day. But he and Regina became an item. There were evenings when he would be at our house and was still there the following morning. Mark and Regina even went to Las Vegas for five days in July.

We started including Mark in trips to Lake Coeur d'Alene and to church on Sunday. That first Sunday had everyone in the congregation checking us out. We arrived in Mark's big Dodge Charger. Would you believe that the Charger is one of the few cars where I can sit in the backseat?

Mark wore jeans, a black turtleneck, and a tan sports coat. And he was packing heat. He had a shoulder holster. He now shot left-handed, but his right hand was getting stronger. His physical therapy included squeezing a rubber ball. He was a confident, cool man.

61

In August Mark bought me a .32 automatic pistol that would fit in my handbag. It had an eight-shot clip. He taught me how to use the small handgun. He said the weapon was used for final defense when an opponent was close enough to touch. Through his security firm, he helped me get a permit to carry a concealed weapon. Of course, you must be twenty-one in the state of Washington to carry a concealed weapon. So, even though I was still seventeen, I had a driver's license that said I was twenty-one. I told Mark that it was illegal to have a false license.

"Your birth certificate is not real," Mark reasoned. "Your last name is Martin, and we have no idea if January seventeenth is you real birth date, so how can one more lie hurt? Besides, the priority is to keep you alive."

Mark enlarged and improved our home security system. He even had more sophisticated security locks and alarms put on my bedroom with fingerprint recognition keys. He used the excuse that these were test items for use by his company. But I knew that it was all about protecting me.

When he and Regina went to Vegas, a black Dodge Charger with two men inside parked behind our barn. They worked eight-hour shifts. I told the twins that they were in training for Mark's company. When I was out with the gang at Pizza Hut, I recognized one of Mark's team members sitting in a corner booth.

Mark's commitment was more than I could have ever dreamed possible, and no one was the wiser. I wondered how I could ever repay him. But soon the opportunity presented itself in the strangest way.

In August, I got a call from Mark on my iPhone. He usually texted me, so we could discuss issues without anyone eavesdropping.

"Hi, Amy," said Mark.

"Hi, Mark, what can I do for you?"

"Right now I'm in Abram's Antiques in Seattle," said Mark.

"Seattle?" I asked.

"Our company has a project protecting a gentleman who works for Microsoft. I flew over for a meeting this morning and plan to come back this afternoon. I also visited my daughter and grandchildren in Newcastle.

"Anyway, I got my business done and had three hours to kill before I needed to be at SeaTac. So I decided to check that ruby out. I have a buyer."

"How much?" I asked.

"Three," he said.

"Only three thousand dollars?" I asked. "Somehow I felt it would be worth more."

"No, three million dollars," said Mark with a chuckle.

I asked him to repeat what he had just said.

"Was that their first offer?" I asked.

"Yes, can you believe that?" he said.

"They said something about King Solomon's mines or something."

"Tell them we want five. Five million or we walk, and they will never see it again," I said.

"You're kidding."

"No, I'm not kidding. I said five million."

"Let me call you back."

Fifteen minutes later Mark called back.

"They said yes," he said. I could hear the excitement build as he spoke.

"Don't forget, Mark, you get twenty percent," I said.

"That isn't going to happen," said Mark.

"Mark, a deal is a deal."

"We'll talk about it when I get back," grumbled Mark.

"Oh, another thing—don't let them use my name on this transaction. No one knows about the gems except you and me. Have the money go to Baker Security."

"My company? Why?" he asked.

"It's the perfect cover, and I just decided I would like to buy stock in your company. All right, I take that back. I want a partnership. I will give you four million."

"You mean five?" asked Mark.

"Four," I said. "The other million is yours. Remember, I'm the boss."

"We'll talk about it when I get back," he insisted.

At seventeen years of age, I acquired a partnership in my first company. *Now, if I could just get time to move faster,* I thought. *I still have to wait five months until I turn eighteen.*

62

I WAS SITTING IN THE FOLEY LIBRARY ON CAMPUS RESEARCHING material for my paper on saints of the twentieth century for my theology course. The problem with attending a Catholic university is that, even if you are not a Catholic, you had to take several courses in religion. Normally I did most of my research on the Internet, but there were a number of excellent books on this subject in Gonzaga's library. It was only eight o'clock in the evening, and normally the library would be crammed with students. But with a basketball game going on in the Kennel, our basketball court, students were either watching the game there or on TV. The team was playing for a berth in the "Big Dance," hoping to be one of the sixty-four teams to play for the national title.

Mark was rather paranoid about me being on the campus after hours. Seated at a table by the front door was Frank Carlson, one of my security guards. Frank was in his twenties and could pass for a college student. He was former military, having just gotten out after six years with the Ranger Battalion at Joint Base Lewis-McChord.

When I had enrolled in the freshmen class at Gonzaga, Mark was not happy. He wanted me to lay low until they could figure out who wanted me dead. But, as I explained to him, not going to college would seem strange, and it helped me pass the time until I turned eighteen. I would not be attending next semester.

I had to admit that I actually enjoyed the courses. Sadly, I was unable to participate in college life. For a day student, that was fairly easy, but I wished I could be just a normal freshman. I avoided close friendships. When invited to one of the events, I used the excuse that I had a boyfriend named Bob Smith who was in the air force. He was stationed at Fairchild. He was an Airman Third Class and spent hours working on planes, so we had no time to participate in college activities. So when I wasn't studying, my time was spent with Regina, Mark, and the twins. The good news was that in two months I would finally be eighteen, and I would begin my quest to discover who—or more like what—I really was.

Mark had detailed information on my immediate real family. On my dad's side, my grandmother, Lindsey Martin, lived in Washington, DC. My dad had no brothers or sisters. My grandfather on Dad's side of the family, Lieutenant General Retired Henry Martin, had died of a heart attack just three years ago. I felt bad that I would never know him.

On Mom's side, her mother, Grandma Dixon, died just one year ago. Mom's father was the multibillionaire former presidential candidate, Senator Allan Dixon. He was living in Kingston, Jamaica. Mom had one brother, Eddie, who lived in Atlanta, Georgia, with his wife and three children.

I didn't know how to deal with these relatives I hadn't known I had. I couldn't imagine approaching a billionaire senator and saying, "Hi, I'm your long-lost granddaughter." That would be difficult, to say the least. I decided to take the easiest route. As soon as possible after my birthday, I would try to meet my grandmother, Lindsey Martin.

63

IT WAS LONG PAST TIME TO GO HOME. I NEEDED TO GET THIS information for the term paper on my tablet. I started to type. After a few moments, I began to sense something was wrong. I couldn't place it. Then I realized it was the silence. Mind you, there were only about a dozen people in the library. But people type and text, open and close books, ask questions of the librarians or tech assistants. Usually I could hear people clearing their throats, coughing, or speaking quietly with someone nearby.

But I couldn't hear anything at all. There was only silence—absolute silence. I looked around, but I saw no one speak or move. People just stared straight ahead as if they had been stopped in time. Even the man assigned to protect me, Frank, was motionless. He sat there staring at the wall. The woman behind the main desk was just standing, staring straight ahead. Not one person moved, not even a little bit.

Then I finally saw some movement by one of the bookshelves on my right. A Catholic priest, maybe in his sixties, walked around the corner of the shelves. He wore the typical white collar, dark shirt, pants, and a sports jacket. Was this all happening in my imagination? I looked around. No, he was the only one moving.

Then I did a double take of the priest. Something was wrong with him. He didn't look right. More than that, it almost seemed like his appearance was changing right before my eyes. It was like there was a glow around his body. I remember the witch Leona saying she could see my aura. I guess that was what I was seeing. I've never taken drugs or even been drunk, but I suspected that those who have may have seen what I was seeing. This aura thing surrounded the priest, but it wasn't just a circle of light. It showed two horns sprouting above the priest's head. The only thing that I've ever seen that even came close to what I was seeing was a demon from a horror movie. Then the aura disappeared, and he returned to being just an ordinary priest. He looked around the room as if he were looking for someone or something.

I froze, pretending to just stare ahead like everyone else. He walked over to one of the girls sitting at a table. With his back to me, I crouched down and moved as quickly as I could to the exit. As I pushed the door open, I heard a voice say, "Stop!" The voice came into my head, not my ears. I dashed out the door, looking around to see where I could hide. The campus is well lit at night, but to the side of the library were flowerbeds filled with rows of shrubs. That side of the building was dark. I got off the concrete path and ran to cover. I ducked behind one of the shrubs and sat down in the bark.

Mark had told me that when police use dogs to flush out a bad guy, the dogs don't usually use scent to find the suspected culprit. Think about it. Unless the bad guy left his coat at the scene, a dog wouldn't know if it was following the scent of a possible criminal or just focusing on one of the people near the scene. A guy gets caught when he moves. German shepherds are hunters. If they see movement, they go for it. If a man bolts and runs, the dogs have him. Mark said that if the target freezes in place and doesn't move, he can escape after the dog passes by. Watch one of those documentaries on Africa. Notice how the antelope freeze and don't move. If the prey holds still, the predator can't see it.

I did the same thing. As I knelt there, the side door to the library opened and the priest came out. He looked up and down the sidewalk. He walked slowly through the grass, approaching my hiding spot. I had already pulled the .32 automatic out of my purse. If he found me, I was prepared to shoot him. He turned toward my hiding spot. In the dark, the aura around his body was back and seemed to glow even more brightly. I didn't know what to do. If I shot the man, and he was just an older priest, I would be in big trouble.

But what I had seen in the library was not human. Somehow, this man had managed to control everyone in sight. Was he looking for me, or was I just the only person not susceptible to his influence? He came closer to my hiding place. It was like he was uncertain if I was really there. He seemed confused; he should have had no problem finding me. Perhaps he didn't expect to find someone that he couldn't control. That made no sense. He took another step closer. I was beginning to understand why the bad guys bolt and run. My instincts were telling me to run and to run fast.

The man stood there, cocking his head like he was trying to hear me. Suddenly, there was shouting and screaming coming from the direction of the Kennel. People poured out the doors, yelling and cheering. The basketball game was over, and the Zags must have won.

I mouthed the words: "Go, Zags!" The priest's attention turned in the direction of the crowd of students who were marching toward the library. I expected the priest to pull out a ray gun. Instead, he jammed his fists into his pockets, walked to the sidewalk, and merged into the crowd of students.

I realized that I was still holding the .32 automatic in my right hand. I put the gun back into my purse and headed back to the library. I noticed that the back of my pants were wet from sitting in the flowerbed behind the bushes. I wiped off the bark chips that still stuck to my pants and joined up with the other students who were coming into the library. When I got to my table, I gathered my study materials and looked around for Frank, who was sitting in the same place he had been earlier.

"Are you ready to go?" he asked.

"Yes," I said.

It was obvious that he had no idea what had happened. I decided to say nothing. What could I say? Maybe something like, "Oh, by the way, an alien from outer space dressed as an old priest froze time and everybody else and tried to kill me." Instead, I followed him to the car. He dropped me off at home. I made sure that I activated the alarm system when I closed the door.

64

WE WATCHED THE TEN O'CLOCK NEWS, AND THEN I HEADED FOR BED. I saw nothing on the news about an alien invasion. Maybe I imagined it had happened. When Mr. P and I got in my bedroom, I checked in the closet, under the bed, and even behind the window curtain. I activated the bedroom's alarm system and made sure the door was securely locked. Mark was so worried about my safety that he had installed a separate alarm system for my bedroom. I thought it was stupid and had never activated it until tonight.

I had never been that afraid before, but what had happened in the library really freaked me out. I grabbed a T-shirt and clean boxer shorts and headed for the shower. The cat followed me. He liked to sit in the warm, moist air. He jumped up and sat on the sink counter.

My bathroom connected directly to my bedroom, so I felt totally secure with the door locked. I spent some extra time in the shower to let the hot water soothe my frayed nerves. Despite everything I had been through this priest thing was too unreal to be true.

After the shower, I dried off using two towels and pulled on my shorts. Carrying my T-shirt, I walked into the bedroom. I leaned over and pulled back the covers. I then pulled the T-shirt over my head.

As I turned around, my heart almost stopped. Sitting behind me at my desk was a man. I dove for my purse, grabbed it, and hit the floor. I rolled to my right and came up with my .32 automatic aimed directly at the son of a bitch. I was ready to empty all eight rounds into the guy. I expected to see the glow of the demon.

The man raised both hands and spoke calmly.

"Don't shoot! I mean you no harm."

"Sure," I said, steadily aiming at his face.

"If I had wanted to harm you," he said, "I could have done it at any time. When your shirt was over your head, you wouldn't have even seen it coming."

Whoa, this guy just watched me get dressed. That made me even more creeped out.

Keeping the gun trained on the guy, I moved to the light switch and flipped on the overhead light. I recognized him from school. No, he wasn't the priest that glowed like a demon. But I had seen him in the cafeteria at noon. When you live at home, you don't get to know the resident students except those in your classes. The only reason I noticed him at all was because he was tall, maybe six foot five or six. He was clean shaven, had short black hair, broad shoulders and a narrow waist. He was definitely a good looking guy. When you're a female who is more than six feet tall, you tend to look for guys who are taller than you. Maybe it's an evolution thing.

Gad, this was even worse. *What is he, some kind of sexual pervert? Well, I'll get to the bottom of this.* I decided to push the panic alarm. Within fifteen minutes, the Spokane County sheriff could find out what he was doing in our house. I pressed the panic button.

"It won't work," he said.

"What do you mean it won't work?" I asked.

"I disabled it when I came in," he answered with a satisfied grin.

"You disabled it? What are you, some kind of serial killer?"

"No, you've got me all wrong."

"Then you're just a Peeping Tom pervert."

"No, no, I had no idea you wouldn't be dressed."

"You just walked into someone's bedroom without knocking," I growled.

I was starting to get really out-of-control angry and was tempted to just shoot him.

"You don't understand," he said. "I had to talk to you, and I couldn't let anyone see us talking."

65

What a load of crap! I thought. I had to figure out how to get help. Keeping my gun trained on him, I walked over and picked up my iPhone. I was about to punch in 911 when he said, "You saw the *endosym* tonight in the library. I knew then that you must be one of us." I stopped, my finger over the nine.

In that crazy dream, the old man warned me about *endosyms*, whatever those were. Then those old witches had asked if I was a *zoutari* or an *endosym*. I decided to try something. I looked at him and asked, "So you're a *zoutari*?"

"Kind of," he said. "It takes many years. I'm only a novice." He had a unique accent. It sounded Scottish to me.

"You're not from here," I said.

"No, I'm from Ireland."

"What are you doing at Gonzaga?"

"There are a number of Irish students there. Didn't you know that?" he asked.

"Not really," I said. "Since I don't live on campus, I don't socialize with other students that much. Why didn't you just come up and introduce yourself at school?"

"With one of the *endosyms* on campus, I couldn't communicate with you. Some *endosyms* can sense if two *zoutari* are together. That's what happened last night. I was downstairs in Crosby Library when the *endosym* came in. There were so few students there that he sensed our presence. He would have never exposed his identity except that apparently with both of us present he realized we were more than just human. He froze the other students to try to flush us out. We're trained not to react emotionally when we encounter an *endosym*. Didn't you realize that once you ran, he knew you were a *zoutari*?"

"I'm new at this," I said. "What was he doing there?"

"I don't know," he said. "We've been told that the barrier between earth and the demon's world has been breached. It must be true. They are showing up even on college campuses. The time is coming when we must gather together to protect mankind."

All right, this conversation had gotten over my head.

"You still haven't told me why you came tonight," I said.

"To warn you not to talk to me in school. That could cause the *endosym* to find us. You also have to not react like you did when you see an *endosym*."

"I've got news for you: I don't know you. I wouldn't talk to you whether or not you told me to."

"Who trained you?" he asked. "You should have been instructed in the proper techniques before being allowed to venture out into the world."

"Sorry about that," I said. "What's your name?"

"Shaun. Shaun O'Kelly," he said. Well, that did sound Irish.

"My name is Amy Brown."

"Well, Amy Brown, perhaps we will get a chance to meet at the next gathering."

The gathering? I wondered what that was, but I was not about to ask.

"Remember, we must not speak or act like we know each other in public. I need to get back to campus."

"How did you get here?" I asked.

"I followed you in my car. It's parked down the road."

So much for my security guys protecting me. He turned toward the bedroom door.

"One more thing, Shaun O'Kelly."

"What?" he asked.

"Don't ever come into my bedroom without an invitation. Otherwise, we'll see if a novice *zoutari* is bulletproof," I said, deadly serious.

216

He blushed. "I apologize, and I shouldn't have done that."

He walked over and placed his hand on the keypad by the door. He stepped out in the hallway. When he closed the door, the system reactivated. *Now that's quite a trick.*

I plopped down on my bed. Life had just taken another twist. There were creatures who walked among us called *endosyms* who were a mix of human and something else. They apparently came from some other dimension. Then there was another group of creatures called *zoutaris* who could see this demon-like creature, the *endosym*. *So where does that put me?* I wondered. *Am I a* zoutari *or something else? Is this all part of why my parents hid in Spokane under false names?*

If I wasn't allowed to talk to Shaun O'Kelly, how would I be able to find out what was happening? My goal had been to trace my roots. I turned off the overhead light and walked back to the side of my bed. I placed the pistol back in my purse and propped a chair under the knob of the bedroom door. So much for Mark's high-tech security locks.

Mr. P stretched out on the bed, watching me.

"Fine watch cat you are," I said. I swear that he looked like he was smiling. Maybe he realized that Shaun O'Kelly was no threat.

I nestled under my covers and closed my eyes, assuming that I wouldn't be able to fall asleep. Surprisingly, I slept very well. But I had a dream. It was a dream about Shaun O'Kelly. It was one I'd never had before and that I never plan on sharing with anyone. It was a dream that caused me to wake up blushing.

66

I WAS SITTING IN THE BACKSEAT OF THE BLACK DODGE CHARGER. WE were parked on a side street a block off Boone and two blocks from the Gonzaga campus. It had snowed the night before, and the sidewalks where we were parked hadn't been cleared. Frank sat at the wheel. Steve, another of my security guards, had gone to locate Shaun O'Kelly. It was ten o'clock in the morning on Monday, January 18.

Yesterday, I had turned eighteen years old. Fifteen months ago, Mom and Dad had been killed.

Regina and the kids put on a surprise birthday party for me. Paul Dino and his wife plus a number of friends from church attended. Paul brought the papers I asked him to prepare.

The first was my will. In the event of my death, my estate would be divided equally among Regina, Sherry, and Randy. I signed, and we had the will witnessed. I never would have thought that I would prepare a will at age eighteen.

The next paper was the contract between Regina and me. Regina was no longer my legal guardian. However, she was now employed as my executive assistant with a salary of two hundred thousand dollars a year. Let me tell you, that woman deserved every penny. She was the one who held me together during my worst hours. She could have just stayed here and lived with me as the aunt I never had. But I wanted her to be more than that.

The final paper concerned Paul Dino and me. I asked him what his salary was working for the law firm. He said two hundred and fifty thousand a year. So I offered him an annual salary of three hundred and fifty thousand dollars and threw in special bonuses. He accepted the contract, so I had a full-time attorney working for me.

I didn't return for the second semester at Gonzaga. Even though I had made this decision when I started college it was still very difficult, but I had to find out who my parents were and if the dream I had last summer was true. For that I had to go to Liberia, West Africa.

For the semester I attended, I earned a 3.6 grade point average. The college bugged me about continuing my education, and I assured them that I was just taking a sabbatical and plan to continue, possibly next year. I wondered how many former college students say that but never go back. I decided to major in finance. When your net worth exceeds six hundred million dollars, it might be a good idea to know how to make that money grow.

Paul also drew up a contract making me a partner in Baker Security. Paul didn't know about the five million dollars I got from selling the ruby and couldn't understand why Mark wanted me to be his partner. But like a good attorney who works for a multimillionaire, he said nothing.

So I am actually sitting in one of my own security cars. I thought as we sat there waiting for Shaun. *Frank and Steve work for me.* Baker Security had also grown to a point where we leased a corporate jet.

Why am I so nervous about meeting with Shaun O'Kelly? Well, first of all, I hadn't called ahead to invite him to this meeting. As a matter of fact, I imagined that Steve would be very forceful in suggesting that Shaun meet with me. I was trying to honor Shaun's reluctance of our meeting—by meeting off campus, we reduced the chances of encountering that *endosym.*

The other problem was the effect that Shaun O'Kelly had on me. OK, I know I was being immature and stupid. The only time I had spoken to him was that night in my bedroom. But then there was also that stupid dream. I'd seen him from a distance a couple of times in the cafeteria. But each time, I watched him like a lovesick puppy. I hadn't felt that way since I had a crush on Bobby Jenkins in fifth grade.

I saw Steve and Shaun coming up the road. Steve was wearing a dark overcoat and looked like a cop. Shaun was wearing a leather jacket, jeans, and boots. He was at least six inches taller that Steve. He was wearing no hat, but the cold air didn't seem to bother him. From the look on his face, I assumed he was pissed about being told that I wanted to see him. This was a great way to start off a meeting with a guy that I had some foolish schoolgirl crush on.

When they got to the car, Steve opened the back door and motioned for Shaun to slide into the backseat next to me. Shaun looked at me.

"Am I being kidnapped?" he asked.

"No," I said. "I just need to talk to you." I spoke too quickly and I was certain that I wasn't making a good impression. I knew I had to be blushing. Shaun seemed uncomfortable. He was so tall that he had to point his legs to the center of the car. We were two tall people. We barely fit into the car.

"Where to, Miss Brown?" asked Frank. *Oops, I didn't think that far ahead.* We could sit in the backseat, but the questions I wanted to ask Shaun were ones I didn't want Steve or Frank to hear.

"Denny's on Division," I said.

Frank dropped the Charger's gearshift into drive, and the car pulled away. Shaun checked out the Charger's interior.

"Nice wheels," he said.

"Yeah," I said. "It belongs to my company."

"Your company?" he asked, somewhat skeptical.

"Yes," I said. "I'm a partner in the business."

"You're a little young, aren't you?" he asked.

"Family money," I said. I knew I was being a smartass, but what I said was true.

We didn't say anything else as we headed north on Division.

67

It only took a few minutes to reach the restaurant. We all got out. Frank and Steve did the security look-around thing. The four of us entered the restaurant.

The hostess asked, "Table for four?"

"No," I said. "The two of us at one table, and the other two gentlemen at a separate table." She looked surprised, but took Shaun and me to a table near the window. Frank and Steve sat two tables away.

Shaun looked over at Steve and Frank, aware that they were far more than chauffeurs.

"Your parents take this security stuff seriously," said Shaun.

"My parents are dead."

"I'm sorry," said Shaun. "I meant whoever takes care of you."

"As of right now, I take care of myself. Steve and Frank work for me. I own controlling interest in Baker Security," I said.

"I can't believe that," he said.

"Why not? I was able to see the *endosym*, wasn't I?" I responded.

"Well, sure, but you're just a teenager. In America you can't own a company," he said.

"Maybe I'm older than I look," I said.

"You're only eighteen, and your birthday was yesterday," he said.

"Oh, really? How do you know that?"

This time he was the one who blushed.

"I peeked at your file in the registrar's office. You had your next of kin as Regina Hanson. I assumed she was your mother, and that guy she's with had to be your stepfather. I've seen you and them with two younger kids."

"Have you been spying on me?" I asked, totally surprised.

He didn't respond right away. That gave me a little time to look at him more closely. I hadn't noticed his blue eyes.

Finally he said, "You are the only person my age who knows I can see the *endosyms*. I just wanted to be sure that you were safe. Then I noticed that everywhere you went, there were like security guys with you. That guy Frank was with you in the library. I thought he was your boyfriend." He nodded toward Frank.

"Well, he's not. I don't have a boyfriend," I said.

"You don't?" he asked with a smile. He had nice teeth. They were so even and white. I liked his smile. My inner voice reminded me that I wasn't there to admire his teeth but to get some information.

The waitress approached, which brought me back to reality. It was almost lunchtime, so I ordered a chef's salad, a piece of chocolate cream pie, and a diet Pepsi. Shaun asked for a cheeseburger, fries, apple pie, and coffee.

"If you're kidnapping me and own a company, you can buy me lunch," he said with a grin.

"Fair enough," I said.

"How come you didn't come back to school this semester?"

I have to go to Washington, DC, to meet my grandmother who doesn't even know I exist. Then I have to travel to Africa."

"Africa?" he asked.

"Well, actually, I think I was born in Liberia," I said.

"You don't know where you were born?" he asked, astonished.

"Not really. Until last year, I thought I had been born in Spokane. I also thought my name was Amy Brown. It appears now that my name is Anaya Martin, and I believe that I was born in Zigda, Liberia, in West Africa."

We ate, saying very little. We both had just finished when I reached in my purse and pulled out the piece of leopard fur. He looked at it.

"I thought you were going to pull that little pistol on me again," he said.

"Not in public," I said. "What do you think this is?" I held out the piece of leopard fur.

"Let me see it," he said. As soon as he touched it, there was that snap of electrical energy. A spark jumped to his fingers. Instead of pulling back, he took the scrap of fur. He turned it over in his hand. "It's a powerful charm," he said. "I can feel its power." He handed it back to me.

"When someone other than me tries to touch it, they receive a powerful electrical shock," I explained as I put it back in my purse. "That's why I needed to see you. I need to know more about the *zoutari.*"

68

"I CANNOT TELL YOU ABOUT THE *ZOUTARI*. I'VE ALREADY TOLD YOU too much, assuming you were one of us. We take a death oath never to divulge the secrets of the *zoutari*. Understand that a *zoutari* who revels themselves will be killed. Amy, this isn't some kind joke. If I tell you about the *zoutari*, and the coven finds out, they will kill me."

"Shaun, someone is trying to kill me. I believe it has something to do with *zoutaris* and *endosyms*. I know that I am more than just a young rich woman, but I don't know for sure what I am or what my destiny is. Isn't there any way you can help me?" I pleaded.

Shaun sat there staring at me. He took a sip of his coffee.

"Have you ever seen the old TV series *Buffy the Vampire Slayer*?"

"Yeah, I guess I saw a couple of shows years ago on the Syfy Channel. What about it?"

"Surprising enough, shows like that can have a foundation in reality," he said. "I can't tell you about us, but I will refresh your memory about the watchers in *Buffy the Vampire Slayer*. In both *Buffy* and its spin-off *Angel*, watchers are devoted to tracking and combating malevolent supernatural entities.

"In ancient times, a group known as the shadow men used magic to infuse a captive girl with the essence of a demon, thereby creating the first slayer, who they used to fight demonic forces. The descendants of the shadow men go on to form the watchers council, which trains new watchers. If you watch the entire series, these facts are revealed."

I interrupted him. "So what's this got to do with the real world?"

He picked up a fry and popped it in is mouth, chewed and swallowed. "Just listen to the story," he insisted. "The council eventually based its headquarters in London, England. It tried to locate potential slayers and then sent watchers to inform and train them. They weren't always successful in doing so. Therefore, some slayers were fully trained when they were called, while others knew nothing of the heritage or purpose of their power. You can find more detail by going online."

"So the watchers in *Buffy* are like your organization?" I asked.

He nodded, taking another French fry.

"Even today there are a number of TV shows and movies on the supernatural," said Shaun. "Of course, these are just stories, but it is surprising how close these stories are to fact. Years ago there was the TV series called *V* that was about an invasion of lizard people that appeared to be human. The *endosyms* are something like the lizard people.

"Then there was the old TV series *Star Trek* that introduced future concepts that today are becoming reality. Some believe that the writers of *Star Trek* were given stories by extraterrestrials. Just think—the easiest way to explain the unknown is to do it in fiction first.

"Myths in many cultures talk about people with special powers who come to the aid of mankind. They have been called such names as seers, sentries, observers, seekers, shaman, and many others."

I began to understand that Shaun was giving me information without revealing the secrets of his organization.

"All right," I said. "I'll get a hold of the series *Buffy the Vampire Slayer*. Now what about the *endosyms*?"

"Do you know what symbiosis is?" he asked. I thought back to my high school biology class before I answered.

"It's when one organism lives on another, like moss on a tree."

"It's also where one partner lives inside another," said Shaun. "There is a term for it. *Endosymbiosis* indicates a symbiotic relationship in which one creature lives within the tissues of the other, either in the intracellular or extracellular space," he continued.

"You're pretty knowledgeable about biology," I said.

"You have to be when your life depends on it," said Shaun.

"So, the *endosyms* are people possessed by that demon thing that I saw?" I asked.

"Yes, but not the demons in the Biblical sense. What do you know about demons?" asked Shaun.

I thought about that before answering. "Well, they're in the Bible. They have them in horror movies. They have horns and a tail. They're minions of the devil, I guess."

"That's what we are led to believe," said Shaun. "Demons have been the nemesis of mankind since the beginning of time.

"But *endosyms* are not spiritual creatures serving the devil. In ancient times human beings didn't know about quantum mechanics or Einstein's theory of relativity, so *endosyms* were thought to be men possessed by evil spirits. The *endosym* is a human and looks like the horned creatures seen up on the walls of caves. Those were drawn as many as ten thousand years ago. They are found in every culture, religion, and country.

"But they were not the devil or his minions. They are from a parallel universe. They live in a world where they are the top predator. They exist by consuming the energy of an animal when its life-force dies. Man has the greatest life-force of all the animals in our world. For this reason, this creature wants nothing more than to kill us for our energy, our essence."

"So, why didn't they kill us off thousands of years ago?" I asked.

"Because on earth, their bodies are not solid, but more like clouds. They must enter the chosen human host, and they live together—two beings in one body. That's how they got the name *endosyms*. Also, it is apparently very difficult for them to cross the barrier between their world and our world. There must be some kind of portal for this to occur. Normally, only a few of these creatures exist on the earth at any time.

"When they and the humans have become one being, the resulting creatures have special gifts. These include superhuman strength and mind power over humans in close proximity. You saw that happen in the library.

"Finally, they almost have immortality. Of course, for these gifts, there is a price—the human must help the creature find and kill other humans to gain their essences. The more humans that are sacrificed, the more spirits are consumed and the more powerful that *endosym* becomes.

"The vampires, the living dead, were men possessed by these beings. They didn't drink human blood but lived from the essence of our souls.

"The *zoutari* can identify the *endosyms* and take the steps to destroy them. Now something has happened that could be catastrophic. Thousands of *endosyms* are coming into our world. We don't know what has changed, but we must stop it."

Shaun paused in his story to take another sip of coffee. I didn't say anything, still digesting everything he'd said. He continued. "All right, that was the twenty-first-century explanation. But that's not the whole story. There is also something mystical in our battle. Things have happened in the past and I believe will happen in the future that can only be directed by the hand of God. To be a *zoutari*, you cannot survive without believing that there is an unseen hand guiding you through the horror of dealing with the *endosyms*.

"Keep your faith, Amy Brown, and if you do not have faith, get it. For I do not know what your role will be in the battle that is coming."

"Neither do I," I said. "But I believe I will find my answer in Africa. Then I may need your help."

"A deal," he said. "Maybe then we can have a real date."

"A real date?" I said, smiling. "We'll see."

I signaled the guys. It was time for us to go.

As we headed back to campus, Shaun said, "Take your cat to Africa with you."

"My cat? Why in the world would I do that?" I asked him, totally surprised.

"If you are what I think you are, the cat is an extension of your body. He is just like a hand. He can be used as a tool to protect you. We have heard old stories of powerful *zoutari* that could cause their familiars to change into horrible beasts that would protect them.

"In the old days, it was believed this was done by magic. But now, many of us believe that a powerful *zoutari*'s mind can manipulate the cellular structure of the familiar. After all, your cat's ancestors were saber-toothed tigers. Cells are mostly empty space. You may have power to make the cat appear to be something else. Maybe he can actually become something else. Take your cat with you."

Frank pulled the car over to the curb.

"Good-bye, Amy Brown. I'm looking forward to that real date."

He quickly kissed me on the lips. That was a bold move. I should have been insulted. Instead I watched him walk away, yet I still could feel his lips on mine. I'd never before felt this intense an attraction for a man.

But right now I had other things to consider. Soon I would be flying to Washington, DC. In the meantime, I had to digest all the information I had learned from Shaun.

Is this part of my destiny? Am I, Amy Brown, the endosym *slayer?*

69

WE PULLED UP TO THE CORPORATE AND GENERAL AVIATION GATE AT Spokane International Airport. Frank drove, Mark sat in the front passenger seat, and I sat in the backseat with Mr. P in his carrier next to me. The guard at the gate requested all of our IDs. We used our Baker Security cards. The guard waved us through, and we headed toward a large hangar at the southwest side of the airport.

I was on my way to Washington, DC, to meet my grandmother, Lindsey Martin.

Mark had initially contacted her to let her know that our security staff had found passports and other personal items in Chad. The items likely were stolen from the plane crash in Liberia eighteen years earlier. He explained that he would be in Washington, DC, on Tuesday and would like to drop the items off at her home. She was delighted to hear the news and was expecting us at one o'clock in the afternoon.

We figured that this would be the best approach, rather than relaying the information by phone, letter, or email. Once there, we would figure out how to tell her that I was her long-lost granddaughter. She didn't even know that I existed. I had a folder with photos taken of our family during the years we lived in Spokane. Even with their changes in appearance, I was pretty sure that she would recognize her son and daughter-in-law. I also had the passports and the leopard tooth, hoping that would help prove that I was her son's daughter.

Based on Shaun's recommendation and Mark's belief that the cat had some kind of powers, I brought Mr. P with me. I felt a little ridiculous taking the cat on the plane. I was pretty sure that the cat agreed.

We drove all the way into the hangar and pulled up next to a small private jet. We got out while Frank pulled our luggage from the trunk and carried it over to the plane. Uniformed airport personnel loaded our bags into the cargo hold. I let Mr. P out of his carrier. I needed to take him for a walk before we left. He was wearing his harness, and I hooked up his leash. We walked to a nearby grassy area. One of the airport crewmen looked at me, frowned, and then walked over and talked to Mark. We walked along the hangar's outside wall. Mr. P stopped by a small shrub. He carefully sniffed it, turned around, lifted his tail straight up, and shot out a stream of pee on the shrub.

"You're spending too much time around Toby. Do you think you're a pit bull or something?" I said. He looked at me as if he were annoyed by my comments. We headed back to the hangar. The crewman who had been talking to Mark approached us. Now he was smiling.

"Right this way, Miss Brown. We will be loading shortly," he said.

"Thank you," I replied.

Mark walked up to me with a wide grin.

"What was that all about?" I asked.

"He told me that my daughter couldn't take her cat on one of the corporate jets. I explained that you were the controlling partner in Baker Security and was, in fact, his boss. I guess that solved any concerns about a cat on the corporate jet," said Mark. I placed Mr. P gently back in his carrier and went up the extended steps at the front of the plane.

Would you believe that that was the first time I had ever been on a plane? Here my parents had been worth millions, yet we had never flown anywhere. We always traveled by car.

I'd seen the inside of commercial planes in the movies, and I guess I expected something similar. I was wrong.

"Wow!" I said as I entered the jet. It was plush, to say the least. There was room for seven passengers. Four of the seats faced each other. Each of the plush leather chairs rotated and reclined. Individual screens provided uploaded movies or data from corporate briefings.

"Cool, isn't it?" commented Mark as he came in behind me. "We normally use one of the smaller jets, but for this trip, I told them I wanted the Gulfstream G200. It has a range of three thousand five hundred miles so we can fly nonstop to DC." Mark sat in one of the plush leather chairs. "Take a seat. It's just the two of us and the pilot and copilot. No stewardess."

I felt the plane moving. "They're towing us out of the hangar; then they'll start the engines," said Mark.

The pilot, who had been talking to Mark, came in along with a young woman wearing a pilot's uniform.

"Good morning, folks. I'm your pilot, Kevin Hicks, and this is your copilot, Emily Ferguson. We would like to thank you for flying Executive Air Jets. Our flying time to Reagan National is five hours and forty minutes. There is a selection of movies available through Netflix, and we have continuous Internet access," said Kevin.

Mark had removed his jacket. He was wearing his shoulder holster with a .40-caliber Glock. The pilots ignored his weapon. Obviously, corporate jets don't require Homeland Security checks.

Emily and Kevin went into the cockpit and left their door wide open. I was glad they'd done that, so I could see what was going on. I was as excited as a kid on her first airplane ride, but I tried my best to act cool. After all, Amy Brown, corporate executive, must act like a corporate executive. *Right,* I thought, *with a gray tomcat and an older guy packing a Glock.*

There was a whining sound as the jet engines fired up. Over the PA system, Kevin said, "Please fasten your seat belts." I glanced at my iPhone. It was early—seven o'clock in the morning. We would be landing in Washington, DC, around four o'clock local time. I looked out my window and watched as we taxied toward the runway. A number of planes were waiting in front of us. I had never seen jet planes that close.

Then it was our turn to take off. The engines roared as we raced down the runway. I felt a sensation in my stomach as the plane's tires lifted off the ground. I almost screamed with the excitement, but I managed to hold it back. I looked out my window, watching the city pass by below me. Then we were flying over Hangman Hills, and there was our home down below me.

"Hi, Regina, Sherry, Randy, and Toby," I whispered as I gave them a brief wave from my window. I then closed my eyes and prayed to God that our trip would be successful.

Once the plane leveled off, Emily came back. She asked if we would like something to drink. I asked for a diet Coke; Frank requested a Heineken beer. She also brought us nuts, cheese, and crackers.

"I've never seen someone fly with a cat," said Emily.

"We're training him to be an explosives sniffer," said Mark.

"Oh, I understand now." Emily laughed. Mark looked over at me and winked.

Five hours passed quickly, and the next thrill was the view of Washington, DC, from the air as we made the approach to Reagan National. I was looking at our Capitol. All those things I had seen in pictures were right below me. For a moment, I forgot why we were there.

There was a rumble as the landing gear came down. The pitch of the engine began to change. If taking off had been a thrill, landing was even more exciting. I could feel the plane slowing down. My cheek was glued to the window as I watched the ground get closer and closer. Then suddenly I saw water running in streaks outside the window.

I braced my feet. Then what seemed like fewer than twenty feet below me, the runway appeared. I felt like, if I turned away from the window, I would find myself out in the open with the runway whizzing directly below me. My toes would almost touch the concrete. Then there was a sharp jolt, a squeal of brakes, and a roar like a giant beast as the jet engines reversed. I saw the terminal go by in a blur. The plane finally slowed but didn't stop completely. We turned off the main runway and headed toward a group of hangars. I looked up. Mark smiled at me.

"You've never flown before, have you?" he asked.

"No," I said, trying not to sound too frightened. "I thought we were going to crash into the water."

"Reagan National was built right along the Potomac River in Alexandria, Virginia. The plane approaches from across the river," said Mark.

"Oh," I said while I looked down at the floor, my hands clutching tightly to the armrests.

"You OK?" he asked.

"Sure," I said.

The plane finally rolled to a stop. I heard the door open and felt the cold January air rush in.

Emily and Kevin came back to talk with us.

"We have an SUV waiting at the terminal. We will have the plane ready to go at ten in the morning on the day after tomorrow. If there is any change in your plans, both Emily and I can be reached on our cell phones."

70

A GROUND ATTENDANT PUT OUR BAGGAGE ON A SMALL VEHICLE THAT looked like a golf cart. We got into the backseat, and we drove to the blue Ford SUV. Everything was packed neatly in the vehicle. Mark slipped confidently behind the wheel.

"We need to let Mr. P potty," Mark said as he pointed to the edge of the parkway.

We pulled over to the edge of the roadway. I opened the carrier and hooked the leash to the harness. I stepped carefully through the snow alongside the road until we found a spot of open grass. Obviously, he really needed to go. This time he got right down to business—no sniffing and no spraying of bushes. He didn't even try to cover it up. He turned and headed back toward the warm SUV. I let him loose inside the car. He jumped in the backseat, stood on his hind legs, and stared out the rear window.

It was just twilight, and I watched the on board navigation screen as we headed north along Route 1 across the Potomac River. Mark seemed to know where he was going.

"I've attended a number of law enforcement meetings in DC. We're staying downtown across from the White House," he told me.

"The White House? Cool."

As we crossed the bridge, I was fascinated by what I saw. Mark took a couple of detours, driving around the Tidal Basin and showing me the Lincoln and Jefferson memorials. Then he drove down Constitution Avenue and turned left on Fifteenth Street to Madison Drive to show me the Smithsonian and the United States Capitol. He gave a running narration as if he were a tour guide.

"You know this pretty well," I said.

"During those conferences, I had a lot of extra time, so I took in all the sights. Maybe after this is all over, the five of us can come back as tourists," said Mark. *Like that'll ever happen,* I thought. *Will it ever be possible for me to live a normal life?*

It was getting darker. Mark headed back down Constitution Avenue and turned right on Fifteenth Street NW. The White House was to our left. We drove by the gate where the president's limo enters. Just past Lafayette Park, Mark turned left on H Street NW, drove one block, and turned right onto Sixteenth Street NW. He pulled up to an old building on the corner across the street from St. John's Church.

The building was constructed with large granite blocks. The entire place was maybe ten stories tall. Out front, I could see a large overhanging porch supported by four pillars that were about twenty feet tall. The massive front doors were made of solid oak. Four flags mounted on large poles thrust out at a thirty-degree angle above the porch.

"Our hotel," said Mark as he handed me a visitor's brochure. I glanced at it.

The Hay-Adams Hotel. The Hay-Adams is quite possibly the most sophisticated hotel in all of DC and not just because it has the most enviable spot in the city across the street from the White House. The property has been the mainstay of the political elite since it opened in 1928. Past guests include Sinclair Lewis, Amelia Earhart, and Charles Lindbergh.

I looked at Mark.

"They don't allow cats, do they?" I asked.

"Nope."

"What do we do with Mr. P?" I asked, fearing that we would have to change our plans.

"There are exceptions, of course," said Mark with a grin. "When you have an explosives-sniffing cat and lots of money, anything is possible."

"Aren't we carrying the explosives-sniffing cat thing a little too far?" I chuckled.

"Not really," said Mark. "They are genetically breeding mice to react to explosives. Not so farfetched for a cat. You should be aware that Baker Security is a cutting-edge company. However, you will have to put him in his carrier until we get to our rooms."

Two bellboys came up as we stepped out of the SUV.

"Mark Baker and my associate, Amy Brown," announced Mark. One of the bellboys glanced at his clipboard.

"Oh, yes, Mr. Baker. Right this way, please. We'll take care of your luggage and park your vehicle in the hotel's garage."

The bellboy, whose nametag read WAYNE, led us through the entrance.

71

FORTUNATELY, THERE WERE NO FLIES INSIDE. WITH MY MOUTH
hanging wide open, I would have swallowed one. The front lobby had
twenty-foot-high ceilings. It was Italian Renaissance design, with curved
supports covered in oak. Spaced around the lobby were polished oak
tables with bouquets of flowers. Scattered about were wide leather chairs.
I felt like I had walked into a palace. Along one wall was the registration
desk that was at least fifty feet long. But we didn't go to the desk. We
headed directly to three banks of elevators. Two were normal elevators
with up and down buttons. The third had no buttons, only a card-insert
slot like the rooms at Northern Quest Casino in Spokane.

The bellboy put in a card, and the door opened. I took Mr. P in his carrier. The door closed softly behind us. He inserted our card into another
slot, and the elevator immediately went up. It took a few moments before
it came to a smooth stop. The doors slid open, and we looked down into
a hallway. The bellboy escorted us to a set of double doors. He used our
card, and the doors swung open. We walked into a living room as large as
our entire house in Spokane.

"The Federal Suite," said the bellboy. "Let me show you the bedrooms."

"Miss Brown will have the Federal Suite bedroom," said Mark. "I will
take the alternate bedroom."

"Of course," said the bellboy with a knowing smile.

I was still in the process of admiring the living room, but I caught
the bellboy's slight grin. Obviously, older men with younger women who
can afford a hotel suite like this are usually more than just associates.

He first showed us my accommodations. The room had a king-sized bed with a partial canopy. The bed was stacked high with color-coordinated pillows. My luxurious bathroom was bigger than some entire houses. The floors were heated granite. There was even a large Jacuzzi tub that could accommodate more than two adults. An armoire held a huge flat-screen TV. French doors led to an outside porch. I stepped outside even though it was cold. I could see the White House, and when I looked to the right, I could see the Washington Monument.

We next went to Mark's room. It was just as plush, but it had no balcony or a view of the White House.

While we were on our minitour, our luggage arrived. The bellboys left. I was surprised to notice that Mark did not tip them.

As I was letting Mr. P out of his carrier, I asked him about the tip.

"You didn't tip the bellboys?"

"It's all covered in the cost of the suite," he answered.

"My gosh, how much does this place cost?"

"Ten thousand a night at our discounted rate," he said.

"You're kidding me?"

"No, Amy. This is the Presidential Federal Suite. It is the most secure place in this hotel. We don't know who's after you. If they followed us, it would be hard to get into this place."

Now, it was Mr. P's turn to examine his quarters. Once out of his carrier, Mr. P. checked out the accommodations. I picked up a plastic briefcase that I had bought at Goodwill last week. I had filled it with clumping cat sand. It was Mr. P's Porta-Potty. He'd have to use the sand if there was no opportunity to go outside. I also took out his water dish and opened three packages of Tender Vittles. He immediately chowed down. He was hungry after his five-hour plane trip. He had had lots of adventures in the past day.

"It's going to cost us twenty thousand dollars for two nights here. How in the world can we afford this?" I said, more to myself than to Mark.

"Amy, the company will write this off as a business expense. That will also include the cost of flying here and charges for the rental car. For someone with your wealth, this is just a drop in the bucket." Mark looked at his watch. "It's dinnertime now. Come on; let's leave the cat here and get something to eat. By the way, meals are also on the expense account!"

To eat in the hotel dining room, you had to be appropriately dressed. Mark looked good—he wore a white shirt, maroon tie, sports coat, and dress slacks. I had a light blue pants suit, a white blouse, and dark blue pumps with four-inch heels. I wore diamond-stud earrings. I had gone to more trouble than usual with my makeup. I added a beige foundation, light blue eye shadow, and coral lip gloss. In my heels, I stood five inches taller than Mark. I thought I looked much older than eighteen.

My purse went well with my shoes. It was small enough to carry in my hands, yet large enough to hold my .32 automatic. We each had a white plastic entry card. There was nothing written on the card. I put mine in my purse. We walked out into the hallway, and the doors closed behind us.

"The walls and doors are lined with Kevlar. It would take major explosives to breach them," said Mark.

We took the elevator to the lobby.

"I'd like a drink before dinner," Mark said.

We headed for the bar. It was a big, comfortable room, yet it wasn't very crowded. The cream-colored ceilings had low-hanging chandeliers. The oak-paneled walls had red velvet accents. Besides the long wooden bar and tables with comfortable chairs, the room had booths along the sides. Up to six people could be seated in semiprivate locations.

Right away, I felt very conspicuous. I recalled how embarrassed I felt when I was ten. I might as well have been wearing a big flashing sign on my forehead that screamed, "She's a minor! Check her ID!"

We were seated at one of the booths.

"Good evening, Mr. Baker, Miss Brown. What would you like to drink?" asked the server.

"Martini," said Mark.

"A glass of white house wine," I said, smiling like I knew what I was doing. I remember that line from an old movie.

"Regina would kill me if she found out that I let you order wine," said Mark.

"Then we won't tell her. Mom and Dad let me drink a glass of wine sometimes. Don't worry. I just plan to sip it. I'll order ice tea with dinner," I told him.

The barmaid returned with our drinks.

"Will you be dining with us tonight?" she asked.

"Yes," said Mark. "We should be ready in about forty-five minutes."

"Very well," she said, "I'll make sure your table is ready."

"How do they know our names?" I asked.

"We're in the Federal Suite; I guarantee you that every employee knows who we are," said Mark.

"Wow, this is cool," I said. "You need to bring Regina here."

Mark laughed out loud.

"Regina and I have beer appetites, not champagne appetites. We are more than happy with a room at Northern Quest Casino."

"So that's where you go when you leave your three poor children at home with a loaf of stale bread and glasses of water," I said.

"Don't forget your starving dog and cat," said Mark.

We sipped our drinks. I couldn't help marveling at how my life had changed. I was sitting with the homicide cop who had been convinced I was a murderer. Now he seemed more like a stepfather or a favorite uncle.

Our server came up to let us know our table was ready. I still had most of my glass of wine left.

"I'll take your glass to your table," she said.

We followed her into the John Hay Dining Room. Like every other place we'd seen in the hotel, the large room could have been in Buckingham Palace. It was already beginning to fill up with dinner guests. We were taken to a table set for two by a window. Each table held a candle and a single red rose. The table settings were impressive—the finest English china, solid silver tableware, and cut-crystal goblets. I had to count the forks, spoons, and knives. There were eight pieces—per person! Obviously, with that much silverware, our meal would be served in multiple courses.

Our waiter was a young man dressed in a tuxedo. He gave me a once-over, obviously more than satisfied with what he saw. His approval pleased me. Unfortunately, he was also probably trying to figure out if Mark was my sugar daddy. He handed us our menus, asking if we preferred English, Spanish, French, or German. We said English, which probably dropped our rating a few notches.

"I don't see any prices listed," I said to Mark. I wasn't sure what to order.

"If you have to ask the prices, you can't afford to eat here," Mark said.

We both ordered the filet mignon. The meal came in seven courses. It was kind of fun, if you had the time. By the time our dessert arrived, we had been there more than two hours.

I was finishing my chocolate mousse when a party of ten men and women came in. A large table had been set up for them in the center of the dining room. Several of them must have already been drinking, because they were rather loud. If you were rich enough to eat there, probably no one would tell you to be quiet. An older gentleman in the party with slicked-back, dyed black hair held a chair for a woman of about his age. He looked in our direction.

I almost choked on the spoonful of mousse. I had no doubt that this man was an *endosym*. Apparently, he was far enough from me that I just got a glimpse of the aura of the creature within him. I remember Shaun's warning of not giving myself away. I shouldn't let him know that I could see what he was. I picked up my napkin and wiped my lips. I didn't dare look up. I kept staring down at my small plate. Even though I was sure that my hands were shaking, I continued to eat the mousse. For a moment, my stomach churned, and I thought I would lose my dinner.

Finally, I was able to calm down. I glanced over to where the *endosym* was seated. His back was toward me. He looked perfectly normal. He was conversing with a man on his right. The other man looked up. Although he did not have the aura of an *endosym*, his eyes seemed to glow. I remembered the glow in the eyes of the two Russians who had tried to kill us in Spokane. *Those in the service of an* endosym *must have a different appearance.* If that were true, I might be able to recognize a potential threat. The person wouldn't be aware that I knew what he or she was. I also realized that if an *endosym* were too far away, I could not identify it as an *endosym*. *I wonder if experienced* zoutari *have more power?* After all, I had only seen two *endosyms* that I knew of. I couldn't really consider myself an expert on the subject matter. I wondered if that meant that the men who had killed my parents were working for an *endosym*.

The party didn't seem to know that we even existed. When Mark finished his coffee, our departure took us away from the group, not closer. I didn't mention the experience to Mark, figuring he was suspicious enough, and I didn't want him pulling a gun and shooting a man in the restaurant.

72

WHEN WE GOT BACK TO THE ROOM, WE WATCHED THE BIG-SCREEN TV in the living room. We saw an old Western movie, and I actually enjoyed it. When it was over, it was one thirty in the morning, but with the three-hour time difference, it was only ten thirty in Spokane.

I excused myself and headed for bed. I had to remove half a dozen pillows just to get down to the sheets. I turned off the lights. I had intended to leave the drapes open so I could admire the city lights. Then I thought of the *endosym* and vampires. That was enough. I got up and closed the drapes after making sure the balcony doors were locked.

Mr. P curled up on the bed beside me.

"You had better be able to morph into a giant cat if that thing I saw shows up in here," I said. The cat just curled up and closed his eyes.

I was sure that I would not be able to sleep, but, the next thing I knew, the sun was shining through a crack in the drapes. In my bathroom I found a fluffy white bathrobe and comfortable slippers. Mark was in the living room, sipping a cup of coffee.

"I thought I would wait until you got up to order breakfast," he said.

"What time is it?" I asked.

"Nine thirty. By the time we order breakfast and get dressed, it will be time to go visit your grandmother."

I ordered a Spanish omelet, orange juice, toast, and coffee. Mark ordered steak and eggs. Within ten minutes, I heard a buzzing sound. Breakfast had arrived. Mark walked over and looked through the peephole before opening the door. A busboy rolled in breakfast on a cart. He laid it out on the dining room table and left.

While we ate, CNN news was on the TV. I wasn't paying much attention until I recognized the man I had seen in the restaurant flashing across the screen.

"Who's that?" I asked.

"Sam Ralston, the new Speaker of the House. Why?" he asked.

"He was in the restaurant," I said.

"Sure, in that group at the big table. Several members of his party were with him. So why are you so interested in Ralston?"

"Because he is one of them."

"Them?" asked Mark.

"The *endosyms*. Remember? I told you about the incident in the library."

"How do you know?" he asked.

"I could see the aura from the creature within him. One of the guys he was talking to also had strange eyes," I said.

"You're sure?"

"Yes, I'm sure."

"Jesus. He's only two sets of heartbeats away from being president. In the event that the president and vice president are killed, the Speaker becomes president. And Ralston is the one pushing for microchipping every citizen," said Mark with a frown.

"Microchipping?" I asked.

"Right, like dogs and cats. That way you no longer have to carry IDs. The chip would be inserted under your skin. Police, airports, military, whoever, could read your ID from a distance. It freaks a lot of people out. They claim it's like the mark of the beast from the book of Revelation in the Bible. But he's getting a lot of backing because of the number of illegal immigrants and potential terrorist attacks along the border."

"I wonder if there are other *endosyms* in Washington, DC," I said.

"God, Amy, you're turning me into one of those conspiracy nuts. We'll talk about this later. We need to get going."

"OK," I said. "But it is kinda scary that the third most powerful man in our country is an *endosym*."

250

73

WE TOOK THE ELEVATOR TO THE LOBBY. I WORE THE SAME OUTFIT
I had on the night before because I liked it. I had cut my hair before
we left for DC. Although I had always worn my hair long, I decided
that as an executive, I wanted it to be short and professionally cut
and groomed. I was worried that the short hair and my outfit would
make Lindsey Martin question my age, so I also packed my birth
certificate. Of course, Mark had discovered it was a fake, and I
believed that I was actually born in Africa. *Gee,* I thought, *maybe
that one president's birth certificate was really fake. Maybe he, too, was
born in Africa.*

I brought along Mr. P in his carrier. For some reason, I didn't
want to leave him in the hotel. I regretted that I hadn't left him
with Regina. Unfortunately, I was stuck with him, and he with me.
Of course, he would be fine in the car while we visited with Lindsey
Martin.

As soon as we reached the lobby, I carried Mr. P to the hotel's front
door. I wanted to be as discreet as possible.

"Is that a cat?" asked a little blond girl who was maybe five or six. She
knelt down and peeked into the cat carrier.

"Yes," I said.

"My daddy said they don't allow pets in here," she said, clearly intent
on reciting the hotel rules.

"Well, he is a special cat," I said.

"What does he do?"

"He's an explosives sniffer," I answered.

"What does an explosive sniffer do?"

"He finds bombs that bad men hide," I answered. I was beginning to believe that Mr. P was actually an explosives sniffer.

"Oh," she said. "My name's Rylan. I'm six years old. What's your name?"

"Amy," I said.

"Are you a police lady?" she asked.

"No, but I work for a security firm."

"Do you have a gun and a badge?" she asked. I couldn't have been this nosy when I was six.

"I have a special ID card," I said as I reached into my purse and pulled my security card.

"Cool! I want to see your gun," she demanded.

"I don't have one today," I said. I wasn't about to pull out my .32 automatic for this precocious little girl.

"Rylan, stop bothering the lady!"

I looked up. A short, stocky man in his thirties approached us.

"Daddy, her name is Amy. She's a special agent spy and has a cat that kills bad guys."

The man looked at me, obviously confused.

"An explosives-sniffing cat," I explained.

"Oh," he said, checking out the cat carrier. "Sorry my daughter bothered you. Come on, Rylan, let's go. Our cab is here."

As they walked away, I heard the father lean over to remind her to be careful. "Didn't I tell you not to talk to strangers?" he said.

I turned and saw Mark come up beside me.

"They're getting the SUV. It should be here in a couple of minutes."

In fewer than two, the doorman came up and handed Mark the keys. I opened the tailgate, set the carrier inside, and opened the carrier door. Mr. P hopped out, glad to be free once again. He jumped into the backseat. I closed the hatch, walked around, and got in the passenger side.

We buckled up, and Mark cranked the engine. He punched Lindsey Martin's address in McLean, Virginia into the GPS. I couldn't help thinking about what would happen when I met my grandmother for the first time. Would she throw us out? Would she be an evil old woman bent on taking over my fortune? Would she be like a fairy godmother?

74

SUDDENLY, A NOISE LIKE I HAD NEVER HEARD BEFORE ERUPTED FROM behind me. I turned around and saw Mr. P, clearly agitated, in the backseat. His tail was all blown up, and he held his ears flat against his head. He was making the most ungodly sound I had ever heard—a growl that, if I hadn't heard it for myself, I would have said a small animal couldn't possibly make.

"What's wrong with the cat?" asked Mark.

"I have no idea," I said.

"Mr. P, what's wrong?" I asked the cat. He stood up on his back legs and looked through the rear window and let out a snakelike hiss. Then a stretch limo pulled up behind us. It had a license plate on the front with an eagle and four stars. Coming out the door was the man I had seen talking to Congressman Ralston.

"That's the same guy that was talking to the Speaker of the House at dinner last night," I told Mark.

"All right," said Mark, clutching the steering wheel and taking control. "We're taking a little detour."

He pulled out into traffic with a squeal of the tires. He drove up about a block and pulled into a loading zone. We sat there for a few moments. Then the limo pulled up by us. Mark let a couple of cars pass by, and then he pulled out and began following the limo.

"We might be a little late meeting your grandmother. If we are, I'll call her," said Mark. According to our onboard navigation the limo headed south on Fourteenth Street. It pulled off Route 1 onto 395 and crossed the bridge over the Potomac River. It took the first right and pulled into the Pentagon South Parking lot.

The parking lot was a secure area, and there was a military police-man—MP for short—at the guarded entry.

"I need your ID card," Mark said. I handed him my Baker Security ID. He took his own card out of his wallet and handed both cards to the MP. The MP used a handheld reader. He ran the cards through the reader and looked at each of us in the eyes. He must have noticed the cat in the backseat, but he said nothing. Apparently, cats don't need IDs.

"Visitors' parking is down lane Four-A."

"Thank you," said Mark.

He returned my ID.

"You'll need it again when we get our visitors' passes."

"How'd we get in?" I asked.

"We've got a Homeland Security contract. We had to provide a list of all employees who would have access. We provided social security numbers and photos. Both of us are in their database. My only concern is that they will know we have been here. But I have to know," said Mark.

"Know what?" I asked.

"I'd rather wait until I'm sure," he said.

We pulled into one of the visitors' parking spaces. Mark took off his jacket and removed his shoulder holster and Glock, placing them under the front seat.

"Put your pistol in the glove compartment, also the extra clip. We will be going through a body scan," explained Mark.

"A body scan? You mean one of those where they see everything?"

"I'm afraid so," said Mark. "Don't worry; it's all computerized now. A real person doesn't watch the screen. It's designed to identify explosives and weapons. If an alarm sounds, you get a physical body search."

As we got out of the SUV, I said, "You stay here, Mr. P." The cat still appeared to be upset. We locked the doors and headed for the entrance.

"Isn't that the limo we followed parked over there?" I asked.

"Unfortunately, yes," said Mark. "It's the chairman of the Joint Chiefs of Staff's personal car. I hope the cat was just having a tizzy fit because he had a hairball," said Mark.

We walked into the Pentagon. I was again duly impressed. The building was huge and had exceptionally wide corridors. We walked to a security post similar to the ones at an airport. The only difference was that the Pentagon's had armed soldiers. We showed our ID cards, and again they were scanned. The woman inspecting the cards handed each of us a visitor's pass. But these were different than the simple student ID cards we used at Gonzaga University. The photo from my security card was on the visitor's card along with my name and company, Baker Security. The top of the card had a red band.

"Access is limited to only red areas," said the woman, who obviously took her job seriously.

We then joined the line waiting to go through the body scanner. When it was my turn, I entered. There was an image on the wall of the scanner. It showed a figure with its legs spread apart about twelve inches and arms held out to the sides with palms up. Apparently that was the stance you had to take in the scanner. As I took the position, I visualized a room on the other side with a bunch of guys drinking coffee and watching the screen., I was standing naked in front of them while they remarked on my body parts. I assumed the requisite position and held my breath. There was a brief hum, then a mechanical voice said, "Cleared. Please exit to your left."

"Now what?" I asked Mark.

"We're going to lunch.,"

"Lunch?" I asked. "We just ate breakfast. Why lunch?"

"Because it's eleven thirty, and everyone eats lunch. I want you to observe who comes in," said Mark.

"I don't understand," I responded, totally confused.

"Just call it a cop's hunch."

Mark knew the building well. He handed me another brochure and filled in more information from his own knowledge.

We had entered on the second floor. I doubt there's anyone in the United States who hasn't heard of the Pentagon. But a person has to visit it to understand the immensity of the building—a five-sided building, five stories high, two basements, and a large central courtyard. No big deal, right? That is, until you discover that twenty-three thousand military and civilian employees work there and that it has nearly four million square feet of office space. The building has more area than three Empire State Buildings.

Floors are numbered one through five. There are five concentric rings of hallways with offices on both sides. A is the innermost ring, and E is the outermost ring. The only offices with windows to the outside are on the E ring. The military leadership of the nation has its offices there.

Mark explained that there are two cafeterias and six snack bars, one on the outside and one in the dining room. Most of the top brass eat in the dining room where they tend to bring visitors. Mark had eaten in the dining room when he was working on the contract for Homeland Security.

The brochure included a map of the Pentagon. Using it and by following the signs along the way, we found the dining room. Unlike the cafeterias, which were self-service, the dining room had servers. Mark asked for a seat near the entrance, explaining that we were expecting two more people. When the waiter came, Mark told him that the other two had been detained. We went ahead and ordered lunch. I ordered one half of a chef's salad, and Mark ordered the fish dinner.

"I still don't understand what we are doing here," I said.

"I want you to watch the people walking by. As we eat, just keep an eye on them," explained Mark. I did as I was told. I saw two men with little eagles on their shoulder boards (full colonels, according to Mark) walk by. When they were within thirty feet, I sucked in a breath. Their eyes were glowing like the people in the dining room last night. I began to suspect what Mark was getting at. Within the next ten minutes, I saw two more people in uniform who had glowing eyes. One was a woman. Then an *endosym* walked in. He looked like a uniformed older man with a chest full of ribbons. He wore three stars on each of his shoulders. All this information, I relayed to Mark.

He put down his fork. "I've seen enough. Let's go," he said.

He signaled to the waiter, got the bill, left a tip, and paid the bill at the cashier. We walked to the exit, turned in our visitor passes, and saw them placed in a shredder.

75

WE LEFT THE BUILDING AND RETURNED TO OUR VEHICLE. MR. P WAS stretched out, sound asleep, in the backseat.

As we drove out, I looked at my watch. It was now half past noon.

"How far is it to McLean?" I asked.

"Twenty minutes," said Mark. "We should make it with ten minutes to spare."

Mr. P had woken up and walked across the console that was between the front bucket seats. He curled up in my lap. Mark admired Mr. P's ability to rest whenever possible, yet to be alert when necessary.

"He's better than an explosives sniffer. That cat can sniff out aliens hiding as humans. Amy, do you understand what we have discovered?"

"Well, there are *endosyms* and people under their power here in Washington, DC," I answered.

"Much worse than that," he said. "They have infiltrated the highest levels of our government. God, are they doing this all over the world? Is this some kind of a takeover of the earth?"

"Maybe it's not that bad," I said.

"It's bad," said Mark. "No wonder they wanted to kill you. You and your cat are like super–lie detectors. You can walk up to a guy on the street and instantly know that he is more than just a human. Unfortunately, who would believe you? All those guys you saw today and last night looked perfectly normal to me. So, how can you stop an invasion when you can't prove to a real cop or soldier that their boss or the leader of a country isn't really human? There must be more to this, and hopefully we can find out who is on our side and whether there is any way to stop what is happening."

Mark pulled off the expressway into a residential area.

"McLean, Virginia," he said. He followed the directions on the navigation system, and we pulled onto a street lined with tall oak trees. The houses had been built sixty to seventy years ago but were still magnificent and immaculately maintained. We stopped in front of a large brick, two-story colonial-style house.

"This is it," said Mark. "Are you ready?"

"As ready as I'll ever be," I said.

76

"I'LL NEED TO LET MR. P OUT IF WE STAY MORE THAN A COUPLE OF hours," I told Mark. We walked up the sidewalk to the house. The temperature was predicted to be in the low fifties so we hadn't worn overcoats. The only snow on the ground was from the blizzard three weeks earlier. What was left had been plowed and then piled along the shoulders of the road. *What a strange weather year it had been*, I thought. Each year, the weather tended to flip-flop more and more. Global climate change continued to baffle the weather people.

Mark rang the doorbell. When the door opened, Mark was the first to speak.

"Mrs. Martin?" asked Mark.

"Yes, I'm Lindsey Martin. You must be Mr. Baker. I understand that you found some items that belonged to my son and daughter-in-law."

"Yes, ma'am," said Mark.

"Please come in," she said graciously.

We stepped into the entryway. Lindsey Martin was not what I had expected. Since she was Dad's mother, I had visualized her as a stooped-over old lady with snow-white hair. According to the information Mark had gotten on her, she was sixty-eight years old. This Lindsey Martin who let us into her house wore faded jeans, running shoes, and a white cotton blouse. Her hair was blond, cut short, and neatly styled. She was wearing small pearl earrings, light makeup, and salmon-colored lipstick. She actually had a rounded rear end and a figure that would put some of my friends to shame. Her voice was strong. If I saw her on the street, I would have assumed that she wasn't much older than Regina.

"Let's sit in the living room," said Lindsey, giving me a strange look. Mark hadn't bothered to introduce me.

We followed her into the living room. It was furnished with contemporary furniture. The hardwood floors were covered with thick oriental carpets. On the fireplace mantel were pictures of two men. Right away, I knew that these men were part of my real family.

A sob caught in my throat. One of the pictures was an older man in a military uniform. The other was of my dad, perhaps of his high school graduation. Along one wall was a banister bookshelf. On top of the shelf was a picture of Mom and Dad, taken the day of their wedding.

I noticed that Lindsey was watching me closely.

From far off, I heard Mark say, "I'm sorry, I forgot to introduce my associate, Miss Amy Brown."

Lindsey Martin came up to me and held out her hand. "It's a pleasure to meet you, Miss Brown."

Something in the sparkle of her eyes and the warmth of her personality reminded me of someone I had known so well—my dad. I stood totally motionless for a moment. Then I reached out and held her hand in mine. I was certain that I was going to break down right then. I felt tears stream down my cheeks. I looked into her face, not knowing what to say or do. I could tell that Lindsey Martin was amazed and puzzled at the same time.

"I know you," she said.

"And I know you," I sobbed.

She embraced me, and I pulled her toward me.

"Twenty-four years ago at Honolulu International Airport, I placed a lei around your mother's neck," my grandmother said. "At that moment I knew that Samantha Dixon would marry Tim. Call it a mother's instinct."

I remember very little of what happened in the next few minutes. I sobbed uncontrollably while my grandmother held me in her arms. By the time I got my emotions under control, even that old tough ex–homicide cop, Mark Baker, was wiping his eyes. At some point, we found ourselves seated by the fireplace.

Grandma Martin and I sat on the love seat. She was holding my hand, and it all seemed so natural.

"When Tim and Sam were lost in Liberia after their plane crashed, I always felt deep in my heart that they had survived. Your grandfather Hank was a soldier. From the statements of witnesses, he was convinced that they could not have lived through the crash. I so wish he could have been here today.

"A year ago, I woke up in the middle of the night. Even though Hank died of a heart attack three years ago, there are still times at night when I can feel him lying beside me. Sometimes I will reach over, expecting to have him there beside me. That night, more than one year ago, it was different. It felt like something had been ripped from me. Tim and Sam are dead, aren't they?"

"Yes," I said, choking back a sob. "It's my fault."

"Dear, I'm sure it wasn't your fault," said Lindsey.

"You don't understand; I can see things that are not human. I know that must sound crazy," I said.

"Not so crazy," said Lindsey. "Your dad could see the evil in people. That's why he was such a good FBI agent."

"No, you don't understand. I can see demons in people," I tried to explain to her.

"Ah, Mrs. Martin, Amy's a little upset. She really doesn't see demons," said Mark in an attempt to protect me. He continued to look worried.

"Oh, I'm sure she does. Both Hank and Tim saw them too," said Lindsey sincerely.

I looked at Mark. I was sure that he was convinced that my whole family was crazy. But that wasn't the case.

"I believe you, Mrs. Martin. From what I have seen since I met Amy, I am not surprised. The question is why does your family see these demons?"

"Oh, dear," said Lindsey. "That is a long story. Can you stay for dinner? I have invited one of your dad's best friends, his wife, and their son. They should be here in an hour. When I first invited them, I only assumed you had items from the plane crash. They will be so surprised to discover that Tim and Sam have a daughter."

I sat there, absorbed in the conversation when the grandfather clock in the other room chimed.

"Oh my gosh, I forgot about Mr. P," I said.

"Who's Mr. P?" asked Lindsey.

"My cat. He's in the car."

"You brought your cat?" asked Lindsey.

"He's kind of a special cat," said Mark.

"I'm sure," said Lindsey. "Cats have a special role in our lives. Ever since Chea Geebe gave me the leopard tooth, our lives have never been the same."

"Is he an old man that lives in a village in Africa and wears a leopard loin cloth?" I asked.

"Lived in Zigda!" said Lindsey. "I'm afraid that he died twenty-four years ago. How do you know about him? Did your father tell you about that old zo?"

"No, I never knew anything about my past until after my parents were murdered last year. Until then I had thought I was born in Spokane. Then I saw the old man in a dream. He said that my name was Anaya Martin and that to find my destiny I must return to Zigda. My cat was in my dream along with a huge leopard."

"Well, Amy—or do you want to be called Anaya?—bring your cat in."

"Call me Amy," I said.

Mark gave me the keys to the SUV, and I went out and got Mr. P. I took him for a quick walk before I brought him into the house. I had him on his leash.

"You can let him loose if you want," said Lindsey. "Do you think he would like a bowl of water and some tuna fish?"

"I'm sure he would love that," I said.

"Come on, Mr. P," said Lindsey. The cat followed her to the kitchen. I heard her talking to the cat. "You act more like a dog than a cat," she said on her way back from the kitchen.

77

We were still standing when the doorbell rang.

"That's Sabo with his wife, Judie, and their youngest son, Joe," said Lindsey as she headed to the front door. Three blacks came in. The man was short, maybe five nine, with short hair graying at the sides. The woman was attractive and about the same age. Their son was a man my age. He was tall, maybe two inches shorter than me. He wore jeans, running shoes, and a black leather jacket.

Lindsey hung their coats in the closet. The woman wore a colorful tie-dyed dress. The older man, apparently my dad's friend, wore slacks and a tie-dyed shirt. The younger man wore a short-sleeved white polo shirt. He had a muscular build, and I had to admit he was very good-looking.

The three joined us in the living room.

"Let me introduce you," Lindsey said. "This is Mark Baker and his associate, Amy Brown. This is Sabo Weah, the Liberian ambassador. This is his wife, Judie, and their son, Joe."

We all shook hands.

"Please sit down," said Lindsey. "I have some startling news to tell you." Lindsey explained to the Weahs that I was her granddaughter.

That afternoon I learned a great deal about my father. When Dad was just a teenager, my grandfather Hank was assigned to Liberia. They were caught up in a plot by the corrupt Liberian government that resulted in my dad and grandmother running for their lives. They hid in a village, deep in the Liberian jungles. An evil group that served an *endosym* captured my dad and Sabo. An old man who was once the greatest witch doctor in Liberia saved them. He gave them a leopard's tooth that had the power to protect them. They became involved in a battle with the men who followed the *endosym*. My dad and Sabo fought against the corrupt regime and helped establish a new government.

Before my parents' disappearance, Sabo and my dad corresponded frequently. Their friendship ran deep. Sabo's uncle was the former minister of defense, and his wife, Judie, was the sister-in-law of the former president of Liberia. Sabo served in Liberia's military for a number of years, and then he had gone on to college. After college he became involved in politics and was appointed ambassador to the United States. He had served in that position for the previous eight years.

Liberia had discovered vast oil reserves and became one of the more prosperous African nations. Yet, despite the increase in the country's prosperity, natives living in the interior still lived much like they had lived for thousands of years.

All this information didn't explain what my role was in this whole mystery, however. There was one piece of information that I believed had to do with the *endosyms*. According to Grandma Martin, when my grandfather rescued my dad from a ceremonial valley where he and Sabo were being held, Grandpa discovered the ruins of an ancient Egyptian-like civilization that existed in Liberia thousands of years ago. In a cavern he found an underground chamber. The passageways were lined with human skulls. Thousands of human beings had been sacrificed there throughout the centuries. From the cavern, my grandfather had taken a statue of a demon. It was about ten inches tall. From Grandma's description of the statue, it sounded like it could have been a statue of an *endosym*. They had kept the statue for years, and then ten years ago it had been stolen during a break-in while my grandparents were visiting family in New York. *I wonder if the theft of the statue has anything to do with what is happening in Washington, DC, now?*

For dinner we had a Liberian dish called jalah of rice. Grandma learned to make the tasty dish when they lived in Liberia. We sat in the dining room. I couldn't believe that I was eating with my grandmother. I couldn't believe that these charming Liberians knew my dad.

The secrets that my parents kept from me for years were mind-boggling. I was having a problem absorbing it all. First, I had never really associated with black people. Spokane did not have a large black community.

From the conversation I learned that rice and spicy foods make up the principal Liberian diet. The meal was something unfamiliar to me. I wouldn't go out of my way to buy food like it. The Weahs, however, wolfed it down and asked for more.

I was seated next to Joe. It was obvious he was more American than Liberian. He was three years older than I and had just started law school in Georgetown. He acted like he knew something about everything. He also made some crude remarks about Mr. P. He asked why I couldn't have just left my "kitty cat" at home. I tried to ignore him and still be polite.

Mark remained surprisingly quiet during the entire time we were there. I noticed that he wrote things in his notebook. After dinner we sat around and heard more stories about my dad and his life.

Several times I found myself tearing up as I realized something had happened that caused my parents to go into hiding. I was pretty sure their disappearance had to do with the *endosyms* and what was currently happening in Washington, DC. Yet at no time during the conversation with Grandma Martin and the Weahs did Mark or I mention that we were becoming convinced that some kind of invasion of *endosyms* was happening. I wasn't sure that Mark totally trusted the Weahs.

Ambassador Weah asked Mark how long we would be in Washington, DC.

"We have to go back to Spokane tomorrow," said Mark.

"Oh, that's too bad. We were just getting to know Amy," said Weah.

"Can't you delay your return trip a few days?" asked Lindsey.

"No, I'm sorry, but we have critical business in Spokane. Our plane is scheduled to depart Reagan National at eleven o'clock in the morning," said Mark.

78

I DIDN'T KNOW WHAT MARK WAS THINKING. WHAT WAS THE BIG hurry? Then it became clear to me—the Speaker of the House and top generals were all *endosyms*. I couldn't help but wonder how many others were there—and where were they? When I was thirteen for Halloween we watched some old horror flicks we ordered fron Netflix. One of them was an old science-fiction movie *The Body Snatchers*. The *endosyms* were like the aliens in that old movie. They were here to do something bad and had to be stopped. *Sorry, Grandma Martin*, I realized, *but we do have pressing business.*

"Amy, you and Mark need to stay here tonight. I won't accept no for an answer," said Lindsey.

I looked at Mark, wondering what he would say.

"I suppose we could check out tonight and go from here to the airport in the morning," he said.

"Amy and I could get the luggage and check out of the motel," said Joe.

"No, that's OK," said Mark. "I'll do it."

"Aw, come on," said Joe. "I know the town, and we won't be gone more than an hour."

Mark looked at me, hoping that I would agree with him.

Actually, I needed to get out of there for an hour or so. It had been quite an emotional evening. I had known Lindsey Martin for fewer than twelve hours—Regina and the twins were more my family than Grandma Martin. She was a wonderful lady, and, in time, I was sure that I would grow to love her like a grandmother. But, at the moment, she was almost a total stranger. Ambassador Weah and his wife were nice people, also, but they had accents, and I found it difficult to understand everything they said. Joe had no accent, and taking a little time off to check out of our suite seemed like a good break.

"No, that's OK. Joe and I can do it. I have the American Express card."

"Great," said Joe. "Let's go."

Joe slipped on his coat. I was about to open the front door so I could get my coat from the SUV, when Mark called out to us.

"Take the cat with you. If he alerts for any reason, get the hell out of there."

"The cat?" asked Joe. "Why in the world would we take the cat?"

"He's a special-bred cat that we use for security," said Mark.

"You're kidding," said Joe.

"Nope," I said firmly.

"All right, he can go, but he won't mess up my car, will he?"

"No," I said. "He's very well behaved."

I hooked up his leash, and we walked out the front door. A brand-new black Corvette was parked in front of the house.

"I came from a class in Georgetown," said Joe, "so I brought my own car."

I slid into the passenger seat. Joe fired it up. It had a nice rumble, a lot like my Mustang.

"Nice wheels," I said as we drove off.

"What motel are you staying in?" asked Joe.

"The Hay-Adams Hotel," I said.

"The Hay-Adams?" asked Joe. "Are you sure?"

"Yes," I said. "It's next to the White House."

"I know where it is. That's a pricey place. I heard the rooms are six hundred dollars a night."

Joe drove the Corvette as if we were in a race. At every multi-lane stoplight, he pulled out first. The way we were passing cars, he was clearly exceeding the speed limit. We took a corner, and the car fishtailed.

"Don't you have stability control in this thing?" I asked.

"I like to feel the traction in the tires when we peel out. Hey, how come a girl knows about stability control?" asked Joe.

"I have a supercharged Mustang GT," I said.

"Did it belong to your dad?" he asked.

"No, it's mine," I said.

"So you really do have a Mustang GT?"

"Yes, I sure do," I said.

We came up behind two cars, both going the speed limit. Joe punched it into a lower gear and floorboarded the Corvette. He crossed the double line into oncoming traffic, racing around the two cars.

"What are you trying to do, kill us?" I yelled.

"Hey, I know how to drive. I had lots of room."

"Well, slow down; I don't need to have myself punched in the face when the airbags deploy," I told him.

"All right, if it makes you nervous, I'll slow down," grumbled Joe. We continued into DC.

"So what's the deal with Mark?" asked Joe.

"What do you mean?" I said.

"Well, he acts like your father or a lover. He always seems to be worrying about you."

As far as I was concerned, this guy was asking far too many questions.

"Mark is Regina's boyfriend. Regina became my legal guardian after my parents were killed," I answered bluntly.

"So, why did he come with you and not Regina?"

I was about to tell him it was none of his business. But instead, I said, "Mark and I are partners."

"Partners?" he asked with a look on his face that said, "He's a sugar daddy, and Regina doesn't know."

"We own a security firm in Spokane. We do work for Homeland Security," I continued.

"Sure," he said with a smirk.

I suspected that he was about to come up with another wisecrack when we pulled up in front of the Hay-Adams Hotel.

"Do we take the kitty cat with us?" asked Joe. *You know,* I thought, *this guy needs a fist in the mouth.* His dad may have been a friend of my dad, but the son was an asshole.

"No," I said. "We can leave him in the car."

We got out of the Corvette. Joe told the doorman that we would only be a few minutes. He pulled out some kind of ID and showed the doorman. He smiled at me.

"Diplomatic passport, and the plates on the Corvette mean I can park anywhere," he said with a grin.

"That doesn't mean you should," I said under my breath.

We walked through the lobby, and Joe hesitated for a few moments.

"There's a great view of the White House and National Monument from the upstairs dining room. It's not open to ordinary patrons, but with my diplomatic status, I could get us up there."

"That's OK. We really don't have time for that," I said.

As we were walking toward the elevators, one of the bellboys approached.

"How are you this evening, Miss Brown?"

"Just fine," I said. "Can you send someone up in about twenty minutes to get our luggage? We are going to check out tonight."

"Of course, Miss Brown. I'll attend to it right away."

As the bellboy walked away, Joe said, "You forgot to tell him your room number."

"Oh, he knows my room number," I said with a smile. *Let this creep think about that one.*

When we got to the elevators, Joe asked, "What floor?" He raised his arm and started to push the up button for the two regular elevators.

"Not those," I said as I walked to the elevator for the Federal Suite.

"That one has no buttons," said Joe.

"I know," I said as I inserted my card. The doors opened, and we stepped into the elevator.

When it stopped and the doors opened, Joe looked confused.

"Where are we?" he asked.

"Top floor, I think," I said. He followed me to the double doors to our suite. I inserted the card in the slot to the right of the doors and the door clicked open. Mr. Joe "Cool" Weah stood there with his mouth open.

"Wow!" he said as we walked in. "This is the Federal Suite? Our president stays here when he visits the United States."

"Oh," I said. "We figured we would rent it for the view. Listen, I need to go pack my clothes, and then I want to get out of this place."

I started to walk to the master bedroom.

"Do you need any help?" he said with a sly grin.

"Help? Like what?" I asked.

"Like getting out of your clothes," he said, still smiling.

I was beginning to get really irritated. What did this guy think I was going to do? Rip off my clothes and fall in bed with him? What a conceited SOB!

I decided he needed a little air let out of his swollen head.

"I am going in there to change my clothes. Sit down and watch TV. If my bedroom door opens even a crack, I will put a bullet between your eyes."

Joe laughed nervously; he seemed a little unsure.

"You don't have a gun or even know how to use one," he said smugly. I reached into my handbag and withdrew the .32 automatic.

"It's a thirty-two caliber; not the most powerful handgun in the world. Mark recommends a headshot. Of course, it's no good at any distance, but I should have no problem at this range."

"Hey, I was just joking," said Joe. "I'll watch TV."

I put the pistol back in my handbag and walked into the bedroom, closing the door behind me.

I pulled out my suitcase and placed it on the bed, removed my suit and blouse, and packed them along with my other things into the suitcase. I put on my jeans, sneakers, and a maroon blouse. I went in the bathroom, applied fresh lipstick, and checked my makeup. I placed my cosmetics in my tote bag. Then I put the cat's two dishes in a plastic bag and put them in a briefcase with Mr. P's extra food. I set the three pieces of luggage by the door. Joe was sitting on the couch, staring at the bedroom door. Maybe he was hoping that I had been bluffing, and he would get a chance to score. *Isn't going to happen, Mr. Joe Weah.*

I needed to get Mark's things. I entered the second bedroom. It was kind of weird packing a man's things. Mark wasn't a stranger, but it felt odd nonetheless. I went through the drawers, packed as best I could, took the shirts out of the closet, and managed to get everything into his one suitcase. I set it in the living room.

When the door buzzer sounded, I opened the doors. Two bellboys were there. They loaded the two suitcases, my tote bag, and the briefcase with the cat sand on a cart. We headed downstairs. When we got in the elevator, one of the bellboys explained that the charges would go on the company's American Express card. We were already checked out.

79

THE CORVETTE HAD ENOUGH ROOM BEHIND THE TWO SEATS TO PACK everything. While Joe was still trying to rearrange the suitcases, all the while cussing under his breath, Mr. P, who was in the front seat, let out one of his deep growls.

Uh oh.

"What's wrong with your cat?" asked Joe.

I had been standing by the side of the Corvette with the passenger door wide open. I turned around and looked behind us. Getting out of a limo was an elderly gentleman. He must have heard the cat and looked our way. I knew he was an *endosym*. He looked directly at me, and a chill passed through my body. A voice in my head asked, "Who are you?"

I yelled at Joe, "Come on! Let's get out of here, and let's do it fast!"

"Fine with me," he said. We slid into our seats. I picked up Mr. P and held him on my lap with my arms around him. He looked over my shoulder and hissed. Joe drove out, using his normal foot-to-the-floor method.

For once I was glad that he was driving fast. I looked out my side mirror, expecting to see the *endosym* coming from behind us, but nothing was following us. The cat finally calmed down. Joe looked at me.

"Your cat has an attitude," Joe said.

"Sometimes," I said.

We headed north. The clock in the Corvette read twelve forty-five. On a weekday night this early in the morning, there wasn't much traffic. Joe was going about fifteen miles per hour over the speed limit. We were crossing a long bridge when I saw a sign up ahead indicating the exit for Washington National Zoo.

"Oh, shit!" said Joe.

"What?"

"Cops."

I looked in the side mirror. Two police cars were coming up fast behind us.

"Maybe they're going to an emergency," I said.

The lead police car pulled up directly behind us and turned on its emergency flashers. Joe pulled over.

"Don't worry," he said. "I have diplomatic plates. They can't even give me a ticket. Stupid cops."

Joe started to open the driver's door when Mr. P began growling. "Joe, we might not be dealing with legitimate cops," I said. Suddenly my own door opened.

Mr. P went wild. He leaped at the cop who still had his hand on the door handle, but the guy swatted the cat away, totally unfazed. Then the cop pulled his Glock and took aim at Mr. P, who had landed unhurt about twenty feet away. The cat was crouched, ready to spring, but when he saw the gun, he turned and ran down a stairway that led down under the bridge to the parkway below. The gun discharged, and I saw sparks fly as the bullet hit the pavement. Before I could say anything, the man turned, holstered his gun, reached in, and lifted me out of the Corvette. His grip was like a steel vice. He threw me facedown on the ground. My hands were pulled behind my back, and I was handcuffed.

Joe was having his own problems. As I was pulled to my feet, I saw another cop grab Joe by his leather jacket and literally lift him off the ground. He threw him down with so much force that I feared for Joe's life. Joe was also cuffed and jerked to his feet.

Joe's face was bloody, and he could hardly stand upright. I didn't need to see the glow in the four cops' eyes to know that they were under the influence of an *endosym*. We were in big-time trouble.

They dragged us down the stairs to the park below. The bridge was lighted by streetlights every hundred feet. Lights along the railing lit up the grassy area below. The cops threw us down on the ground next to a tree. Joe tried to talk his way out of it.

"This is an outrage! I'm a diplomat!" he screamed.

"Shut up, asshole, or I'll put my boot in your mouth!" barked one of the so-called cops.

The man wearing sergeant stripes turned to another man, who was maybe only a few years older than I am.

"Find that damn cat, and kill it!"

The young cop, seemingly pleased with his orders, headed off into the woods. The sergeant pulled out a cell phone, punched in some numbers, and waited a few minutes before he began speaking.

"We've got them! We're in Rock Creek Park. You'll see our vehicles along the road."

He flipped the phone shut and stuffed it in his pocket. The three cops stood about thirty feet from us. They were talking quietly among themselves.

"What's going on?" whispered Joe.

"Something bad," I said.

"We've got to do something," said Joe, gasping for breath. "God, I think they cracked some ribs." I took another look at Joe. He looked bad. When they threw him on the ground, he must have hit his face on the curb. His nose was bleeding, and there was a cut on his forehead that would require stitches—if we survived long enough for him to get stitches.

The cops looked toward the stairs. They had heard someone coming down the steps. As the man came into the light from the streetlights, I recognized him. It was the *endosym* from Hay-Adams. He wore a long black overcoat, under which I could see that same white shirt and dark tie. He looked like a white gentleman in his early sixties. He had neatly trimmed hair. I caught a glimpse of the Rolex on his left wrist. On his right middle finger, he wore a large ruby ring.

As he came closer, he looked down at us. I stared up at him. This close, I thought I was looking at a double-exposure print. I could see both the man and the aura of the demon-like thing that coexisted within him.

He looked directly at me.

"Who are you?" I heard him ask, but his lips didn't move. I continued to stare at him.

"You have no power to resist me," the *endosym* said. "If you resist, I will enter your mind. I will find out and destroy your very being."

My God, I thought. He was talking in my mind, but I wasn't hearing him with my ears. I tried not to think; I tried to focus on something else. He stared at me, and then I felt something crawling within my brain. It's hard to describe the feeling. It was like a huge spider wrapping me in its silk web, just before it began to suck out my life. I closed my eyes and held my breath. I could feel the thing probing my mind. My flesh broke out in goose bumps.

The probing continued. I opened my eyes. The *endosym* was still staring at me.

"Go to hell!" I said.

He blinked and momentarily seemed confused.

Then that voice in my head said, "It doesn't matter. Tonight you die."

He turned toward the police sergeant and said aloud, "Kill them both. Make it look like a mugging. You can do what you want with them before you kill them. I'll send a team to clean up and stage the site."

"What about the cat?" asked the sergeant.

"Forget him," said the *endosym*. "Once she is dead, it is of no consequence."

The *endosym* turned and walked back up the stairs. I heard a car drive away.

The sergeant spoke into his shoulder mic for his radio.

"Steve, forget about the cat. Just get back here. It's party time. We get to waste them."

80

OK, Amy, think—what can we do? My thoughts went to Mr. P. Shaun O'Kelly had said that some *zoutari* had cats that could morph into unique creatures. Mark was convinced that Mr. P was some kind of supernatural beast, and the cat could spot *endosyms* and those under their control.

But right now, the cat was hiding in the woods. Did I call him and say, "Sic 'em, Mr. P!"? *Maybe I just have to concentrate.* I closed my eyes and tried to visualize my cat as a monster. *OK, what kind of monster? Crap.* All I could think of was Godzilla in that hokey movie. Mr. P—a giant lizard with cat whiskers.

Then I remembered Mark talking about the autopsies of the men who were killed in the storage unit. They indicated that a large tiger with sharp claws had ripped them apart. I closed my eyes, squeezing them shut as hard as I could, and imagined a large gray-striped tiger, maybe a large gray saber-toothed tiger. Say, it weighed about a thousand pounds.

I visualized this huge gray monster cat stalking the four cops, attacking them, and tearing them apart. With my eyes still closed, my thoughts were interrupted by the most god-awful sounds—birds cawing and what might have been chimpanzees screeching mixed in with other animal sounds. I opened my eyes to check the source of the noise. It seemed to be coming from the north. I assumed it was just my own imagination, but the cops had heard something too.

"What's that?" asked one of them.

"The zoo," said the sergeant. "Something must be upsetting the animals. Don't worry about it."

Then as quickly as the noise started, it suddenly ceased. There was absolute silence.

"Weird," remarked one of the cops.

I thought that this was quite a statement, coming from a guy who served an *endosym*. Then the silence was broken again by a kind of a grunting sound, repeated over and over.

"That's just one of the lions in the zoo," said the sergeant.

"Sounds kind of close," said another cop. Then I heard two gunshots.

"What the hell is Steve doing?" asked the sergeant. He talked into his mic. "Steve, what are you doing? I told you to forget the cat."

He waited, listening for an answer. Whoever was supposed to answer hadn't responded. He turned to the other cops.

"Go find out what that idiot is doing," said the sergeant. The two men headed into the woods.

It was just the sergeant guarding us. *If I can get my hands free, I might be able to do something.* I pulled on my handcuffs. The cuff on my right wrist felt a little loose. With small bones and long, thin fingers, maybe I could slip the cuff off my wrist.

Gripping the chain on the cuff in my left hand, I tugged hard on it at the same time as I pulled up with my right hand. That didn't work. The corner of the cuff was sharp, and it cut into my wrist. I had no choice. We were going to die if I didn't get free. I pulled harder. I could feel skin ripping away from my wrist, but I continued to pull. I closed my eyes and tried to ignore the pain. My fingers felt wet and sticky. My wrist was bleeding.

I felt the cuff slip farther down my wrist. I gritted my teeth. The cuff continued to move a little farther. I pulled harder. The cuff was now hung up on one of my knuckles. I had become obsessed with getting it off. I was willing to tear off my knuckle, if necessary. Then, oblivious to the pain, I felt my skin tear. With one more pull, my hand was free. I almost brought it around to see how much damage I had inflicted on myself, but I resisted the urge to look. I kept my hands behind my back as if I were still handcuffed. I kept my head lowered, trying to appear totally defeated. I wiggled my fingers. I could still feel blood running down my hand. I prayed that I hadn't cut a major vein or artery and was now bleeding to death. It made no difference. In the cuffs, I was dead anyway. Free, we had a chance. I breathed in slowly; all the while I checked to see if the police sergeant was aware of my movements.

Then we heard shots and a loud commotion coming from the thick woods. A man screamed loud and long. The sergeant turned to look. It was now or never. I slowly moved my legs under me. Using my hands, I pushed myself up onto my feet and rushed toward the sergeant. My right leg was numb from sitting on the ground for so long, and I almost fell flat on my face. I struggled to continue forward.

I struck the sergeant with every ounce of strength I could muster. It was as if my body had crashed into an immovable light pole. The impact caused me to fall backward. Fortunately, as I collided with him, my body rotated, and my left hand struck his Glock. It flew out of his hand, landing on the ground six feet from me. I dove for the gun, grabbed it, rolled, and fired five shots into the cop. He laughed. He had taken five shots from a 40-caliber Glock, and it didn't even knock him back. He must have been wearing a bulletproof vest. I lowered my aim and fired two shots at his left thigh. That got his attention. I aimed at his head and missed. I fired another shot that struck his neck. I saw spurts of blood. The next shot struck him in the shoulder. He finally went down. I pulled the trigger again, but nothing happened. The gun was empty. I knew cops' guns only carried ten-round magazines. I threw the weapon on the ground and turned to help Joe get on his feet.

"Can you walk?" I asked.

"I think so," he said. I held his arm and guided him toward the steps.

"You're both dead!"

The police sergeant hobbled toward me, his eyes glowing with the power of the *endosym* he served. I couldn't understand how he could stand, let alone walk.

Then I heard a roar from the trees. I looked in the direction of the sound and saw two red eyes glowing in the darkness. A gray blur came out of the thick brush. The police sergeant managed to reach the small grassy spot in the trees on the other side. The creature followed, and they both disappeared. Then I heard a scream and a sound that I am sure was the crunch of bones.

81

"Up the stairs! Quick!" I said as I pushed Joe ahead of me. Two police cars and the Corvette were still parked by the curb. When I tried the door, I found it was locked.

"Where's your key fob?"

"In my coat pocket," said Joe. He couldn't get into his pockets with his hands cuffed. I patted the pocket.

"It's not there," I said.

"Must have fallen out," he said.

I ran around the other side of the Corvette. No keys. They must be down in the grass by the tree. I was about to head down the steps when I saw Mr. P come bounding up the steps. He ran directly to me. Then I noticed that one of the police cruisers sat nearby with its motor running and its emergency lights flashing.

"The police car," I said. "Come on!"

I pushed Joe toward the passenger side. I had to help him get in. It wasn't easy sliding into a car with handcuffs behind your back. I closed the door, ran around to the driver's side, and fell into the seat. The cat jumped into my lap. I set him on the console between Joe and me. I needed to turn off the flashers, so I checked out all the police controls. I pushed a button. The siren wailed. Then I tried another button, and the lights went out. I pulled out around the Corvette.

"What about my Corvette?" asked Joe.

"Right now, every cop in DC knows the license number of the Corvette. We are better off in this police car."

I crossed the bridge, still heading north.

I was going to call Mark but I was worried that they might be able to monitor my cell phone. "How do we get to Grandma Martin's house?" I asked.

"Turn left at the next light," said Joe. "I thought we were going to die back there. I can't believe what you did."

"What?" I asked.

"You were the one who attacked that guy, and then you shot him with his gun. You were so badass," said Joe.

"Apparently, I wasn't too good of a shot. He got up and came after us again."

"No, you don't understand. He was something like a zo—you know, a witch doctor. Bullets couldn't kill him," said Joe.

Joe had no idea how close that was to the truth, I thought.

"Well, we got away," I said.

I think we would have been better off if Joe had just kept quiet, but I was worried about how badly he had been injured, and he didn't seem to want to stop talking. Maybe getting his mind off all this would help get him through his injuries.

"When I was twelve, my dad made me go through bush school," Joe said.

"Bush school?" I asked.

"Puberty rites. When boys and girls become adults in our country, they go to bush school. Anyway, I wasn't happy about that. We lived in Monrovia, not Zigda. I have three sisters. Mom is from a different tribe, and she wouldn't let her daughters go through bush school, but my dad insisted that I go.

"I was sent to Zigda. That was the home of our relatives on my dad's side. The bush school was shorter than when Dad went, but it was still four weeks of hell. We learned all kinds of secrets and took a death oath never to divulge what we learned.

"The final test in bush school was to battle a mythical beast called the Nangma. I know that this sounds like a bunch of nonsense, but my people still believe that monsters live in the jungles. They believe that powerful zos still exist. You guys call them witch doctors. They can do both good and evil.

"Anyway, the time came when we would meet the great Nangma. We were taken deep into the forest, and each of us was required to drink a special potion. When my turn came, I opened my throat and let the liquid flow freely into my body.

"I leaned back against a tree and waited my turn. I prayed that I would live so I could once again see my father and mother. I fell into a deep sleep. A short time later, I awoke. I was no longer in the compound, but on a jungle trail. Even though it was deep into the night, I could see enough to make my way along the path. I walked forward, listening intently and choosing each step with care.

"Without warning, a huge leopard appeared before me. It growled, crouched, and then lunged toward me. I knelt with my spear pointed forward like they taught me in bush school. The beast fell against my spear. My blade plunged deep into its massive chest. The shaft snapped under the animal's weight. The leopard howled with pain and kept coming toward me. It threw me to the ground. Its razor-sharp claws slashed my chest. I plunged my knife into its throat, twisting the blade as it entered. It gave up its charge and fell lifeless to the ground before me. My arms and legs trembled, yet I rose to my feet. My broken spear was still embedded in its chest, and my knife protruded from its throat."

Joe laughed. At first I couldn't figure out why he could laugh at this frightening story, but soon I understood that he was only marveling at his own courage.

"Understand I was a town boy, born and raised in Monrovia. The first animal I ever killed was a small deer in bush school. We had to learn how to hunt and kill our own food. I cried when I killed it, so killing this leopard was quite a feat.

"I ran ahead, down the trail. Within moments, I heard a low growl. I turned in time to see the leopard rise again to its feet. It still lived! Pure hatred gleamed from its eyes. As it neared, I ran. I sensed its nearness. I ran even faster, my lungs laboring as much from fear as from fatigue. Ahead, a large tree blocked my route. I panicked, crying for a way to escape. Then I saw an opening to my right. Heedless of the unknown, I left the trail and dashed into the bush.

"The forest opened up, and I found myself in a dark passageway. It sloped downward. I continued to run. I could hear the beast thrashing through the brush behind me. Despite the darkness, I could still make my way ahead.

I glanced over at Joe. The talking was at least keeping him from passing out.

"Panting, I continued my downward path. Ahead I could see a reddish glow. I knew it was the Nangma itself. Behind, I smelled the humid breath of the wounded beast. But my fear of the beast paled compared to what loomed before me. No nightmare could ever be this frightening! Even the leopard gave up its chase. I trembled as I became aware of the presence of the great Poro spirit ahead.

"I reversed direction and followed the leopard's hasty retreat. I felt the Nangma follow. My foot struck a branch, and I lost my balance. Sharp fangs pierced my shoulder. At that moment, I was sure my spirit was destined to serve Nangma for eternity.

"I awoke. Once again I was inside the hut where we lived during bush school. I moved to one side. Spasms of pain ran up my spine. My arms and legs throbbed in rhythm to my heartbeat. In the distance, I heard the moaning of my brothers. I heard a man say that the Nangma had chewed us up and spit us out. Yet I would live. In two weeks, I would be welcomed into the Poro. A sense of well-being came over me, and I fell into a deep slumber."

Joe seemed to shake himself out of his reverie.

"I'm sorry. I'm probably boring you," he said.

"No," I said. "I lived a quiet, ordinary life in Spokane, Washington. The most exciting thing I did was to tryout for cheerleading. I can't even imagine what it would be like to survive in the jungles of Africa."

"Take a right at the next street," said Joe.

"Tonight, I think I saw a Nangma."

"What?" I said.

"You remember the noise of the animals in the zoo? You remember the silence that followed? You remember that strange woofing sound?" asked Joe.

"Yeah. Wasn't that a lion from the zoo?" I asked.

"No," said Joe. "I heard that same sound when I was in bush school. Tonight I saw the Nangma rush out of the woods and grab that cop who was coming after us."

I looked at Mr. P who was stretched out on the console between us. If Joe knew my story, he might be more freaked out. Were the words of Chea Geebe true? Was I a witch doctor or zo? Was I able to create a Nangma or whatever it was that attacked those cops?

I saw Grandma Martin's house up ahead. I pulled into a side driveway. I ran around the car, opened the passenger door, and helped Joe get out. I supported him as he slowly struggled up the stairs to the front door. All this time, I kept looking around to see if we were being followed. The police cruiser was hidden from the main road by the shrubs along the side of the house. I hadn't seen anyone following us.

82

I RANG THE DOORBELL. LINDSEY OPENED THE DOOR.

"My God, what happened?" she gasped. I pushed Joe inside.

"Big trouble," I said. I'm sure that was obvious. Here was Joe with his hands cuffed behind his back. I stood there beside him with my right hand coated in blood and a handcuff dangling from my left hand.

"Mark!" shouted Lindsey. "I need your help!"

"My God!" he said when he saw us. He reached into his back pocket and pulled out his wallet. He took out a small key and used it to unlock Joe's handcuffs. Then he took off my remaining handcuff.

"Get them both into the kitchen. We need towels and hot water," said Mark.

When the Weahs saw their son, I expected them to freak out. To my surprise, I was the only one who freaked out. Lindsey, Mark, and the Weahs had all seen death and injuries in the past. As they got Joe seated, Mark pulled me aside.

"What happened?" he asked.

"I ran into an *endosym* at the Hay-Adams. He knew that I had seen him. When we were coming back here, four cops pulled us over and took us into Rock Creek Park. Then the *endosym* came and wanted to know who I was. He tried to get into my mind. When he couldn't, he told the cops to kill us," I explained.

"How did you get away?" he asked.

"With a little bit of luck and with the assistance of my helper from the storage unit," I said.

"You mean the cat thing?"

I nodded my head.

"How did you get here?" he asked.

"In a police cruiser. We had to leave Joe's Corvette on the bridge."

"Uh, we have to hurry," he said. We went back into the kitchen. Lindsey had washed the blood from Joe's face. She had applied antiseptic and had bandaged his cuts.

"I'm calling the secretary of state," growled Sabo. "I will not tolerate this police brutality."

"Don't do that," said Mark. "I need your help. Come with me, and I will tell you why I think that would be a bad move."

"Where are you going?" I asked Mark.

"We have to get rid of that police cruiser," said Mark. "They have GPS locaters. Come on, Sabo. Let's ditch the cruiser. You can follow me and bring me back." Within minutes, I heard the cars start up and pull out of the driveway.

I walked back into the kitchen. Grandma Martin looked at my hand.

"Let me see that, young lady."

I held up my right hand.

"It doesn't seem to hurt that bad," I said. She made me sit down and washed my wrist. "My goodness, it looks like it has almost healed. I guess it wasn't too serious." She wrapped my hand in a bandage—for good measure, she said. "I think your cat was shot," she said as she put the supplies away.

"What?" I asked.

"He's all covered with blood too."

Sure enough, his chest and face were caked with dried blood. I picked him up and gently picked at his fur. I could find no wounds.

"Can I wash him in the sink?"

"Sure," said Lindsey.

Cats don't like water, and Mr. P definitely objected. I used the sprayer attachment and saw the blood pour off. I dried him with a towel.

"I can't find any injuries," I said.

"Strange," said Lindsey. "He had so much blood on him."

"He must have gotten it from Joe and me."

"I wonder..." Lindsey didn't finish her thought out loud.

I didn't wonder. I was pretty sure that there were four shredded rogue cops in Rock Creek.

After Mark and Sabo returned, we sat at the kitchen table. Mark was clearly running the show. As a retired homicide cop, he knew how the bad guys thought. And right now he was considering us bad guys. I don't know how much Mark told Sabo, but it was apparent that he was following Mark's advice. The first thing Sabo had done was to call the police and report that his son's new Corvette had been stolen. He provided the license number and told them that it had been parked in Georgetown. Eventually the security cameras at Hay-Adams might show us loading up the Corvette. However, Mark believed that the *endosyms* would not want to blow their cover and there would be no mention of the cops being killed.

Joe looked like he had been in a war. His head was bandaged. Even his dark skin showed deep purple areas. They had wrapped a torn sheet around his chest. Grandma Martin was convinced that his ribs weren't broken, but he might have cracked one. Mark said that there was no way this could be traced back to Lindsey Martin. Nothing in our itinerary indicated a visit to her house.

Unfortunately, that wasn't the case with Mark and me. It would be easy for someone to find out who we were, and they might try to stop us at the airport. He had contacted the pilots and told them to have the plane ready in two hours. We would be flying out at four o'clock in the morning, much to Grandma Martin's disappointment.

I assured her that I would come back, but I could tell that she realized that this was a bad situation and there was a chance we might not survive. Mark had not told them everything, assuring them that the less they knew, the safer they were.

The final issue was Joe Weah. Mark recommended that Sabo send Joe back to Liberia on the first available flight. He told the Weahs that he was fairly confident that the disappearance of the four cops would never be reported, and he was sure that some very powerful people would be trying to squelch the whole thing. All the diplomatic immunity in the world would not save Joe if they found him.

The only positive thing for Joe was the fact that Mark wanted to get me to Liberia, and he needed someone in Liberia to escort me. Joe would be that person. He would have help from his great-uncle, who now served as the paramount chief after retiring as the country's defense minister. His uncle lived in Zigda.

It was both a joyful and a sad good-bye as we left the warm people who seemed more and more like family with each passing minute. When we were ready to leave, everyone hugged each other.

The Weahs taught me how to shake hands, Liberian style. When Liberians shake hands, they add an extra gesture. As they pull their hands away, they slide their middle fingers back and then make a snap with their fingers. Apparently the tradition goes back to ancient times when warriors would pop their fingers to show that they had no poison under their nails. I wasn't too good at the popping of fingers, but they all laughed with me and seemed satisfied.

As I was getting in the SUV, Joe came over before the car door closed. He stroked Mr. P's head.

"Your cat will be welcome in Zigda," he said.

It was obvious he was serious. I think Joe had an inkling that Mr. P was more than just a regular cat. We backed out of the driveway and headed for Reagan National Airport.

I wondered if I would ever see my grandmother again.

83

OUR PLANE HAD JUST LEVELED OFF AFTER OUR TAKEOFF FROM Reagan National. We were headed back to Spokane, and I was anxious to get home.

Mark unfastened his seat belt and entered the cockpit. I saw him talking to our pilot. Both Kevin Hicks, the pilot, and Emily Ferguson, the copilot, had been waiting near the plane when we arrived. Despite the early hour, they had the plane ready for takeoff. Within the hour, we were in the air.

I wondered what Mark wanted to tell Kevin. I didn't think a passenger was supposed to approach the pilot during a flight. When Mark came back, he smiled and sat down. I heard the pitch of the engines change. Then I felt the cabin tip to the left. We were making a turn.

"What's going on?" I asked.

"We're taking a little detour," Mark said.

"Where?" I asked.

"To Charlottesville, Virginia. It's about a twenty-minute flight. Then to Newburgh, New York, and finally we will go back to Spokane," explained Mark.

"What's in Charlottesville?"

"Well, actually, we will be going to Johnsonville, Virginia. It's a forty-five-minute drive from the airport," said Mark.

"I don't understand," I said.

"While you and Joe Weah were gone, your grandmother told me something that happened the year your mom and dad were married. A cult leader named George Sarday kidnapped your mother.

"Apparently, this Sarday guy established a New Age school in Johnsonville. He claimed he could channel an ancient god from Egypt. Turned out that this Sarday was from Liberia. He was part of that corrupt government, and I'm certain he was an *endosym*.

"Apparently, your dad, the local chief of police, and some noncommissioned officers that your grandfather knew rescued your mother and killed Sarday. It was a pretty messy thing, and several hundred of Sarday's followers died. The official story was that they perished in a methane gas explosion. I want to talk to this retired chief of police who still lives in Johnsonville. Your grandmother gave me his name and address."

"How come you didn't say anything to me earlier?" I asked, definitely miffed.

"Sorry; I didn't think about it until we were airborne," said Mark. "Then as I was going over my notes, I realized that if we changed our flight right now, the bad guys who may be tracking us would not be able to react fast enough to stop us. I decided to ask the pilot if we could change our flight plan. He said it wasn't a problem." Mark looked pleased with the change of plans. "I'll do the same thing after we leave Charlottesville. Our destination will again be Spokane, and then we will change to Newburgh in the air. That should keep them guessing."

"OK," I said. "I now get Johnsonville, but why Newburgh, New York?"

"Actually we are going to Garrison, New York, to visit a retired general who was in Liberia when your dad and grandparents were there. It seems that six months before your parents disappeared in Liberia, your dad helped this general when he was stationed at West Point.

"According to your grandmother, it had something to do with what happened in Liberia, which again tells me that an *endosym* was somehow involved. I'm trying to gather enough evidence to see if I can shine some light on what happened to make your parents go into hiding. Hopefully, we'll be able to find out who ordered them killed."

"All right, Mark, you're forgiven, but I like to be informed," I said.

"Sorry, Amy; like I said, I hadn't really considered it until after we took off from Reagan."

Mark was right about it only taking twenty minutes to get to Charlottesville. As my second time landing in a plane, it was still exciting. Charlottesville Albemarle Airport was smaller than both Reagan National and Spokane International. We taxied past the main terminal and headed for the general aviation and executive terminal.

Our jet pulled up alongside a smaller Learjet. Emily opened the plane's door and extended the steps.

84

ONLY FOUR OR FIVE PEOPLE WERE IN THE TERMINAL. IT WAS COLD outside, and the skies were clear. We approached the counter. A woman in her midfifties asked if we needed fuel.

"No," said Kevin. "We should only be here on the ground for five or six hours."

"Is there a place where I can get a rental car?" asked Mark.

"Sure, I can call the main terminal and have them deliver one. Any preference?" asked the woman, whose nametag read JOAN BLUSHING.

"I would like a full-sized sedan," said Mark.

"Is there anywhere for our pilots to stay until we get back?" asked Mark.

"We have two options. I can arrange for a shuttle to a local motel for the pilots, or we have a lounge, showers, and a full-screen TV here," she said.

"We'll stay here," said Kevin.

"Great," said Mark.

Mark signed papers for the car, and we waited for it to show up.

"Do you have a map of the area?" asked Mark.

"Where are you going?" asked Joan.

"To Johnsonville," said Mark.

"The GPS navigation in the car will have the map," she said. "Not that many people go to Johnsonville in the winter. The large crowds come for the summer solstice on June twenty-first. Of course, people also come to the site of the Great Transformation at the start of the fall, winter, and spring seasons."

"What's the Great Transformation?" asked Mark.

"It's when the followers of Doctor Sarday vanished twenty-four years ago. I remember that day as if it were yesterday," said Joan.

"You worked here twenty-four years ago when it all happened?" ask Mark.

"I've been working for general aviation for thirty-two years," said Joan.

"Back then I was just an assistant. Richie Moore was my boss. He's been retired now for ten years," said Joan.

"It must have been quite an event," said Mark. "I was only in my early twenties and don't remember much about it."

"Oh, I will never forget the day that it happened. We felt the ground shake right here at the airport," said Joan.

"So what happened?" asked Mark.

"At first, it was so sad," said Joan. "All those rich and famous people were killed by a freak methane gas explosion. Apparently, Sarday's school was located on top of a large limestone cavern. Methane gas built up in the cavern and ignited. Hundreds died. They were never able to recover any of the bodies. Then New Age people began to come to the site, claiming it was the exact place where the ley lines converged, opening the door to the cosmos. Of course, I don't really believe all that, but it makes me feel better believing that all those poor people are now in a better place."

Joan went to the wall and took down a picture frame. Inside was a sheet of paper with what looked like an autograph. She handed it to me. Scrawled on the paper were the words To Joan, from your friend, Zack Trevor.

"Who's Zack Trevor?" I asked.

Joan looked at me, shocked at my ignorance.

"Oh, that was probably before you were born," she said. "Zack was a superhero movie actor. We all had crushes on Zack Trevor. I remember that day. Richie and I were working the desk. Zack flew his own Boeing 737. It parked right where your plane is now. It looked as big as a 747 jumbo jet when it rolled up next to our smaller corporate jets.

"On a normal Wednesday, the general aviation side of Charlottesville Albemarle Airport would have four or five corporate jets and a number of smaller aircraft parked on the tarmac. But on that day every slot was filled.

"Richie and I had watched a steady stream of the rich and famous arrive, disembark, and drive out in limos. We recognized the movie-star couple that adopted all those kids from Africa. Then there was that former action-hero-turned-producer. We also recognized a blond singer, but now I've forgotten her name. Leading this group of some of Hollywood's most famous personalities was Zack Trevor. Trevor himself owned at least a dozen planes and piloted his own 737.

"I remember when Zack came up to the counter. He was just like an ordinary person. He signed that autograph for me that day.

"We even saw Chuck Washburn, the famous producer. He was dying from cancer but was cured by Doctor Sarday. What a great man Doctor Sarday was! Of course, I never met him, but all the rich and famous came to his school. Had he lived, he would have been the next Martin Luther King Jr.

"Why are you going to Johnsonville, mister...?"

"Mark, Mark Sampson. This is my associate, Amy Johnson. We are considering investing in a real estate development in Johnsonville."

"That would be wonderful. After the Transformation, the town lacks enough motels to accommodate the summer visitors. It would be great to see some new motels. You know, the mayor and most of the city council also 'transformed' that day. The event really changed things here. Well, I hope you have a successful trip," she concluded. "Oh, here's your car."

"Wonderful!" said Mark. To me, he said, "Bring the cat."

I walked back out the door to the plane, got Mr. P out of his carrier, and hooked up his harness. We got ready to return to the terminal.

"I've never seen a cat on a leash before. Why, he acts just like a dog!" Joan commented.

"He's very well trained," said Mark. "We use him in our advertising, just like that insurance company with its digital gecko."

"Why don't you use a digital cat?" asked Joan.

"Oh, we do, but having a live cat for investment trips pays dividends," explained Mark.

"I never thought of that," said Joan.

Mark and I climbed into a white four-door sedan.

"Joan Blushing must be some kind of New Age loony," said Mark. "Never heard of this 'Transformation' site."

"Well, I guess you could call *endosyms* some kind of transformation," I said.

Mr. P cuddled on my lap and looked up at me affectionately.

"From bomb sniffer to TV personality—is that a promotion or demotion, cat?" I asked Mr. P as I patted his head and then scratched behind his ears.

Mark started the car, and we headed for our next stop—Johnsonville.

85

WE LEFT CHARLOTTESVILLE AND HEADED WEST. IN SPOKANE WE HAD pine trees. When we went into Idaho, we saw fir trees. In Charlottesville, most of the trees were maple and oak. The trees were bare of leaves in January. The hills were more rolling, less rugged. But at the same time the area where we were traveling was beautiful. I would have loved to see it in the summer.

We traveled Highway 64 through the Blue Ridge Mountains. Then we drove through the Staunton/Waynesboro metropolitan area, which looked about the size of Spokane. We continued west. It was now seven thirty, and the sun was coming up behind us. Ahead were the Alleghany Mountains.

Once we left the urban area, we traveled another fifteen miles and topped a hill. Below us was Johnsonville, Virginia. It was nestled in a valley. Part of the town was still hidden in the shadows of the hills.

We drove into town and stopped at a McDonald's for breakfast. I ordered an Egg McMuffin and a coffee. Mark ordered two Sausage Egg McMuffins and coffee. As we ate, Mark told me that the old police chief was a man named Brian Bishop. He and his wife lived just outside of town.

"Are you going to call them and tell them we're coming?" I asked.

"No," said Mark. "I've found that surprise is on your side when you arrive unannounced. Bishop has been retired for fifteen years. I doubt they are up and around at half past eight. We'll finish breakfast and get there by nine."

After breakfast we headed out to Bishop's house. It was only three miles from the McDonald's. We turned off on a paved dead-end road, drove about a half mile, and took a right into a cul-de-sac with three homes. On the right was a ranch-style home. A large metal garage sat to the right of the house.

We pulled up and started to get out of the car. When I opened the door, Mr. P bolted out of the car and ran up the walkway. He sat on the front porch.

"What in the world has gotten into that cat?" asked Mark.

"I don't know," I said. "Let me go get him."

I hurried up to the front porch to get my cat. As I bent over, the front door opened. Standing, looking out the glass storm door, was a thin, older man with white hair. He wore pajama bottoms, a white T-shirt, and slippers. He held a cup of coffee.

Talk about feeling stupid—I was at a stranger's front porch on my knees, trying to pick up a cat that was squirming and trying to get out of my hands. To add insult to injury, the man opened the door even wider, and Mr. P broke free and rushed inside the house.

By now, Mark was running up the sidewalk. This had turned into a disaster.

"I'm so sorry," I said. "My cat got away."

"Well, don't just stand there. Go get him," said the man.

I cautiously entered. Mark remained on the porch.

"Mr. P, you come here!" I demanded.

"What did you say?" asked the man, somewhat startled.

"Mr. P," I said. "My cat's name is Mr. P."

"Impossible," said the man. "Who are you anyway?"

Oh God, now what do I do? I told myself to think quickly. "My name is Anaya Martin. My dad was Tim Martin, and my mother was Samantha Dixon-Martin."

"That's not possible," said the man. "The Martins died eighteen years ago."

Just then a woman shouted from the kitchen.

"Brian, there is a gray cat in here! I swear to God he looks just like Mr. P."

Mark stepped in the front door.

"Chief Bishop, I'm Detective Mark Baker. This young woman is the Martins' daughter."

Brian Bishop took a second look at me.

"You do look like Samantha Dixon," he remarked.

"Care to tell me what's going on?" said an older woman with white hair who came out of the kitchen with Mr. P in her arms. *"I couldn't believe my eyes. I have never seen my cat that friendly with a stranger."*

She looked at us all standing there, not moving or speaking.

"Well, come into the living room," said Ann Bishop. "Let's sit down and sort this out." She put down my cat. He ran over to a stuffed chair and stretched out like he had always lived there.

For the next hour, Mark and I told the Bishops what had happened to bring us to them. Again, we left out the potential invasion of the *endosyms*.

Cop to cop, Mark did explain to Brian that he believed the murder of my parents was some kind of conspiracy linked to what happened in Johnsonville.

Although I explained that my dad had named my cat Mr. P, the Bishops were mystified by the fact that a gray cat named Mr. P had saved them from Sarday and his cult. That had happened when my dad and Brian Bishop had rescued mom from the endosym George Sarday over twenty-four years ago. When they had first acquired him, the cat was already old. He lived with them for six more years. One night, he simply disappeared. All that had happened eighteen years earlier. There was no way this could be the same cat.

For the next hour, Brian Bishop told us what had really happened at the place he called the Plantation. When Doctor George Nah Sarday, the leader of the New Age cult Dacari Mucomba purchased the old Johnson Plantation in Johnsonville, Virginia, as the site for the School for West African Spiritual Studies, no one had had a clue that so many lives would be changed.

When Brian stumbled onto the realization that human sacrifices were taking place at the Plantation, he was accused of dealing drugs. Then he was marked for assassination. Strangely, he found an unlikely ally in my dad, who at that time was a senior at the University of Virginia. When my mother and her brother were kidnapped by Sarday's cult, some retired Special Forces soldiers from Fort Bragg, North Carolina, helped Brian and my dad rescue them and stop Sarday.

At first Brian didn't know that they were dealing with what he ended up calling demonic possession. Sarday had sacrificed young acolytes from the school in a huge cavern while hundreds of his followers watched. Something or some substance had caused the rescue team to pass out as soon as they entered the cavern. He remembered very little of what had happened during that time. He did remember that the cat had been instrumental in turning the tables on Sarday.

He said that my dad had claimed he had killed Sarday. But as they were leaving this cavern, they all heard a voice in their heads saying, "Kill them." At first they were confused until they realized that that voice wasn't directing them—it was directing Sarday's followers.

Mark and I looked at each other. "Voices inside one's head" was a phrase all too familiar.

After rescuing Mom and her brother, they had run for their lives from Sarday's crazed followers, who acted like zombies. Brian said that my dad and he had been forced to kill dozens of the followers as they had tried to escape. He said that he had never told anyone this story. Some of the followers had been people he knew, and he still had nightmares about that night.

He added that the followers had superhuman strength. The only way to kill them had been by shooting them in their heads. *That's why the cop I shot didn't die,* I realized. The only way to kill one of them was with a headshot.

Finally, when they thought they had escaped, Oscar Jalah, Sarday's Liberian henchman, had confronted them. Some strange force had possessed Jalah, making him seem almost not human. *Obviously an endosym,* I concluded.

Several guards had accompanied Jalah, and it had looked like the rescue team was not going to survive. Then the cat had attacked Jalah. As

Jalah had struggled with the cat, my dad had jumped into the fight. But Jalah had overpowered Dad. Then Brian had shot Jalah with his pistol. When Jalah had died, the other evil men had just stood there as if Jalah had been controlling them with his mind. The team had confiscated their rifles. They had run for the helicopter that they had brought from Fort Bragg. They had all piled on board and had just taken off when a huge explosion occurred. Brian said it had been like a small nuclear bomb had gone off. Fire had consumed the buildings at the school and a huge sinkhole had appeared in the ground.

They had flown back to Fort Bragg. The people who had framed Brian were now dead and no proof existed that he had been involved with drugs. Brian had been reinstated as chief of police.

No one from the outside had ever known the true story of what had actually happened.

86

"WOULD IT BE POSSIBLE FOR US TO SEE THE SITE?" ASKED MARK.

"Sure," said Brian. "It's only a fifteen-minute drive from our house. I'll take you over there."

Brian drove Mark and me to where my dad had killed Sarday. He had a fifteen-year-old Jeep SUV. Mark rode in the front seat, and I sat in the back with Mr. P. To my surprise, Bishop didn't seem at all concerned that we were taking the cat with us.

Brian's wife, Ann, stayed home. Arthritis in her knees made walking quite a chore.

On the way, Brian gave us a brief history of the Plantation. It sat on sixty acres. The house was located at the end of old Johnson Road, seven miles from downtown Johnsonville. Twenty-four years ago when Sarday purchased the house, four thousand people lived in the town, which was named after its founder, Brigadier General Nathanial Johnson.

In 1842, Johnson and several other families settled in the valley.

Johnson was killed in the Battle of Shiloh. His oldest son tried to maintain the Plantation, but after the South's defeat and with the slaves freed, there was no labor to plant and harvest the crops. The Plantation, as a business, withered and died. The Johnson family became as poor as the former slaves who worked as sharecroppers.

In 1914, Walter Smith, an executive for Reynolds Tobacco, bought the property. The Smiths restored the Plantation to its original glory, but they elected to sell off all but sixty acres of the adjoining farmlands.

When the Great Depression occurred, Walter Smith, who had lost his fortune in the stock market, killed his wife and then committed suicide.

Their daughter and only child, Martha, returned to the Plantation after their deaths. She became a recluse. For seventy years, she seldom left. The townspeople called her Crazy Martha. Well into her nineties, fell down the basement stairs and broke her back.

The Smiths had no other children, and the Plantation remained vacant for years. It became a hangout for teenagers. Some fearfully tried to spend a night in what they considered a haunted plantation. Then twenty-seven years ago, six teenagers put on an all-night drug party. Something went wrong. Bad crack cocaine, too much booze, and a sharp Samurai sword somehow contributed to a ghastly scenario. The old kitchen became a blood bath. A search party eventually found the bodies—likely due to the horrible smell. The bodies had been in ninety-degree heat for five days.

The plantation house was labeled a crime scene and declared off-limits to trespassers. A distant relative made an attempt to unload it, offering it on the market at a reduced price of $2.2 million. Sarday bought the Plantation as soon as he saw the property. He put millions of dollars into refurbishing the main house and constructing additional facilities. One addition was a large pavilion that could be used for large gatherings or performances. He sought to recruit students for the School for West African Spiritual Studies.

87

WE DROVE THROUGH SEVERAL HOUSING DEVELOPMENTS, AND THEN we came to a fenced-in area. The eight-foot-high chain link fence hadn't been maintained. In a number of places, it had been knocked to the ground. A narrow, paved road lead up to the remains of the school. Surprisingly, the road was in pretty good shape.

Brian explained that because of the fixation on the disappearance of Sarday's cult, the city limited the number of people permitted on the road. A reasonable effort was made to locate any heirs. Eventually, the city assumed control of the property. The parks department did minimum maintenance on the road, kept the trails open, and placed garbage barrels at viewpoints.

We pulled into a grassy clearing. It was large enough to park hundreds of cars in. Patches of dried grass poked up through the melting snow. Overflowing garbage barrels sat on wide places along the shoulder. A number of collapsed buildings huddled together in a low spot. At one time, this was an impressive campus. Now it was only haphazard piles of broken lumber. Fences circled the deteriorating buildings. Signs nailed to the leaning fence posts explained the buildings' former uses.

"The city has capitalized on the stories of the cult transforming to another world. Now the community makes lots of money from the gawkers," said Brian. "Of course, it's all hocus-pocus, but the tourists love it."

We walked to the ruins of the Johnson house. On a signpost was a picture of the remodeled house before it had been destroyed. There was nothing left but a hole in the ground filled with debris.

I had my cat on his leash. He kept pulling on the leash and looking to the left.

"That's the old slave quarters," said Brian, pointing ahead. "Behind us is the old Negro cemetery."

"I wonder..." He paused. "If you let the cat go, will he run away?"

"No; he never has before," I said.

"Let him go, and let's follow him. I believe you will be surprised," said Brian.

"OK," I agreed.

When I released his harness, the cat raced off behind the ruins of the old slave quarters. An old cemetery lay behind the quarters. Mr. P ran through the gate along the row of tombstones. He sat down in front of one of the markers. I checked out the engraving. The name read MICHELLE JOHNSON.

"That's Grandma Johnson's grave," said Brian. "She was ninety-eight years old when she died. She was a midwife and healer for those too poor to receive treatment from a doctor. Many believed she was a witch. Mr. P lived with Grandma Johnson before he moved in with us."

I thought of my dream where I saw that old lady in Africa. The old woman had laughed about Mr. P being with me.

"What happened to her?" I asked.

"She died of a heart attack," said Brian. "On her deathbed, she told her grandson that he had to find your dad. She kept with her a strange statue of a demon."

"A statue?" asked Mark. "What did it look like?"

"It was weird. It was about ten inches tall and had horns and a tail. Your dad said that his dad had one just like it," said Brian.

"Could we see it?" asked Mark.

"If I had it, of course you could," said Brian. "Unfortunately, it was stolen from our house about ten years ago."

I had to stop and think about this. Both my grandmother and now Brian Bishop say that the statues were stolen about the same time. I wondered what was going on with these statues.

"Anyway," said Brian, "after Grandma Johnson died her grandson took her cat. When Sarday's henchmen tried to kill us, Ann hid out with Grandma Johnson's grandson and his wife while Tim and I went to Fort Bragg. During that time the cat kind of adopted Ann. That's why we had him for six years. I know that this is impossible, but I believe that this is the same cat."

"If it is," said Mark, "this has got to be the oldest cat in the world."

"Could be just a coincidence," I said. Even as I said it, I was pretty sure that my cat had been here before. This whole story was getting more and more eerie.

88

WE WALKED AROUND THE RUINS, READING THE SIGNS IDENTIFYING the purpose of each building.

"You still haven't seen the main attraction," Brian said.

He led us behind the old Johnson house, down the hill, and to a small stream. A bridge had been built over the water, and a smooth gravel pathway led to the top of the hill. The two of us, plus Mr. P, followed Brian. As we crested the hill, we came to an abrupt halt. Both Mark and I stood speechless. No one could have prepared us for the enormity of the event.

The crater was more than a mile in diameter. Its depth exceeded seven hundred feet. In the twenty-four years since the explosion, brush and trees had grown up along its sides, but nothing grew in the center.

Smoke rose from the crater's center.

"What is it, a volcano?" asked Mark.

"No, it's the crater created when the cavern collapsed," Brian answered. "The smoke comes from the burning coal vein. It has burned continuously for twenty years. That's why the New Age movement is so mesmerized by this place. It's so big that you can see this gigantic hole from the International Space Station. The believers say that this is one of those special places on the earth like Stonehenge in England or Machu Picchu in Peru."

I stood mesmerized, staring into the crater. I didn't know if it was the effects of the fumes or the fact that I had had little sleep, but I suddenly I started feeling dizzy.

"I don't feel too good," I said. "Do you mind if I sit down for a few minutes?"

Mark looked at me, suddenly worried.

"Let's get back to the car," he said.

"No, I'll be fine if I sit down for a while."

"OK," said Mark. "Brian and I are going to walk around the rim of the crater. You should be able to see us. If something happens, just yell for us."

I sat down on a flat slab of rock. Mr. P jumped in my lap and stared into my eyes.

It began to feel like twilight, although it was only around one o'clock in the afternoon.

I squinted to check the position of the sun. It still shone brightly overhead.

I felt sleepy, and I closed my eyes.

89

A FLASH OF BRIGHT LIGHT MADE ME SUDDENLY ALERT. I TRIED TO move, yet I couldn't force my body to work for me. I also couldn't hear anything. I sat in the silence. Finally, I seemed to move along, but not out of my own volition. I couldn't do anything but watch what was occurring before me. I felt as if I was sitting in an IMAX surround-sound theater. I had no choice but to allow the camera to carry me through an adventure. My head seemed locked in a vise, and my eyes felt like they had been taped open.

There was no color. The scene was like a sepia photograph. I moved through a yellow-brown forest of huge trees with twenty-foot-wide trunks. Then my body entered a clearing where an old house stood at the end of a wide, paved road.

Was this the Johnson house before it was destroyed? As I moved closer, the steps leading up to the main door seemed out of proportion. At first, each step seemed exceptionally high—perhaps four-feet tall for each one. The front door stood wide open.

I slipped into the house through the doorway. Although there was less light inside, everything stood out in sharp contrast. A chair fit for a giant stood alone in the hallway. To the right was a ceiling-to-floor mirror that exceeded three stories in height. The scene paused in front of the mirror for a moment. Looking out from the mirror was a large gray cat, identical to my own Mr. P. Suddenly I realized there was nothing behind the cat—I must have been seeing all this through the cat's eyes.

That's why everything seemed so out of proportion. The visions flowed before me through the cat's eyes. I wondered if that was the way the demon sees the world—looking at its surroundings through the eyes of the possessed human being as they become an *endosym*.

But why can't I control the scene or speak or move? Perhaps it's because I'm seeing something that happened in the past. I guess all I can do is go along for the ride. The scene moved down a hallway to a kitchen. Again, although unlighted and without color, everything stood out sharp and clear. That must have been because cats can see in the dark.

We—the cat and I—moved toward an open door that led to the basement. We entered a large, open room. Flickering candles marked out a pathway to a wall. A slight push allowed another door to rotate, revealing a tunnel that sloped downward. We quickly moved along the tunnel and came to another set of steps leading even more deeply into the earth. We hurried down those steps and continued through the narrow tunnel.

Candlelight was our only source of illumination. There was no sound. I assumed I could only see, not hear, what was happening. The tunnel went deeper and deeper into the earth before widening into a natural underground cavern. Mr. P could see far ahead into the darkness. We saw a maze of stalactites and stalagmites and pools of water on both sides of us. If there had been sound, I imagined we would have heard the drip-drip of water in the darkness. We were able to make out wet footprints from bare feet on the ground. Then there were no more candles, but the walls glowed brightly, and we could see a great distance before us.

We rounded a corner and discovered a gigantic underground limestone cave. In the center of the cave were hundreds of naked people, standing with their backs to us. We ran forward to join the crowd. From a cat's height, the people's legs looked as big as tree trunks. We ran in and out among the legs, finally bursting through the crowd. We took up a position at the front of the group. We saw a stone altar.

A black-hooded figure held a sword in its right hand. More people in black robes and hoods stood near the altar. With our superb eyesight, we saw the faces of the men and women.

My stomach churned as I watched two of the hooded individuals pick up a headless corpse. A pile of naked, headless bodies of men and women were stacked like firewood behind the altar. Blood flowed freely from the altar top and formed rivulets on the cavern floor. I tried to close my eyes to avoid the gory scene, but I was frozen in place. I couldn't do anything but watch through the cat's eyes.

At the end of the altar was a hideous statue, resembling a dwarf demon. Protruding from the top of its head were two horns, one on each side. The face had thick ridges on the brow line. It looked similar to an artist's depiction of a Neanderthal. Large yellowed buckteeth stuck out from the grinning mouth. Blood covered the eye sockets, hiding any expression.

Far worse than the decapitated bodies were the severed heads that were loosely stacked in a basket that sat between the statue and the altar. Some of the heads had rolled out or had been kicked out of the way. Some sat scalp up; some lay on an ear; and some exposed a severed neck. Like rotting fruit, the useless skulls no longer served any purpose.

In a brilliant flash of light, we caught a glimpse of a bolt of lightning making a direct strike on the altar. What appeared to be a dark circle formed behind the altar. No, that wasn't true. I squinted. It wasn't a simple circle; it appeared to be the opening of a large pipe. It must have been twenty-five feet in diameter. We were drawn to a light coming from inside the pipe. It seemed to beckon us to enter. We stepped inside.

One moment we were in the cavern; the next moment we had entered another world. We saw a rugged terrain, similar to an arid desert landscape. Strange, deformed trees towered high above us. On the horizon we saw double moons. We looked up in the sky toward the sun. But it wasn't our sun. It was huge: three times the size of our sun, but not nearly as bright. I assumed that it was an older sun giving off less energy. This planet was much closer to its sun than earth was to our own sun.

We continued to climb a small hill until we were able to see a substantial village in the valley before us. Each building was of a different size and shape. The dwellings had rock walls and irregular openings that I assumed were windows.

There were people milling about. Running heedlessly down the hill, we saw that these beings were not humans, but the demon-like creatures that inhabit human bodies to become *endosyms*. We ran down an irregular path that served as a street. We were close enough to see the physical anatomy of these naked beings. Their skin was grey. They had two horns poking from large bald-heads. Their bodies were completely hairless and appeared human in shape except for the tails that came out of their back above their butts and trailed on the ground. Males, females, and children lived with no tools or modern inventions. They were more primitive than even the most remote villages on earth. I wondered how these primitive creatures could be invading a civilization as sophisticated as ours.

We passed calmly through the primitive town. Children played a running game, kicking an object ahead of them. As we approached, we discovered that it wasn't a ball—their plaything was a human skull. We neared what appeared to be a coliseum and entered through a large crack in the wall. Inside, we saw holding pens that contained domestic animals. But on closer examination, we saw that they weren't animals—they were male and female humans who wore the skins of animals.

The humans looked like images of the Neanderthals that disappeared from earth more thousands years ago. I wondered about their "disappearance," assuming that they were somehow "transferred" to this strange world.

The creatures ignored us as we explored the area. We moved carefully and discovered a location that allowed us to look back into the center of the amphitheater. The seating area around us was composed of crudely built stands. An audience of demons of all ages and both genders sat quietly as if waiting for the action to begin.

Being led to the altars was a number of the Neanderthals. They were controlled by their own kind. I suspected that the possessed beings were *endosyms*.

As the Neanderthals lined up and came forward, they were individually forced to kneel at the altar. Three demons, each carrying a sharp instrument, beheaded the unfortunate victims. I tried to turn away, but I had no control of what I saw. As a head was severed from its body, a light—the person's essence—arose from the body. So many sacrifices had been made here that a fog of essences filled the stagnant air in the arena. Members of the crowd seemed to absorb this essence.

We turned and ran back toward the hill where we had first entered this world. Standing near the black hole were three of the demon-creatures. Two of them were male and one was a female. Two of them were shorter and appeared younger. The other, older and more imposing, was obviously in charge. The three appeared to be deeply involved in discussion.

We slipped back unseen through the hole between the two worlds. We were once again in the cavern, running through the legs of the naked worshipers. We saw five humans lying on the ground. They wore police-style uniforms, and they had helmets on their heads like those seen in photos of SWAT teams.

We ran up to one of the humans and began licking its face. I recognized him instantly. It was my dad. Only much younger.

Dad opened his eyes and slowly got to his feet. We turned and ran back toward the worshipers. We kept looking back to see if Dad had followed us. We ran out of the crowd toward two people—one was a young black man; the other was my mother. They were both in some kind of trance. As we watched, one of the robed figures reached out and took my mother's hand. Dad lunged ahead to separate them.

As Dad grabbed the figure, its hood fell back, and I saw that the creature inside was a woman. The glow of her eyes revealed that she was under the influnce of an endosym. Dad quickly assumed a defensive martial arts posture. The creature didn't stop her attack. She charged, driving him back. It seemed that Dad was incapable of stopping her. Finally, he struck her on the jaw. She went down and didn't get up.

Dad turned and tried to get Mom's attention, but she just stared straight ahead. She seemed unaware that Dad was even there.

Other robed figures approached him. Dad pulled out his pistol and fired a shot into the first one. The round knocked it over backward, but it stumbled and then quickly got to its feet. In an effort to gain the upper hand, Dad aimed at the dark hole in the hood where the face should have been, and he fired again. When it went down, it didn't get up.

Dad didn't hesitate—he pointed the weapon to the right and took on two more of the hooded figures that had approached simultaneously.

The headshots threw both backward, and they crumpled to the ground. Then the creature wielding a sword charged. I could see the aura around its body. It was an *endosym*. Dad was knocked backward. The impact was so great that for several seconds, Dad didn't move. We saw the flash of a sword through the air as the *endosym* tried to make contact once again. Dad rolled on the ground just as the sword's blade struck inches from his shoulder. He scrambled to his feet and whirled to catch another glimpse of a sword that whizzed by his left ear. Dad ducked and fired his pistol. He missed. Dad kept fighting, but his opponent was too strong. Dad slipped and landed on his back. The *endosym* raised the sword, ready to make the kill.

We rushed toward the *endosym* and flew through the air, landing on its hidden face. We saw only a blur of blood and claws as we tore at the creature's face. We were again flying through the air before we submerged into the crowd of worshipers. Too many legs obstructed our field of vision. We couldn't see what happened. Finally, the area cleared, and we saw my dad and mom with the young black man make their way through the crowd.

We followed them back where the other men lay. The men twisted and turned, apparently beginning to wake up. Once they finally got to their feet, Dad spoke to them. He finished, and then everyone turned and ran away. One of the men with Dad fell down. It seemed like something was wrong with his ankle. He rubbed it with his hand. He tried to stand, but he couldn't support the weight on his leg. He sat back down. He was now alone at the back of the cavern.

The *endosym* staggered to his feet with the sword embedded in his body and looked toward the opening to the other world. We followed his gaze. The three demons stepped out of the hole between the two worlds. The *endosym* pointed his finger toward us, and all the worshipers turned and started to come our way.

Six hundred naked people chased after us. The man with the injured ankle was trapped on the floor, unable to escape. He carried a funny looking gun. He put a large shell in the gun and aimed it over the heads of the advancing worshipers. We saw a flash as the gun fired. We looked up. The round hit the ceiling of the cavern and exploded. Then pieces of the ceiling began to tumble around us. Cracks opened up overhead.

90

"AMY, ARE YOU OK?"

"What?" I opened my eyes. I was sitting on the edge of the crater. Both Brian and Mark looked closely at me. "I'm OK," I said. "Just haven't gotten much sleep lately."

"We're ready to leave," said Mark. "Do you need any help?"

"No," I said with determination. I put Mr. P on the ground and stood up. We headed back to Brian's car.

I sighed with relief as we drove back to civilization.

While Brian drove and chatted with Mark in the front seat of the Jeep, it was just Mr. P and me sitting in the back. The cat stretched out beside me, appearing totally calm and content despite what we had just experienced. I took advantage of this opportunity to think through the past months. From Spokane to Johnsonville, my life had certainly taken a surprising twist. A year ago I never would have expected to have an out-of-body experience like I just had. But I could not deny that something strange had occurred. I had experienced a dream sequence far removed from reality.

I looked down at my left hand. I had been chewing on the knuckle of my ring finger—an old habit I'd had since I was ten years old. I resorted to this thoughtless action when I was upset or bothered by something.

"Amy, get your hand out of your mouth!" my mother always said, eventually wearing me down. She told me that she had spent a fortune on braces and that this bad habit might change the alignment of my front teeth. It also didn't look good on my hand, as the knuckle was often red. Her persistence had paid off, and my knuckle stayed out of my mouth for the most part. But Mom was gone, and I didn't have her to say those words. I wiped the tears from my eyes, wishing I had the comfort that only comes from a mother's love.

"Brian?" I said.

"Yes, Amy?"

"When you and Dad were in the cavern, was there any lightning?" I asked.

"Yeah, I forgot about that. It was really weird. As we got closer to the cavern, we could feel the static electricity in the air. When we escaped, bolts of lightning crashed from the ceiling directly to the ground in front of the crowd. Despite the fact that we were going the other way, the lightning seemed to intensify. We could hear the cracking sound when it touched ground," Brian said. "Why do you ask?"

"I was just trying to figure out what caused the explosion of the methane gas," I said.

I brought my knuckle back to my mouth. So, there was lightning flashing just like I saw in the vision. OK, what else had I seen that Brian forgot to mention? Oh, yes, the old man shooting the strange gun. It had looked like he was going to get himself killed.

"Brian, did you lose anyone from your team when you got away from Sarday?"

"Yeah, we lost Bill Catfield," Brian said, turning around to look at me. I could tell that the death of this man still bothered Brian. "We probably shouldn't have taken him. He had problems seeing at night. Then he sprained his ankle, but he kept trying to keep up. When we were running through the caves, we heard an explosion from an M203 grenade."

"What's that?" I asked.

"It's a high-explosive round fired from a launcher below the barrel of the rifle. Anyway, Bill had wanted an assault rifle with a grenade launcher. The rest of us didn't think it would be needed. When we heard the explosion, we realized that Bill wasn't with us. We turned to go back to see what had happened when we heard automatic weapons fire. Bill was firing his assault rifle on full automatic.

"Then there was a scream followed by silence. Tiny, one of the other Non Commissioned Officers, insisted that we go back to find Bill. We hadn't gone very far when we saw the worshipers coming after us. We didn't think twice. We ran for our lives. You'd never think that a bunch of old guys like that could run so fast.

"It's hard to lose a member of the team. Until Tiny Sprague and Mike Kellogg died several years ago, we would try to get together once a year to toast Bill Catfield. Now I'm the only one left," said Brian.

"I'm sorry," I said.

I brought my knuckle back to my tooth. Oh my God, what I had seen in my dream really did happen. The other world and those demons were part of the story. A door opened between worlds, and the evil creatures tried to enter our world. Somehow, another opening must exist. That's why we had seen the *endosyms* in Washington, DC.

91

We pulled up in front of the Bishops' home. Ann had made submarine sandwiches, opened some chips, and popped a few beers for the guys and a soda for me. After lunch we said our good-byes.

"You take care of Mr. P," Ann said as she hugged me. "I loved my Mr. P."

She wasn't done yet. She turned to Brian.

"I want another cat, a gray cat."

"We don't need a cat," said Brian.

"Well, I'm getting a cat."

"We'll talk about it," said Brian.

As we drove off, Mark said, "He'll lose. Men always do."

On the drive back to the airport, I told Mark what had happened to me while he and Brian walked around the crater. One thing I like about Mark is that he believes me without question.

"Jesus, they sound like sharks," said Mark.

"Sharks? I don't understand what you mean," I replied.

"Whatever kind of creature they are, they only care about their place in the food chain. Just like sharks, they attack for the bloody pleasure of killing.

"You said this world, or whatever it is, is very primitive. No electricity, no TVs, no cars or anything modern. You said that they don't even wear clothes, yet the Neanderthals or whatever those human types were wore animal skins. The demons seem to only want to kill for the victims' essences. Is that the plan for those of us who will not serve the *endosyms*? They offer wealth or power to humans who are willing to serve them, then those humans look the other way as the rest of our race is enslaved and killed."

"I hope you're wrong," I said. Yet I had a gut feeling that Mark had hit the nail on the head.

Mark had called our pilots, and the plane was ready when we got to the airport. Joan Blushing helped check us out, and we paid for the rental car.

"Was your trip successful?" she asked.

"Very successful," said Mark.

"I hope you can build some new motels," she said.

"We'll see," said Mark.

Mr. P stood beside me on his leash. He'd been wanting to stay close to me.

"Can I pet him?" asked Joan.

"Sure," I said.

She started to reach for the cat. He let out a low growl.

"Whoa, he doesn't seem to like me," said Joan, pulling back quickly.

"Oh, he has an upset stomach," I said.

"Well, we're off to Spokane, Washington. Should be there in six hours," said Mark.

"Well, you have a good trip," said Joan.

"What was that all about?" I asked Mark as we walked to our plane.

"I don't know," he said. "Did she look funny, like she was possessed or something?"

"No," I said, "but Mr. P is a good judge of character."

As I climbed up the steps, I looked back at the terminal. Joan had her cell phone to her ear as she watched us board.

I was beginning to be as paranoid as Mark.

92

I STOOD AT THE WINDOW OF MY ROOM ON THE SIXTH FLOOR OF THE Hilton Garden Inn. I could see the runway lights of Stewart International Airport in Newburgh, New York.

It was five thirty in the morning and not yet light outside. I had already showered, dressed, and began to apply my makeup. We planned to meet at the hotel restaurant at seven o'clock for breakfast. Then we would head for Garrison, New York, which was about a thirty-minute drive from the Hilton. Mark had told General Parkinson that we would arrive around ten o'clock.

I would still be sleeping if it hadn't been for the dream. Maybe something I ate had disagreed with me. I had gone to bed before midnight. I had texted Sherry throughout our trip, just as if she were a younger sister.

Of course, I only told her about the good things. Meeting my grandmother, our visit to Washington, DC, and meeting Ambassador Weah and his family were all highlights. Obviously, you wouldn't tell your thirteen-year-old sister that our planet has been invaded by some kind of demon-creatures from another world, that my cat had morphed into a monster, or that I was almost killed.

We had come into Stewart International yesterday at five o'clock. According to Kevin, Stewart was a former air force base. It had been converted to a civilian airport in 1991. The airport had been designated as an international airport because it handles passengers, airfreight, and livestock. It is the state of New York's animal import center.

After we landed, we rented two cars. One was for the pilots, and the other one for Mark and me. We checked into the Hilton, which was adjacent to the airport.

The four of us met for dinner in the hotel's dining room. After dinner we stopped by the bar to listen to the live music. We ordered drinks. I stuck with diet Coke.

It was actually fun. I sat in a bar with three adults and talked about adult stuff. Actually, I spent most of the time listening to the three of them. Kevin had worked for Executive Air Jets for twenty-five years. God, he had been flying for more years than I had been alive. He already had grandchildren. He had lived in Spokane all of his life, only leaving for a tour in the air force where he flew C-17 cargo jets.

Emily Ferguson's life was far more interesting. She had just started working for Executive Air Jets. She was thirty-two years old and had graduated from the US Air Force Academy. When the air force was looking for female pilots to fly the new Raptor supersonic fighter, she applied and was accepted into the program. She flew a jet fighter that could exceed two thousand miles per hour. It had the most sophisticated weapons systems in the world.

She had fought in the Middle East wars, shooting down four enemy fighters in aerial combat. During one encounter, her plane was hit with shrapnel from the exploding enemy jet, and she lost power. She had to bail out over enemy territory. She escaped capture and was rescued a week later by a special operations force sent to find her.

She was married to a fellow air force pilot. Her husband, Ted, was the wing commander at Fairchild. Rather than be separated, she resigned her commission from the air force last year and was hired by Executive Air Jets. She was really a cool woman. I couldn't imagine the things that she had done. Her life seemed so exciting. By the time we left the bar, she definitely had gained a fan.

What was really neat was that Mark had suggested that she might consider coming to work for Baker Security. He had considered purchasing a helicopter and would need to hire experienced pilots. What almost embarrassed me was the fact that when he suggested she consider his offer, he looked at her and then nodded at me.

"My partner, Amy, and I would sure like to have you on our team."

Whoa! Is that ever neat! I thought. *Here I am offering "Wonder Woman" to come and work for me.*

It turned out the Hilton had no problem with accommodating Mr. P. Since people fly with their pets all the time, more and more hotels were allowing pets. So Mr. P joined me as we looked out the hotel window. The two of us watched the outside lights as a large jumbo jet came in for a night landing. It wasn't like watching birds fly around outside a bedroom window, but Mr. P still found it entertaining. Finally, I had enough and curled up on the king-sized bed and dozed off.

But my sleep didn't last long.

Once again I had one of those crazy dreams. Considering what had happened during the week, it was really going to take something to make it into the crazy category. But I couldn't make any sense of this one. It scared me so much I couldn't get back to sleep. In my dream, which couldn't have lasted very long, I saw a man carrying a canvas-like bundle out of a house. He moved through a low-lying fog. It was a colonial-style house, just two stories high. The entrance was made of cobblestones. By the way the man was dressed, it looked like he was an actor in a scene from colonial Williamsburg. Several years ago, I'd seen a documentary on the History Channel about life in colonial times. He could have played a starring role.

Chills ran down my spine every time I recalled what happened next. The man was driving a horse-drawn wagon. Other men forced him to come to a stop. They inspected the back of the wagon and apparently didn't like what they saw. They yanked the man from the wagon, bound his hands, and set him on horseback. They took him to a nearby oak tree. A thick rope was fashioned into a noose and placed around the man's neck. When they threw the rope over a limb, it became clear they intended to hang him right then. Another man in the group pulled out his whip and struck the horse's rump. In the split second between the crack of the whip and the snap of the rope, the victim turned and looked directly at me. I knew instantly that he was an *endosym*, and I knew that he hated me with a passion I'd never seen before. The nightmare seemed so real. I couldn't seem to shake the image of that evil look in his eyes even after waking.

I turned from the window and walked into the bathroom and cleaned out Mr. P's cat box. I closed the portable cat box, washed my hands, and applied my makeup. I decided to wear the small pearl earrings I'd brought from home. We were meeting a retired general, and I wanted to be dressed more formally. I closed up my Tote Bag and set everything next to the door. I assured Mr. P that I would be back for him after breakfast. I then took the elevator to the lobby.

I was the first of our group to arrive, so I wandered over to a stand that displayed tourist brochures. I was shocked when I saw a photograph of the house from my dream.

Under the photograph the caption called it the McDougal House, and it expressed a greeting to all tourists: "Welcome old and new occult practitioners to a unique opportunity."

Inside, it gave more information:

Only four miles north of Newburgh, New York, off of Highway 87, the McDougal House offers the believer a unique experience. The spiritually enlightened may relax with a cup of herbal tea, have a tarot reading, and shop for books, herbs, candles, organic soap, crystals, tarot decks, incense, and much more. Come any time! Visitors are always welcome.

I folded the brochure, put it in my purse, and headed for the dining room. Emily, Kevin, Mark, and I took our seats and ordered breakfast. After breakfast, Emily and Kevin planned to take our luggage to the plane. Mr. P would go with Mark and me to visit General Parkinson.

We intended to fly out of Stewart that afternoon. I brought my cat down to the lobby in my arms. Once outside, I took him for a short walk on his leash. When we got in the car, I turned to Mark.

"Would you mind taking a short detour before we head off to Garrison?"

"Sure," said Mark. "Where?" I pulled out the brochure for the McDougal House.

We followed the directions from the brochure and pulled up a dirt road. The house looked exactly like the one in my dream.

"All right, Amy, what's going on?" Mark asked.

I told him about my dream and the fact that this house looked just like the one in the dream. It also seemed to be too much of a coincidence that the house sold things used in witchcraft.

"After what we've been through, I suppose anything is possible," Mark concluded. "I'll go with you."

"No, that will make them suspicious. I need to go alone."

"All right," said Mark. "But take your cat."

"What if they won't let me bring Mr. P into the house?" I asked.

"Amy, they sell occult stuff. Tell them that you are a practicing witch, and the cat is your familiar."

"You're serious?" I asked.

"Yes," said Mark. "The cat will warn you if there is an *endosym* in there. If you sense anything dangerous, get out of there fast."

"I'll be OK," I assured him.

I hooked the leash to Mr. P's harness. He walked beside me just like an obedient dog. I looked down at Mr. P.

"Well, cat, you've been downgraded from a morphing killer saber-tooth cat to just my familiar."

93

THE HOUSE WAS OF THE SALTBOX DESIGN WITH A WIDE FRONT PORCH. The windows were small with leaded glass, maybe the originals from the time of the Revolution. The red door was tall, maybe eight feet, and decorated with a white pentagram. Crystals dangled in the windows. I rapped the large brass knocker to let the proprietor know I was there.

After two knocks, the door opened slowly. A young woman about my age stood before me. She had a tattoo of a pentagram on her forehead. For jewelry she wore nose and eye rings. No pink or coral lip gloss—she wore a thick, black lipstick.

"Hi," she said. "Welcome to McDougal House." She looked at Mr. P. "Cool cat. Please come in."

Mr. P and I stepped into the entryway. Right away, I smelled a strong odor of incense. The lighting was dimmed, and it took my eyes a moment to adjust. I felt like I had just stepped into the eighteenth century. There were no electric lights, only candles.

We walked into what was once the living room. It was stocked with all kinds of occult things for sale.

"My name's Sabrina. What's yours?" asked the girl.

"Amy," I said.

"Mom's gone to Scotland to meet with my father and won't be back until next week. But I can sell you things. So how can I help you?" she asked.

"I saw your brochure at the hotel and just had to visit," I said.

"Oh, wonderful! Let me show you our house."

In the living room were at least a half dozen small tables, indicating that this was also a café.

"Would you like a cup of tea?" asked Sabrina.

"Oh, no thank you. I can only stay a few minutes. I have a meeting at ten," I said.

"Well, at least let me show you where it all began," said Sabrina.

"Began?" I asked.

"Haven't you read our blog?" she asked.

"No," I said.

"Oh dear, you need to do that. Just go online and type in 'end days,'" said Sabrina.

"OK," I said with a smile. "What does 'end days' mean?"

"Why, when the horned gods claim earth," she said as if I should have known what she was talking about. I checked out Mr. P to see if he was displaying any warning signs. His tail had not blown up, but I assure you, every hair on my arms stood up. I tried to remain calm.

"I'm rather new to Wicca," I said. "Perhaps you can briefly tell me what's going on. Then I can get the rest of the information from the Internet."

"Of course, silly of me to assume you knew about Duncan. Let me explain his role in opening the door to the other world," said Sabrina.

"Duncan McDougal lived in this very house until the Reverend Samuel Marsh hanged him on March 28, 1779. Most agree that Duncan was the greatest warlock to ever live.

"He was a genius who was on the verge of opening the door to the other world. He had learned that five statues of the horned god had been created thousands of years ago. Anyone who possesses a statue is able to communicate with the horned god. If ever someone managed to possess all five, that person would have immense powers.

"If all five statues were placed on the points of the pentagram that had been drawn on sacred earth at precisely where the ley lines converge, a window would open and the horned god would appear at that spot and claim his kingdom."

"How do you know all of this?" I asked, unable to grasp all that she said. It seemed too overwhelming to imagine that we were that close to unlocking this mystery.

"My great-great-great-grandmother was a member of his coven. Duncan had started the process of revealing these secrets when a member of the coven betrayed him. Twenty men led by Reverend Marsh hanged Duncan. He was buried in an unmarked grave at what is now West Point. Andrew Wyatt, the silversmith, created a large silver cross that was placed on Duncan's coffin. It would keep his soul captured for eternity. But once again, this was not to be. The women of the coven excavated his remains and hid them in a secret place.

"They passed down the story of that fateful night, confident that Duncan would rise again. That fateful day occurred nineteen years ago. Duncan now rules the Covens of the New Order from his castle in Scotland. He is my father. I have just turned eighteen. When Mother returns, I will go to Father's castle and become one with the horned gods. He has told his followers that on December twenty-first of this year, a New Order will begin, and the horned gods will once again claim their kingdom on earth.

"But you need to get back to your coven and let them know that only the true believers will be saved," Sabrina cautioned me. She apparently feared for the fate of earth's people.

Sabrina's story didn't include anything that we had not heard before. There were all kind of nuts predicting the end of the world. For example, I remembered reading an article about a prophecy of the Second Coming of Christ on May 21, 2011. According to the believers, the Rapture would occur on that day, and on October 31, 2011, the world would end. People sold their homes, quit paying their debts, and waited for that day to come. May 21 came and went. In October, a number of the followers committed suicide.

Anyone listening to Sabrina would have dismissed her rants as just another wild prophecy. But I had seen the *endosyms* and had experienced the other world. All this was going to happen.

"Gee, Sabrina, I really appreciate the information. I'll get together with my coven as soon as I get home. Thank you for your time," I said.

I purchased two small crystals and a scented candle. I paid in cash. Then Mr. P and I headed back to the car.

As I slid in the front seat, Mark asked, "Find out anything?"

"I'm not sure," I said. "Let's visit General Parkinson. Then I'll tell you whether this has anything to do with what I think is happening."

Unfortunately, in my mind, I had no doubt that I had found the man responsible for the murder of my parents.

That person was someone named Duncan McDougal.

94

MARK PROGRAMMED IN THE DIRECTIONS TO GENERAL PARKINSON'S
house on the car's navigation system. We left the McDougal House and
turned back south on 9W to Interstate 84. We then headed east on 84
and crossed the Newburgh Beacon Bridge over the Hudson River. Mark
paid the bridge toll and exited onto State Route 9D going south toward
Garrison. We passed through the towns of Beacon, Nelsonville, and Cold
Spring. All were small whistle-stops along the road. I'd never been in this
part of the country, so I didn't realize how rural New York State could be.
We made good time despite the fact that it was snowing lightly. It still
wasn't sticking to the road.

I should have been enjoying the view, but I could not get Sabrina's
story out of my mind. It began to seem possible that this Duncan
McDougal could be more than two hundred years old. Obviously, an
endosym was using the covens to create havoc on December 21.

I had to admit that Mark's conspiracy theory about the *endosyms'* infiltration of all levels of government was sounding more and more feasible.
It was a potentially successful strategy for taking over the world.

We turned right onto County Road 14. After about a mile, it turned
in to Upper Station Road. We got to the top of a hill, and I was surprised
to see an oceangoing freighter on the Hudson River this far into the rural
countryside.

"The river carries ocean ships all the way to the capital, Albany,"
commented Mark who must have noticed my amazement.

On the other side of the river were huge granite buildings. At first I
thought we were looking at a factory or industrial area.

"What's that?" I asked.

"West Point," said Mark. "That's the United States Military Academy."

"I didn't realize it was so big," I remarked.

"It's been there two hundred years. During the Revolutionary War, several forts were built on the site. They were defensive fortifications to prevent the British from coming up the Hudson River to Albany."

Mark slowed the car and turned left onto a single-lane paved road that wound along the tops of the hills. We drove about a half mile and came to an impressive house. One side was nearly all windows that looked out across the Hudson. The place also had a clear view of the military academy.

"General Parkinson was the dean of West Point before he retired. I guess he wanted a house where he could always stand watch over the academy," said Mark.

I nodded. "It's a beautiful place."

A circular driveway made a loop in front of the house. We pulled up and got out.

"You stay in the car," I told Mr. P. The cat yawned and stretched out on the backseat. We walked up the wide front steps to the porch. Mark rang the doorbell.

A tall African American opened the door. He wore a black sweater, black slacks, and spit-polished shoes. His white hair was closely cut to his head. He stood ramrod straight.

"General Parkinson?" Mark asked reaching out to shake hands. "I'm Mark Baker, and this is Amy Brown."

"Please come in. Call me Jim," said the general.

He had a strong, deep voice. I immediately liked him. We walked into the exquisitely furnished living room. We had seen the windows from outside the house, but looking out from the inside was even more amazing. He had an impressive view across the Hudson to West Point. I could visualize Jim Parkinson sitting by the window and admiring the institution where he had served as dean. He offered us a choice of chairs near the upholstered recliner that was clearly his viewpoint. He asked if we would care for coffee. I declined. Mark asked for a cup of black coffee.

We'd barely settled in when a woman came into the living room carrying a tray with a coffee pot, cups, and a plate of cookies.

"This is my wife, Maggie," said the general. Mrs. Parkinson was an attractive woman, about five four, and had the same dusky complexion as my own mother. We stood up and made our introductions. Maggie took a seat next to her husband.

"I understand your company has some questions about the incident at West Point eighteen years ago," said Jim.

"Yes," said Mark. "Amy is Tim Martin's daughter."

"That can't be possible," said Maggie. "Hank and Lindsey never mentioned having a granddaughter. Besides, Tim and his wife, Samantha, both died in a plane crash seven months after that terrible incident at the Point."

"That's the reason we are here," said Mark. "Amy's parents were murdered a little more than a year ago. During our investigation, we discovered that the Browns were actually the Martins. We have no idea why they were in hiding."

"I don't see how I can help," said Jim. "Tim only helped me on that one incident. We were as shocked as everyone else when we heard that they had been killed in Liberia."

"Our research leads us to believe that the incident may have something to do with not only their disappearances but the reason why they were killed," explained Mark.

"Well, I don't know if this will help, but I have no objection to telling you what happened," said Jim Parkinson.

95

JIM LEANED BACK AND CLOSED HIS EYES. HE RUBBED HIS FISTS ON HIS eyelids as if trying to conjure up a clear memory of the event. Then he began to tell us the most unbelievable story.

"When I became the dean of the United States Military Academy, I was the first black to ever fill that prestigious position. We had had a black president and black four-star generals, even a black chairman of the Joint Chiefs of Staff, but never a black dean. I had a responsibility to every African American to be successful.

"The staff and faculty members sponsor cadets while they are here at West Point. It's sort of like creating a home away from home. We sponsor eight cadets each year. One of the cadets we sponsored, Ambrose Wiggins, came to me the day before he died. He told me that he was being initiated into a witch's coven that conducted ceremonies in the tunnels."

"The tunnels?" I asked, trying to downplay my initial shock.

Jim explained the history of the steam tunnels and how, over the years, the cadets found their way into them. Miles of these tunnels ran beneath the grounds. Some of them connected with old Revolutionary War tunnels that had connected the forts.

"Anyway, Cadet Wiggins came to me and said that he was pledging membership in this coven. Apparently several upper classmen, all first-year cadets or seniors, held ceremonies in the tunnels that supposedly enhanced their physical and mental abilities. Of course, I assumed that this was just BS, and we always try to discourage such activities.

"The problem was that, according to Cadet Wiggins, part of the initiation was a requirement that he accompany two of these cadets on a trip to New York City to kidnap a homeless person and bring him back to the tunnels to be used in the ceremony. They tried to kidnap a bum in the Bowery. It turned out this man was tougher than they realized, and they found they were lucky to only end up with a few bruises.

"Cadet Wiggins decided that he wanted out and came to me. I was ready to recommend that the commandant initiate an Article Thirty-two investigation. I told Cadet Wiggins that I would need the names of the cadets involved. He said he would bring me the names the next morning. That never happened. They found Wiggins dead in his bunk. Although it was ruled an accidental death, I planned to talk to other cadets about this coven.

"The same day, I was jogging after dark. A female cadet came up alongside me. As we neared a wooded area, she shoved me into the brush. I'm a big man. Twenty years ago I was six five and weighed two hundred and sixty pounds. All right, I may have been a little overweight and not as tough as I used to be, but this cadet couldn't have weighed more than one hundred and twenty pounds and was barely five four, maybe even shorter. But she had unbelievable strength. She shoved me against the tree and warned me to stop asking questions about Cadet Wiggins.

"Then she said that she hoped my mother-in-law would get better. It would be unfortunate if my wife, Maggie, had an accident and was unable to care for her. Maggie was in Baltimore staying with her mother who was dying from cancer. She let go of me and ran into the dark. It was then I felt the pain in my arms where she had grabbed me. There was blood on my sweatshirt. I headed back to the house. When I got my shirt off, the marks on my arms looked like a person with small hands had gripped my arms and squeezed so hard that the fingers had broken the skin.

"I was faced with a major dilemma. I had no real proof that this had happened. All I needed was for the superintendent to begin wondering if I was playing with a full deck of cards. Then I saw an article in the *New York Times* where your dad, who was an FBI agent, had just stopped a hostage situation in the Chase Manhattan Bank. Of course I knew your dad when he was a teenager when your grandparents and I were serving together in Liberia. I figured that he would listen to my story and keep it confidential. I called the FBI office and invited Tim to come visit at West Point. When I told him what was going on, he not only believed me, but he also said he would volunteer to help me.

"By the time you dad arrived, I was certain that Cadet Butch Langston was the ringleader. He had begun to make some incredible strides on the football team. Just the year before, he was second string, and then he became one of the best backs on the team. His grades also did a turn-around. He'd been in the bottom of his class. Then, amazingly, he maxed his thermodynamics test.

"Your dad wanted to see Langston without him knowing he was being watched. I took your dad to the cadet mess for lunch. I was going to point Langston out, but your dad insisted that if he was what he thought he was, he would recognize him.

"I selected an athletes' table. They got bigger servings than the other cadets. Your dad sat down next to me. We chatted while we observed the cadets. When we had finished our apple pie, your dad claimed that several in the group had been possessed by a creature he called an *endosym*. I don't know how he did it, but I would soon learn that he was right.

"After lunch, we walked back to my quarters. I asked Tim why he wouldn't let me point out which cadet was Langston. Your dad identified Langston as the young man with freckles sitting at the third table to our left. I asked him how he knew. He told me that there had been several cadets there who were controlled by *endosyms*, one of whom was a woman. I thought Tim had gone off the deep end. There were no such things as *endosyms*.

"Then your dad said, 'Look at your arms again. As you said, no human could have done that.' Your dad warned me not to ask any questions about what happened to Cadet Wiggins and to not tell anyone what I had just told him. He said that he had to get back to the city. He told me that the two of us would address the problem.

"A week later, in the middle of the night, we entered the tunnels. I had managed to obtain keys to the tunnel access doors from the facilities

engineers. We were well armed. As we checked our weapons, I was beginning to realize how serious the situation was. Your dad cautioned me that
if one of these creatures came at either of us, we needed to shoot for the
head. Only headshots would stop them. I felt a chill of disbelief come
over me; these were young cadets, weren't they?

"I had blueprints, maps, and crude drawings of what we knew about
the tunnels. We had several LED flashlights that were good for up to
sixteen hours. Yet I had no idea how we would be able to find anything—
nor any idea of what we were looking for.

"Strangely, your dad insisted that he would be able to find where the
cadets were conducting their rituals. Now, this is the weird part. I never
believed in the African witchcraft stuff, but your dad had this leopard
tooth that he believed would guide him to the source of the witchcraft.
Already what we'd seen was spooky. The tooth seemed to glow in the low
light from the tunnels. It reminded me of those watches with radium
dials. Your dad would hold the tooth in his hand, and when we came to a
place where the tunnel split off, he would take a few steps each direction.
One way the glow would fade; the other way, the glow would brighten.
It was like using a water witch to find a well.

"We traveled deeper and deeper into the tunnels. We found ourselves
in an older tunnel completely made of old brick. It was no longer a steam
tunnel but one of the old readout tunnels from the Revolution-era forts.

"I was sure that that we were in an area that was never on any map.
The leopard tooth began to glow so brightly that your dad placed the
leather thong with the tooth around his neck and concealed it under his
T-shirt. We turned off our lights and listened. It was then that I heard
the chanting. We carefully followed the sounds. Stepping cautiously, we
saw a light up ahead.

"We rounded a bend in the tunnel and walked straight into hell. Up
ahead was a room that likely served as an old cell from the Revolutionary
War. The only illumination came from Coleman lanterns. The cadets
stood close to a crude altar built of old and broken bricks. The cadets
were naked; they all chanted, but the words were indecipherable. An old
man bound at the hands and feet lay facedown. His head hung over the

edge of the altar. One of the cadets held a sword over his head. It appeared that they were preparing to execute the old man by beheading him.

"I stood immovable, frozen, unable to react. Then your dad shouted, 'FBI! Drop the sword!' They didn't even look our way, seemingly unaware of our presence. Your dad aimed his pistol and fired one shot. The blast was amplified by the confines of the tunnels. The bullet struck the hilt of the sword, knocking it from the cadet's hand. That got their attention. They all turned toward us, not as individuals, but as an entire group. I swear, their eyes froze the blood in my veins. They were no longer cadets. They were not human. They all began moving slowly toward us. I recall hearing your dad say, 'You must shoot them in the head.' My God, there was no way I could shoot unarmed cadets. Even if I aimed the pistol at them my hands trembled so much that I couldn't have hit the broad side of a barn.

"I would have probably died within moments except the strangest thing happened. The tunnel began to collapse, burying the cadets. Only one, Langston, the one who had held the sword, survived. A brick from the ceiling struck his head, and he fell unconscious to the floor. We knew we had to get out of there, but the collapse had damaged a twenty-inch water main. Water began to flood the tunnel."

"Then what happened?" I asked.

"Your dad was very upset—not over the bodies, but because the leopard's tooth no longer glowed. It was clear to him that the *endosym* that had possessed the cadets had escaped. We had no choice but to run for our lives, dragging Langston with us. When we got back to the surface, we told the emergency personnel that we discovered some cadets had been fooling around in the tunnels. Whatever they were doing caused the tunnels to collapse and had ruptured the waterline. We were only able to save one cadet, and he was in poor condition. No one, besides your dad and I, knew the truth."

96

Jim Parkinson stopped talking. We sat there for a moment, trying to absorb what we had just heard.

"Jim, what finally happened to Cadet Langston?" asked Mark.

"He had suffered a terrible head injury. He had no memory of what happened. Of course, the academy wanted to keep the lid on the whole thing. Langston kept insisting that a warlock more than two hundred years old had recruited the cadets and offered them great powers to serve him. But with his injuries, doctors considered his story just the ramblings of a seriously brain-injured man."

"You mentioned this two-hundred-year-old warlock. Did he have a name?" I asked.

"Gee, I guess so, but I don't recall what he said his name was. You could ask Butch," said Jim.

"Butch?" I asked.

"Yes, Butch Langston," said Jim. "He's in Four Winds Hospital in Katonah, New York, which is a twenty-minute drive from here."

"What's he doing in a hospital?" I asked.

"It's a mental hospital," said Jim. "He's in the insane ward and has been there for the last eighteen years."

I turned to Mark.

"Do we have time to talk to Cadet Langston?"

Mark looked at Jim.

"Is he dangerous?"

"Oh, no," said Jim. "I visit him once in a while."

"Once in a while?" Maggie corrected him. "You have been going there every month since you retired."

"She's right." Jim smiled. "I feel sorry for him. He is really a nice guy, and everyone else abandoned him. Not one family member has ever visited him. Besides, he plays a good chess game. If you want to see him, we can leave right now."

"Let's go," I said.

97

WE DECIDED TO DRIVE THE RENTAL CAR TO FOUR WINDS HOSPITAL in Katonah. As we started out the front door, Maggie handed Jim a Ziploc bag full of cookies.

"They're chocolate chip, Butch's favorite," she said to Jim.

"He'll be surprised," said Jim. "This isn't my normal visiting day."

When we reached the car, I stopped.

"I better let Mr. P out for a quick walk."

Jim looked at me and asked, "Who's Mr. P?"

"My cat," I said.

"Your cat? You brought your cat with you?" asked Jim, totally surprised.

"The cat's a special tool we use in our business. He's a bomb-sniffing cat, and we combined business with this trip, demonstrating his skills to the FAA," explained Mark.

"Oh, I never heard of a bomb-sniffing cat," said Jim.

"A special breed," said Mark, with a grin.

As we walked back, Jim smiled. "Wow, we once owned a cat, but I've never seen one that responds like a dog."

Jim got in the passenger side, and I got in the backseat with my cat. Mark started the car and pulled out of the driveway. Twenty minutes later we arrived at the front gates of Four Winds Hospital.

It wasn't what I expected. It was located on a large expanse of acreage. Jim explained that all of the multistory brick buildings had been built following World War II. Even in the winter, the grounds were well tended. Thick mulch had been spread to protect the flowerbeds. Although the trees were bare, there wasn't a stray or withered leaf on the ground.

We pulled into a parking lot. From our angle we couldn't see the buildings. An eight-foot- high wall in front of us was topped with a coil of razor wire.

"This is the building that houses the insane," said Jim, nodding toward the structure inside the wall.

We stopped at a guardhouse next to the door. After we showed our IDs, the guard pressed a button to give us permission to enter. Again we admired the well-mown lawns and neatly prepared flowerbeds. *Inmate labor?* I couldn't help but wonder. At the main entrance, we waited to speak to another guard inside the secured doors. Jim said a few words to the guard. Again we waited. A few minutes later, a man in whites came through the door.

"We didn't expect you today, General Parkinson. Butch will be happy to see you," said the man.

"I have two guests with me who would like to meet Butch," said Jim.

The man introduced us to Fred Robinson, one of the attendants at the hospital.

"Are either of you carrying?" asked Fred.

"Why?" asked Mark.

"The last thing we want is for one of the inmates to get his hands on a gun. We require even law enforcement to place weapons in a lockbox until they are ready to exit," he explained.

Mark pulled his Glock from his shoulder holster. I reached in my handbag and took out my .32 automatic. They were both placed in a secure box, and Mark was given the key. Jim looked at me as if I had just robbed a bank.

"I have a permit," I assured him. Jim just shrugged.

We heard a click and stepped into the hallway. The floors were highly polished, excellent-quality wood. The hallway was wide, and each of the doors had coded locks.

"Butch is in the greenhouse," said Fred. "You know how he loves plants. You can talk to him in the greenhouse office if you like."

"That would be fine," said Jim.

The greenhouse was hot and humid and smelled of decaying plant material. I'd never seen such a variety of tropical plants in a single location.

"Butch, you have a visitor," shouted Fred.

"I'm coming," said a voice from behind a wall of thick green fronds.

I don't know what I was expecting, but Cadet Butch Langston didn't look like a cold-blooded demon-possessed killer. Far from someone sinister, Butch could have just stepped out of a Robin Hood movie. All he would have needed was a monk's robe, and I would have called him Friar Tuck. He was a big man, maybe six five, overweight with red hair—at least what was left of it—a big smile, and twinkling blue eyes. The most striking feature was the rugged scar that ran across his scalp. It looked like a part of his skull was missing.

When Butch saw Jim, he acted like his own father had just walked in.

"Dean Parkinson, I didn't expect to see you until the end of the month," said Butch with a wide grin.

"Hi, Butch, good to see you," said Jim, giving the man a bear hug. "Hey, I brought two people who would like to ask you a few questions," said Jim.

"Anything for you, Dean," said Butch.

"Let's go in the office where we can have a little privacy," said Jim.

The "office" was more like an employee break room. We clustered around a small metal table and teetered on wooden stools.

"Butch, this is Amy Brown, and this is Mark Baker," explained Jim.

"Pleased to meet you, Miss Brown and Mr. Baker," Butch said politely.

"Cadet Langston, Amy and Mark would like to have you tell them about what happened in the tunnel eighteen years ago."

"You know I have to tell the truth," said Butch.

"Of course, just the truth," said Jim.

"Doctor Sanchez says if I stop telling the truth about what happened, I could leave here. But a cadet never lies, cheats, or steals; isn't that right, Dean?"

"That's right, Cadet Langston; so tell Amy and Mark the truth."

98

LANGSTON HESITATED A MINUTE TO GATHER HIS THOUGHTS. THEN he began his story.

"I had gone to a movie at the mall and got back to Highland Falls around eleven thirty. I was hungry and stopped by McDonald's for some burgers. I met her there. She was small, like a pixie. Her name was Kelley. I like small women. Sorry, Miss Brown," he said as he looked at me.

I wasn't upset by his frank comment. I nodded, and he continued telling his story.

"She was really hot for me, and we left and went up in the woods and had sex. But something went wrong, and she stopped breathing. I thought I had killed her. I didn't know what to do. So I put her body in my duffel bag and decided to hide it in the tunnels.

"I carried the bag deep into the tunnels to a place I had never been before. Part of the wall had fallen away, and I decided to hide her body behind the wall. I was pulling away bricks when she started moaning. She wasn't dead."

Now a frown came over Butch's face.

"I think I hit her with a brick to keep her quiet. Maybe I did it more than once. I had never done anything like this. She stopped moaning. I pulled more bricks away. Then I pointed my flashlight into the opening behind the wall. I saw an old man lying there on his back. He had long white hair and a beard. His fingernails had grown to more than two inches long. He was dead.

"I leaned in to get a closer look when he reached out and grabbed my hand. I think I screamed. I also peed in my pants. Then I heard his voice in my head, and suddenly I was no longer afraid. He asked me what year it was. At first, I didn't understand, then I told him the date. I heard him laugh inside my head. He told me that he had slept more than two hundred years."

I couldn't wait any longer.

"What was his name?" I asked.

Butch stopped talking and looked at me as if he had been surprised by the question. Jim also looked a little shocked.

"I'm sorry," I said. "I just wondered if the man told you his name?"

"Of course, he did," said Butch. "It was McDougal, Duncan McDougal."

"Oh my God!" I cried.

"Did you know him?" asked Butch.

"No, but I've heard his name. Please, I'm sorry, go ahead with your story."

Both Mark and Jim looked at me as if I had lost my mind. I smiled weakly and focused my eyes downward.

Butch continued his story.

"Duncan promised me power and wealth if I would help him return to this world. Over the next few weeks, I brought him food and water. I provided him with clothes. I cut his hair, beard, and long nails. I helped him get inside the barracks to take showers. When we were in public, he had the power to make people unaware of his presence. He could go almost anywhere he wanted.

"At first he looked like he was a hundred-year-old man, but he told me he would become younger. In order for that to happen, he had to take a human life to obtain its essence. He had the power over me to make me want to do his bidding. But how could anyone just go out on the street, drag someone back into the tunnels, and kill him? I needed help, so I approached three of the other tunnel rats."

"Tunnel rats?" asked Mark.

"It was a secret group of cadets at the bottom of our class," explained Butch. "We had a special place in the tunnels where we could meet. We went through sort of an initiation. You know, kind of like a fraternity, only for dummies." He continued his story. "Once the guys met Duncan, they were under his power. He insisted that he needed a victim to sacrifice, but we had to prepare an appropriate place for the ceremony. We used the old materials that were inside the tunnels to build a makeshift altar. Someone located an old broadsword. He told us that to capture the full essence of a human's soul at death, the victim must be publicly beheaded.

"Apparently when I killed Kelly that night, her spirit had revived Duncan but had failed to provide him his full power. We finally came up with a plan to find a victim. The three of us went to New York and walked through the Bowery where the homeless people hang out. We found one potential victim passed out in a doorway. We tied him securely, put a gag in his mouth, and stuffed him into the trunk of my car. When we got back to the Point, we carried him down into the tunnels and presented him to Duncan.

"Duncan designed an appropriate ceremony. He had us all get naked and learn a chant that was required during the ceremony. We placed the unconscious bum on the altar, and then the ritual commenced. Soon I could feel a strange power coming over me. Duncan used the broadsword to cut off the victim's head. At the precise moment of death, the tunnel assumed a red glow. I felt a power like nothing I had ever known before. From then on, each of us was hooked. Duncan grinned with pleasure and demanded that we find more victims.

"During this time Duncan began learning about the modern world. At first, he talked funny and could not understand the concept of electric lights or how to operate a car. I taught him how to use a computer. He spent more time learning on the Internet than anyone I have ever known. He was like a visitor from another planet who comes to earth and learns our ways.

"Duncan was also changed with each victim's death. Just as we were growing stronger and smarter, he was becoming younger. Although his hair was white, he looked like a man in his forties. He told us that he had a spirit that lived in him and that they mutually shared one body.

"He told us that there would be a special ceremony where another spirit would be brought here. One of us would be chosen to share his body with the spirit. Jointly we would become immortal.

"For us, things had changed for the best. We aced our tests and each of us gained the strength that would make us superheroes. Then we made our first mistake when we decided to initiate a new member. We invited Cadet Wiggins to join our ranks. As part of the initiation, before he would meet Duncan, we took him to New York to assist in the kidnapping of another homeless person.

"By now we had taken more than a dozen homeless off the streets of New York. We figured we were doing the city a service. We picked an old guy sleeping in the old subway tunnel. When we tried to take him, we found out that he had some kind of martial arts training, and he kicked our butts. We returned to the Point empty-handed.

"Then Wiggins got cold feet and talked to you, Dean. Duncan was really mad at us for doing that. He said that he would take care of Wiggins. I don't know what he did, but Wiggins turned up dead. Then we warned you, Dean, not to ask questions.

"A week later, Duncan told us that he was going to visit his old home in Newburgh to retrieve a small statue that would allow him to open a doorway so that another spirit could enter this world. Duncan borrowed my car. We were all down there, relaxing in the tunnel, when we decided to kill one of the guys we had stored in the cells. We decided to do the ceremony without Duncan. We believed that each of us would gain more power without Duncan.

"So we started the ritual just as Duncan had taught us. I was just about ready to lop off the guy's head when that guy with you, Dean, shot the sword out of my hand. We were going to kill both of you when I heard Duncan's voice in my head.

"'You fools,' he said in anger. 'Now the secret will be out. You have failed me, and you all must die.'

"I felt a pain in my head like it was going to explode. Then it went away, and I knew immediately that Duncan had abandoned us. Then the tunnel collapsed. That's all I remember.

"So here I must spend the rest of my life. But it's OK. Bad things are going to happen outside soon. Is there anything else you want me to tell you?" asked Butch.

"No, Butch; unless Amy or Mark has any other questions, that's all." Jim looked at Mark. He shook his head. He then looked at me.

"Butch, did Duncan ever tell you where his home was before he came to America?" I asked.

"Edinburgh, Scotland," said Butch. "Duncan was born on June 21, 1739."

I stared at Cadet Langston. His story had just confirmed my suspicions. Then Butch said something that shook me to the core of my being.

"You're just like Duncan, Miss Brown."

"What?" I said totally shocked.

"You're more than just human, just like Duncan. I can see it in your eyes," answered Butch.

"I'm just a teenage girl," I whispered.

Jim interrupted the conversation.

"I think we have taken enough of your time, Butch. Maggie sent these chocolate chip cookies."

"Oh, tell her thank you," said Butch, tears in his eyes. "I love her cookies."

99

WE GOT UP AND WALKED OUT OF THE OFFICE, TO WHERE THE attendant waited. After picking up our weapons, we were escorted out of the building and headed for our car. We drove off the hospital grounds and headed back to Garrison. No one said a word on the way back to the Parkinsons' house.

When we pulled up in front of the house, Jim turned to me in the backseat.

"I may be an old man, but I am not senile. Something very strange is going on, and I would like to have you two tell me what it is."

I looked at Mark and nodded my head.

"All right," said Mark. "But what we are about to tell you will make Cadet Langston seem like the sane one."

For the next hour, we told Jim what we had found out. When we had finished, Jim shook his head and sighed deeply.

"All right, if you went public with this, you would be committed. Before that night in the tunnels with your dad, I would have considered you two conspiracy nuts. But right now, I am afraid that what you are saying is true.

"You claim that the chairman of the Joint Chiefs is possessed by one of these demon things," said Jim. "I happen to be acquainted with this man. His name is Fred Hutchinson. He was a cadet at the Point when I was dean. He turned in three cadets for cheating on a final exam."

"That would make him a straight arrow," said Mark.

"Yes," said Jim. "I was on the honors board that heard the case. What bothered me was the fact that Cadet Hutchinson seemed to enjoy nailing the three cadets. When I was a cadet, the worst thing I could have imagined was turning in a fellow cadet. Even though the honor code would require it, the whole process would have torn me up.

"I never forgot that day. When Hutchinson went on active duty, he was a fast riser, making all of his promotions early, and then became the youngest chairman since Alexander Haig. So what do you want me to do?" asked Jim.

"Right now, nothing. Discuss this with no one, not even Maggie. We have to find a way to address a threat to all of humankind, and we have to do it soon. Get a disposable cell phone, and call me at this number," said Mark, handing him one of his cards.

We all shook hands. As I took General Parkinson's hand, he held my hand longer than I had expected. He seemed to have skipped ahead to a new thought.

"What's the date of your birth?" asked Jim.

"What?" I asked, temporarily astonished by this change in subject.

As for the birth date, I was about to lie, but with what we had already discussed, I told him the date that was written on my birth certificate.

"On the day of your birthday, the strangest thing happened to me," said Jim. "Maggie and I had both been reading in our den at West Point. Suddenly, I began to perspire. I stepped outdoors for a few moments.

"It was a crisp, cold winter night with the temperature around twenty degrees. There was still snow in spots along the road. I stepped down onto the shoveled sidewalk. I could see through the trees that the lights were on in the cadet barracks. Four thousand cadets were preparing for the next day's classes and activities.

"The streetlights cast a yellow glow on the freshly fallen snow. I looked toward Washington Road. The gaping hole from the collapsed tunnels three months ago had been filled. New sidewalks and curbs were formed up, readied for the pouring of concrete. The road would be paved in the spring.

"The Corps of Engineers had restored power and heat to all buildings. Sadly, the bodies of the three cadets and the victims would remain buried beneath the plain forever.

"I was still having nightmares of that horrible night. In them, the *endosym* was a member of the faculty. I was trying to find out which one of my fellow officers was not human, but really an *endosym*. I would just be ready to open the office door to where I knew the *endosym* was hiding, and then I would wake up, only to return to a similar dream again another night.

"I couldn't shake it, although I tried. I looked up at the clear night sky, and I could see the brighter stars even though the streetlights were on. Then I felt dizzy. I closed my eyes.

"All of a sudden, I was floating near the thatched ceiling of a hut. There were no sounds, no smells, no feeling. I looked down. Two Coleman lanterns lit up the interior. Lying on a grass mat was a woman, flat on her back. Two other women held her feet to the ground. She wore no clothes, and her legs were spread apart.

She was giving birth. I couldn't see her face. I watched as the child was expelled from her womb. The baby, a female, was washed off and wrapped in a thin towel. She was light-skinned, a white child, yet clearly this was an African hut. It reminded me of the huts that I had seen when we were stationed in Liberia twelve years before.

"The baby's eyes opened to mere slits, revealing a striking green color. They were your eyes, Miss Brown," Jim said.

"With everything else that has happened to me I'm not surprised," I said.

"There is more," he said. "I felt joy as I looked into your eyes. You smiled. Then the scene vanished, and I was in a modern hospital room. There was a woman in stirrups giving birth. Again I could not see the woman's face. Medical staff surrounded her. Again I floated above the brightly lit room.

"All of a sudden, this child was expelled from this woman's womb. A doctor in blue scrubs cut the umbilical cord and carried the child to a hospital crib. He gently laid the child in the small bed, and he took a step backward.

"This, too, was a girl, but something was wrong. Her skin was a gray color. Her head was way too large and two small bumps protruded from the sides of the skull. Then I saw the tail. The baby had a long tail, an extended tailbone. I wondered what had happened. Then I was brought closer. I examined the small creature—that's what it was; it couldn't have been human. It stared in my direction and opened its eyes. They appeared to be only black holes in the head. It opened its mouth in a pitiful cry, revealing two rows of tiny razor-sharp teeth. It was like looking into the mouth of a shark. It was pure evil. I could feel it in my bones.

"Darkness surrounded me, and I felt a moment of sheer terror until I realized that my eyes had been closed, and what had happened was only in my imagination. When I came back to reality, I found myself standing on the sidewalk by my quarters."

I've never been a religious man and even after all these years it seems so weird. I'm really sorry, I shouldn't have brought this up," said Jim.

"No, that's OK," I said. "I think I just met the other child."

Now both men seemed shocked.

"On our way here from Newburgh, I asked Mark to stop by Duncan McDougal's original homestead. There I met a young woman named Sabrina who said she just turned eighteen. She told me that Duncan was her father. She was planning to go to Scotland to meet the 'horned god.'

"That's why I asked Butch where Duncan had come from. God, I don't know if you had a vision or what. I'm scared. I don't know what is wanted of me."

We were all speechless until Mark broke the silence.

"We have to get back to Spokane. I'll keep you in the loop, Jim."

100

OUR FLIGHT FROM NEW YORK WAS UNEVENTFUL. AS WE BEGAN THE approach to Spokane International Airport, I looked out the window. The ground was covered in fresh white snow.

Yet in places, I could see patches of brown grass, cracked sidewalks, dilapidated roofs, and other indications of all that had been hidden under the layers of snow during the winter months.

It was just like the evil demon- creatures that lie hidden inside the willing hosts. They become *endosyms*, hiding their evil in a human disguise.

When we landed, I was thrilled to see Regina and the twins who had come to meet us. There were hugs all around. I had picked up some gifts for the twins, and I had an emerald necklace and earrings for Regina.

We stopped by Applebee's for dinner before going home. Sherry wrapped a piece of her fish filet in a napkin for Mr. P. She gave it to him when we got back in the car.

When we got home, Toby was so excited to see us that he even went up and licked Mr. P's face. The cat scowled but reluctantly accepted this touch of affection from the big pit bull. After we got settled in, we sat around watching TV. I was amazed that, after all that happened, we could return to our comfortable home as if we'd never left it.

I had taken pictures of Grandma Martin and the Weahs. Sherry thought Joe Weah was cool. All of a sudden, every good-looking guy she saw was cool. I tried to remember if I ever went through that phase when I was thirteen. Funny, after what I had learned on this trip, I couldn't remember what I was like at thirteen. *God, that was only five years ago.*

After the twins had gone to bed, Mark and I sat down and told Regina about everything. She knew some of what was going on, but she couldn't accept the idea that *endosyms* truly did exist. In the end, she just sobbed while Mark held her.

Finally, she wiped away her tears.

"Let's keep this from the twins as long as we can," she said. Then, typical of Regina, she added, "All right, let's plan for the worst case and pray for the best case." She was now part of the team. Together, we had a brainstorming session.

In the worst case, the *endosyms* would win, and the world would be lost. Our only chance of surviving and not becoming raw meat for these demon-creatures was to develop a siege mentality. You know, like the survivalist groups that crop up every once in a while. But we couldn't do this in Spokane. We needed to focus on Northern Idaho, Montana, or Canada. We needed to find an easily defendable, remote ranch and be prepared to hunker down and live like pioneers.

The best-case scenario would be to destroy the *endosyms*. Most likely we would come up with something in between these two possibilities.

Regina looked at Mark and me and said, "Gold."

"Gold?" we asked.

"Yes," she said. "US currency, stocks, and bonds would be worthless in a world where we were no longer the top dogs on the planet. We need to convert our assets into gold and not rely on banks or financial institutions."

"We will also need to amass an arsenal of weapons and ammunition. I'll be able to do that through the company," said Mark.

"We need to identify a list of friends and relatives who will join us. The larger our resistance force, the better we can defend ourselves," I said.

"We also must be discreet about who we include and when we tell them what's going on. I'm pretty sure that the *endosyms* are planning to take over the world on December twenty-first. They will want to eliminate the opposition. They'll want a population that submits to their tyranny. I'm betting that big cities will be the first to fall," said Mark.

Our discussion went on for hours. When we finally decided to call it quits for the night, we were exhausted, yet none of us got much sleep that night.

101

OVER THE NEXT FEW WEEKS, WE BEGAN TO IMPLEMENT OUR PLAN. Mark discovered a white supremacy compound in Canada just north of the border. Following their court loss in Idaho a number of years ago, this group had moved into Canada. They were not well received, and the government had confiscated their property. We picked up the three hundred acres with all buildings for pennies on the dollar. We then started relocating employees of Baker Security to the site, preparing it for what might come.

I began buying up gold in the form of coins. I had to be careful not to buy too much too soon, because it could cause prices to rise. Obviously, I couldn't dump three hundred million dollars into gold, but I aimed at putting one quarter of my portfolio into bullion.

Although we were deeply involved in the plan to defeat the *endosyms*, we also had a happy change in the structure of our extended family. Mark made it official and proposed to Regina.

Reverend John conducted the wedding ceremony at Hills United Methodist Church. We kept it low-key, inviting just close friends. I was the "best person" for the wedding, standing up for both Mark and Regina. The twins had been legally adopted by Regina over the course of all this, and after Mark and Regina got married, they also had a father. They, too, participated in the ceremony. Reverend John even had a part for them where they said that they would love honor and obey Mark as their true father. Since they had no idea who their biological father was, it was a special day for them, too. I spent most of the ceremony wiping tears from my eyes. Obviously, with the world possibly ending in less than eight months, we stayed close together and celebrated the reception in the safety and security of our home.

The twins continued to attend school at Freeman High School. Their lives, like the rest of the world, seemed normal. They were unaware of the changes that had been taking place, but, just by watching the evening news, anyone could guess that changes were in the wind.

Three nations in Africa and two in South America endured bloody coups that resulted in governmental changes. Five upheavals within three weeks was exceptional. Then right on our doorstep, the Mexican government collapsed. Drug cartels filled the void. Terrorist attacks along the Mexico-US border intensified. The conflicts became the headline stories on every news channel. Suddenly, just like after 911 when many Middle Eastern men were viewed with suspicion Mexican Americans men were viewed with suspicion.

Death tolls from attacks on malls, shopping centers, and public schools along the border resulted in border closings. The president ordered troops to patrol the danger zones.

What really caught our attention was the proposal to microchip all US citizens as a tool to protect the country from terrorist infiltration. Government officials argued that inserting microchips into all US citizens would make life easier for the good guys and impossible for the bad ones. Airport scanners would permit cleared passengers to walk directly to their planes. Police roadblocks would target suspects. Even at grocery and department stores, scanners would eliminate the need for people to carry ID. The microchip would even eliminate the need to carry a driver's license or passport.

There was talk about the microchip replacing the social security card. What was really scary was that more and more people were in favor of this plan. Several European countries and China were also looking at microchip data to monitor population movement.

That was scary. If this happened, no one could hide or escape. The exact locations of individuals could be determined via helicopters or cars. They might be able to track you just like the GPS in an iPhone or by cell phone. Sadly, the advantage went both ways: with the use of microchips, *endosyms* could keep better track of their human cattle.

So we did our homework, keeping our attention focused on websites and information from foreign and domestic sources. We met regularly to discuss our findings and planned for the inevitable. By April we were totally focused on survival. But I also believed in my heart that God would not let this happen.

What I did not understand was my role in these frightening developments. I had come to the edge of understanding the horror of these demon-creatures.

Was my dream about the village of Zigda in Liberia, West Africa, just one part of the great plan to defeat the *endosyms*?

102

I PULLED MY MUSTANG UP TO THE CURB IN FRONT OF AN OLDER TWO-story house just south of Mission Avenue. Although it was dark, the low street lighting was good enough to see the house through the bushes. It was just a short walk from here to the Gonzaga campus. The clock on the dash read eleven thirty. I shut off the engine. Mr. P had already gone to sleep for the night. He was curled up in the passenger seat. He went everywhere with me.

We had been back in Spokane for two months. It had been a mild spring, and some of the trees were already budding. For most people, this was a time to celebrate new growth. Mark, Regina, and the twins took advantage of spring break and skipped town, heading for Disneyland. I had opted out. I know they wanted to keep things as normal as possible for as long as they could.

In some ways, it was like keeping secret the fact that a child has terminal cancer. If the child didn't know, he or she would have a few more days or weeks to enjoy a carefree childhood. In this case, the world had its own brand of terminal cancer in the form of the *endosyms*.

Mark had abandoned his mission to incessantly guard me. We realized that this threat was far bigger than any of us. He knew that I possessed some power or ability that allowed me to recognize the *endosyms*. With Mr. P by my side, I had the added advantage of his ability to change into something that could protect me better than armed guards could. Unfortunately, I had no idea what triggered Mr. P's ability to sense the danger. I wish I knew.

In June, I would be going to Liberia to find out if there was something there that would help us defeat these demon-creatures that 'wanted our world. God, it was so bizarre. People were going about their lives unaware of what was coming.

We had been hiring a larger staff for Baker Security. We had more than two hundred combat veterans working for us and training for what was to come. Yet, only a handful of us truly knew what the enemy was. We told our employees that we had intelligence indicating that terrorists were planning a massive attack. We wanted a crack team to be trained and ready to go. At least for now, that satisfied their curiosity.

If the *endosyms* were indeed planning to enslave the human race, once that happened there would be nothing we could do. We would become a small survivalist group vanishing into the Canadian woods when the whole world collapsed. A better plan would be to stop the *endosyms* from doing whatever they had planned for December twenty first.

There were two main problems. First, only the cat and I could spot an *endosym*. Yet I knew from Shaun O'Kelly that there were others out there who could also identify the *endosyms*. But Shaun had avoided me since I came back, and I had to meet with his people and get their help to save the world.

The greater problem was we couldn't just walk up to an *endosym* who might be a prominent member of the community or maybe even the head of a government. We would have to shoot him or her twice in the head. If we went public and disclosed the threats, the government would lock us up and throw away the keys.

And that was why I was parked in front of a two-story house just south of Mission Avenue. Shaun O'Kelly and I needed to talk. If he wouldn't answer my calls, then I would go to his apartment. I was not going to take "no" for an answer.

And besides, I was a little pissed off. I hated to admit it, but I had a crush on Shaun O'Kelly. I know—we had only met a few times. Of course, one of those times was in my bedroom, and Shaun had seen a lot more of me than any other boy had ever seen. I also related to Shaun, who like me, could see *endosyms*. He was the only other person I knew outside my family who wouldn't consider me a freak. *So why is he avoiding me?* It's kind of like that guy who invites you on a date then never calls you again. Finding out where Shaun lived was a piece of cake. After all, owning a security firm made finding personal information take only a matter of minutes.

Many of the old houses around Gonzaga had apartments that were rented to students. Shaun lived in a second-floor apartment across the street from where I had parked. His apartment had a private outside entrance. A set of stairs led to his door.

I opened the car door.

"Come on, cat. You go with me."

After everything we'd gone through together, Mr. P had started accompanying me without requiring a leash and a harness. He followed me like an obedient dog.

Being a weekday night, no one was on the street. Once the sun went down in Spokane, it got cold. It had been in the midsixties during the day, and at this hour it must have been twenty degrees colder. The stairway was unlit, but I could see light coming from the window in the door at the top of the stairs. I cut across the street and took the stairs two at a time. That's easy to do when you have long legs. I wore jeans, sneakers, and a blue-hooded sweatshirt. Actually, I could have used a coat, but I didn't plan on standing on the porch to talk. Hopefully he would ask me to come in.

When I reached the top of the stairs, I saw a window next to the door. There were no curtains on the window. I looked through the glass. The door opened into a small living room. It had a large flat-screen TV against one wall, an outdated sofa, several mismatched chairs, and a kitchen table with wooden chairs. A small kitchen was also visible. The room was a living room, dining room, and kitchen all in one.

Another door on one wall stood wide open, revealing a bedroom. A small nightstand near the bed had a lamp with a tilted shade. I started to knock, and then I smiled. Shaun had come in to my house by bypassing our security system and then had had the nerve to sneak into my bedroom. He had scared the daylights out of me.

Turnabout was fair play. I tried the door, assuming that if he didn't put curtains on the window, he wouldn't bother to lock the door. Wrong. The door was secured with a deadbolt. Well, Mr. O'Kelly, I have a surprise for you. I reached in my handbag and withdrew a small leather case. I opened the case and withdrew the special lockpick. It was a state-of-the-art tool that could only be purchased by law enforcement and government agencies. I figured that access to special tools was one of the perks of owning my own security company. I inserted the device into the keyhole and pressed a button on the side. I felt a slight vibration. I turned the tool to the right, and the lock released.

103

I PRESSED DOWN ON THE DOOR HANDLE AND PUSHED THE DOOR OPEN. Mr. P zipped around my feet into the room and stretched out on the carpet. I entered, and then I closed the door. The TV was on, but there was no one in the room. I looked around. The place was surprisingly neat for a guy's place. I was about to call out when I heard water running in the bedroom. *Can fate be smiling on me?* He was taking a shower. That was truly payback.

Wait a minute I though, this isn't right. I had only come to speak to him about *endosyms.* I was about ready to turn and get out. I was suddenly embarrassed that I had picked his lock and walked right in. What in the world was I thinking? I stepped back and started to head for the door when the shower stopped. I stood there frozen in place. Then I saw Shaun O'Kelly walk out of the bathroom buck naked, drying his hair with a towel.

I stood there staring, my mouth wide open. I mean I had never seen a naked man for real. You know, like, in the flesh. I let out a squeak like a mouse. He looked in my direction, and the towel went from his head to his crotch. Then he turned and dashed back into the bathroom.

Well, I'll be! He was embarrassed to see me standing there. Big, cool Shaun O'Kelly.

A few seconds later, Shaun came out of the bathroom wearing jeans and a T-shirt.

"How did you get in here?" he growled.

"The door was unlocked," I lied.

"No, it wasn't," he said.

"Well, maybe I can pass through secure doors just like you can," I said with a sly smile.

"I doubt that. What do you want?" he demanded.

"To talk. You wouldn't return my calls, and we have things to discuss."

"Mother told me not to have anything to do with you," he said.

"Mother? Your mother told you not to have anything to do with me? How old are you?" I asked, starting to get mad.

"Twenty-one," said Shaun.

"Well, Mr. O'Kelly, you're old enough to make you own decisions."

"You don't know my mother," said Shaun.

"Well, I think I need to meet her and soon," I responded.

"That's not going to happen," he snapped.

Now I really was mad.

"You listen to me, Shaun O'Kelly, the world is going to end on December twenty-first, and you're worried about your mother? We need to be working together to stop the *endosyms* from taking over the world."

"What do you mean by taking over the world?" asked Shaun.

"They have infiltrated the highest levels of our government, and I would bet the other governments in the world. The Speaker of the House of Representatives and the chairman of the Joint Chiefs of Staff are both *endosyms*. They're being controlled from a castle in Scotland," I yelled.

"You're not making sense, Amy. You need to sit down." Shaun looked more worried than I'd ever seen him before.

I plopped down on the sofa. Shaun sat down slowly next to me. I could see the dampness of his dark hair and smell the scent of his body wash. I had a quick visual memory of seeing him come out of the bathroom with nothing on. *Whoa, I need to calm down.* I took a deep breath.

"All right," he said. "Why don't you start at the beginning?"

At that moment he saw Mr. P.

"I see you brought your cat with you?" he said.

"I don't go anywhere without him," I said. "He's saved my life three times and killed seven guys."

Shaun paused and then just stared at me. "All right, start at the beginning. I'll listen."

I told him about my trip to Washington, DC, and my abduction by the henchmen of an *endosym*. I told him I knew that key people in our government were now *endosyms*. I described my vision of the other world where demon-creatures enslaved humans to be used as sacrifices. Finally, I told him what I had found out about Duncan McDougal. I believed that he was the cause of the rise of the *endosyms*.

I must have blabbed away for close to an hour. Then I stopped talking. I looked at Shaun. He was frowning.

"So that's why they want me to come home as soon as school is out. They never told me anything. When I told Mom about you, she was angry, saying that it wasn't possible for you to see *endosyms*. I got a call three days ago telling me that the *zoutari* from the covens in Scotland, England, and Ireland would gather on June twenty-first in Glastonbury."

"Where's Glastonbury?" I asked.

"You've never heard of Glastonbury?" Shaun asked, totally astonished. "Glastonbury is a small town in southwest England. It's considered the center of the metaphysical world. It's the site of the first Christian church in the British Isles. It is believed that at one time the Holy Grail was hidden there. The history of my people the *zoutari* can be traced back to the Druids that lived near Glastonbury.

"Glastonbury is the vortex of four powerful energy sources, or ley lines. The electrical energy from these lines flow outward from Glastonbury. The covens will gather at the base of the Tor, a conical hill topped by a fourteenth-century tower.

"My people believe that this is the site where the door opened to the underworld. Avallach, ruler of the underworld, was driven back by our ancestors at this very site. It's a place where fairy folk lived. Glastonbury is a focus of spiritually for Christians and pagan alike."

"So what is the purpose of the gathering?" I asked.

"From what you have told me, they want to come up with a plan to battle the influx of *endosyms*," he said.

I sat there unable to speak. I had just reached meltdown. The last twenty-two months had changed my life in so many ways. My parents had been murdered. I had discovered that I was not who I thought I was.

I was having out-of-body experiences. And, to top it off, there were monsters in the world that made movie monsters seem like Muppets.

I had no idea what my role was in this whole crazy business. I was sitting next to a guy I really liked and would like to know better. But it probably didn't matter. Most likely I would be dead before my twentieth birthday. Oh, yes, one more thing: I was also some kind of witch with a cat that could morph into a monster saber-tooth cat. I would never live to have my own family, never experience the simple joys in life, and I would never know a man's love. I would die a virgin.

Shaun looked somewhat confused. After talking nonstop for more than an hour, I was suddenly speechless. What could I say? *"Could you Druid types go kick the butts of those* endosyms*?"* That was a start but somehow I believed that it would take a lot more than that.

My attention shifted back to this man beside me. *God, he has beautiful eyes.* Then it occurred to me. *If I die tomorrow, I'm not going out as a virgin.* I got up and ran for the bathroom.

In the bathroom, I looked around. It was a man's bathroom. No womanly things. All masculine. I looked in the medicine cabinet. I saw a bottle of mouthwash. I took a slug from the bottle, rinsed my mouth, and spit it out into the sink. I was feeling weak-kneed. Maybe I wasn't his type. But I recalled how he had looked at me in my bedroom. I know desire when I see it.

In that moment, I wanted to forget what the future held, and I wanted Shaun O'Kelly. I returned to the living room. Shaun stood by the refrigerator, holding a can of Pepsi in each hand.

"Want a drink?" he asked.

"Later," I said. "Right now, I want to forget about *endosyms*."

I threw my arms around him and kissed him hard on the lips. I had to stand on my tiptoes to do that. I have a thing for tall men!

It was like I had lit a match in a room full of gasoline. As my lips touched his, I felt his arms wrap tightly around me. His tongue brushed my teeth. I thrust my tongue into his mouth. I felt his hands under my sweatshirt reaching for the hook on my bra. It came loose. Then his hands were caressing my breasts. I couldn't breathe evenly. Nothing like this had ever happened before, but it felt so right. As he pressed against me, I could feel a fullness in his jeans. I imagined him naked before me. I started unbuttoning my jeans. I would give myself to Shaun O'Kelly. No more virgin here.

The kissing quickly came to a halt. He held me at arm's length.

"I can't," he said.

"You can't?" I asked, shocked by this sudden turn of events. "Why? Is it the cat? We can lock him in the bathroom."

"Not the cat," he gasped.

"I'll help you! We've got to do it!" I moaned, stomping my feet in frustration.

"You don't understand," said Shaun, "As a *zoutari*, everything we do must be for the purpose."

"Am I not good enough for you?"

"No, no. Amy Brown, I love you," said Shaun, his eyes filling with tears.

"Love me? We've only met four times."

"I fell in love with you that night in the library," he said.

"OK, if you love me, let's do it," I protested, deciding to just go with it.

"It's not that simple. We were both born *zoutari*. I know you don't believe it, and Mother doesn't believe it, but what you have done surpasses the greatest of priest and priestess.

"Our survival has been based on each generation marrying only another *zoutari*. But to ensure that the offspring are *zoutari*, the two must become one where the Mary and Michael ley lines cross. We first unite in Glastonbury," explained Shaun.

"What? On some altar or something?" I asked sarcastically.

"No, no—in a bed and breakfast, in a house. Hopefully, in a bed. If not, in the backseat of a car or on a grassy field in the woods. It's just that the first coupling must occur in the town of Glastonbury."

I faced him, disappointed beyond words.

"I guess we can't get there tonight," I said.

"No, I'm afraid not, but I do want to take you there, and the sooner the better," said Shaun as he held my hands in his.

"All right," I said. "Scratch that idea."

It looked like my plan was a bust. I needed to get myself put back together, so I headed back to the bathroom. I looked in the mirror. My face was beet red. Still aroused, I splashed cool water on my face. I rehooked my bra and adjusted my shirt. I ran my fingers through my hair and returned to the living room. Shaun held Mr. P in his arms. He didn't just let anyone pick him up. Then again, if the cat had been observing our antics, he must have assumed that we weren't strangers.

"Let's go," said Shaun.

"Go where?" I asked.

"I don't care," he said. "We're going on a date."

"A date? It's two in the morning."

"There are places open," he said with a grin.

"Oh, well, if I can't lose my virginity except in Glastonbury, I guess you can buy me an early breakfast."

We headed down the stairs to the Mustang. Shaun carried Mr. P in his arms.

104

IT HAD BEEN A WEEK SINCE SHAUN O'KELLY HAD ENTERED MY LIFE, like, big-time. Was I in love with Shaun? Well, not like love at first sight as Shaun claimed it was for him, but over that week, all I could think about was Shaun.

I hadn't felt like that since I had had that crush on Bobby Jenkins in fifth grade. With Shaun, what with the world possibly coming to an end it sure seemed like Shaun might just be the man for me.

After my aggressive pass at Shaun in his apartment and his rebuff, we reverted to progressing like two young people getting to know each other, kissing and making out, going to movies, and just hanging out.

To tell you the truth, I was thankful that Shaun turned down my advances that night. I had been at a low spot in my life and had believed that giving myself to Shaun would make everything all right. It hadn't taken long to remember what Mom had told me when I was twelve years old. She had been really cool in her approach to sex. Of course, we had discussed what changes were taking place in my body when I had my first period, and Mom had always been open about sex and totally honest with me.

But some of Mom's words had really stuck in my mind.

"Amy, your body is a gift from God," she had told me. "Young men will always want more than you may be willing to give. You can always say no, but the first time you give in and go all the way, the gift you gave is one that can never be retrieved. Make sure that you want to give that gift before you say yes."

I ended up pretty happy that we didn't go all the way that night. Will I give my virginity to Shaun O'Kelly, or will there be someone else? I don't know at this time. What I do know is that I want to be the one that makes that decision.

Surprising enough, Shaun and I had a lot in common. We even enjoyed the same music. Of course, I knew very little about Dublin, Ireland, Shaun's home. I had so much to learn about it but also about the *zoutari*. Shaun had hinted about some of their history, and I began to learn about the *zoutaris'* legendary battle with the *endosyms*.

Shaun believed the demons of Christianity were derived from stories of these beings. They were not minions of the devil. He was surprisingly well versed in the Bible and showed me scriptures where the demons could have been the creatures from another world. When Jesus was tempted in the wilderness, the devil offered him great power and wealth and control over mankind—which is what the demons offered their human hosts. When Christ drove the demons from the man into the pigs, it implied that the demons were living within the man.

My biggest surprise was to find out that Shaun s father was a multimillionaire, owning a string of car dealerships in Ireland. They lived in a magnificent home in Dublin. His mother was a stay-at-home mom. Nowhere on their résumés was the notation that they were members of a coven of *zoutari*, whose mission was to identify and destroy *endosyms*.

Shaun explained that his parents' ancestors were Druids. For thousands of years, they had had the ability to see the *endosyms*. There had been a constant battle between the *zoutari* and the *endosyms*. Since there were not that many *endosyms*, when one was discovered, it was destroyed in ways that made it look like it was simply an unfortunate accident. Some *zoutari* were trained assassins who could make a prominent person appear to have died in an accident.

The *zoutari* didn't know what happened to a demon once its host was killed. Demon-creatures could not survive long on earth without a host. The *zoutari* also knew that the *endosyms* recruited ordinary humans to serve them. They granted those humans special powers. That explained the extraordinary powers of the cops who had abducted Joe and me in Washington, DC.

Hundreds of years ago, the *zoutari* cowered in small, hidden covens fearing for their lives. In those days, those accused of witchcraft were hanged or burned at the stake. They were unaware that other covens like theirs existed throughout the world. In modern times, groups of *zoutari* lived near the ley lines, the magnetic anomalies that bisected the earth. *Zoutari* dwelled throughout Europe. The *zoutari* have spread throughout South America, China, Australia, and Africa.

With the wider acceptance of New Age religions, the *zoutari* started saying that they were just members of Wicca covens. They even communicated between covens via the Internet. The primary goal of their powerful organization was to keep *endosyms* under control. But something had gone wrong now there were hundreds of *endosyms* and they had infiltrated positions of power and wealth and it was becoming difficult for the covens to stop them without being exposed. I was convinced that Duncan McDougal had discovered a way to open a doorway between the two worlds.

Shaun and I spent many hours together, having fun and discussing the fate of our world. The *zoutari* were a closed religious society that protected their secrecy. They were willing to commit murder to ensure that no outsiders infiltrated the covens. Marriages occurred between members of the covens but never with outsiders. The organization was big enough that marriages never occurred unless the two were at least cousins fourth generation removed. Children were homeschooled until they were old enough to keep the coven's secrets.

Shaun attended school at Gonzaga in Spokane so that he could become an outside operator for the coven. His parents were practicing Catholics, and their neighbors had no idea that they were into the occult. That's how they kept the society a secret.

A number of wealthy businessmen and women throughout the British Isles were *zoutaris*. I had to admit that Shaun's passion for his religion, as a *zoutari*, was commendable, as was his desire to honor my virtue. Now, as

I learned more about the *zoutari*, more convinced that they might be the ones to stop the *endosyms*.

In a month, I was leaving for Liberia. Depending on how long I was gone, Shaun would be back in Ireland when I returned. Would our short-lived romance fade away as did so many other first loves? Being on two separate continents would be a real test of our relationship. I wondered if I would ever see Shaun O'Kelly again.

Well, if I got my way, on June twenty first I would meet him in Glastonbury, England. That scared him. He said that the coven would not be happy to see me. Apparently he was still afraid that his mother the high priestess would no accept me as a zoutari. That didn't make me happy. Less than an week ago I had assumed that he had invited me to Glastonbury. I told Shaun that if I found my destiny in Liberia, and if I believed that I could stop Duncan McDougal, then the covens had better watch out. Besides, I expected him to be waiting for me if he truly loved me.

Perhaps the funniest thing was Mark's reaction to Shaun. I don't believe my own dad would have been as suspicious of the men in my life. When Mark, Regina, and the twins got back from Disneyland, I had invited Shaun to join us for dinner. Sherry was gaga over him, Randy liked his cool accent, and Mark grilled him like he was Jack the Ripper. He wanted to know what Shaun's father did and what Shaun's plans were for the future. Mark and Regina both knew that Shaun could see *endosyms* and were somewhat aware of the fact that he belonged to a group that tracked *endosyms*. We all knew that the world as we knew it could come to an end in a few short months yet for a short period of time, it was enjoyable just to have my family give my new boyfriend the third degree.

105

THE CITY OF SPOKANE STOPS EVERYTHING ON THE FIRST SUNDAY IN May. Since 1977, millions of people have participated in the Lilac Bloomsday Run, and the current race was no exception: sixty thousand people were expected to join in the frenzied excitement.

Bloomsday was an annual, timed road race. The course was twelve kilometers—seven and a half miles—long. It started downtown and headed west and north to Spokane Community College, before crossing the Spokane River and heading up the one-mile "Doomsday Hill" past the Spokane County Court House to finish on the Monroe Street Bridge.

Runners, walkers, stroller-pushers, and wheelchair drivers comprised an organized riot, all moving in the same direction. To provide some kind on order to the chaos, the race organizers broke the race into eight categories. In the first group are the elite runners who compete for large cash prizes. They start at nine o'clock in the morning; the final group begins at ten o'clock.

Despite attempts to place the runners in groups by their running ability, some runners tended to fudge their times. Every year, within forty minutes of the start of the race, the entire course was jammed with thousands of runners of all ability levels.

All finishers were awarded the coveted Bloomsday T-shirt. Afterward, the masses gathered in Riverfront Park to eat, drink, and play. Participants proudly showed off their T-shirts to their fellow runners and families.

The race was multigenerational; parents who participated in the early days of this race ended up running with their grandchildren years later. Race weekend sold out every hotel and motel. The event brought in millions of dollars for the Spokane economy.

The weather varied year to year, anything from mixed rain and snow to sunny and temperatures in the seventies. Current temperatures were projected to be in the low seventies by afternoon, and the day promised to be bright and clear.

We arrived about an hour before the start of the race. We parked up on Third Avenue and walked down to the race site. We were lined up in the green number group between Wall Street and Howard Street on Riverside Avenue.

Shaun, Sherry, Randy, and I were all running the race. For Shaun, Sherry, and Randy, it was their first Bloomsday. It was my fifteenth. Mom and Dad had loved Bloomsday. I had started out in a stroller years ago. When I was in junior high and high school, we ran as a threesome.

I couldn't convince myself to even register for the race the year my parents died. I still had moments where I choked up.

Shaun was being a big baby. It was more than three weeks before I would leave for Liberia, but he was acting as if it was our last night together. He had wanted us to spend the day together, just the two of us. But I had promised Sherry I would run with her, and I wasn't going to back down. Besides, I loved this event.

Sherry and I wore new running outfits. We both had short shorts and matching singlets. When the weather was warm, people bought thousands of dollars in running gear for the Bloomsday race. It was a great time for tush watching, for both the guys and the gals. I had purchased Sherry a sports bra for the race. She definitely needed the support. Sherry had blossomed into quite a foxy number. I could almost be jealous. I noticed that a number of guys were checking her out. Unfortunately, despite the vivid colors of my outfit, not all guys didn't seem to notice long, tall Amy Brown.

Well, at least one guy was admiring me. Shaun looked me up and down, admiring my outfit. Shaun's running clothes were pretty simple; he wore a white T-shirt one size too small and cutoff jeans. It didn't really matter. With his muscular build, it was obvious that the women approved. Randy was too embarrassed to wear shorts and didn't want anyone to see his white legs. Sweat pants seemed to satisfy him.

I ran into several friends from my high school days. I introduced them to Shaun and received approving glances. I guess they had concluded that wallflower Amy Brown hadn't done too badly for herself.

Twenty minutes before nine, the starting gun went off for the wheelchair race. Wheelchair racers were given a twenty-minute head start. At exactly nine o'clock, the elite runners took off.

Everyone else moved up and began to crowd the start line. The yellow group took off. We were next. Once the yellow runners crossed the start line, our whole group moved forward to the starting line. Everyone could feel the tension and excitement building.

Randy had linked up with three guys from Freeman.

"We'll meet you girls at the finish," said Randy. "Do you want to run with us guys, Shaun?" asked Randy.

"No, Randy, I'll run with Amy and Sherry," replied Shaun.

"OK!" he said with a wide grin. "See you guys at the finish line."

"Someday, he'll be more interested in running with a girl," I said with a laugh. I turned to Shaun. "You may not be able to keep up with us girls, big guy."

"Think so?" said Shaun, laughing along with me.

Then it was the announcer's turn.

"On your mark, get ready—" There was a pause, and then the crack of the starting gun. We were toward the middle of the green group, which probably numbered five thousand. In the old days, everyone wanted to be at the front of the group, thinking that would improve their times. Of course, if your time was slow, you could always say that you started at the back of the line. No more.

Modern runners attached an adhesive tab to their running shoe. It contained a microchip with the runner's name and age. The start and finish lines were rubber mats. As runners crossed the mats, their exact times, names, and ages are recorded. No more excuses, and the times were accurate for the entire distance.

We started walking toward the starting line as the mass of humanity surged forward. By the time we reached the starting line, we were running. I could see Randy and his buddies dashing around other runners. We charged west down Riverside in a solid mass from curb to curb. When we reached Monroe, we jogged to the left across the street in front of the Catholic church. People stood along the sidewalks, cheering on the runners.

Riverside headed downhill toward Latah Creek. We passed the two-mile marker. Sherry jogged along beside Shaun and wasn't even breathing hard. She had been turning out for the school's cross-country team.

"Sherry, why don't you stretch it out? We'll meet you at the finish line," I told her.

"OK," she said with a confident grin.

I checked out Shaun's reaction.

"You're not looking at Sherry's ass, are you? She's only thirteen," I scolded him.

As we started up Government Way, Shaun was obviously impressed.

"This is quite an event. You know we have Bloomsday in Dublin."

"You're kidding!" I said.

"Nope. It's a weeklong festival. It starts June sixteenth."

"Is there a race?" I asked.

"No. It celebrates the day in 1904 that James Joyce's novel *Ulysses* takes place. It all happens in Dublin. On June sixteenth, it is traditional to dress up and go out for the day, visiting all the locations in the book. People take part in readings, walks, and carnival activities that in some way connect with *Ulysses*, its author, and its world."

"Oh," I said. "I think I like a Bloomsday race better."

Riverside changed to Government Way. We passed milepost three and then turned on to Fort George Wright Way. As we passed the community college, we caught up with Randy and his three buddies. He waved at us as we ran by.

"Where's Sherry? Did she give up?"

"No," I said. "She left us at milepost two. You must have missed her when she ran by."

"Oh," said Randy, disappointed.

At milepost four we started downhill toward the Spokane River.

"This isn't such a tough run," said Shaun. "I thought you said this race whips people."

"Just wait," I said, smiling back at him.

We rounded the corner and took the TJ Meenach Bridge across the river. On the other side was Pettet Drive—known as Doomsday Hill to runners. Within a mile, the road climbed steeply a good four hundred feet.

"Holy smokes!" said Shaun.

"The goal is to not walk, but run, the whole length of Doomsday Hill," I said.

"If you can do it, I can," boasted Shaun.

We crossed the bridge and started uphill. With fifteen Bloomsdays under my belt, I knew how to handle the hill. Rule one: keep a steady pace; think one foot at a time. Rule two: don't look up; let the top of the hill be a surprise. Rule three: use steady breathing.

I leaned into the hill. I could hear Shaun's breathing increase. I looked over at him and smiled.

"Beautiful day for a run," I said.

"Yeah, sure," he gasped.

We were almost to the top when I looked for Shaun. He wasn't there. I turned around. He had dropped back. I slowed down and allowed him to catch up.

"Don't look up the rest of the hill. Look at the ground," I said as I coached him to the top of the hill.

When we reached the highest point, he gasped for breath. "We can stop now?"

"No," I said. "We have about two more miles to go."

"God," he moaned. "That was a killer!"

"That's why they call it Doomsday Hill," I said.

On Lindeke, we passed milepost six.

"Only about one and a half miles to go," I said, smiling. Shaun appeared to have caught his breath.

"Do you want me to take your arm and help you?" I volunteered with a sweet smile.

"I'm fine," he whispered.

I slowed down. I decided I'd had enough fun. Pretty soon we were doing a leisurely jog. On Broadway we hit milepost seven near the county court house.

"Let's increase our pace," said Shaun. He took off.

"Oh, no, you don't!" I hollered.

We turned the corner onto Monroe Street. The two of us were now in a two-person sprint to the finish line. He was starting to pull away from me. Longer legs and more muscle were winning out; he was going to beat me. Then he slowed, reached out, and took my hand. We crossed the finish line together, hand in hand.

I looked at him. I realized that he was more interested in finishing together than he was in beating me. That was something Dad would have done for Mom. *That's a big plus for you, Shaun O'Kelly*, I thought. We crossed the rubber mat of the finish line. Race officials directed us to move along toward the race shirt tables. They told us to remove the bottom part of our race numbers. It had to be turned in to get the T-shirt.

Sherry came running up, beaming.

"I loved the way you guys finished. That was so romantic!" she gushed.

"It was," I said. *It really was.*

The race ended on the Monroe Street Bridge. We stood at the railing and looked down at the falls. In May the falls were at full volume from the snowmelt in the Idaho mountains. Randy and his buddies came up, and we all headed to the T-shirt tables. Everyone was laughing.

Then I saw them, and my heart almost stopped beating. I'd missed them at first because they had been standing in the bright sunlight. Then they had stepped back into the shade from the buildings. Auras surrounded their bodies. I glanced away, hoping that they wouldn't see my fear and disgust. I knew what they were.

Three *endosyms* stood on the sidewalk just as we neared the T-shirt tables. One was the priest who was my first encounter with an *endosym* in the Foley Library. The other was a woman I recognized. She was the mayor of Spokane. The third was an older gentleman wearing a suit. I did not recognize him.

What are they doing here? I glanced over quickly. They were smiling. *Oh my God,* I thought. They were looking at us humans like ranchers would admire the cattle being taken to the slaughterhouse.

No, I decided. *I'm not going to let those bastards spoil this day with Shaun and my family.* I looked at the runners in front of me and smiled. I handed in the bottom of my number and was given my T-shirt.

"Eat, drink, and be merry, for tomorrow we may die," I said to myself as Shaun and I headed toward the park.

106

WE SPENT SEVERAL HOURS IN THE RIVERFRONT PARK FOLLOWING
the race. Then we headed back to the house. Mark and Regina wanted
to take us to the Golden Corral buffet to celebrate the race. Shaun and I
declined, deciding instead to do a late dinner at the Red Lion Barbecue
and Pub on Division. It had been selected as one of the best places to eat
in Spokane. Shaun had never eaten real Western barbecue. It was a cool
place to go. Shaun had driven the Mustang back to his place to clean up
and change clothes. I puttered around the house until he picked me up
at eight thirty.

Mark didn't want me to loan Shaun the Mustang. I asked Mark how
much I was worth on the last audit.

"I guess close to one billion dollars," he said.

"So my three-year-old Mustang is worth what?"

"I don't know," answered Mark. "I guess around thirty thousand
dollars."

"So at my current net worth, I probably wouldn't be too devastated
if Shaun shipped the car to Ireland. Except, of course, I would kill him
since I love my Mustang."

Mark grumbled. "Yeah, but I just don't think it's right for a young
woman to loan her car to a guy."

I laughed.

"It's OK. I'll deal with it."

We headed to town following Grand Boulevard, turned by Sacred
Heart Hospital, and then went down the hill until we linked up with
Division, which was one-way going north. When we reached downtown,

the streets were jammed with people. It was a warm spring night, and there were thousands of out-of-town visitors.

Up ahead on the old brick four-story building that housed the restaurant was a large sign painted on the bricks. It had a yellow background with a shied with a red lion like on an old British knight's battle shied. Beneath the lion were the words EST. 1960. The large red letters on the sign read RED LION BARBECUE.

People were actually lined up along the sidewalk to get into the place.

"Maybe we should go somewhere else," said Shaun.

"No," I said. "You're going to eat barbecue tonight. Besides, you can bet every other place will be equally crowded."

The light turned red at Spokane Falls Boulevard.

"Amy, get out and get in line. I'll find a parking place down by the convention center."

"Oh, gee!" I said. "That's almost two blocks away. Are you sure you will be able to hobble all the way back here?"

"I'll do the best I can," he said with a laugh.

"I'll see you in a few minutes," I shouted as I got out and zipped across the street before the light changed to green. I walked back toward the Red Lion Pub.

What a wonderful night. Everyone was wearing Bloomsday shirts. It was cool, though, so I also wore a Gonzaga sweatshirt over my running shirt. I had on jeans and sneakers. I left my phone in the glove compartment of the Mustang. It was just Shaun and me tonight. All I had was my credit card and driver's license. Everyone on the street was smiling and laughing. This was going to be a great night.

A sudden screech of tires caught my attention. I looked to my right. A police car had come up right next to me with its emergency lights flashing. Two policemen got out of the car. I wondered what was going on. They looked around as if they were searching for something. Then I saw their eyes and their unmistakable glow. I stepped out of the line and turned into the alley. I began to run. I had to warn Shaun.

Oh, great, I left my phone in the Mustang. I cut down to the next street. As I rounded the corner, I almost ran straight into another cop. I slowed down. He walked toward me. I glanced up. Thank God; he was a real police officer.

"Excuse me, officer, there are two men back there who are impersonating policemen."

He spoke into his mic on his lapel. Then he looked at me.

"Miss, you are going to have to come with me."

At first, I thought he had called the real police, and then I saw the two fake cops walking toward us, grinning. I turned and started to run. Then I doubled over in unbelievable pain. My teeth chattered. I was being electrocuted. Then everything went black.

107

IOPENEDMYEYES.IWASSITTINGINAMETALCHAIRATAMETALTABLE.ACROSS
from the table were two chairs. I was in a room about twelve feet square.
The walls and ceiling were covered with white acoustic tiles. Fluorescent
lights were embedded in the ceiling. Directly in front of me was a
large mirror. I assumed it was actually a one-way mirror. I was in an
interrogation room. My hands were tied behind my back. My feet were
also bound. I looked down. Double plastic ties had been wrapped around
my ankles. I assumed that my wrists were also bound with the plastic ties.

"Hello, is anyone out there?" I shouted.

I waited. It seemed like hours. *What the hell is going to happen?* An
interrogation room can be creepy. It was soundproof. I could almost hear
my heart beat. My God, was this it? Was I going to die? Then I thought
of God. *Can he save me? Should I pray?* I looked up at the ceiling.

"I'm sorry, God. I guess I haven't really talked to you in a while. I just
don't know what to do. What do you want from me?"

I do believe that I felt some comfort surround me. I felt less tense.
Then the door opened. In walked Edith Dorson, the mayor of Spokane.
She sat down in one of the chairs. This was the closest I had ever been
to an *endosym*. I could clearly see the outline of the demon aura projected
around her body.

"Well, Miss Martin, you have indeed been a problem."

"My name is Amy Brown. I don't know what you are talking about."

"Come now, Miss Martin; do you think I'm stupid? You know what
we are. We observed your reaction this morning. Don't you realize

we have been watching you since those foolish idiots botched your elimination last year?"

The door opened once again. The older *endosym* I had seen that morning stepped inside. From the look on his face, I could see that he was furious. Edith stood up and stared at him. It's almost impossible to explain what happened next.

Their lips were not moving, yet I could hear their words inside my head.

"What the hell are you doing?" he said.

"I'm trying to clean up your mess. You weren't able to kill her, so I'm taking care of it."

"You heard the council's orders. We are to do nothing that might create suspicion before the final days," he said.

"She was supposed to die when we tased her. The Taser would have killed a horse. They were going to claim that she had been drunk."

"Why the hell did they bring her here?" he asked.

"A nonfollower got involved and called the station. They had no choice but to bring her here."

"Is there a chance that someone will find out where she is?"

"No chance. We were discreet."

"This has to look like an accident," he ordered.

They both walked out, not even looking at me. They closed the door when they left. I was alone again.

Oh my gosh. They were speaking telepathically and apparently had no idea that I could hear them. But what good would this knowledge do me? They planned to kill me.

Can I break my bonds? I remembered slipping out of the handcuffs in Washington, DC. I moved my wrists, pulling on the plastic ties. They cut into my wrists. I strained harder. I felt blood running down my fingers and drip on the floor. It was no use. I couldn't slip my hands out of the ties, and I lacked the strength to break them. They were too tight.

I stared at the one-way mirror. I heard the door creak, and I saw it begin to open. Was this it? The door swung wide open. The two cops who had brought me to the station carried a funnel attached to a three-foot-long rubber hose. One of them held a bottle of Crown Royal.

"Jesus, look at the blood!" said the older one.

"We should have just left her to bleed to death," said the younger one.

Now he looked at me and spoke softly.

"Honey, unless you serve one of the masters, there is no way you would have the strength to break those plastic ties.

"Now, listen carefully. We're going to shove this hose down your throat, then pour a half bottle of this good booze down into your gut. We'll wait until the alcohol gets in your bloodstream. Then you're going to fall off your chair and break your neck. Ain't that a bitch?"

The older cop turned to the younger one.

"Come on, Chuck; all we've got to do is kill her. We don't need to torture her. Let's get her drunk, and do it as painlessly as possible. We need to make this look like an accident."

"Screw you, Zack. I just want to get this done."

"I've still got seniority. We do it my way," growled Zack.

"Fine. I'll be in the other room. Let me know when it's done. I've got better things to do than coddle a dead woman."

The young cop walked out and slammed the door behind him. Zack sat down in the chair across from me. I could see the glow behind his eyes, yet he still wanted to spare me undue agony. All he wanted to do was to kill me.

He opened the bottle of Crown Royal and took a long drink.

"OK, you have to take a drink. Otherwise, it's the tube down the throat," he said.

In the back of my mind, I wondered if I could I get him drunk and then convince him to let me go. I had nothing to lose. He held the bottle to my lips and tipped it toward me. I swallowed a gulp of the liquor. *My God, it tastes like sweet gasoline.* I started coughing.

"You don't drink much, do you?"

"No," I gasped as the warm liquor flowed into my body.

"Well, tonight you'll drink, and it will be a painless way to go."

He took another swig.

"It's your turn," he said.

"I don't want any more," I told him.

"You don't understand. It's this way or Chuck's way with the rubber hose and funnel."

I was about to tell him to go to hell, but I still held out a small glimmer of hope. I took another swallow. This time it went down more easily. I could feel the warmth in my stomach.

"Why?" I asked.

"Why what?" he asked as he took another drink.

"Why would you sell out the human race for those monsters? You're a cop. You're supposed to protect us."

"For nineteen years, I've protected and served this town. Protected what? The mothers on crack who have just had their fifth kid so they can continue to draw money from the state? The asshole who buys his way out of a DUI by paying big bucks to his lawyer or the dickheads who run the government?

"Hell," he continued, "the human race is reproducing like fucking rabbits. There are over seven billion humans polluting what's left of the earth's resources. You've got teenagers shooting up shopping malls, and then they plead insanity and end up in a plush psychiatric ward for a few years before they get released."

He took another swig.

"Drink!" he commanded.

I took another drink. I was starting to feel a little woozy.

"What you're serving is not even human. They're creatures called *endosyms*, part human and part alien."

"I know that. Otherwise they couldn't give me this additional power."

"You know they get their power by killing humans," I argued.

"Sure," he said. "So what? We need to reduce the world's population by a couple of billion. For you, it's too late, but soon people will get to make a choice. Serve the *endosyms* or die. They're everywhere. Through the years, they have infiltrated key positions in every major city and in every country. Next year, the entire world will be in the hands of the masters that you call *endosyms*. There is no way to stop them, so I've gotten on their bandwagon. Now, drink up. It's time for you to leave this earth."

108

TEARS RAN DOWN MY CHEEKS. I WAS GOING TO DIE, AND THERE WAS nothing I could do about it. For the first and last time in my life, I was drunk, but it didn't do anything to dull that fact. Then I heard a crash, and the one-way mirror cracked in several places.

"What the hell?" shouted Zack.

He stood and moved to the door. Once he opened it, he left the room. I heard another loud crash, then nothing more. The room was spinning.

The door swung open. It was Shaun. I started to speak, but I slurred my words. He approached me, pulled a knife from his pocket, and cut the ties around my ankles and wrists. I was able to move my hands and flex my fingers. My wrists were covered with blood. Shaun, concerned, held my hands tenderly and examined my wrists.

"It's OK," I mumbled. Then I started laughing.

"My God, Amy, you're drunk. Can you walk?"

"I think so," I said before I began giggling again.

He took my arm and led me out the door. The two cops were lying on the floor. They were either dead or unconscious.

We were in the Public Safety Building, but for some reason, the walls continued to spin. We walked down the hallway to the elevators. When we got in, he pushed B. The elevator started down.

"I'm going to be sick," I gasped. Then I proceeded to vomit the contents of my stomach. It smelled horrible. It got on my sweatshirt and pooled on the floor beside my shoes. Liquid oozed out my nose. I coughed and gagged.

"You'll feel better after getting some of the alcohol out of your system," said Shaun.

The elevator doors opened. We were in the police garage. Before us stood Mark and ten of our guys, all packing automatic weapons. I was escorted to one of our three Dodge Chargers. We all piled in the cars and slowly drove out of the garage. We headed back toward the south hill.

I made it to Twenty-Ninth before I asked them to stop. I was sick again. I opened my door and barfed on the street. When we got to the house, there were security guys everywhere. I was relieved to see Regina.

"Oh my God, Amy, what have they done to you?" she cried out.

"What?" I looked down. There was blood on my jeans from my damaged wrists.

"She smells like a distillery," said Regina. "She needs hot coffee, and we need to clean her up and examine those wrists. What did they do to torture her?"

"No," I mumbled. "I tried to get out of the ties. They cut into my wrists."

Regina took me upstairs, stripped off my clothes, and helped me into the shower. After I cleaned up and toweled off, she helped me dress in a comfortable sweatshirt and sweat pants. She treated and bandaged the wounds on my wrists, worrying all the time that I might need stitches. Finally, she steadied me as we walked slowly back to the kitchen.

As I drank my third cup of coffee, I looked seriously at Shaun.

"How did you find me?" I asked.

"I didn't. It was Mark. When I found a parking spot, I went to the Red Lion Pub. I didn't see you and assumed you had already been seated. I walked to the front of the line and asked the doorman if he had seen you. He said he hadn't seen anyone matching your description. Someone in line said that they thought the police had arrested you.

"Another couple overheard and joined the conservation. They reported saying that a woman of your description had been tased and taken away in a police car. When they heard my accent, I got the feeling that they believed that you and I were terrorists. I think if I had hung around any longer, they would have called the cops.

"I got out of there and headed back to the car. I used Amy's phone to call Mark. He told me to get back to the house."

"When I got there, he had a ten-man team all formed up. They were ready for action: black Kevlar assault suits and weapons. Mark told me that he had called some of his buddies on the police force. They hadn't heard of any arrests. Then he got a call from a sergeant working the night shift. He said that something was going on down at the Public Safety Building. It involved the mayor and the two cops who had been assigned as a security detail. When he nosed around, they restricted him from entering the interrogation area. They claimed it was special government business. When Mark heard that, he figured that was where you were," explained Shaun.

"I was ready to storm the place," said Mark. "Then Shaun said that he had been trained on how to enter a secure place and not be detected. I was about to tell him to blow off. Yet I realized if we stormed the building, every cop in town would be on our trail. I told Shaun to see if he could get in. Next thing, we find the two of you coming out of the elevator."

I looked at Shaun.

"Did you kill those two cops?"

"No," said Shaun. "I only incapacitated them. To kill an *endosym* or one of their followers gets messy. This way they lost you but have to be careful since they have no idea how we got you out."

"We've still got big trouble," said Mark. "They know where you live. We've got to get out of the country."

"I don't think so, at least not yet," I said.

"Why?" asked Mark.

"When the mayor grabbed me, the old *endosym* was angry with her. They have been told to keep a low profile until after December twenty-first."

"Who told you that?" asked Regina.

"I overheard them talking. Well, not exactly talking. I think they are telepathic and can communicate without speaking. Apparently, humans would not know what they are saying. But for some reason I could hear them communicating."

"You mean you can read *endosyms'* minds?" asked Mark.

"No, I don't think so. But I can understand their telepathic communication."

"Well, whether they come or not, I'm increasing the security around you and our entire family," said Mark. "We need to get ready to head for the ranch in Canada at a moment's notice. We should be packed and ready to go."

109

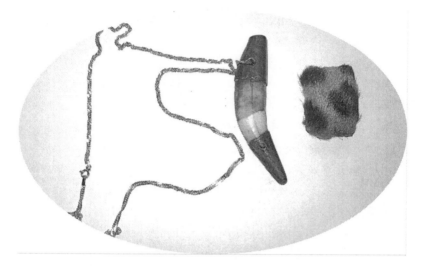

SHAUN STAYED IN MY ROOM THAT NIGHT. NO, WE DIDN'T SLEEP together, and the door to the bedroom was open the whole time. One of our security team was posted outside. We did end up on the bed together, fully clothed. He had his arm around me, and Mr. P was curled up at the foot of the bed. It had started out as a beautiful day, and then everything changed. I was so happy to see Shaun come through the door of the interrogation room.

"Shaun?" I asked. "Remember when I sent one of my security guys to get you?"

"Yes," he said.

"If you had not wanted to come, no matter how well trained my security guys were, they wouldn't have been able to take you, would they?"

"No," said Shaun. "But we are told to never use our full powers."

I laughed. "I must be dating a superhero."

"No, Amy, you're the superhero. You can read the *endosyms'* telepathic messages."

"Whatever," I said as I closed my eyes.

The next morning we sat in the kitchen watching the local news. There was nothing about what had happened the night before. There were no wanted pictures of me. There was also nothing on the police scanners or any bolos out on us.

While I sat at the table, I unconsciously unwrapped the gauze bandages around my wrists. When we had gotten back to the house the night before, Regina had treated my cut wrists. She had washed the wounds and treated them with antiseptic cream. She was worried that my wrists might be permanently scarred. When I removed the gauze, my wrists were red, and the cuts were beginning to close. Shaun looked at my wrists.

"Wow, do you ever heal fast!" he said.

"I guess so," I said. "I have always healed fast."

The days passed by quickly. I had been right. No one seemed to be after us. But I kept remembering what the cop Zack had said.

"They're everywhere. Over the years they have infiltrated key positions in every major city, in every country. Next year, the entire world will be in the hands of the masters that you call endosyms. *There is no way to stop them, so I've jumped on the bandwagon."*

The next morning I was set to leave for Liberia, West Africa. I will be carrying an old leopard tooth given to my family over thirty years ago by the witch doctor named Chea Geebe and a piece of leopard hide given to me by the same old zo.

Will the leopard tooth point the way, and will the leopard hide be the key to the secret hidden in the Mountain of Darkness in the ancient village of Zigda? I wondered.

The *endosyms* are taking over the planet.
Book five coming fall 2015.
See endosym.com.

EVERYTHING YOU BELIEVED IS WRONG

BOOK FIVE

REVELATION

AMY BROWN CAN SEE PEOPLE WHO ARE MORE THAN HUMAN. THE majority of the human race cannot see them or know that they are different. These creatures called *endosyms* are a combination of human and demon and have infiltrated positions in the highest levels of leadership in governments all over the world. Yet will anyone believe her?

Following the murder of her parents, Amy Brown begins having dreams that her real name is Anaya Martin and she must travel to Liberia, West Africa, to learn how she can save the world from the invasion of the *endosyms*.

As the United States recovers from a terrorist attack on Washington, DC, and the new president of the United States is an *endosym*, Amy and Joe Weah travel to the ancient village of Zigda.

There, hidden beneath the Mountain of Darkness, they discover a secret that will change everything they thought they knew about the human race.

Armed with the knowledge of the location of Duncan McDougal, the leader of the *endosyms*, they travel to Glastonbury, England, to elicit the help of the *zoutari,* members of an ancient Druid cult that has battled the *endosyms* for thousands of years.

But her task will not be an easy one. With time running out, will she be able to save the world?

24397701R00241

Made in the USA
San Bernardino, CA
23 September 2015